FIRE IN THE
HOLE

To Josie for evermore.

FIRE IN THE HOLE

A NOVEL

DOUGLAS CLARK

Southern West Virginia Counties

PART ONE

Displaced striking coal miner families at Holy Grove during the Paint Creek & Cabin Creek Strike of 1912-1913.

CHAPTER 1

Paint Creek, West Virginia | June 1912

Paint Creek is one of hundreds of small rivers flowing through the Southern Appalachian Mountains as part of the greater Mississippi watershed. From the earliest times of native Americans, these creeks defined the passageways through the mountains. Paint Creek runs north 42 miles from its source at over 2,000 feet elevation in Raleigh County through Kanawha County to empty into the Kanawha River at an elevation of 600 feet. The Kanawha runs westward to empty into the Ohio River.

Like so many other counties of West Virginia, the economy of Kanawha County is dominated by coal mining. The mines are typically located in remote locations accessed by primitive roads and by the later 19th century with a broad network of rail tracks necessary to transport the coal.

Irish born Joseph Burke emigrated from Ireland to West Virginia with his family in 1883. In that year, Burke worked as a coal miner in County Lancashire not far from Liverpool, England. He was age thirty-four that year. Married with three children. His oldest son was sixteen and worked alongside him in the mine. A typical age for entering into adult manual labor. Burke's wife Maude and two youngest children remained in County Cork, Ireland.

Coal mining is a dangerous and poorly paid occupation often generational. Joseph Burke became a miner the same as his father, working at a mine in Kanturk, County Cork. Maude taught school affording the family the ability to eke out a subsistence existence. Her youngest children aged nine and six at least benefited from receiving an education. Political circumstances had much to do with how Joseph and Maude Burke lived. Both were fervent Fenian radicals. The term Fenian derived from the Irish Gaelic term of mythological warriors. The name applied as a pejorative to members of a secret, outlawed mid-19th century movement known as the Irish Republican Brotherhood. The IRB sought to secure Ireland's independence from the British Empire that had exploited Ireland for hundreds of years.

Joseph and Maude Burke and their oldest son Liam all became active participants in the IRB. More than just political revolutionaries in the Irish cause of independence from Britain, they were willing to take violent action to bring that about. Both Joseph and Maude came from a family heritage of Irish rebellion. They knew each other because their fathers fought together in the Fenian Rising of 1867.

Joseph was eighteen at the time but did not directly participate in the brief fighting with his father in only a single day's confrontation in Cork City in March. Not much of a rebellion. Only twelve people were killed that day across all of Ireland. Poorly organized, the revolt proved a military failure as the Constabulary supported by British regulars easily defeated the rebels. It never materialized into widespread popular support of the Irish population. With the arrest of most of the Fenian leaders, the fervor of armed rebellion died away in favor of pursuing other means of asserting Irish rights.

However, Joseph Burke still retained the nationalistic fire for violent rebellion. He was one of many that came under the influence of hardened Irish nationalist Jeremiah O'Donovan Rossa.

After the failed Fenian Rising of 1867, the British sought to rid themselves of this troublesome rebel by exiling him to America. By the 1880s, a strong Irish nationalist movement already existed in America because of the earlier influx of Irish immigrants driven from the motherland because of the Great Potato Famine of the 1840s. With cooperation from Irish revolutionaries in America, the unrepentant rebel Rossa set out to organize a bombing campaign in Britian.

Local IRB members in County Cork conspiring with Rossa recruited Burke to find work in the Lancashire Coalfield mines in Northwest England outside of the port city of Liverpool. Joseph Burke possessed the skill in the use of dynamite and the political will to become a willing participant in Rossa's plan to raise havoc in Britian. The series of attacks that became known as the Fenian Dynamite Campaign was an exercise in terrorism. The strategy meant to intimidate the British public into pressuring those in government to make changes in policy by attacking soft targets rather than directly confronting British authority.

In 1881, Joseph Burke, with his son's assistance, began a series of bombings in the Liverpool area. In early May they set off an explosion at Chester Police Barracks south of Liverpool. A week later they repeated with a bombing of the Liverpool Police Barracks. Six weeks later they planted explosives aboard the steam and sail cargo vessel the SS Malta in port at Liverpool. They followed this two days later by attempting to sabotage the SS Bavaria also docked at Liverpool.

The explosives were discovered on both vessels before detonation. The failures caused Joseph Burke to conclude these ventures far too risky to endanger his son. If discovered, they could go to the gallows. Their terrorist exploits already made headlines in English newspapers. Scotland Yard came under intense pressure to identify and arrest the perpetrators. In response, Scotland Yard Special Branch was created as a special unit responsible for investigating matters of national security.

Burke and his son returned to County Cork in Ireland to resume coal mining around Kanturk. While remaining secretly involved with the Irish Republican Brotherhood, the organization curtailed engaging in the bombing campaign for over a year before resuming in early 1883. However, during the period of relative calm, Scotland Yard Special Branch relentlessly pursued efforts to identify those involved in the bombing conspiracy.

Several arrests were made in Liverpool in March 1883. Two of these individuals came from County Cork, Ireland with the news published in the *Cork Examiner*. Burke was well acquainted with these individuals. Immediately, Burke and his family went into hiding with the help of the local IRB. Within weeks, the Royal Irish Constabulary raided the homes and businesses of individuals with associations of any of those individuals.

Joseph Burke knew it was only a matter of time before anyone connected with the Irish Republican Brotherhood in Cork was detained. That would lead to discovering he and his son had been in the Liverpool area when the bombings began in 1881. This left no choice but to leave Ireland.

With assistance from Jeremiah O'Donovan Rossa in America, the family of five caught passage to America, eventually making their way to the coalfields of southern West Virginia. Burke and his oldest son easily found employment as coal miners among the vast numbers of coal mines in this sector of the Appalachian Mountains. Outside the Irish conclaves of Boston and New York, West Virginia was sufficiently remote to disappear from scrutiny from British police and possible extradition.

The Burkes settled in the Paint Creek area south of the town of Pratt on the Kanawha River in West Virginia. Coal mining in America offered nothing better than the same difficult poverty existence but with more opportunities with its dozens of coal mines than in economically distressed Ireland. Mining coal was among the most dangerous and demanding work in the late 19th century so there was always available employment for those willing to engage in the demanding work for subsistence wages.

The Burkes' circumstances were substantively not much different than impoverished County Cork in Ireland. They were comparatively better off financially with two male wage earners and a second income from Maude Burke teaching the children of miners. Teaching also provided the means of educating the two younger children, Noreen and Alan. Perhaps providing them the opportunity to escape the generational cycle of poverty.

As with most coal mines in the rugged mountain terrain of West Virginia, miners and their families mostly lived in company provided housing and bought goods at company owned stores close to their place of work. The arrangement served to bind the workforce into a form of labor servitude in the remotely located coalfields. Mine operators also extracted additional profits by providing goods and services at uncompetitive prices. Even Maude Burke's meager teaching salary came from the mine operator but indirectly came from the miners by extracting a tuition fee for each child from the miner's wages. The practice discouraged the sacrifice necessary to earn an education and regrettably further promoted child labor.

—

Joseph and Maude Burke lived in relative peace outside of Mucklow in the Paint Creek region for the next ten years after immigrating from Ireland. It was in the 1890s that competing mining labor unions ultimately merged into the United Mine Workers of America. The injustices and the social structure of corporate feudalism struck responsive nerves for the radical militant Irish rebels Joseph and Maude Burke. Both saw the direct parallels of mine operator oppression of their workers to centuries of British oppression of the Irish population. Finding this new cause Joseph and Maude devoted themselves to union organizing. Passivity was not in their nature. Their backgrounds of militant resistance in the cause of social justice found a new voice in union organizing activities over the next twenty years.

By 1912, daughter Noreen followed her mother into teaching and married. Now thirty-eight, Noreen found her life disappointing. Choosing marriage instead of pursuing an education beyond her training at a teacher's normal school in Charleston proved a mistake. Fergus Hannigan was a miner and close friend of her brother Liam. Their marriage made ever escaping from West Virginia unlikely. Eventually discovering her inability to bear children profoundly changed their relationship.

Alan Burke finished high school by making the three and a half-mile walk each way to Pratt every school day. In 1896 at the age of eighteen, he enlisted in the United States Marine Corps.

Joining the Marine Corps was the best way to get as far away from the backward West Virginia mountains as possible and experience the world. He saw the Marines as an elite military organization. By his reading of American history, the Marines afforded a career with opportunities for experiencing foreign travel.

By 1912, Alan Burke was in his seventeenth year of military service with the United States Marines. That service had taken him to many foreign places. Locations vital to American interests experiencing conflict. Those deployments afforded the opportunity to distinguish himself in repeated combat situations resulting in his promotion to master gunnery sergeant with several decorations for valor. Yet the inability to visit his family because of his almost continual foreign postings left a void in relations with his family. In those seventeen years, he only visited three times. Each time was difficult. The West Virginia coalfields now felt just as alien as his postings. He mostly missed his siblings. Having little appreciation for his parents' union militancy made interaction with them seem as if talking to strangers. Both were now in their early sixties and working hard yet energized by their activism to promote better conditions for coal miners. His father still went into the mines to dig for coal. Strong as a mule but noticeably slowed by advancing arthritis.

Alan's older brother Liam worked alongside his father digging coal for many years before becoming an organizer for the United Mine Workers union. Encouraged by his parents to escape the manual work of a miner, Liam Burke found a career with better prospects. Unfortunately, the demands of constant travel proved difficult to consider marriage and a family. As years passed, he never married. Liam Burke lived his life in the shadow of his parents. He travelled widely throughout the Kanawha River coal fields along Paint Creek and Cabin Creek organizing for the United Mine Workers.

—

Paint Creek and Cabin Creek comprised 96 coal mines employing 7,500 miners. Liam devoted most of his efforts to the unorganized Cabin Creek region to the west of Paint Creek. The 41 mines comprising the Paint Creek coalfield were all unionized by the UMW by 1912. The 55 mines on Cabin Creek were not unionized. Not just open shops, but where union miners were not hired. Joining the UMW made them became subject to immediate termination. Recruitment was a hard sell.

Although the Paint Creek mines were unionized, miners received 2 ½¢ less per ton of coal extracted than other unionized mines in Southern West Virginia. In union negotiations, the UMW demanded compensation parity for Paint Creek miners with the other union miners of the region. They also demanded several fundamental work rule changes. Discontinuation of blacklisting of discharged workers, discontinuation of compulsory trading at company stores, and several measures to rectify mine operators cheating on tonnage weights. Miners were not paid by the hour but rather by tonnage produced and brought to the surface and weighed by company officials.

The increase of 2 ½¢ per ton would equate to costing mine operators 15¢ per miner per day. The mine operators refused. Although the UMW did not call a strike, all the miners along Paint Creek walked out on April 18, 1912. Collectively and with little debate, the miners of the Cabin Creek mines declared their own strike and joined the walkout of the miners of Paint Creek.

Unrest among coal miners had been escalating for years. Although striking meant inflicting economic hardship for miners already existing on close to a subsistence level, there existed overwhelming support for going out. Even with emotions running high, there was surprisingly little violence in the first month of the strike. With widespread support from miners across the region, the UMW wanted to take advantage of the solidarity to achieve gains peacefully.

Any such thoughts became dashed when on May 10, 1912, the mine operating companies collectively hired the Baldwin-Felts Detective Agency to break the strike.

Baldwin-Felts was a private security service company. It had its origin around the turn of the 20th century. Patterned after the Pinkerton Detective Agency, predominate in the field in the second half of the 19th century, Baldwin-Felts established in 1890 initially began providing security and investigative services to railroads in Southeastern United States. The firm became well known to the mine operators because of their armed security for payroll trains to the remotely located coalfields. It was to Baldwin-Felts that West Virginia mine operators turned to as labor unrest reached a tipping point with the widespread strike in the Paint Creek and Cabin Creek coalfields.

Both Pinkerton and Baldwin-Felts also provided investigative and even quasi-law enforcement functions to federal and state government agencies. During the early decades of the 20th century, criminal elements used geographic boundaries as a means of thwarting law enforcement. Most law enforcement at the time was administered by county-level agencies, making escape across jurisdictions a widespread criminal tactic. Private security agencies had no such restrictions. They also had fewer constraints than official law enforcement in the manner with which they dealt with suspected felons.

With declining demand for their services by the railroads, Baldwin-Felts turned their efforts to providing security for mining companies. Typical of the time, public law enforcement in labor disputes involving large numbers of workers fell to the mine operators. The scope of such disturbances went far beyond the resources to maintain public order by local law enforcement, or even by state-level law enforcement. However, the mine operators used Baldwin-Felts to go beyond providing security for company property. Not bound by enforcing the law, this private army of well-armed men practiced in violent confrontation could use their services for other means of coercing the workforce. Eviction from company-owned housing, harassment, and protecting strikebreaking replacement labor from intimidation by striking miners.

Baldwin-Felts detectives carried an array of weapons that went beyond mere defensive protection. Their basic weapon was a Smith & Weston Model 3 .44 caliber revolver. A massive six-round weapon 12 inches long and weighing 2.9 pounds. Many were also armed with a large clip-point knife such as a Bowie knife that might be up to 20 inches in length and weighing 2 pounds. At their disposal was a typical compliment of Winchester Model 1886 lever-action .45 caliber repeating rifles and Colt 10-gauge shotguns. As the need may arise, they also had access machine guns.

The company headquarters of most of West Virginia's mining operations were located outside the state. Each mine was one of any number of profit-producing assets spanning the region. There existed no attachment between management and the workforce other than profits. Even during this advanced time of the industrial revolution, labor was considered as a necessary cost of doing business. Often an expendable commodity, easily replaced. In coal mining, even more so. Labor represented only modest capital investment compared to other great industrial enterprises such as making steel, railroad lines and rolling stock, or industrial textile looms. Its product was a natural resource, not subject to higher levels of worker skills as for manufactured products.

Forced into adding a substantial non-value-added expense in armed security, the mine operators proactively made use of this necessary resource in the coalfields that had only minimal official law enforcement. West Virginia was largely lawless territory. Except for remote coal mining communities, sparsely populated. What little official law enforcement existed was often in the pocket of the coal mining companies. Baldwin-Felts had experience in suppressing strikes by armed force with typically no governmental interference. As a detective agency, Baldwin-Felts was also well practiced in gathering intelligence on the miners and the UMW union. The hired security also prevented union organizers from entering company grounds and guarded strike-breaking replacement miners arriving by train. Observing no operational boundaries, Baldwin-Felts attacked union organizers and other troublemakers indiscriminately.

The most disturbing use of Baldwin-Felts was the evictions of miner families from company-owned housing. Not only did the miners lose income but forcing families from their homes provided an insidious means of intimidating a rebellious workforce.

Within a couple of weeks, Baldwin-Felts had a force of more than 300 heavily armed agents employed as mine guards in Paint Creek and Cabin Creek. The Burkes lived in company housing provided by the Paint Creek Mine since it opened in Mucklow in 1902. Early in the morning of May 21, two dozen Baldwin-Felts agents converged on the rough cabins housing miners' families. Conducted like a military operation, a handful of Baldwin-Felts agents entered a house forcing the occupants out at gun point. An array of additional agents stood outside in strategic positions to prevent interference from the miners. Many of these agents were armed with rifles and shotguns. Beyond evicting the occupants, the agents systematically began removing all household goods. Outside, several agents wielded axes to destroy furniture and household goods.

Joseph Burke and his son Liam could only look on with simmering hatred. For Joseph Burke now sixty-three, the old fire of taking violent retribution against his oppressors reignited. This act of being evicted while unable to fight back was the last straw. When news spread of Baldwin-Felts flooding into Paint Creek by train, the old revolutionary Joseph directed Liam, Fergus Hannigan, and a group of likeminded miners to hide firearms in strategic locations outside of company land. He rationalized that if they kept weapons close at hand, they would be cut down piecemeal in a firefight by better armed Baldwin-Felts agents. Tactically it seemed wiser to keep their arms secure and available to act collectively at the appropriate time. For Joseph Burke that time had now arrived.

Maude and Noreen gathered what goods they could salvage while Joeseph commandeered a wagon to assist them and fellow families in relocating off company land. Among the chaos, Noreen's husband Fergus Hannigan arrived as the evictions were in its final stages. As an organizer for the UMW, he learned of the eviction attack on the miner's housing and returned to Mucklow by train immediately. He brought news that the Union was setting up a tent camp a mile and a half north in a place called Holly Grove to provide shelter for displaced mining families.

Fortunately, it was springtime with modest temperatures, however, the rains made adjusting to already dismal circumstances further demoralizing. Joseph Burke wasted little time before planning an armed response to the outrage. Courageous throughout his violent background, Joseph Burke was also reckless.

The Burkes hid a cache of weapons and ammunition in a well-hidden cave. Packed in a box, the weapons were wrapped in oiled butcher paper to prevent corrosion. Other miners hid their arms in similar fashion.

Immediately following eviction, the miners retrieved their concealed weapons enroute to Holly Grove. They would now keep firearms at the ready in their tent community, Joseph Burke organized a defensive perimeter with outlaying pickets manned around the clock to warn of any incursion by armed Baldwin-Felts guards. The evictions were a de facto declaration of war by the mine operators.

It had been two months since the eviction of miner families from their homes in Mucklow. The strike continued with no progress with the mine operators refusing to negotiate with the UMW union. Hostilities escalated as wholesale evictions commenced throughout the Kanawha Coalfield provoking violent responses from the ousted miners. Sniping at the hated Baldwin-Felts mine guards and random acts of sabotage to mine assets became regular occurrences. In retaliation and to invoke terror, Baldwin-Felts agents freely moved outside of company-owned land to harass miners with unprovoked beatings and destruction of miner's property. The sheriff of Kanawha County did nothing to curtail the excesses committed by Baldwin-Felts. William Baldwin and Thomas Felts soon became the two most feared and hated men in the mountains.

Although a good many of the striking miners did not belong to the Union, there was no other means for negotiation. Restless to do something, Joseph Burke assembled a group of more than thirty of the most militant miners one evening in late July. They gathered at some distance from the tent encampment to avoid being overheard.

Standing on a large rock, Joseph Burke addressed the miners. "This strike is now three months old. The mine operators have hired an army of thugs. Driven us from our homes. Destroyed our property. Now they are taking away our livelihood by hiring scabs. We live no better than slaves. Time has come to take up arms. Been listening to that old woman Mother Jones. She's preaching that it's time to fight back."

One miner yelled out, "Damn little good she's accomplished. That march to the state capitol with thousands of miners didn't do jack shit. Fuckin' Governor's on the side of the mining companies."

"Right you are about that," Burke replied. "An old woman and demonstrations only show the mine companies how weak we are. Time to show 'em we can bite back sharply. Stop the flow of strikebreaking scabs coming in. Time for us to draw real blood."

"What you have in mind?" another miner yelled.

"Begin a campaign of organized attacks on the trains bringing in the scabs. Scare the shit out of anyone thinking they can come here and take our jobs. First of all, we need to send a strong message. Attack these Baldwin-Felts hired guns. Kill a few of the fuckers. Let them know we have arms and are ready to use them. They have set up camp on the north end of the creek to fortify both the Paint Creek and Scranton Mines.

"I chose you blokes because I believe you have the sand to show these fuckers they have a real fight on their hands. I want to hit the Baldwin-Felts camp at daylight tomorrow morning. My son Liam has scouted the camp. Gather around and let me show you how we go about this."

Joseph Burke was energized for the first time in years. Subconsciously, perhaps feeling his age and mortality, inflicting violence on the enemy played into his fierce nature.

—

As daylight broke the following morning in late July, Burke's well-armed miners positioned themselves in the tangled underbrush on a rise within rifle range of Baldwin-Felts sentries. The miners watched as the Baldwin-Felts agents lit campfires in their tent encampment at the outer perimeter of the Paint Creek Mine. Soon there was the smell of coffee brewing and bacon sizzling in frying pans.

Liam was a crack marksman. His first shot would signal the attack. The miners would then rush toward the tents coming down the hills attacking from both flanks. There were six large tents. Liam appeared to have had done a good job of reconnoitering the battlefield a few nights previous. Estimated possibly a dozen Baldwin-Felts agents. However, it was a dark overcast night with only a half-moon. Liam failed to miss one critical detail. High up on the right hillside overlooking the encampment, Baldwin-Felts constructed a machine gun emplacement with breastworks of railroad ties. Even in the morning light, it remained concealed behind carefully placed shrubbery, appearing as only another sentry outpost. By its location, potentially a sniper position.

The attack plan called for Liam to kill a sentry posted further out on the right side then scale the hillside under covering fire to remove any threat of a sniper on the high ground.

Liam took out that advance sentry with a shot to the head signaling the start of the attack. All the miners began pouring rifle fire into the camp.

Taking the lead, Liam and his brother-in-law Fergus Hannigan begin scampering up the hillside to remove the sniper threat. Joseph directed several miners with rifles to train fire on the Baldwin-Felts concealed position.

Because of the angle of the hill's elevation, the miners' shots went over the heads of the two-man machine gun team. Using the U.S. Army's standard Hotchkiss machine gun firing .30-06 caliber ammunition at a rate of over 400 rounds per minute, one Balwin-Felts agent fired the weapon while a second man loaded 30-round feeder strips for an almost continuous rate of fire.

First to be cut down by the withering fire was Liam Burke leading the attack. Following closely behind him, his father, brother-in-law, and three other miners all fell victim to the machine gun. Wounded, some tried to escape back down the hillside only to be repeatedly hit.

The miners' attack lasted no more than fifteen minutes before they withdrew carrying their dead and wounded. The battle left twelve miners dead, four others wounded, and four Baldwin-Felts agents dead.

Joseph Burke, Liam Burke, and Fergus Hannigan were among the dead as the surviving miners struggled for hours to carry the casualties back to the Holly Grove tent encampment.

—

Strong-willed Maude Burke aided by her daughter Noreen, stoically attended the burying of Joseph and Liam Burke and Noreen's husband Fergus Hannigan. Maude had lived a life of rebellion alongside her husband all her life. His dangerous acts of rebellion imbued her with a fatalism of the possibility of his sudden violent death. Her daughter did not share the militant activism of her parents. In silence, she resented her father for leading her brother and husband in the ill-conceived attack that took their lives.

It was Noreen Burke that kept in regular correspondence with her younger brother Alan serving in the U.S. Marine Corps. They were kindred spirits sharing a hatred for the oppression of working-class life in the coal mines but realizing that violent conflict could not remedy the social injustice. They sustained each other while growing up in the depressive environment of the coalfields of West Virginia.

Alan Burke was currently serving with a contingent of U.S. Marines in Nicaragua. It was weeks after the incident at Mucklow and burying their dead that his mother and sister made their way to Pratt and Noreen wired her brother. The telegram to Marine headquarters was eventually relayed to the *USS Annapolis* anchored off the coast of Nicaragua then delayed further before reaching him. *Family disaster beloved brother. Father, Liam, and Fergus killed by mine guards. Mother and I relocated to Pratt. Plans uncertain. Reach me through UMW District 17 headquarters Charleston. Mother is bearing up stoically. Noreen.*

CHAPTER 2

Charleston, West Virginia | December 1912

Sergeant Major Alan Joseph Burke was in the mess tent eating breakfast in the U.S. Marine encampment in Managua, Nicaragua. Another hot October day in the tropics. His unit had been in combat skirmishes with insurgents for several weeks since arriving in Nicaragua. They were being resupplied and resting, waiting to see if further hostilities would resume. A private came up to him and said, "Sorry to interrupt, Sergeant Major. The Major wants to see you. Said it was urgent."

"Very well," Burke replied. Taking a last sip of coffee, he donned his campaign hat and set off to the command tent.

Major Smedley Butler sat behind a field desk as Burke stepped inside the tent and saluted.

Butler looked up with a grim expression on his face. "Afraid I have some disturbing news, Sergeant Major." Handing it to Burke, he added, "Telegram arrived an hour ago. Sent months ago, but just caught up with us after leaving the Canal Zone."

Burke read the typed note. Without comment he just exhaled and the muscles in his jaw clinched.

"Sit down, Sergeant Major," Butler said. "Nothing anyone can say can ease the pain of unexpected loss of a family member."

Burke was shaken by the terrible news. Could not say he was surprised though. He knew the temperament of his father and brother. From the regular letters from his sister Noreen, he kept abreast of the festering hostilities between the coal miners and the mine operators. Nonetheless, the loss hit him deeply.

He pulled up a camp chair as his commander ordered.

"You'll be wanting to put in for compassionate leave. Unfortunately, I can't spare you until orders come through to pull us out of Nicaragua. Sometimes I believe you run this outfit more than I do. We've been together for lots of years. Seen how you perform in combat."

Alan Burke was a recipient of the Congressional Medal of Honor, earned in China during the Boxer Rebellion at the Battle of Tientsin in 1900. The recommendation came from his commanding officer Smedley Butler, at the time a first lieutenant. After their Captain was killed and Butler was wounded, Staff Sergeant Burke took charge of the company until reinforcements arrived after two days of heavy fighting.

"That's okay, Major. Need some time to get my head around how to deal with this. My sister will take care of my mother. Both are strong women."

"I take it you have some idea what might have happened to your father and brother?"

Burke nodded. "I'm sure you've read in the newspapers about what's happening in the coal fields of West Virginia, Major. If you're a coal miner, the situation's much worse than what makes it into the newspapers. The workingman there is no better off than the people of these *banana republics* where Washington sends us. The mine operators hire their own private militia. The miners are hardened mountain men. Now armed in great numbers. The place is a powder keg. Somebody just lit the match."

Butler nodded. "Tough place you come from. When your leave is up, find transportation back to Camp Elliott. Panama is backwater garrison duty but at least we're not fighting for a bunch of crooked American businessmen. They manipulated Washington to send us into Nicaragua again to prop up a government they can buy off to give them monopolies. A rotten business all around."

Major Butler then stood and shook Burke's hand, laying his left hand on Burke's shoulder. "That'll be all, Sergeant Major. Take care of yourself," Butler said and saluted. Although protocol directs subordinate ranks to initiate salutes to a superior officer, this is reversed for medal of honor recipients.

—

Burke first arrived in Panama in December 1909 as part of a U.S. Marine contingent of 250 men of the 3rd Battalion, 1st Marine Regiment under the command of Major Smedley Butler. They were there to protect American interests during the construction of the Panama Canal. In May of 1910 Butler was ordered to take his battalion to the Atlantic coast of Nicaragua as a show of force against Liberal Party President José Zelaya. Allegedly to protect American citizens located there, it was a thinly veiled excuse for Washington to demonstrate support for the revolt led by a Nicaraguan Conservative Party regional governor named Juan Estrada. Zelaya resigned and went into exile in Mexico and Estrada became president months after the landing of the U.S. Marines. American private financial investment to exploit Nicaraguan resources increased.

However, Nicaraguan internal political strife between liberal and conservative factions soon deteriorated threatening loans to Estrada's coalition government. Pressure forced Estrada to resign bringing his conservative vice president Adolfo Diaz into the presidency. His popularity quickly deteriorated as he faced opposition from his Secretary of War, General Luis Mena. Mena gained support in the National Assembly with a nationalistic platform condemning Diaz from selling out the nation to New York bankers. To stay in power, Diaz requested another intervention by U.S. military forces.

As another Nicaraguan political crisis erupted, Washington ordered Major Butler to mount an expeditionary force of Marines from Camp Elliott, Panama to disembark at Managua to support a smaller force of Marines already in Nicaragua. The current Nicaraguan crisis involved another insurgency, this time to a government friendly to the United States. Nicaragua had taken on increased importance for U.S. strategic military interests with the construction of the Panama Canal now in its final stages of completion. A never-ending cycle of colonial instability.

Transported from Panama by the supply ship *USS Justin*, Major Butler landed with 250 U.S. Marines and an artillery battery to reinforce the 100 Marines already in Nicaragua on August 15, 1912. They completed their mission to seize the city of Granada held by rebel forces on September 22. Butler's battalion saw further action until the insurrection was completely suppressed a month later and his Marines returned to Panama where Burke would then return to the States on a thirty-day leave.

Alan Burke was the senior non-commissioned officer. He had served with Butler since the Spanish-American War and in a variety of foreign postings since then. Major Butler was four years younger and held great respect for Burke as a soldier, promoting him to the most senior non-commission officer rank as the most essential member of his command.

—

The defeat of the miners at what became known as the Battle of Mucklow did not end hostilities. A month later, 5,000 miners from the north side of the Kanawha River began marching south to join the striking miners of Paint Creek and Cabin Creek. The massive growing assemblage of striking miners with untold numbers openly bearing arms caused Governor William Glasscock to panic and declare martial law in southern West Virginia. 1,200 West Virginia State Militia descended into the area disarming both sides and temporarily forestalling a full-scale confrontation.

The martial law declaration effectively suspended civil rights guaranteed under the U.S. Constitution. Under martial law, miners were forbidden to congregate. Indiscriminate arrests by troops untrained in policing subjected miners to summary trials without legal representation. Tried before military tribunals by officers untrained in legal proceedings, they often handed down excessive prison sentences without observing limits imposed by state statutes.

Governor Glasscock misreading the situation as stabilized, lifted martial law on October 15. Armed hostilities immediately returned forcing him to reimpose it on November 15.

Throughout his term as governor of West Virginia, William Glasscock faced political challenges that went far beyond his limited abilities. His background consisted of education until acquiring a law degree at age 41. A short stint as an attorney for a U.S. senator resulted in an appointment as internal revenue collector for West Virginia. Three years later he ran for governor of West Virginia. In 1908, he ran as the Republican nominee for governor beating out his Democratic rival and taking office in 1909.

By early 1912, Glasscock had already decided not to seek a second term in office as the Republican candidate. When the strike commenced in April, the circumstances and explosion of violence overwhelmed him. Throughout the rest of the year, he demonstrated a lack of leadership thereby adding to events going unchecked by any governmental action. By the fall, he could only resort to declaring martial law to quell violence between miners and coal company guards. Even with this tool of using the West Virginia State Militia to maintain order and by suspending constitutional civil liberties, Glasscock demonstrated his inability to produce meaningful results. By December, he was looking only to turn over the office to his elected successor on March 4, 1913.

—

It was late November before Alan Burke shipped out from Nicaragua. He was able to catch passage on a warship to the Norfolk Naval Station in Virginia. Butler was able to grant him a 30-day leave before he was to report back to duty in the Panama Canal Zone. He wired his sister at the United Mine Workers headquarters in Charleston West Virginia. *Arriving at Norfolk Naval Base Virginia after Thanksgiving. Will train immediately to Charleston. Anticipate arriving Charleston Sunday Dec. 1. Alan.* The day before he left Panama, his sister wired back. *Staying at boarding house close to Charleston train station. Mother is in Pratt. Will explain when you arrive. Noreen.*

It was late in the afternoon. A cold day with a wind blowing as the train pulled into the railroad station on the south side of the Kanawha River. The early sign of approaching winter with the leaves gone from the trees as his train pulled into the station. Grabbing his duffle bag, he jumped down to the platform. Immediately his sister came running toward him. Dropping his bag, they embraced.

Noreen burst into tears as she kissed his cheek. "So glad to see you, Alan. You look so handsome in your uniform. It's been so long since you've been back. Everything has changed. All for the worst. I feel so alone."

"Well, I'm here now and you're no longer alone. Let's get out of the cold."

"We can walk to where I'm staying."

"Is Mother in Pratt?"

"Yes. I'll explain when we get somewhere warm. Hungry?"

"That I am. Know a good place where we can have dinner and talk?"

As they walked inside the railway station, Burke saw several armed men in military-style uniform. Assuming they were West Virginia State Militia, Burke said to his sister, "I read in the newspapers that martial law was lifted over a month ago."

"It was but the Governor reimposed it again over a week ago."

One of the militiamen nodded to him recognizing him as a fellow soldier since he wore his Marine khaki field uniform with wrapped puttees over high laced brown leather boots. Yet the distinctive Marine squat pattern cap with the eagle, globe, and anchor insignia and short brim distinguished him from the standard U.S. Army uniform. Burke acknowledged the militia troopers by raising his hand in a loose salute.

Noreen took him to the Hotel Kanawha not far from her boarding house. Depositing his gear in a room, he returned to the dining room of the hotel's small restaurant. Given the renewed declaration of martial law and the Thanksgiving holiday, there were few guests.

Sitting down across from Noreen, "Okay, so what's Mother doing in Pratt? Did she know I was arriving?"

Noreen let out a sigh. "Yes. I told her. Said to say she was sorry not to be here to meet you but hoped to see you soon. Likely involved with some union activity but she didn't explain."

Burke's relationship with his mother was always somewhat distant, but he thought under the circumstances she would want to embrace her only remaining son. They had not seen each other for three years.

Noreen could see her brother's imperceptible reaction by his expression of disappointment. "It's about her union work. Since the deaths, she has immersed herself in it day and night. She's working closely with an older woman Mary Jones who goes by the name Mother Jones. A nationally known union activist. A real force of nature. Mum and Mother Jones are staying in Pratt with another union activist, Sarah Blizzard, the mother of an UMW official. All three are right in the thick of things. They risk being arrested each day."

"Rebellion was a religion for Mum and Dad. I appreciate your letters that gave me a sense of what was going on." Laying his hand on hers, "How are you getting on, Noreen?"

"Good as can be expected. Mum is a constant worry. Losing Fergus was a shock but I'm over that. Things between us were not good for years. Ever since learning I could not bear children, he gradually turned away. Like you, he looked up to Liam. Followed him and Dad to a bad death. You ask how I am, I'm angry as hell. At all three of them getting killed for their stupidity."

"What happened that day?" Burke asked as a waitress came over.

"You folks be orderin' dinner?"

"Yes, we are. Could we get something to drink first," Alan said.

"Can't get you any alcohol because of the martial law."

Noreen said, "How 'bout coffee then?"

"Be right back. Got beef stew or chicken with dumplings for dinner if you're interested."

21

Noreen answered her brother's question. "The strike was hard enough but Dad went over the top when they evicted us from our company housing in Mucklow. The Baldwin-Felts hired mine guards destroyed much of our belongings. It was Dad that organized and led about thirty armed miners to retaliate against the Baldwin-Felts encampment outside the Paint Creek Mine.

"Liam as usual was right by Dad's side. Fergus of course followed. Got nine other miners killed and others wounded."

"Did you learn more detail of what happened?"

Noreen nodded. "Fergus' best friend was there that day. Helped bring Fergus' body back to our tent camp at Holly Grove about a mile and a half north of Mucklow. Oh God, Alan, it was somethin' awful looking at their bodies. Smashed up bad by machine gun bullets is what Fergus' mate said. All three cut down trying to climb a hill to get at that gun. Mum broke down and wept like she was going to die herself."

"How is she now?"

"Wouldn't know. Haven't seen much of her lately. Mum's tough but she just lost a husband and son. We argue too much. Better to leave it be. She's caught up in the maelstrom created by that rabble-rousing old woman Mother Jones. Challenges the miners to take action. Marching in protest is one thing, but encouraging miners to take up arms to fight mine guards that are better armed is criminal. The miners look to Mother Jones like someone larger than life. She has the gift of oratory alright. Speaks to the emotions of the miners using common language. Makes it sound like she's been anointed by God when she speaks. Mum has become a devoted follower. Personally, I can't stand the foul-mouthed old bitch. Talks as if she's the second coming."

"Is Mum still teaching school?"

"No. Not since Mucklow. UMW District 17 pays her a small wage for organizing. Mum found she has persuasive skills much like Mother Jones uses when speaking to groups of miners. As the widow of a miner, they embrace Mum as one of them. Plays the role of martyr."

"Are you sure you're not being a little hard on her?"

Noreen smiled. "I sound that angry, huh?"

Burke said, "Listen, you have the right to be angry. Mum and I never saw eye to eye either. It was you I looked up."

Noreen made a sour look, "Don't know about that. You looked up to Liam as your big brother. Taught you how to shoot and handle yourself with your fists. Together you two could be a fearsome pair."

He recalled his older brother fondly. Liam was six feet two and muscled from working in the mines from age sixteen. Alan was strong in a wiry sense but shorter. As a teenager attending school, many boys his age from miner families were already employed in the mines. Some taunted him for his privileged life of being able to attend high school. Many fights resulted. Liam taught him how to win by fighting dirty.

Burke smiled, "Yeah, I learned a lot from Liam. But I learned a lot from you, Sis. You taught me other things. How to use my brain. Your idea of rebelling against injustice was to use your intellect. You taught me to love books."

"That didn't get me very far. I am thirty-eight, widowed, no children, teaching children in the most depressed place in America, with no prospects."

"Listen Noreen, what happened to Dad and Fergus has changed everything. I hope to convince Mum to leave this place. She's spry enough to resume teaching in some decent place not torn by violence. You also need to be free of this life, Noreen."

"I need to be free of Mum. I can't abide listening to her continual union preaching. Yet I feel responsible for looking after her even if she doesn't want my help."

They paused as the waitress interrupted to serve them their dinner.

Noreen wanted to change the conversation from depressing family affairs. "Tell me about what you've been doing these last months in Nicaragua."

Burke and his sister corresponded regularly but that was interrupted with the deployment from Panama to Nicaragua.

"Panama is just garrison duty. The Marines are there to backup Navy warships in protect the canal construction project. Boring and uncomfortable duty. Panama is close to the equator and hotter even than Nicaragua. Same circumstances I've experienced my entire career as a Marine. Boredom in uncomfortable climates frequently broken by occasional calls to combat.

"The United States Marines are the elite shock troops of America's military might. We are the best trained and the most mobile. Saw my share of more combat in Nicaragua. Couldn't say why we were in Nicaragua other than to protect American interests. That can mean all sorts of things. Glad it was a short deployment like the first time I was there three years ago. Yet not particularly enthused about returning to duty in Panama."

They talked back and forth about personal matters while eating dinner. Although separated for significant periods of time, they remained exceptionally close as brother and sister through correspondence. Not only was Alan emotionally close to his sister, but he also respected her intelligence. Although Noreen was only three years older, that difference was important in his early development and an alternative to the charged militant views of his parents.

After eating dinner, Noreen said, "Shall we take the train down to Pratt to see Mum in the morning?"

Burke replied, "Sure." He paused before adding. "It's been wonderful seeing you, Noreen. I'm not just here for Mum. It's also about you. You've got a life ahead of you. We both have a responsibility to look after Mum, but you can't ignore your own wellbeing."

—

Burke and Noreen arrived in Pratt the following morning. A small town on the banks of the Kanawha River, it remained largely unchanged from the time when Burke left West Virginia to join the Marines seventeen years earlier in 1895. He trudged from home in Mucklow to Pratt every school day to attend high school. As the train pulled into the station, he saw a large building with a sign reading Shaw Steel & Iron Works. Turning to Noreen, "Looks like the old Shaw blacksmith shop has prospered. That wasn't here when I went to high school. My best friend in high

24

school was Cameron Shaw. Maybe he now runs the business. I'll try looking him up while I'm here."

As the train came to a stop with a great release of steam, Burke saw his mother standing on the platform. With her was a younger woman stylishly dressed in a broad- brimmed large hat. Burke and his sister disembarked as their mother hurried toward them.

Maude Burke embraced her son. She might be toughened by all that life threw against her, but tears flowed freely down her cheeks. It had been a long time since she had seen her son. Noreen walked over to the other woman and shook hands as Maude followed behind leading her son arm in arm.

With martial law again reimposed just ten days earlier, several militiamen with rifles stood on the platform smoking cigarettes. As Maude passed, she shouted, "This here's my son. He's a real soldier not the likes of you boys just pretending as part timer warriors."

Burke pulled his mother's arm, "Easy, Mum. Not the time or place for making trouble."

The soldiers made no response to Maude's comments, but they looked quizzically at Burke trying to understand his uniform. The tunic of his dress uniform was dark navy blue outlined by a standing red collar and matching red at the sleeve buttons. At the upper arm was the Marine Corps oversized insignia of rank consisting in his case of three peaked chevrons up and three horizontally on the bottom in striking yellow outlined in red. His cap was the distinctive compact Marine cap in matching blue with red band and short brim. Visible even from a distance, his impressive array of campaign and valor ribbons on the left breast of his tunic made a bold statement.

Once all four gathered on the platform, Noreen said, "This is Miss Keara Murphy. She's a lawyer and writer from New York. And this is my brother, Keara. Sergeant Major Alan Burke of the United States Marine Corps."

Burke took Murphy's extended hand saying, "A pleasure meeting you, Miss Murphy. What brings you to West Virginia?"

"Researching the labor strife here in West Virginia by following the campaigning activities of Mother Jones. Like me, Mary

Jones is a crusader against child labor. Nothing worse than children engaged in the dangers of coal mining. The UMW were gracious enough to provide your mother as my liaison. We just returned from Mingo County last night. Mother Jones is off working west of here in Cabin Creek."

Still holding her son's arm, Maude Burke said, "The situation is much worse in Cabin Creek. I fear for her safety. These militia buggers do nothing to keep the Baldwin-Felts thugs in check. Better that I didn't take Miss Murphy there. Besides, it was more important that I was here to see my son."

Murphy smiled at Maude still clutching Alan's arm. "Everyone has been so helpful to me since I arrived. Is there a place I could buy us lunch and we can chat? I'd like to get your opinions about what is going on in West Virginia, Sergeant Major Burke. You're from here but somewhat of an outsider considering you've been absent for so many years. Your sister has lived her life here. Her perspectives about the corrupting influences of coal mining and railroad interests are insightful. She explains the underlying circumstances that make West Virginia seem like a place apart from the American ideal. What some call corporate feudalism."

Noreen said, "Well, West Virginia is a place apart. At least the coalfields. The origins for that are complex. Not easily rectified. However, Keara, lunch sounds like a grand idea. I suggest Alice's Restaurant. It's only a short walk up the street. Good food with a large fireplace."

They enjoyed lunch. Since Maude had been with Keara Murphy for several days, the conversation naturally turned to Alan Burke's foreign adventures during the last couple of years. Everyone welcomed talking of something other than the coal mine strike and the violent circumstances leading to the reinstituting of martial law.

Murphy commented, "Your mother said you've been in the Marine Corps for seventeen years. Those ribbons on your uniform attest to an illustrious career."

Burke smiled, "Not sure you could call it illustrious. It attests to the role of the Marine Corps. We are usually the first military

forces deployed in foreign lands. Part of the Navy so we are mobile. I've been involved in a good many combat missions."

"Most of those ribbons are quite colorful, except for that pale
blue one with the stars. What was that for?"

Noreen answered knowing her brother's modesty. "That is
the Congressional Medal of Honor. The highest American citation
for valor. Awarded to Alan in 1900 for an exceptional act of hero-
ism in China during the Boxer Rebellion."

"Oh, my! That is extraordinary."

"I'm so proud of my boy," Maude said. Those purple ribbons
denote wounds received in battle. One he got in China when he
received the Medal of Honor. A second time while serving in the
Philippines.

Murphy asked, "Is sergeant major a senior rank?"

"It's the most senior rank for a non-commission officer. The
commissioned officers give the orders and it's my job to see that
the troops carry out the mission."

"What did you do to receive the medal of honor?"

"I was part of a battalion of Marines that arrived on the cruiser
USS Brooklyn at the large port city of Tientsin in Northern
China on the shore of the Bohai Sea. Weeks earlier the dowager
empress declared war against foreign occupation of China. Our
orders were to dislodge Chinese regulars and Boxer rebel forces
laying siege to Tientsin. From the port it was a 20-mile march to
reach Tientsin. Our orders were to relive other U.S. forces defending Tientsin.

"Advancing toward the city we were ambushed by Chinese
forces. My company commander was killed, and two platoon officers were wounded. As the most senior non-commissioned officer, I took charge." Burke paused for a moment caught up in the
memory. "It was a vicious fight at close quarters. My citation was
for leading a counterattack that inflicted heavy casualties on the
Chinese causing them to break off their repeated attacks. In combat you do your duty to survive. If you don't die in the process,
they award you a medal."

All three women listened in silence trying to visualize what
Burke was relating. Even his mother and sister had never heard

this much detail about that singular event in his many letters over the years.

Burke paused for a moment caught up in the memory. "I apologize for recounting that experience considering how much we have lost as a family here in West Virginia. As Marines, we are bound together as brothers and feel their loss as such."

Changing the subject, he said, "With the state militia patrolling, will this tone down the violence?"

Maude replied, "No. Nothing has changed. Once the uniformed troops leave, we must still contend with the Baldwin-Felts thugs. Governor Glascock was a weakling. Don't expect much better from this new governor. The state house, the police, and the courts are all in the pocket of the collieries."

"Where then do you think this is going Maude?" Keara Murphy asked.

Maude shook her head. "Can't foretell that. This is a war for freedom. Freedom for miners to live a decent life. They and their families are treated no better than the mules hauling up coal out of the mines. The mules are led by young boys that should be in school. Neither the mules nor the boys will ever leave the mines."

Murphy commented, "Well, Maude, people like you and Mother Jones, and even activists like me can only continue to bring pressure to bear on those that exercise oppression."

With lunch over, Maude said to Alan, "I have some union business to attend to this afternoon then Keara and I will return to Charleston with you and Noreen on the four o'clock train."

Noreen said, "Fine, Mum. I'll stay with Alan. He might want to look around Pratt for old times' sake since he went to school here. Care to join us Keara?"

"I'd like that."

"Okay, Mum. We'll see you at the train station no later than 3:30."

After Maude left for the local UMW office, Alan said to his sister and Keara Murphy, "I'd like to look up Cameron Shaw at the iron works. Maybe show off a bit by escorting two beautiful women."

Although it was the coming of winter and a cold day, there was no snow yet on the ground and the sun was out. A good day for a walk. Pratt was a quiet place on the Kanawha River belying its proximity to a center of so much violence. Both Noreen and Murphy smiled, and each took his arm.

Before entering the larger, newer building with the sign Shaw Steel & Iron Works, Burke pointed to a small older building a short distance away. "That's the old blacksmith shop. My friend Cameron learned blacksmithing from a young age by helping out in the shop. Yet like my dad, his father made him complete his education. The family had the money to send Cameron off to college. I went into the Marines instead. Haven't kept in touch all these years. That's a shame. Don't even know if the family still owns the business."

Inside the office, Burke said to a woman behind the counter, "Might Cameron Shaw be in the office today?"

The woman said, "Yes, he is. Whom should I say you are?"

"My name is Alan Burke. Went to high school with Mr. Shaw. Haven't seen him for many years. Would just like to say hello."

"Let me check with Mr. Shaw. I'll be back in a moment."

The woman had left for only a short time when she returned with a man dressed in a suit.

"Well, I'll be damned!" the man said coming from behind the counter extending his hand to Burke with both then embracing. "Look at you. Been years since I last saw you. Still in the Marine Corps?"

"Yep. Been all over the world. Difficult to get back to West Virginia."

"Heard about your father and brother. A terrible loss. Guess that's why you're here."

Burke nodded. This is my sister Noreen Hannigan. Regrettably, she also lost her husband in the same incident. And this Miss Keara Murphy a lawyer and journalist from New York."

Shaw extended his hand to Noreen, "My condolences, Mrs. Hannigan for such a great family tragedy." Turning then to Murphy, "Pleased to meet you, Miss Murphy. Please come into my office."

Once everyone was seated in comfortable chairs, Shaw said, "Suffered my own loss with the death of my father several years ago to a heart attack. I took over management of the business. His health was not good for some time. He and mother spent time away from here traveling on doctor's orders to get away from the stress of our growing business."

Shaw turned Murphy, "What brings you to this remote corner of West Virginia, Miss Murphy?"

"Been researching the violence surrounding the coal miners' strike. Following the rallies of the labor activist Mother Jones. Mr. Burke's mother has been escorting me through the coalfields to gain an understanding from the miners' perspective."

Shaw said, "I have heard of your mother's involvement with the United Mine Workers, Alan. I'd have thought she and your sister might have left West Virginia given everything that's happened."

Noreen replied, "One would think that to be the case, Mr. Shaw. I for one have tried to convince my mother to do just that. Unfortunately, she's managing her grief by becoming more deeply involved with the miners' cause. I do not share that commitment. I'm a teacher not a labor activist. I stay only to watch over my mother."

"Are you a labor activist, Miss Murphy?" Shaw asked.

"You might say that since I am a vocal opponent to child labor. That's what drew me to Mother Jones. She is the loudest voice right now against child labor. The problem exists throughout American industry, but the practice of employing children in dangerous coal mining work is particularly horrific in the twentieth century."

"Couldn't agree more," Shaw said. Tiring of discussing nothing else but the ever-present coalfield wars, he changed the subject. "It's been seven years since I last saw you, Alan. Where are you serving now?"

"Panama. Guarding the construction of the canal. Arrived there after spending several years in Cuba at the Guantanamo Bay Naval Base on the eastern tip of the island. Guantanamo was strategically located to position a strike force of U.S. Marines for rapid deployment anywhere in the Caribbean. Now Panama serves the same purpose while guarding the canal construction nearing completion.

"President Roosevelt applied the Monroe Doctrine from a hundred years ago to exclude European powers influence in the Western Hemisphere. That meant the Caribbean, Central and South America. American colonial expansion started after defeating the Spanish. We gave Cuba its independence in 1902. Not entirely. The United States retained the right to intervene in Cuban affairs. That includes controlling its finances and dictating foreign affairs.

"Teddy took American expansionist destiny further as a basis for justifying our meddling in other countries in the hemisphere. That included sending the U.S. Marines to enforce United States interests. His next imperialistic venture was taking Panama away from Columbia. President Taft continued Roosevelt's Monroe Doctrine strategy. With the Panama Canal nearing completion that now becomes even more important. Now we have a strong military presence based in both Cuba and Panama. That's why I was I was in Nicaragua when eventually learning of the tragic events at Paint Creek."

Murphy spoke up, "You sound as if you disapprove of American foreign policy."

Burke nodded. "Let me answer that this way, Miss Murphy. I disagree with how we exercise American might. Goes far beyond ensuring America's defense. It serves to establish these poor countries as virtual U.S. colonies to serve American economic interests. Typically, private corporate economic interests."

"You're very well informed, Sergeant."

"Every soldier should always be well informed. We may be sent to risk our lives because of Washington foreign policy. All the more important for U.S. Marines. We're always the first troops to enter a combat zone."

They chatted for the next hour over coffee before Burke said they must be leaving to meet his mother and catch the train to Charleston.

31

Shaw said, "This has been wonderful seeing you, Alan. How long will you be in West Virginia?"

"Couple of weeks. Must be in Norfolk a week before Christmas. Then back to Panama."

"Wonderful. Let's plan on having dinner in Charleston before you leave. I'll bring my wife Edith. Where are you staying?"

"The Kanawha Hotel."

"Excellent. In the Arcade Building on Virginia Street. That's where I stay on my business visits to Charleston. Edith loves the shops at the Arcade. I hope you and your mother can also join us, Mrs. Hannigan."

CHAPTER 3

Charleston, West Virginia | December 1912

As they waited inside the small Pratt train station, Maude Burke arrived twenty minutes before the scheduled train to Charleston. Sitting down on the bench next to Alan she took his hand, "Told them I'd be back Wednesday when Mary Jones returns. Miss Murphy is leaving to return to New York on Wednesday, but I must help with getting food to the tent camps. I'll be back at the end of the week then be free to spend all the following week visiting with my wandering son."

Arriving at the Charleston train station, they walked over the bridge to the Hotel Kanawha on Virginia Street where both Alan and Keara Murphy were staying.

Noreen said to Murphy, "Alan and I are going to take Mum back to our boarding house tonight and catch up on family affairs. Since you are leaving Wednesday, would you like to have dinner with Alan and I tomorrow night? I'd love to talk to you more about New York."

"That would be wonderful," Murphy responded. "I have plenty of work to keep me busy working on my newspaper article."

"Excellent. The restaurant here at the hotel is the best in Charleston. We'll fetch you around seven tomorrow evening," Noreen said.

Murphy extended her hand to Maude. "Thank you so very much for showing me around, Maude. You have been invaluable. If I don't see you before I leave, once again I hope you can find your way to work through your terrible tragedy."

Maude shook Murphy's hand then hugged her. "That's what I'm doing, Keara. Fighting for justice for West Virginia coal miners is now my purpose."

—

Alan walked his mother and Noreen to their boarding house. Everyone was sitting down to dinner. The landlady insisted Alan join the other tenants. The other guests consisted of four men of varying ages. They welcomed the opportunity to question Alan about his many military ventures of which his mother was so proud.

Following dinner, Alan, Maude, and Noreen wanted to discuss personal matters privately. Finishing the simple meal of chicken and dumplings, the landlady said to Noreen, "You and your mother go along into the parlor with your brother. I'll clean up the dishes. If you gentlemen will be so kind, might I ask you to let Maude and her family have some time alone? God knows they have much to discuss after all they've been through."

Seated in the parlor with a fire in the fireplace, Alan got right to the point. "What are your plans, Mum?"

"Working for the Union. It's my duty to do all I can to make things better."

"Mum, I've been reading yours and Noreen's letters for years. The situation for coal miners has only gotten worse. The colliery operators have a strangle hold over everything. The violence only stops temporarily with martial law. Only miners are arrested. Never any of the Baldwin-Felts mine guards. It's a rigged game. With the government supporting the mine operators there is no path for the miners to achieve their objectives."

"What would you have me do, Son?"

"Leave this place. Teach school somewhere that's not at war."

34

Maude shook her head. "Noreen has been saying the same thing ever since ... since your father, brother, and Fergus died. If I left West Virginia, I'd feel lost. This place holds me hereafter almost thirty years. Union organizing work is now my life. Working alongside Mary Jones showed me that I have a calling to continue the fight.

"Mary and I are kindred spirits. It's as if I was meant to do this work. Like me, Mary is Irish. Born in Cork in the old country. Came to America as a young girl when her family fled Ireland during the Great Famine some sixty years ago. She's much older than me but with the energy of a woman half her age.

"Mary has suffered tragedy all her life. Lost her husband and four children to yellow fever soon after the civil war. Turning to dressmaking, she then lost her home and livelihood in the Great Chicago Fire of 1871. That's when she became a union activist. Now she has saved me by her example of service to coal miners. Do you not see the parallels in our lives?"

Alan let out a sigh. "Mum, you can't continue doing this. It's too dangerous. Besides, everything is against union organizing efforts. You wrote to me about the yellow dog contracts the mining companies force all the miners to sign. Means being fired if they joined a union. You wrote that the courts have upheld such contracts. How can you win with even the government against the labor union?"

Yellow dog contracts became a condition of employment for miners among most of the coalfields of West Virginia. Recognized as legal by the West Virginia Supreme Court, these employment contracts prohibited miners from joining any union on penalty of immediate termination. The United Mine Workers of America was also unsuccessful in getting the courts to suppress injunctions filed by mine operators which also legally prohibited UMW organizing efforts where these contracts existed.

Maude replied, "That's oppression of the worse kind when corporate money corrupts government. The rights given to the people in the American Constitution are denied to the coal miners of West Virginia. I follow Mother Jones' lead in rebelling against any unjust practice, legal or otherwise. Working people cannot forever live under the yoke of tyranny."

Noreen interjected, "I have had the same argument many times with Mum, Alan. It's like arguing religion to a convert."

Maude smiled condescendingly, "I know you both are trying to look after me. But I've been fighting oppression since I married your father. Even before that, both our families had a history of rebelling against the British. That's what forced us to leave Ireland. After what happened to your father, your brother, and Fergus, I must not shy away from carrying on. The role of grieving widow does not suit me."

"Alan responded sharply, "Mum, the coal miners can never win this fight. The UMW will not be successful. The miners will suffer through this strike only to return to the mines. Probably no better off. No guarantee that violence will not resume once martial law is removed."

"You've been a teacher all your life, Mum," Noreen said. "A good teacher. More benefit is to be done by returning to teaching than trying to sell miners on joining the union."

Maude pursed her lips before replying, "Hard to explain, but fighting against mining company oppression is necessary for me. This is my way of way of enduring the unendurable loss of Joseph and Liam. Noreen found her own path of survival by devoting herself to teaching. For me, it's fighting against those that oppress us."

To end the debate, Maude switched the discussion to Alan. "When your leave is up, where will you then go?"

"Back to Panama. Boring duty. I detest the place. A tropical disease-ridden jungle. The Marines are there to protect the construction of the Canal. You see the United States stole the narrow isthmus of Panama from Columbia ten years ago. This was to take over the earlier failed excavations of the French to dig a canal connecting the Caribbean to the Pacific Ocean."

"Stole? Is that true?" Maude asked.

"Essentially. Columbia was fighting a civil war. The United States supported the rebels that led to the creation of the Republic of Panama which was a remote province of Columbia. With the new government of Panama, the United States drafted a treaty giving us control of what is called the Canal Zone. American imperialism."

"Obviously you are against that," Maude said.

"In many ways. International politics is complicated. Every country attempts to justify its reasons for imperialistic conquest. One reason given is that the people of the foreign land become better off under the protection of the more powerful nation. It usually ends instead becoming some form of oppression. Not much different circumstances than what coal miners endure in West Virginia."

Noreen knew of her brother's evolving feelings as his military career progressed. In choosing to serve in the U.S. Marine Corps, this assured repeated foreign postings to protect American foreign interests.

Noreen asked, "Have you ever considered leaving the Marine Corps?"

"Sure. The question remains as to what else I would do if I resigned. Soldiering is all I know. I'm approaching twenty years of service in a couple of years. Maybe then."

Maude said, "I'm a little tired. I'll let you and Noreen chat. I've got to take the train back to Pratt tomorrow morning. Need to meet with Mother Jones. I'll be back in Charleston at the end of the week. I promise to spend all next week with you, Son."

With that, Maude stood up and embraced Alan.

After their mother retired to her room, Noreen said, "See what I tried to tell you in my letters? Mum won't budge. She sees Mother Jones as fearless and feels she must do the same."

"Is the situation in West Virginia as bad as you described in your recent letters?" Alan asked.

"Worse. You'd have to have lived here these last few years to appreciate just how far West Virginia coalfields have descended into something alien to the American experience. This is the second time the Governor has invoked martial law. That provided the ability for the state militia to arrest and try miners in military courts martial proceedings. Civil liberties suspended. But you know all that. A depressing place to live."

Alan nodded in agreement, "After high school, I wanted to leave West Virginia. Not because of labor violence but just everything about coal mining. The dirt, the danger, the isolation in these remote mountains. Even going to school in Pratt brought a sense of living away from the mines. Saw what life could offer away from the coal mines."

"They weren't. However, the foundations for what goes on today started long ago before the turn of the century. While away at college in Danville, I studied the history behind the coalfields of West Virginia. Why did this oppression exist? The answer was converging factors. Advancing technology. The growth of industrial demand for energy fueled by coal. The sparsely populated remote locations where coal exists. The opportunity for corporate greed to flourish.

"Going back several decades, farsighted corporate entrepreneurs from outside West Virginia formed syndicates and purchased large tracts. Bribing local officials, they evicted people that had logged, hunted, and farmed the region for generations. Once the railroads penetrated into the Appalachians, it created a coal rush. West Virginia offered easily accessed exposed coal seams of bituminous coal. Along with cheap non-union labor, West Virginia coal undermined higher-priced union-mined coal from elsewhere.

"Today, West Virginia coal mines are the most dangerous coal mines in America, and with the lowest pay. Over 90 percent of miners live in company towns allowing the mine operators to control all economic life of the labor force. Medieval serfism. Like what Mum and Dad described of tenant farms in Ireland the last century."

Alan chuckled, "How is it you know so much about West Virginia history?"

"Started when I went to college. In the last few months since the killings, I immersed myself in trying to understand how this environment came about. Talking with Keara, she suggests I try writing. Not a history book, but a first-person account of life in this corner of America. How it's like to live under oppression that denies civil liberties and the very idea of what America represents."

"You're a smart one, Sis. You should write a book. From someplace like New York where you can publish while continuing teaching. Maybe further your education and teach at a university. Why do you stay here?"

"Well, life is complicated, little brother. Truth is, I'd welcome the chance to live elsewhere Would do just that in a heartbeat if it weren't for Mum fixed on remaining in West Virginia."

"Doesn't seem like she needs much looking after."

"Maybe not but she's still my mother. Getting up in age. She tries to keep up with Mother Jones. For whatever else I think of Mother Jones, the old woman has the stamina of mule. Mum is sixty-one, Mother Jones says claims to be eighty-two. Mum looks to her as a mentor. Ignores the physical dangers of union organizing. Easy enough to become an accidental victim.

"Mother Jones has even been talking about working to organize the miners along the Tug Fork River to the south. That's where she and Mum were before you arrived. That is especially hostile country to union organizing. The mine operators there have been successful in excluding the UMW."

"Listen, Noreen, I came back to see about you as much as Mum. You've suffered just as great a loss as Mum. You have a long life ahead of you."

"I shared the same feelings about leaving given only poor prospects for a future as you did, Alan. As a young woman I did not have the same options as a man. That's why I got an education to expand my horizons. Made the mistake of succumbing to the attractions of a handsome man that was interested in me. Our marriage deteriorated after I learned I was incapable of having children. I was okay with that, but Fergus wasn't. As we drifted apart, I devoted myself to teaching. Mum was also a teacher, but she did it more as a job. I on the contrary find it a rewarding calling. Regrettably, I did not take the opportunity to leave years ago. Circumstances now make that more difficult."

"Since you love teaching that provides the perfect means of relocating far from this troubled place. Maybe Mum will tire of this union organizing work. Might start feeling her age and look to an easier life in her later years. Once you are established elsewhere, that might entice her to join you."

"A tantalizing idea that I fantasize about often. Mum would never admit she needs some looking after, and maybe she doesn't. With me settled at some distance but still close enough by train, she might see the advantage on her own. If I relocated outside West Virginia, I'd worry constantly. More than that, I'd feel guilty for abandoning her for my own selfish reasons."

"Damnit, Noreen, that's no way to think."

"Perhaps not, but emotionally that's what keeps me at Mum's side." Standing up, Noreen announced, "I'm going to call it a night. What are you doing tomorrow?"

"Going to check out Paint Creek. Where you and the family lived for a time after eviction from the mine-owned housing where we grew up. Want to also have a look at where this gun battle took place. Where our family died."

Alan Burke knew the truth about what happened that day where his father and brother died. His sister related in detail the events that day gleaned from survivors of the attack. Their father instigated the ill-fated attack. Although their mother surely knew, none of the other families of the dead miners ever laid the blame on Joseph Burke.

Surprised and apprehensive, Noreen replied, "Not sure that'll be possible. That's mining company property. Guarded by Baldwin-Felts agents. Maybe also by state militia troops."

"I'll be careful. I'll see you tomorrow evening at the hotel for dinner with Miss Murphy."

Noreen embraced him and planted a kiss on his cheek. "Be careful. I love you, Alan."

—

The next morning, Burke found a car for hire. Setting out for Mucklow, it was 25 miles from Charleston to Mucklow. Following a decent road running alongside the Kanawha River, the last three miles were a slow go over the rutted frozen road as he turned south at Hangford to follow along the Paint Creek tributary. Familiar country even after seventeen years. He walked this every week to get to high school in Pratt, a mile further east from Hangford.

Within a mile he came upon the displaced miners' tent encampment of Holly Grove. This was where his family came after being evicted soon after the strike was called in April. He stopped to take in the depressing sight. The road on the opposite side of the creek from the rail tracks on the other side with the tent enclave beyond crawled up the hill to the west. It was cold and overcast. The ground covered with patchy areas of snow. The water in the shallow creek was partly frozen over at the edges.

Smoke curled from cooking fires. Several women tended a very large cast iron pot Burke assumed might be for boiling water to wash clothes. A couple of men moved about carrying firewood. A few children appearing engaged in chores rather than play.

Burke did not linger yet the image made vivid the conditions under which his family was forced to live after eviction. A mile further on as he entered the small hamlet of Mucklow, two militiamen in campaign hats carrying rifles waved him to a stop. Behind them stood several men in cheap suits armed with rifles. Burke assumed these to be Baldwin-Felts agents hired by the mine management. The mining company owned Mucklow.

A state militiaman came up to Burke's car. "What's your business in Mucklow?"

"Just looking about. Someone I knew died here in a gun battle early this year."

The militiaman looked at Burke's distinctive Marine cap. "You some sort of soldier?"

"A sergeant major in the United States Marine Corps."

"You armed?"

"No."

The second militiaman with sergeant chevrons came up to them followed by the Baldwin-Felts agents. "What the fuck's going on Lester?"

"This fella's a United States Marine sergeant major."

The militia sergeant said, "Out of the car."

Burke complied. "Just wanted to see where someone I grew up with died in a gun battle."

One of the Baldwin-Felts standing next to the militia sergeant then spoke up, "What's your friend's name?"

"Burke."

"What's your name?"

Burke turned to the guardsman sergeant. "You in charge here, Sergeant, or this hired gun?"

The Baldwin-Felts agent held the rifle in his left hand and pulled back his coat to reveal a revolver on his hip. "Any more shit out of you and I'll teach you a lesson soldier man."

Burke looked into the man's eyes. "You goin' to shoot an unarmed man? Maybe just work me over? Hear tell you are good at beating and killing miners. Ever come up against someone that knows how to handle himself?"

Not prudent to be this aggressive, but the sight of the Baldwin-Felts guards going about armed when martial law outlawed civilians displaying firearms made him angry.

Turning to the provocative Baldwin-Felts agent, the militia sergeant said, "Back off." Turning to Burke. "Now, what's your name?"

"Sergeant Major Alan Burke."

"Jesus! Was the fella that died a relative?"

"My father and brother."

"Fuck! You here to make trouble?"

"Not at all. Just wanted to see the place where they died."

The militia sergeant said, "Afraid you can't do that. Turn around and go back the way you came."

The Baldwin-Felts agent spoke up. "Ever kill anybody in battle, Sergeant Major?"

"Killed my share of the enemy. How about you?"

"You look'n for a fight smartass?"

"Not under these circumstances. The best I could do is kill you, but your colleagues would then gun me down."

"How the fuck could you kill me? With just your hands?"

42

"That's right. You'd be dead in seconds. I taught Marines how to do that." Somewhat of an exaggeration, unless he had a knife, but Burke's expression reflected confidence in the threat.

The militia sergeant saw the situation getting out of hand, "Shut the fuck up, both of you! Now you get back in your car, Sergeant Major, and drive back north before I put you under arrest."

Burke understood he pushed further than warranted and left without incident. The experience provided a visceral appreciation of the tensions that existed. He did not recall with fondness his early years growing up here, yet the environment had deteriorated into something far worse. This remote pocket of America now resembled a war zone.

—

Burke spent the rest of the day exploring Charleston. With a population of 25,000, it was not a large city, but at least an American city of sufficient size to offer a feeling of returning to familiar ground. As the state capitol, only the occasional presence of state militia troops reflected the imposition of martial law focused primarily in the rural areas of the coalfields.

Having been away for so many years, West Virginia seemed as if just another foreign place. What struck him was the sheer natural beauty, a counterpoint to the poverty and the desperate circumstances of the coal miners. With his limited time before returning to Panama, he wanted to better understand the environment in which his mother and sister now lived. With his mother preoccupied for the next couple of days, he planned to visit the Tug Fork Valley, a tributary of the Big Sandy River that eventually dumped into the Ohio River. With so much of West Virginia isolated by the Appalachian Mountains, it was also well-served by a network of rail lines necessary to access the coalfields and move coal.

Armed with maps, he planned on training south 60 miles to Williamson in Mingo County sitting on the Tug Fork River. This was the region spilling over into Kentucky made infamous in the later decades of the 19th century for the long-running violent feud of the Hatfield and McCoy clans. The lurid stories of the feud told when he was growing up made him feel like he lived in a primitive backwoods corner of America. West Virginia was just that. If his mother was contemplating on participating in union organizing in this place, he wanted to get his own impression of how hostile the environment might be.

Tonight however, he would enjoy *civilized* Charleston in a grand hotel having dinner with two interesting women. His sister was his lifeline to the family. Through her letters, he came to appreciate her exceptional intellect. She was the first woman he knew that forged a life beyond managing a household and raising a family. As he grew into his teens, he became closer to Noreen than his older brother Liam that he worshiped as a younger boy.

Keara Murphy was like his sister in many ways. As a lawyer and writer, she did not fit the stereotypical woman of the time. That she was also very attractive was not lost on Burke. Moving about the world from one trouble spot to another left little time for interacting with women like his sister and Murphy. He could not deny a physical attraction to Murphy.

Before dinner, he arranged for hotel staff to press his dress uniform and polish his boots. Shaving for a second time since the morning, he grinned in the mirror acknowledging the reason for his vanity.

Descending the staircase, he saw Keara Murphy sitting on a sofa in the lobby. As he approached with his cap tucked under his arm, she gave him a broad smile. "Oh my. You do look dashing in your uniform, Sergeant Major."

He returned her smile, clicking his heels while giving a sharp nod of acknowledgement. "Thank you. However, it is you that that looks exceptionally lovely this evening, Miss Murphy."

She offered her hand that he held then brushed with an air kiss.

"Please sit down next to me, Sergeant Major."

Burke sat down as Murphy said, "May I call you Alan? I think I know you well enough from the glowing praise of your adoring sister. Please call me Keara. Referring to you throughout the evening as Sergeant Major and you replying with Miss Murphy sounds so tedious."

He smiled broadly, "I couldn't agree more, Keara."

Moments later, Noreen appeared. Alan noticed that she also dressed to impress. She was a handsome woman that had a studious look since she wore glasses. Alan smiled as she approached. "My, you look splendid, Noreen." He kissed her on the cheek. "I shall be the envy of the other dining guests escorting two such beautiful women to dinner."

As they entered the hotel dining room, Alan discreetly slipped a bill into the hand of the matre'd. Once seated, a waiter came over with a tray of three cocktail glasses.

Noreen looked at her glass and realized it was champagne by the bubbles. "Is this champaign, Alan?"

"Of course. I'm celebrating being back here."

"But I thought selling liquor was prohibited during the martial law declaration?" Murphy said.

"Well perhaps it is, Keara. Possibly it was my charm or maybe the tip that persuaded the matre'd to suspend that restriction. Drink up, the rest of the bottle is on ice out of sight behind the bar."

Noreen raised her eyebrow and smiled at her brother for calling Murphy by her first name. "Did you go to Paint Creek today?" she asked.

"Yeah. Didn't get as far as Mucklow though. State militia troops have the place sealed off. Saw the tent encampment at Holly Grove. Truly a depressing sight."

Taking a sip of the champaign, he commented, "I could use a whiskey but this champaign is pretty good." Interested in Murphy, he asked, "As a lawyer in New York, what kind of legal work do you do, Keara?"

"Most of my work comes in the form of defending women's suffrage activists that are arrested for protesting to have the right to vote. Filing lawsuits on behalf of women's rights groups to assert all manner of other rights denied to woman. I filed lawsuits for victims' families of the infamous Triangle Shirtwaist Fire in New York last year. I also file lawsuits against employers using child labor. That is how I came to be interested in the activist efforts of Mother Jones. Apart from her union organizing activism, Mother Jones is a strong voice condemning child labor. However, having come to West Virginia, the coal miners' strike and the associated violence has exposed something that is difficult to describe. I fear that few people outside the coalfields of West Virginia can appreciate the stark oppression that exists for coal miners."

Noreen interjected, "The situation in West Virginia is unique to other coalfields in the country. The mines are geographically more remote. That provides the mining corporations extraordinary power over controlling wages and working conditions. Most are headquartered outside of West Virginia with no vested social interest. Yet collectively they wield monopolistic political power."

"Your mother makings that same observation," Keara said, "Described the strike as almost a rebellion."

Noreen replied, "Regrettably, the Governor sees it as an insurrection. Uses state laws to prosecute striking miners on sedition charges by military tribunals."

Murphy nodded and turned toward Alan. "Your mother made many references to me regarding how arduous and dangerous coal mining is. I couldn't very well go into any mines and see things for myself. Few photographs exist that describe exactly how coal is extracted. Can you give me some verbal descriptions that I can use in my articles? Important to give readers a sense of what coal miners endure underground then are made to suffer further above ground."

Alan responded, "Sure. Bear in mind I was never a miner or even went into a coal mine. My mother and father didn't want that for me. However, my older brother gave me some idea of what it was like.

"Each mine consists of a long central tunnel or shaft. Perhaps several such central shafts depending on the size and shape of the seam of coal. Some coal seams are near enough to the surface to permit a central shaft to start at the surface and angle downward. If the seam is at greater depth, some mines employ an elevator to carry miners below. The miners work in specific areas called rooms branching off the central shaft. It is here that they remove the coal from the surrounding rock. A seam might have a thickness of only a couple of feet to well over eight feet. Now this room must be dug by hand. Timber shoring is necessary to secure the walls and ceiling from collapse."

"How's the coal removed from the rock? Murphy asked.

"Picks, hammers, shovels, and explosives. Tools each miner must supply on his own. Typically, a hole is hammered into the coal seam with a chisel. The hole is then filled with dynamite or black powder. Lit by a fuse, the explosive charge fractures the coal. Then the real hard work begins. Sometimes shafts start at just a couple of feet in diameter. The miner shovels the loosened coal often hunched over on his knees. Remember, the air is full of choking dust with the darkness lit only by each miner's open-flame headlamp."

Murphy held up her hand. "Wait a moment. I've got to write this down." After she extracted a notebook and fountain pen from her handbag she said, "Please continue, Alan."

"The coal is then shoveled into cars on narrow tracks and hauled to the surface using mules tended by young boys. The coal is then weighed establishing the miner's pay based on the weight of the extracted coal. The mining companies often short the weight to cheat the miners.

"Now throughout this process there exists all sorts of deadly hazards. Opening up a deposit of flammable gas might ignite by the headlamps sending a shock wave through the shafts. Other gases might be toxic and overwhelm the miners. Or a new mine shaft might break into an unground reservoir of water drowning the miners. The most common disaster is the collapse of a shaft ceiling. And finally, if you don't die in an accident, you probably will contract black lung, a disease that destroys the lungs from years of breathing coal dust. A wasting disease resulting in a slow death."

Murphy laid down her pen then said, "Good lord! This is a hellish job."

Alan replied, "That it is. I was fortunate that my father and mother sacrificed much to ensure that I never went into the coal mines."

The evening passed too quickly for all of them. As they broke up to retire for the evening, Murphy said to Alan and Noreen, "My trip here has been most enlightening. It has also been a pleasure meeting both of you. I wish to keep in touch with all of you." Reaching into her handbag, she extracted two business cards. "Here is my address in Brooklyn. Write to me soon and give me your addresses which I suspect might be different then your current residences."

Murphy embraced Noreen then surprisingly did the same to Alan.

Surprised but thrilled by Murphy's embrace, Alan said, "This has been a wonderful experience for all of us meeting you, Keara. I will cherish this part of my return to West Virginia as something special. I believe your presence has been particularly beneficial to Noreen and Mother for many reasons. Thank you for coming."

As Murphy left, Noreen turned to Alan with a grin, "You were smitten by Keara. Admit it."

"Does it show that much? She reminds me of you, Sis."

"I don't know the details, but she confided to me that she is a widow. Husband of only a few years died earlier this year in some sort of train accident."

Surprised, he replied, "She hides her grief well. Thank you for telling me. I'm going to stay in touch with her. You do the same. Maybe she can give you reason to consider leaving West Virginia. Now let me walk you back to the boarding house."

—

Alan Burke stayed on in West Virginia for two weeks before returning to Norfolk to arrange passage back to Panama. The trip proved a satisfying experience to reconnect with his mother and sister. Yet it still left unanswered questions about their immediate future. He more than ever wanted to see Noreen pursue a rewarding life. Her life had been filled with little joy. Now feeling the obligation of looking after their mother becomes another burden. Made more difficult with their mother's obsession with union organizing. Meeting Keara Murphy hopefully may have provided Noreen with incentive to look to her own needs.

For Alan Burke meeting Keara Murphy was also an unexpected experience. She left with pleasurable thoughts that brightened his outlook while managing through this family tragedy.

—

Governor Glasscock lifted martial law again on January 10, 1913. However, just weeks later on February 7, Mucklow was again attacked by armed miners, killing one person. That same evening, Kanawha County Sheriff Bonner Hill led a group of Baldwin-Felts agents in a retaliatory attack by train on the Holly Grove miners' settlement.

The *Bull Moose Special* was a previously outfitted train used as an instrument for quickly bringing decisive armed forces into play to facilitate evictions of striking miners from company-owned housing. Fabricated in the C&O Railroad's Huntington Works, it consisted of a locomotive, a passenger car, and an iron-plated baggage car equipped with two machine guns. With the tent community situated close to the railroad tracks, the attacking force steamed into the area and began raking the settlement with machine gun fire resulting in the killing of one miner.

After withdrawing, a group of enraged women led by union activist Sarah Blizzard inflicted damage to the railroad tracks to forestall another immediate attack. Two days later, armed miners again attacked Mucklow killing two people.

On February 10, beleaguered Governor Glasscock imposed martial law for a third time. Only a month before leaving office, Glasscock was relieved to hand over authority come March to the new governor-elect, Henry D. Hatfield, a native of the southern West Virginia coalfields.

On February 13, Mary G. Harris Jones, also known as Mother Jones, was arrested along with 166 striking miners. The defendants were brought before a military court in direct violation of

Sections 4 and 12 of Article III of the West Virginia Constitution and the Fourteenth Amendment of the United States Constitution. Section 4 Article III read: *The privilege of the writ of habeas corpus shall not be suspended. No person shall be held to answer for treason, felony or other crime, not cognizable by a justice, unless on presentment or indictment of a grand jury.* Section 12 Article III read: *The military shall be subordinate to the civil power; and no citizen, unless engaged in the military service of the state, shall be tried or punished by any military court, for any offence that is cognizable by the civil courts of the state.* The Fourteenth Amendment to the United States Constitution reads in part: *No State shall make or enforce any law which shall abridge the privileges or immunities of citizens of the United States; nor shall any State deprive any person of life, liberty, or property, without due process of law; nor deny to any person within its jurisdiction the equal protection of the laws.*

The blatant unchallenged disregard for standing state and federal constitutional statutes provided clear evidence that the State of West Virginia was an outlier to American civil liberties. All of which derived by the economic strangle hold of corporate coal mining interests corrupting the function of government.

Forty-eight defendants were prosecuted in Pratt in a military court before three West Virginia State Militia officers serving as judges. Twelve defendants were found guilty and convicted of various conspiracy charges with many sentenced to long terms in the state penitentiary. Mother Jones was convicted of inciting to riot and sentenced to twenty years in prison. She was eight-three in 1913.

CHAPTER 4

Brooklyn, New York | Summer 1913

When Keara Murphy journeyed to West Virginia during the violent coal mine strike in Kanawha County, she too was recovering from her own personal loss earlier in the year. Like Maude Burke and Noreen Hannigan, her partner died unexpectedly that July. They lived together in a fashionable brownstone in the Cobble Hill neighborhood of Brooklyn as a married couple but were never married. Only their parents knew the truth. The subterfuge was largely of Murphy's making. Robert Cooke did not mind. He completely understood Murphy's need to remain independent. Independent in the real sense of the term by avoiding the social and legal restrictions imposed on a woman by the institution of marriage.

Murphy fiercely resented the social norms that relegated women at the turn of the twentieth century subordinate to men. This was the Edwardian Era, a transformative time of technology and social change from the Victorian Era of the prior century. Yet changes in the social stature of women remained decidedly inferior to men. In 1913, women still did not have the right to vote. While the women's suffrage movement became a dominate issue, there remained a long list of other rights denied to women by law and social convention.

Murphy shunned marriage in favor of an education and pursuing a career. A husband diminished all manner of freedoms and legal rights. Children held no interest. However, she was not celibate making engaging in intimate relations socially problematic. In the first two decades of the new century, particularly in New York City, it was not unusual for middle class educated professional women to postpone marriage or shun the institution entirely. Murphy found the transfer of legal rights of a married woman to her husband outrageously anachronistic. Many professional women found physical intimacy with likeminded women. However, Keara Murphy's sexuality was decidedly heterosexual. With sexual intimacy an integral part of her life, such relationships for an unmarried woman proved challenging.

Robert Cooke proved the perfect partner. Connecting intellectually and physically, they fell in love. He was also an attorney allowing them to engage at a professional level. More importantly, Cooke totally embraced equality for women in every aspect of life. Neither of them felt constrained by conventions they found inconvenient. As their relationship progressed, it was Robert's idea to create the fabrication of having eloped and married. Neither had siblings requiring only confiding the truth of their unmarried cohabitation to their parents.

Their short time together ended in tragedy when Robert fell victim to a major railway accident. Even in a time of numerous railway catastrophes, the Corning Train Wreck was unusually deadly with 39 deaths and injuring another 88. Robert was on a business trip traveling on train No. 9 consisting of ten passenger cars of the Delaware, Lackawanna & Western Railroad running from Hoboken, New Jersey to Buffalo, NY. After a brief stop in Elmira, NY, the train departed at 4:47am heading west on the morning of July 4, 1912.

A sequence of compounding mishaps began an hour earlier when freight train No. 393 with 55 loaded freight cars left Elmira at 3:50am also heading west. Experiencing steam problems, it pulled onto a siding at East Corning just 12 miles west of Elmira at 4:46am to investigate. Attempting to pull all the cars onto the siding, a coupling broke leaving several cars stranded on the main line. The automatic blocking signal system activated the appropriate warning semaphore signals to stop any oncoming trains. Unfortunately, there was a dense fog that early morning.

Passenger train No. 9, with Robert Cooke onboard, heeded the warning signal and stopped behind the disabled freight cars.

A third train, express mail train No. 11, departed Elmira at 5:00am, also heading west. Inexplicably, the engineer of train No. 11 did not heed the warning signal, slamming into stationary passenger train No. 9 at full speed.

The rear three passenger cars of passenger train no. 9 suffered catastrophic damage. The collision derailed the cars of train no. 11 bringing down the telegraph lines. It took an hour before news of the crash reached Corning. A special train arrived at 7:00am with medical personnel. Even with large numbers of rescue manpower, many injured victims remained trapped even hours later.

Keara Murphy only learned of the disaster in the *New York Times* the following day. Robert Cooke was listed among the dead.

The newspaper accounts of the Corning Train Wreck were troubling. The coroner's inquest held the engineer of the No. 11 mail train responsible for the crash. He not only failed to heed the working automatic warning semaphore signal flags, a flagman with a colored flare from the stopped passenger train or following company procedure that required reducing speed in order to identify warning signals given the dense fog. Further evidence offered that the engineer appeared drunk earlier at 12:30am that morning then reported late for work just hours later.

She and her father immediately took a train to Corning to retrieve Cooke's body. Keara went further. Donning working clothes and men's boots, she climbed among the twisted rail cars amid workmen beginning to dismantle the wreckage. Conducting her own investigation, she would eventually agree with the findings of the inquest that the accident did not result from misconduct of the Lackawanna Railroad, but the negligence of the mail train engineer.

Her depth of despair was no different than that of anyone losing a soulmate. Keara Murphy cared nothing for observing expected protocol for dealing with the death of a loved one. She only wished to be left alone. Her parents understood and did every-thing possible to pick up the burden. The entire funeral process served only to add further emotional distress. They were Irish-Catholic but non-practicing making the funeral mass difficult as a forced public display of devotion for the departed. Nothing com-forting for someone without religious feelings, only an added bur-den to be endured. She refused to comply with imposed social pressure. Her only concession was to dress in black to avoid pro-voking unnecessary controversy. Her parents covered for her by claiming she was overcome with grief.

The death of Robert Cooke came on the heels of her profes-sional disappointment with the outcome of the criminal trial con-nected to the Triangle Shirtwaist Fire the prior year. To her dis-may, the company owners were acquitted of manslaughter charges in December. Hers and other civil lawsuits would take longer to pass through the courts. However, without a finding of criminal responsibility, those suits lost much of their strength for assigning financial liability and recovering compensation for the victims' families.

Part of her reason going to West Virginia only months after Robert's death was to absorb herself in something distracting. Taking firm control of managing her affairs was in her nature. West Virginia was also a good reason to leave New York for a couple of weeks before facing the endless expressions of sympa-thies at holiday social events. The loss of Robert left her unsettled and depressed.

With the mantle of widowhood, Murphy joined a unique so-cial category of women. She was single but now looked upon in a different light. She was thirty years old. An experienced profes-sional as both an attorney and writer. Society would likely accept an accomplished attractive woman engaging in male relation-ships after becoming unexpectedly widowed at an early age. However, she was not yet over the loss of Robert. She harbored no thoughts of seeking a romantic relationship. Downplaying ex-pectations of eventual remarriage proved an excuse for avoiding male companionship. Whatever increased freedom to engage in intimate relations that might exist as a widow held little interest.

Devoting herself instead to professional pursuits became her way of coping.

—

In March, Murphy received a letter from Noreen Hannigan.

Dearest Keara,

Following Governor Glasscock imposing martial law for a third time, I am sure you read of the arrest and trial of Mother Jones. She was returned to Pratt and tried by a military tribunal of three officers of the West Virginia Militia. According to her, she attributed her conviction to a speech she made months earlier in Cabin Creek. As much as I did not like Mary Jones, a sentence of twenty years in state prison to an old woman in her eighties attests to the oppression of coal miners in West Virginia. They imprisoned her in the military encampment in Pratt where she contracted pneumonia. Moved her then to Charleston for medical treatment. Once recovered, she was returned to Pratt and remanded to house arrest in Mrs. Carney's boarding house where we previously stayed. Still in poor health, I assume Governor Hatfield was hesitant to send her to the state penitentiary where she might die.

Yet the old warhorse was still bent on making trouble. As a frequent visitor regularly looking in on Jones, my mother smuggled out a message. Mother transcribed the message then sent a telegram to Democratic Senator John Kern of Indiana as instructed by Mother Jones. Kern is already pushing for a congressional investigation into the labor violence in West Virginia. Kern used Mother Jones' words from prison to pass a resolution that led to the Senate Committee on Education and Labor recommending an investigation into conditions in West Virginia coal mines. Mother Jones' words focused attention on West Virginia causing newly elected Governor Hatfield to pardon her and the other miners convicted by military courts. Since the trials violated the West Virginia Constitution, Hatfield was just avoiding bad press when the convictions were later overturned on appeal.

Mother Jones has since gone off to Colorado. Hired by District 15 of the UMW. She is part of a cadre of union organizers going after unionizing Colorado Fuel & Iron. Thankfully, my mother decided to stay in West Virginia. Wants to continue organizing efforts for UMW District 17. The UMW agreed to an unsatisfactory agreement after the strike and reign of martial law imposed in Kanawha County. The coal miners are not happy with the deal that was never even put up to vote of rank-and-file miners. Nonetheless, the UMW refocused organizing efforts to the coalfields in the Tug Fork Valley in the southern counties. That is where my mother is bent on going. Specifically, the town of Matewan in Mingo County. I have done everything possible to dissuade her. Argued that something smelled fishy about the District 17 leadership caving into the mine operators with an agreement that achieved no concessions to the miners. When I suggested it appeared as possible collusion with the mine operators, Mother defended the union leadership, but I knew she too was troubled by the outcome.

Mother and I are now in Mingo County in the town of Matewan. You might ask why we have relocated to an even more depressing place than Pratt? The answer is because of Mother. She took up Mother Jones' incarceration as reason for her to assume the role of spreading unionizing gospel. And it is like a religion. I have lived all my life in a household consumed with rebellion. First against the British then here in America against coal mining companies.

Mingo County sits on the Tug Fork of the Big Sandy River. On the border with Kentucky. The entire Tug Fork Valley on both sides is dotted with coal mines. None of the mines are unionized. This is a bastion of corporate coal interests. The new battleground between the mine operators and the UMW.

I read your article in McClure's Magazine. An exceptional piece that captured the desperate realities of life in the West Virginia coalfields. The events of the strike last year settled nothing. The underlying circumstances have not changed. Coalminers and their families will continue to suffer. Union organizing by the UMW will not become successful. My mother's efforts will achieve nothing. Tensions will only continue. I fear some greater cataclysm lies in the future. I fear for my mother's safety but can do nothing.

Everything this past year has proved a tipping point for me. Mother's obsession is an unbearable burden, yet I cannot entirely abandon her. I have therefore hit upon a temporary solution. I have accepted a teaching position in the town of Bluefield. About 90 miles west of Matewan by train. Makes for interacting with Mother largely by telephone, but it's not that far that we cannot occasionally visit.

I apologize for unburdening my personal issues. You seem the only one other than my brother that I can have a candid conversation with. Although we were together for only a short time, I feel a deep personal connection with you, Keara. You never spoke much about the loss of your husband, but I imagine you may still be contending with your own grief. The worst part of grief seems to be the management of one's unbalanced existence. You are my lifeline. Let us please stay in touch.

Your dear friend,
Noreen

The introduction of Keara Murphy's article appearing in McClure's Magazine referred to by Noreen Hannigan read:

As a longtime resident of New York City, I recently journeyed to West Virginia to investigate the spreading labor strife between coal mining companies and coal miners. The strike started in April of last year. Subsequent events after almost a year transformed part of West Virginia coalfields into a vicious

58

place of violence between armed guards hired by the mine operators and armed miners. The former West Virginia governor attempted to suppress the violence through imposing martial law on three different occasions. Nothing has been resolved. The underlying fundamental issues remain unchanged. If anything, the hostilities are only exacerbated by arrests made under the declaration of martial law that created circumstances favorable to the mine operators.

The following article does not attempt to adjudicate the arguments of the warring factions. My first-hand observations point to a situation far more troubling than typical labor issue disputes involving wages and working conditions. What I found in the state of West Virginia is a place alien to what it means to live in the United States. A place where coal miners and their families live in what has been called corporate feudalism. A type of serfdom induced by employment conditions imposed by corporations that go far beyond mere wage issues. Where their dwelling and basic living conditions are controlled by their employer.

Many of the several coalfields of southern West Virginia lie within inaccessible valleys of the Appalachian Mountains. For most miners, they must rent their places of residence from property owned by the mine. Adding to that, they most often must purchase food and goods from a mining company-owned store. These arrangements afforded mine operators another profit stream by setting uncompetitive prices. The strike in Kanawha County affected 96 mines and 7,500 miners with an unknown number of dependents. Striking miners and their families were immediately evicted from their homes by armed mine guards that frequently engaged in destroying miner's personal property.

The evicted mining families were then forced to relocate off mining company property to live in tent communities. I observed atrocious living conditions. No sanitation facilities with inadequate sources of fresh water existed in these makeshift hovels. All this while facing survival in unheated tents with the onset of winter. Meager food supplies purchased with Union subsidies do not go far enough to stave off malnutrition.

By the force of necessity, the mining companies can thereby add the weight of eviction and possible employment blacklisting as bargaining pressure points in a work stoppage. The mine operators refused to even meet with the UMW much less negotiate. These and a long list of other oppressive mining company practices reached such extremes that half of the striking miners were not even members of the United Mine Workers of America Union.

Murphy's sojourn to West Virginia proved enlightening. A place that could not be more different than Murphy's life in New York. It also exposed her to a wider appreciation of the diversity of the Irish diaspora. She was second generation Irish American. Her paternal grandparents left Ireland during the Great Famine in the late 1840s. The same origin as Mother Jones. The Burke family represented that continuum of Irish emigration. Metropolitan New York held the greatest urban concentration of ethnic conclaves in America. In this diverse mix, removed by generations, she thought little about her own connection to Ireland.

Murphy's paternal grandfather was a blacksmith in Ireland and left with his new wife during the potato famine before having children. Her father Thomas Murphy put himself through college then law school by working nights at his father's prosperous blacksmith shop in the Bronx.

Murphy's mother was also of Irish ancestry but going back more generations to New York starting with the early decades of the 19th century. From a middle-class family her maternal grandfather was a reporter for the *New York Times* and her mother received an education becoming a high school teacher. Teaching was one of few professions available to women before the turn of the new century, yet her mother soon realized this was not to be her career. Attending the College of the City of New York, she obtained a degree in journalism. Her aspirations to follow her father as a reporter never materialized given gender bias against female newspaper reporters. Nonetheless, determined to expand her horizons, she left teaching for a copy-editing job at the *Times*. Murphy's mother currently holds the position of copy-editing supervisor at the *Times*. Alison Murphy became her daughter's example by persevering in pursuit of challenging interests.

With strong feelings about women's rights, Alison Murphy saw the restriction disallowing the right for women to vote as the fundamental gender issue that must first be overcome to fully emancipate women. The controversial issue that threatened male domination in affairs of government and business made active participation in the suffrage movement impossible without endangering both her and her husband's jobs. Alison Murphy therefore turned to writing articles under different pen names using elaborate cutouts to conceal her identity.

Thomas Murphy enthusiastically supported his wife's devotion to women's rights advocacy. Coming from immigrant working-class beginnings to eventually develop a highly successful corporate law practice left him an appreciation for self-determination. Institutionalized male domination inherently offended his sense of social justice. That view further extended to his daughter. Keara Murphy was therefore blessed with enlightened parents. Unlike many girls pressured to pursue conventional marriage and family, her formative years became an exploration of career options encouraged by her parents.

—

The death of Robert Cooke profoundly unsettled Keara Murphy. For the years they were together she felt both in command and comfortably fixed with her unconventional life choices. His death not only unsettled her sense of wellbeing but caused her to examine her career focus more critically. Admittedly, she had lost enthusiasm for defending suffragette activists. Her advocacy against child labor held greater interest. That became part of the reason to make the trip to West Virginia to liaison with Mother Jones, a strong advocate against child labor. Murphy found the use of children coal mining particularly loathsome. Yet Murphy was also becoming interested in the broader labor abuses of corporate interests. Coal mining stood out as a striking example.

It was clear to her that the industrial revolution brought change in the dynamics of market-based economic democracy. Technology changed the relation of labor to enterprise ownership. Trade guilds were being replaced with labor unions to preserve jobs impacted by technological advances. Vital industries increasingly demanded massive capital investment. Skilled trades progressively lost ground to automation.

Murphy did not possess strong political opinions. She was a thinker that thought in pragmatic terms. Rights codified in the United States Constitution held greater meaning than political ideologies. That was how she practiced law. Argue from the position of legal rights and the language of statutes rather than make impassioned emotional appeals. While she understood the inequities of the coalminers circumstances as with other industries, she did not ascribe to socialism as a socio-political solution. On that she differed with Mother Jones and others in the labor movement. Murphy had no clear solution but understood that market economy dynamics must find the means of reconciling the relationship between corporations and their workforces. Profits should not override an equitable social contract.

Submitting articles for publication to the *Saturday Evening Post*, *Collier's*, and *McClure's Magazine*, Keara Murphy joined a new breed of investigative journalists. The article on the West Virginia Coalmine Strike of 1912 published by *McClure's* received much acclaim. It established her as a part of a community of investigative journalists that became known as muckrakers. The label referred to journalists expending considerable research to objectively explain the cause and effects of social injustice, corruption, and other abusive business practices of social significance.

Among those writers was Ida Tarbell. Trabell was a generation older than Murphy but a journalism legend. Tarbell's 1904 bestselling book *The History of Standard Oil* exposed the illegitimate business practices of John D. Rockefeller. Her diligent research efforts contributed to the breakup of Standard Oil for violating anti-trust statutes enacted by Congress ten years before the turn of the new century. Tarbell became an inspiration even before Murphy began to write seriously. Not only an investigative journalist, Tarbell also wrote highly regarded biographies. Tarbell even sent Murphy a letter congratulating her on the West Virginia article. Publication brought Murphy into the informal fraternity of the many highly respected contributing writers to *McClure's*.

Adding to her writing credentials was another article published in the *Saturday Evening Post* within a week of the *McClure* piece. She was close to the tragedy of the deadly Triangle Shirtwaist Fire two years earlier when she began representing the families of many of the victims in civil suits. For those families, the first denial of justice was the acquittal of the two owners of the garment business on criminal manslaughter charges. Over 100 witnesses testified they knew the exit doors were locked yet the plaintiffs failed to convince the jury. Although the business was found liable for wrongful death damages in a subsequent civil suit, the families received an awarded of only $75 for each deceased victim. Adding further insult, Murphy discovered the insurance company settlement to the owners amounted to $60,000. For the deaths of 146 victims that amounted to over $400 per each death.

While Murphy's article was regarded as excellent journalism, as an attorney she deemed her efforts toward seeking justice for the victims of the fire a failure. It reinforced her developing view that her efforts to pursue solutions through the courts for social issues were less effective than the power of the press. Her legal work focused on women's suffrage, child labor, redress for rapacious business practices suffered from entrenched convention, and legalized inequity. Changes to these fundamental elements required societal changes necessary for changes in law to take place. The reception of her recent journalism articles pushed her to reexamine where best to direct her efforts to affect change.

—

Those thoughts caused Keara Murphy to embark on a new course of investigation. A letter from Noreen Hannigan informed her of the aftermath of the Paint Creek & Cabin Creek coalmines strike in West Virginia. Hannigan wrote to Murphy:

Dearest Keara,

Hope you are doing well. My circumstances unfortunately remain unsettled. Mother's continued involvement with the UMW is the final straw for me. I have no interest in union organizing efforts. Nor am I willing to follow my mother into another environment of contention that very likely will result in further violence. The mines operating along the Tug are virulently anti-union. I cannot live in such a place. Therefore, I am taking a high school teaching position in the town of Bluefield in Mercer County about 90 miles east of Matewan. Easily reachable by train but far enough away to establish my independence and find some measure of peace.

Announcing my move to Mother undoubtedly hurt her, yet you could not tell by her angry reaction. She can be a real terror, but I am no longer the obliging daughter. She declared Mercer County was the devil's den controlled by mining interests. Bluefield is even the headquarters of the hated Baldwin-Felts Detective Agency the mine operators hired as armed guards. The very thugs that murdered my father, brother, and husband. Maybe true but I am not fighting that war any longer. Silently, I blame Papa for leading those that died on such an ill-conceived venture. Then again, that was Papa's nature. Mother is being *selfish, wanting to keep me close. I understand but I have my own life to consider. That is what Alan tells me. He encourages me to follow my own path.*

Bluefield is a prosperous and pretty community. Not isolated in a secluded valley. It has economic interests other than coal mining. The Norfolk & Western Railroad has a major repair facility and switching center located there. Just nine miles north is the 'Millionaires' Town' of Bramwell created from the wealth of Bluefield.

On my own I have taken charge of my life. I'm trying my hand at writing. Started working on a first-person fictional account about what it means living in this dreadful environment. Not intended as a memoir, I am inventing a more interesting protagonist. A good deal of that motivation comes from your encouragement to begin writing. Hope you are doing well. I so miss being able to talk with you, Keara.

Warmest regards,
Noreen

Surprisingly, Murphy received a letter from Alan Burke just weeks later. His first letter.

Dearest Keara,

I apologize for not writing sooner. Returning to West Virginia under those circumstances months ago was more difficult than I expected. That my mother is adamant in continuing her union organizing efforts is disappointing. Noreen forwarded your published magazine article. An exceptional piece of writing that explains the oppressive environment of those working the coal mines. You have an extraordinary writing style that captures the very essence of what is going on in West Virginia.

It is Noreen that most concerns me. She deserves a new life after all she has sacrificed. That she decided to pursue her own life is encouraging. Not only moving to a more peaceful location with a good teaching opportunity, but her turning to writing is a welcome surprise. From her letters, we have you to thank for that encouragement. Noreen is especially fond of you, Keara. I believe your friendship has done wonders for her to weather the difficulties of this past year.

I apologize for not writing sooner. Got caught up in my duties after returning to Panama. I do not enjoy this posting. Garrison duty for a soldier is exceedingly boring. The tropical climate adds to the discomfort. I spend my time training my Marines. I call them mine because I am responsible for their wellbeing. As a soldier that means I'm trained to survive combat. As a Marine that becomes even more meaningful. If Washington must call on its military, it is the Marine Corps that becomes the sharp end of the spear. My job is instructing and keeping the fighting skills of my charges sharpened.

Been keeping myself informed on deteriorating circumstances in Mexico for some time. For the past year, the political situation has worsened. The current president of Mexico Huerta, a former general commanding the Federal Army, came to power by a military coup in February. He's now contending with widespread revolution from different revolutionary opponents. Should Huerta fall from power, a civil war becomes likely. That is what happens in a political vacuum. The United States shares a long border with Mexico so what happens there has ramifications. Where American interests become involved, U.S. Marines are often called upon. Huerta is in serious disfavor with President Wilson. Some sort of incursion into Mexico becomes a distinct possibility should the situation worsen.

Forgive my rambling. I have such little opportunity to engage intellectually with someone like you. A soldier's life unfortunately becomes isolated, especially in postings to remote foreign lands.

I remember our dinner in Charleston with fond memories. Please write and tell me what is going on with your life.

Sincerely,
Alan Burke

CHAPTER 5

Bluefield, West Virginia | Autumn 1913

Noreen Hannigan and her mother prepared to depart from the Charleston railroad station together. For Noreen a journey undertaken with hopes of finding a new beginning after tragic events upended an already dreary life. A bright warm September morning in Charleston made her feel hopeful for a new future by leaving behind the worst of the labor unrest of the West Virginia's coalfields.

They were taking the same Chesapeake & Ohio train to Huntington. Changing trains in Huntington to a Norfolk & Western train, they would then make their way southeast through the Tug Fork River Valley that represented the border with Kentucky. They were leaving the Kanawha Coalfield where they had lived since coming to West Virginia from Ireland thirty years ago. Although the circumstances of leaving Charleston were emotionally troubling, for Noreen the promise of a brighter future on her own in a new place was exhilarating.

Maude Burke however was not leaving behind the coalfield wars. Relocating to the Williamson Coalfield of Mingo County to the town of Matewan was just a new battleground. At age sixty-two she once again became a refugee. Apart from her outward expression of toughness, the thought of living alone without family consumed her private thoughts. Yet dedicating herself to selfless struggle drove her to sacrifice emotional comfort. She embraced her husband's lifelong rebellion against oppression for the forty-two years they were together. First the British then the colliery operators of West Virginia. With her husband dead and the family shattered, continued rebellion sustained her purpose in life.

For Noreen, leaving Paint Creek held no nostalgia. For someone of her intellect, the place stifled her spirit from her formative years. Leaving to attend college was her brightest time. Marrying was a mistake. That the marriage failed only added to depression. That her husband died in a stupid venture initiated by her father created mixed emotions. Freed by his death only added a sense of guilt for harboring such thoughts. She rebuked herself for emotionally questioning if remaining in West Virginia to stay close to her aging mother was penance for her selfish thoughts. She felt that living separate from her mother while remaining reasonably close by train was a considerate compromise serving her interests as well as discharging her responsibilities.

The catastrophic events of the last year profoundly changed Noreen's behavior. The violent deaths of her family members unconsciously freed her from the constraints of her quiet reserved demeanor. Her intelligence provided her with a sense of confidence that now gave way to expression. She was thirty-nine. A good many years ahead of her with which she intended to forge a new life.

While taking the same train with her mother, Noreen was only spending one night in Matewan to get her settled. Maude Burke was relocating to Matewan to take up union organizing with the mines along the Tug Valley that had historically resisted UMW efforts. Maude hoped to replicate the oratory successes of Mother Jones by using her own tragic background to draw miners to join the union.

The following day, Noreen planned to board the same train traveling eastward from Matewan to Bluefield in Mercer County. To a new life that she alone would shape. Teaching while pursuing her new challenge of writing. Bluefield allowed being close enough to watch over her mother but far enough to distance herself from living within the likely next battleground of the West Virginia coalfield wars.

Once onboard the train as it left Charleston, Noreen asked her mother, "Anytime you want to quit working for the UMW, you can return to teaching, Mum. You've in good health with many good years left."

Maude patted her daughter's hand. "We've had this discussion before, Dear. For now, this is what I need to do. Can't entirely explain why. Since I lost your father and brother, my life has changed."

"So has mine, Mum. That's why I can't stay with you. You're off to your own war. It's not my war."

They sat in silence for the remainder of the trip until the train pulled into Matewan. Disembarking, Maude remarked after looking at the buildings spread along the tracks, "Well, not exactly Charleston, but larger than Pratt. There's a boarding house on Mate Street. If they have nothing available, there's the Urias Hotel."

Matewan was indeed a small town. Population 650. 15 miles southeast from the larger county seat city of Williamson with a population of 4,000. These numbers did not include the thousands of coal miners and their families working in the mines of Mingo County living mostly in remote company-provided housing close to the mines. What served as Matewan's downtown was nestled between the Norfolk & Western train tracks and the Tug Fork River. The river served as the border with Kentucky with the Appalachian Mountains rising on either side.

When her mother first told her of the UMW offer to work in organizing efforts in the Williamson Coalfield area, Noreen silently questioned why Matewan? It would seem the most important center for UMW activity would be the larger town of Williamson. She concluded it was maybe the UMW District 17 throwing a bone to her mother for her loss of husband and livelihood. More likely it was to exile Maude Burke from district headquarters where her guarded criticism of the questionable agreement made with Governor Hatfield to end the strike remained a contentious issue.

The miners of Kanawha County West Virginia harbored resentment for the agreement never brought to the rank-and-file for ratification. Allegations of United Mine Workers Union leadership corruption abounded. Maude Burke was untainted by these suspicions. Given her personal losses, no one questioned her integrity.

Noreen also found it odd that Mother Jones did not publicly repudiate the agreement. Once pardoned by the Governor and released from incarceration, she took an organizing position with UMW District 15 and left for Trinidad, Colorado. There she would pursue organizing the coalmines of the large steel conglomerate Colorado Fuel & Iron Company that had broad holdings in steel, coalmining, coking plants, and railroads.

Maude Burke also demonstrated a surprising energy and enthusiasm. Not in the same league as Mother Jones as an orator, Maude Burke could nonetheless hold a crowd. A longtime friend of UMW official Bill Blizzard's mother Sarah, an activist known affectionately as Mother Sarah, Maude took on the name of Mother Burke. Speaking to miners at gatherings during the strike and periods of martial law then with Mary "Mother" Jones having left West Virginia, Maude Burke became useful in organizing efforts along the Tug.

Maude found a room at the only boarding house in Matewan. She and Noreen then spent the day walking about Matewan. Noreen thought Matewan a dreary place. Larger than Pratt which was the town nearest to Paint Creek where she grew up after coming to America, but still a backward remote hamlet. Not at all like Bluefield with a population of 12,000 that she visited when interviewing for the teaching position.

The day passed without tears or any disagreeable exchange. They ate a fine dinner at the Urias Hotel restaurant before spending the night together at the boarding house. The next day turned overcast adding to their already saddened mood.

As the train arrived pulled to a stop, Noreen said, "Once I get settled, Mum, I will call you at the boarding house with a telephone number where you can reach me." Beyond that, there was little else to say. No more harsh words. All those exhausted over the previous weeks. Two strong-willed women each pursuing what they must. "I love you. Be careful and write often."

However, neither could hold off the tears as they embraced with the conductor motioning to get onboard. Maude said, "You take good care of yourself, Dear. Stay in touch with your brother. Thank goodness you and Alan are so close. I love you."

Noreen stepped up into the railway carriage. Finding a seat, she waved to her mother. The parting was more discontenting than she anticipated. Even with the sense of freedom to pursue a new course in her life she felt unmoored. Leaving her mother alone left her more despondent, feeling that she was in some manner shirking responsibility. Intellectually understanding the imperative of finding the best alternative for fulfilling her own needs did not lessen the emotional discomfort.

—

During her previous visit to Bluefield when interviewing for the prospective teaching position, Noreen scouted suitable places of residence close to the school should she get the job. Once accepted at Bluefield high school to teach history and geography, she sent a letter to her selected choice of residence announcing her date of arrival and the availability of a room for long-term rental. It was a lovely boarding house with all the occupants being women.

The owner, Olivia Snyder was a congenial middle-aged widow that Noreen later learned also owned a local clothing and dry goods business. Her late husband a successful lawyer having died prematurely of a heart attack years earlier, left her financially secure. Rather than selling their large mansion with six bedrooms, she decided she did not want to live alone. She loved the magnificent house that had been her home for twenty years. The solution was to rent the rooms to single women thereby providing for continual upkeep of the home while establishing an environment of interesting women. Snyder employed a cook, housekeeper, and handyman to maintain the residence. As the arrangement served to satisfy Snyder's social inclinations, she set her rental rates to

cover only expenses and upkeep. Noreen thought it an enlightened approach for a woman to leverage her comfortable financial
means to create a fulfilling life.

Starting her teaching job as the new school year began, Noreen
felt immediately satisfied that she had made the right decision. In
her first letter to her mother in Matewan, Noreen described her
newfound circumstances. The teaching position and staff made
for an environment that could not have been better. She particularly welcomed the congenial atmosphere of Olivia Snyder's
boarding house and her fellow tenants. If her mother was put off
by Noreen's enthusiasm, then maybe she might consider abandoning her union organizing and return to teaching. Perhaps even
joining her in Bluefield. Noreen said as much in her letters.

Weeks after settling in Bluefield, Noreen received a letter from
her brother, Alan.

Noreen,

Received your letter with much pleasure. So glad
you are forging a new life. Never been to Bluefield
but it sounds like the perfect place with your new
teaching position. Wonderful that you are residing
in a place that affords stimulating companionship. Seems a different environment from where we
grew up in Kanawha.

Mother's relocation to Matewan comes as no
surprise. We are never going to dissuade her from
devoting herself to the plight of coal miners. If she
finds personal rewards in that, then so be it. We
can only do our best to look after her as best we
can while pursuing our own lives. Should anything

urgent ever come up, wire me at headquarters here in Panama City.

The Canal is close to completion. Next month they are projecting to destroy the Gamboa Dike that is holding back the waters of the Charges River. This will flood the Culebra Cut. An amazing massive eight-mile excavation taking years that created a valley and waterway across the continental divide. Once flooded, this will link the Atlantic and Pacific Oceans across the narrow Panama isthmus. You teach geography so be sure to explain the significance to your students.

As for me, I can only hope for reassignment somewhere more appealing than Panama. Garrison duty in this hellish climate is depressing. Don't be surprised though if Washington calls on the Marines to intervene somewhere soon. Mexico has been in the throes of a revolution for several years. A continuing struggle for power with different players that shows no sign of resolution. The United States shares a 2000-mile border with Mexico. Lots of American economic and strategic interests are involved. I've been sent to Cuba, the Philippines, Nicaragua, and Panama. Why not Mexico?

Enough of my soldiering speculation. I wrote to Keara Murphy a month ago. Thanked her for her friendship with you. Keep in touch with her. One smart lady. She wrote back saying that she hoped Noreen would find herself. That's how she put it. Delighted that you are trying your hand at writing. You have the talent to write and certainly have a lot of material to work with.

Do me a favor and get yourself a camera. The Sears Roebuck catalog sells a small easy to use Kodak camera. Called the Vest Pocket Kodak Camera or VPK, it measures only 2.5 x 5 x 1.0 inches. It's a bit costly at $6, so I've enclosed a ten-dollar bill. I'd like to see pictures of you and Mum and where you live. Going to purchase one myself.

Write often and give Mum my love.

Love,
Alan

CHAPTER 6

Trinidad, Colorado | February 1914

With her successful publication of articles on the Coalfield War in West Virginia, Keara Murphy found a new subject with which to focus her journalistic attentions. After the labor strife between mine operators and coal miners originating in Kanawha County abated a year earlier, violence erupted in the southern coalfields of Las Animas Counties, Colorado. Circumstances were much the same as in the West Virginia coalfields. This newest outbreak of labor dispute in the country's coalfields occurred in September 1913. Just a year following the strike in Kanawha County West, Virginia, the widespread strike in the southern coalfield of Colorado would turn exceedingly violent in succeeding months. Ambushes and assassinations became commonplace. From the onset, the stage was set for a major confrontation between the mining corporations and the coalminers. The largest employer, Colorado Fuel & Iron began eviction of as many as 20,000 miners and their families from company owned housing.

District 15 of the United Mine Workers prepared for just that eventuality by shipping in tents sufficient for establishing eight tent colonies. A rainstorm drenched the region the first day of the strike. Unfortunately, the shipment of tents and associated construction materials was delayed. For unknown reasons, the UMW went forward with the walk-out on schedule. The displaced mining families suffered terribly in the winter cold, creating whatever makeshift sheltering possible while contending with the mud.

CF&I President Jesse Welborn publicly announced that he would never meet with the striking miners. Before the strike, Mother Jones responded by leading a march on the Trinidad town hall. In one of her typical colorful speeches, she incited the miners to, "Rise up and strike! If you are too cowardly, there are enough women in this country to come in here and beat the hell out of you."

Murphy's research revealed certain differences between the circumstances in Colorado and West Virginia. Whereas the coal mines throughout the various coalfields of West Virginia were owned by comparatively small mining companies, those in Southern Colorado were dominated by just a couple of large corporations. This included the largest Colorado Fuel & Iron, controlled by John D. Rockefeller Jr., working in unison with the Rock Mountain Fuel Company and Victor-American Fuel Company to collectively resist organizing efforts of the United Mine Workers...

CF&I top management took a hands-off approach to employee relations resulting in widespread abuses and corruption by middle-management to increase profits at the expense of the miners. In addition to all the other wage and working condition issues, the region was notorious for cost saving practices that substantially degraded safety in the mines. Already among the most dangerous forms of labor, Colorado fatalities in the coal mines were more than double the national average at 6.8 deaths per 1,000 miners. Three years earlier, CF&I suffered two mass-casualty events in Las Animas County resulting from explosions. 75 miners died in the Primero Mine followed months later by another 56 killed in their Starkville Mine. Within weeks, another explosion at the nearby Victor-American Fuel Company mine in Delagua killed 76.

Murphy discovered that as the largest coal mining producer in Colorado, CF&I held exceptional influence in the Colorado state government. CF&I President Jesse Welborn and Chaiman of the Board of Directors Lamont Bowers along with fellow mine operators John Osgood of Victor-American and David Brown of Rocky Mountain Fuel had the ear of newly elected Colorado Governor Elias Ammons. Even newspapers commented on mining interests dominating political life in Colorado. As for the coal miners, they lived under the oppression of the worst aspects of corporate feudalism.

Murphy's editorial pieces avoided arguing the bargaining positions of either labor or management. The basis of her published work attempted to expose the sociological and political environment as the source of the violence. While coal mining was not the only industry suffering labor turmoil, it exhibited certain aspects that held wider societal implications. Implications that went to the heart of a functioning democracy in a market economy. The all too human tendency toward abuse of power. The inherent struggle between ownership and labor. Those that held the wealth created by others. How can the intrinsic rights of life, liberty, and the pursuit of happiness expressed in the United States Constitution have universal meaning to everyone? That remains the fundamental existential question that defied any simple answer.

The larger picture of the conflict in Colorado mirrored the same conditions of West Virginia. Corporate mining interests controlled all economic and political life in the state. Coal miners worked under the same oppression that could only be defined as serfdom. Once sufficiently familiar with the background, Murphy prepared to go to Colorado after Christmas. Violence had erupted after a strike months earlier that involved thousands of miners and their families. Subsequently, the Colorado Governor Elias Ammons called in the Colorado National Guard to the region to keep the warring factions apart. That temporary measure did nothing to alter the entrenched position of Colorado Fuel & Iron, Victor-American, and the Rocky Mountain Fuel Company. They collectively refused to negotiate with the United Mine Workers. The situation was the same as in West Virginia where local law enforcement was firmly under control of the mine operators. Striking miners had no legal means of seeking redress for their grievances.

Murphy styled herself a thinker. She did not embrace either extreme on the political spectrum. Her writings attempted to provoke thoughtful argument. In hindsight that may have been a subconscious reason for pursuing law as a career. As the body of laws could never achieve a perfect balance for legitimate competing interests, it was a never-ending work in process. The U.S. Constitution was an exceptional blueprint. What she found in these labor wars in the coal mining industry was a fundamental disregard for the rights expressed in the Constitution. The perpetrators were the mining interests using their economic leverage to gain hegemony over local and state government institutions. Murphy sided with the position of the miners on legal grounds. The framers of the Constitution could find nothing more reprehensible than corporate feudalism.

According to newspaper accounts, the threat of random unexpected gunfire violence encountered in West Virginia became no different in Colorado. As a freelance journalist with her recent magazine publications critical of coalmining business interests and corrupt public officials, she expected to be unwelcome. Easy to speculate that some hothead might wish her harm. Her solo venture into Colorado labor unrest might prove more hazardous than her West Virginia experience following the high-profile activist Mother Jones. In Colorado she was poking around to uncover newsworthy material and take photographs. Material decidedly unfavorable toward the coal mining corporations. She needed a means of personal protection. If nothing else to provide some peace of mind.

Weeks earlier when forming her plan to go to Colorado, she wrote Alan Burke. Her letter dealt with her long-distance close relationship with his sister. Stating her professional interest in writing about the labor strife consuming the coal mining industry, she told Burke of her impending plan to visit Colorado. Expressing safety concerns, she asked his advice for his recommendation of a firearm to carry.

She did want his recommendation but more than that, it provided an excuse to write to him. Their brief meeting in West Virginia a year earlier left a lasting impression. Something about this articulate and thoughtful soldier stayed with her. When writing the letter, she smiled at the thought that it was perhaps as much the visceral attraction of a handsome man in uniform decorated for valor while fighting in exotic foreign lands.

Burke responded weeks later with a letter from Panama.

Dearest Keara,

Delighted to hear from you. Noreen tells me much about how much your friendship has encouraged her to move forward with her life. She has also forwarded your published articles. Showed them to my commanding officer, Major Smedley Butler. I have served with him for many years in several theaters of conflict and I value his opinions. He remarked that the articles were exceptionally well written. Insightful into the greater issue these coal wars are exposing. My assessment as well. I spend my off-duty time reading. Particularly classics and scholarly works. I believe therefore that I can recognize the essence of important writing.

Your plans to travel alone to Colorado in the middle of that region's coal mining related violence leaves me concerned for your safety. Especially since you feel the need to go armed for protection. However, following the exploits of my own mother, I can understand the compelling need to pursue what one deems important work.

I recommend you secure a small .38 revolver. Avoid the inclination to consider a smaller caliber. If faced with a serious personal threat, you need to put your attacker down. A smaller caliber can still leave you vulnerable. A revolver is bulkier than a semi-automatic pistol but is simpler and always reliable. I recommend a Colt Police Positive Special with a four-inch barrel chambered for .38 special cartridges for greater stopping power. It weighs about a pound and a half so it's not light. About 9 inches in overall length. Not sure how you can wear it concealed on your body, but you will need a holster. You can find the weapon in the Sears Roebuck catalog to give you a sense of what it looks like. Any gun shop in New York should offer them for sale. If you have never fired a handgun, you should find a shooting range and get accustomed to handling it safely. Wish I could be there to instruct you. If I was, I would also accompany you to Colorado as your bodyguard.

Lastly, keep the revolver on your person with the means to access it quickly. For a man that would mean in a holster affixed to the belt of the trousers and located at the back for concealment if wearing a coat. For a woman, not sure where best to place *the weapon. Needs to be on your person for quick access rather than in a handbag.*

Please write to me as you leave for Colorado and wire me upon your safe return to New York. Already feeling anxious about your safety going to Colorado under these circumstances. I shall worry until you safely return to Brooklyn. Take care of yourself and do good work.

Fondest regards,
Alan

Reading Alan Burke's letter brought a smile to Keara Murphy. *Bodyguard? Fondest regards* instead of his previous less personal *warmest regards?* She must be sure to return his affectionate subtleties in her next letter. A decorated career soldier that reads classics? He was an intriguing man.

Murphy's research into the situation in Las Animas County, Colorado revealed the mine companies had also hired the Baldwin-Felts Detective Agency for security. The brutal Baldwin-Felts agents engaged in far more than security from Murphy's observations while in West Virginia. Since her journalism might likely take her into unwelcome conflict with these armed thugs, she would take Alan Burke's advice. A woman of her appearance could not expect the same deference given to grandmotherly union agitator Mother Jones.

As to the use of a firearm, she already had some basic experience. Her father possessed guns and belonged to a hunting club east of Brooklyn on a wilder part of Long Island. In her younger years, she fired shotguns shooting clay pigeons at the club and revolvers on the shooting range. By no means an accomplished gun user, she at least possessed a functional understanding of the basics and the feel of discharging a firearm.

Concealing the revolver should not be a problem. Wearing dresses in the Colorado coalfields did not seem practical. Men's trousers seemed better suited. In deference to her gender, she chose instead to wear female riding breeches with a belt. Both feminine and practical. After all, this the American West and she might have need of using a horse. This was winter so wearing a loose-fitting jacket or sweater made sense making concealment of the weapon possible with a holstered revolver situated at the small of her back. She set about to immediately purchase the weapon from a local gun retailer. With a box of .38 Special cartridges, she familiarized herself with firing the weapon at the underground shooting range in the basement of the gun shop.

She informed her parents only that she was going to Colorado to gather material on the current labor conflict like the events she reported on in West Virginia a year earlier. She said nothing about her assessment that the circumstances in Colorado might expose her to greater danger, enough to warrant arming herself for protection.

—

Murphy outfitted herself for the rigors of venturing into the Western wilderness. Colorado was experiencing one of coldest winters on record. Except for a single dress and comfortable shoes, her attire was geared to moving around the rugged coal mining environment. She packed riding breeches, flannel shirts, sweaters, and a warm wool coat with a hood. Sturdy calf-height riding boots instead of urbanized stylish shoes with heels better for outdoor work in this tough rugged land.

Her destination was the town of Trinidad, Colorado in the southeast corner of the state. In a valley on the eastern slopes of the Rocky Mountains, the town was still at an elevation of 6,000 feet. In the middle of winter, nighttime temperatures dropped well below freezing with occasional snow. However, the winter of 1913-14 was proving to be one of the most severe in Colorado history causing her to revise her travel clothing to include men's wool work socks and fleece-lined gloves. In December a storm dumped more than four feet of snow with wind creating epic snowdrifts in Denver.

It was late February 1914 when Kear Murphy boarded the train to Denver. The situation in Colorado had only become worse since the start of the strike before winter with both warring sides firmly polarized. Her luggage consisted of a single suitcase with an additional duffle bag holding her Corona portable folding typewriter and riding boots. She boarded a New York Central train from Penn Station in Midtown Manhattan. The train would take her through St. Louis then onto Denver in two days on a Pullman sleeper car. She would change trains in Denver heading south to Trinidad, a city of 10,000 people located 200 miles south of Denver close to the border with New Mexico.

—

For a town of reasonable size, Trinad still had the look of a frontier town. It was situated in a valley below Fisher's Peak, a distinctive spur of the Ratón Mesa with its flattened peak to the south and east, rising to an elevation of 9,600 feet elevation. When Murphy arrived, it was a cold windy overcast day. Trinidad in Las Animas County was at the center of a regional coal mine labor uprising that extended north to the town of Walsenburg in Huerfano County. Murphy had followed events in Colorado closely during the months since the strike in September through subscriptions to the *Denver Post* and the *Trinidad Chronicle-News*.

Violent episodes occurred even before the calling of the strike on September 23, 1913. In August, two Baldwin-Felts detectives employed by CF&I killed a UMW organizer in Trinidad, claiming justifiable homicide. Upon the calling of the strike, as many as 75 additional Baldwin-Felts detectives were brought in and sworn in as Las Animas County sheriff deputies.

As in West Virginia, Colorado also allowed private enterprises to pay the wages and costs for local law enforcement. The rationale for locations dominated by mining explained as the need to maintain public order involving large numbers of imported workers with the financial burden born by business interests. For the coal mining corporations, it ensured that they could maintain an armed security force to not only do their bidding, but in many cases, function under the legal cover as official law enforcement officers. Beyond providing property security, Baldwin-Felts operatives freely intimidated striking miners and union organizers while facilitating the introduction of non-union strikebreaking replacement miners.

The largest of the striking miner tent camps was near a place called Ludlow. 200 tents housed 1,200 miners and their families. A Colorado & Southern rail line servicing the coalfields on the eastern slopes of the Rocky Mountains ran through Berwind Canyon passing near the Ludlow colony. The railroad now served as a firing platform from which to harass striking miners moving along the road parallel to the train tracks.

On October 22, the Stag Cañon Coal Mine No. 2 near Dawson, New Mexico suffered a massive explosion and collapse killing 263. Although not within the Colorado strike zone, the disaster made nationwide newspaper headlines. The publicity caused outcries in support of coal miner grievances concerning the appalling safety record of Colorado mines.

Violence erupted leading Governor Elias Ammons to call in the Colorado National Guard. Once mobilized, the Guard immediately began field operations in late October. The strategy was to separate the warring factions by setting up their own tent encampments between the mines and the various miner tent colonies strung out between Trinidad and Walsenburg.

While some striking miners welcomed what they assumed to be a neutral intervention by the National Guard, violent episodes continued. Several buildings including the post office and a mine structure were set on fire in the town of Aquilar immediately following the deployment of National Guard troops. It was one of many incidents illustrating the depth of miner animosity challenging government authority. The terrible winter weather did not slow the violence during the remaining months of 1913. At the Oakview Mine in the La Veta Pass, three CF&I company men were killed by pro-union gunmen. That same morning a strikebreaker was shot dead. A clerk at the McLaughlin Mine was assaulted. In Piedmont, the home of a miner quitting the strike was dynamited. A Baldwin-Felts detective was assassinated. At Delagua, a mine guard was shot dead.

Succumbing to mine corporation pressure, Governor Ammons allowed strikebreakers to resume entering the strike zone in mid-December after a brief period of restriction. The move only served to exacerbate hostilities.

In January, fiery Mother Jones returned to Trinidad. Arrested on orders from the Governor for incitement under the martial law declaration, she was immediately incarcerated at the Mt. San Rafael Hospital.

In late January, the National Guard discovered an unexploded bomb concealed near their encampment outside of Walsenburg. The incident punctuated the change in attitude to one of open hostility by striking miners toward the Colorado National Guard.

Keara Murphy understood the dangers she might face. Those holding power would see her as a threat given her published ideological position accusing the mining corporations of blatant oppression of coal miners. Contrasted to her experience in West Virginia, the striking miners in southern Colorado were proving exceptionally aggressive by regularly engaging in violent attacks against the mining corporations. This also included targeting law enforcement under control of mining interests.

The introduction of the National Guard did little to suppress the situation. It soon became evident to the striking miners that the state militia was allied with the mining corporations. Leading the National Guard was Adjutant General John Chase, a virulent anti-unionist. General Chase was the same commander in charge of suppressing the Cripple Creek Strike of 1903-1904 where he repeatedly exceeded his authority. A decade later had done nothing to alter his aggressive stance against striking miners. Making no attempt to hide his allegiance, the National Guard routinely used CF&I vehicles and other resources.

Murphy disembarked the train in Trinidad late in the afternoon along with several other passengers. Bitter cold with snow embankments compacted into ice were visible everywhere. Inside the train station she saw three armed men dressed in military uniform. Obviously, Colorado National Guardsmen, they eyed her intently with one clearly leering.

Approaching the ticket agent, she said, "Can you recommend a good hotel nearby?"

"The best hotel is the Columbian just down Commercial Street. Less than a half mile. Unfortunately, the streetcars aren't running on Commercial Street, or Main Street for that matter. A bit of a walk since you're carrying luggage. That fella over there in the yellow cap is a taxi driver keeping warm until he gets a fare if you're interested."

Murphy understood why the streetcars were not operating from reading accounts of the violence in the *Trinidad Chronicle-News*. It was simply too dangerous. The striking miners had brought violence to the very streets of Trinidad. In response, the National Guard positioned sentries and snipers strategically on roof tops of buildings in the center of the town.

Turned out to be a cold ride in the Ford Model T, but better than walking with luggage and navigating snow piled on the sidewalk. Murphy entered an impressive lobby into the three-story brick building that held almost 100 rooms. Two guardsmen lounging near the front desk looked her over as she approached. The only others in the lobby were three seated men.

The clerk behind the front desk greeted her, "Good afternoon, Madam."

"Good afternoon. I'd like a room if one is available."

The clerk smiled, "Lots of rooms available with all the goings on. How long are you staying?"

"Not sure. Probably for a couple of weeks."

"Really? Might I ask what brings you to Trinidad?"

"As you pointed out, the troubles going on with the coalmines. I'm a journalist from New York."

The clerk nodded. "Bad for the hotel business, that's for sure."

After checking in the clerk summoned a teenager in uniform. "John, take Miss Murphy up to room 212."

As the young man carried her bags up the staircase, he said, "Don't have many lady guests right now."

"I can understand why."

"Heard you say you're from New York. This must be something different from such a big city. You're now in the Old West. Lots of history right here at the hotel. In the basement we have a gaming room, a fine gambling establishment. Of course, that is more suited to our male clientele than a lady like yourself from New York City. Yet it's somewhat famous. The famous gunfighter Doc Holiday spent time gambling there in 1882. Wyatt Earp, living up in Pueblo at the time arranged for his friend Bat Masterson who was chief of police of Trinidad at the time to assist Holiday in escaping extradition to Arizona for participating in the murder of Frank Stilwell back in Tombstone, Arizona. You of course know of the famous gunfight at the O.K. Corral?"

Murphy responded, "I recall reading something about that. Those old-time gunfighters would feel right in their element given what's going on in Trinidad today."

Once at her room, the bellboy said, "You have one of the best rooms in the house. Got your own toilet right in there with a bathtub and everything. Stove is over there with coal in the hopper. Want me to start you a fire to get the place warm?"

"That would be nice. Thank you."

While the talkative bellboy took some newspaper and kindling and struck a match, he stood back to let the fire get started before placing in the coal with a set of large tongs. Continuing his rabbling commentary, "On this same floor at the other end of the hallway is our most important guest, General Chase. He's the commander of the National Guard troops sent to Las Animas and Huerfano Counties."

After giving the bellboy a generous tip and finally getting rid of him, she changed into her only dress to explore the hotel and get some dinner.

Inspecting the luxurious saloon, she drew glances from the all-male clientele. Beyond the grand bar was the entrance to a gentlemen's smoking room and a lady's lounge. Before coming to the dining room, she passed a wide staircase of polished wood leading to the basement with a sign overhead reading *Gaming Room & Barber Shop*.

The dining room was sparsely attended with only a few tables occupied. Again, all the customers were men. At one table sat a portly man in military uniform with a large white mustache and thinning grey hair. On his shoulder a single star indicated his rank as a brigadier general. From a newspaper photograph, Murphy recognized General John Chase. At his table were two other army officers. All three men looked toward Murphy as a waiter seated her at a nearby table. Chase acknowledged her with a nod.

At least Murphy knew where to locate her first interview subject.

CHAPTER 7

Las Animas County, Colorado | April 1914

After a good night's rest in the surprisingly well-appointed room, Keara Murphy planned to use her first full day in Colorado to survey the area of conflict. The coal mines stretched mostly in a straight-line running north from Trinidad to Walsenburg for approximately forty miles. According to her map, a road ran parallel to the railroad tracks. Most of the mines and miner camps representing the troubled locations ran along this route since the rail line was necessary for shipping the coal. For her purpose, she would need sturdy automobile transportation. Ideally with a driver familiar with the area.

As a working day traveling the region subjected to the cold weather, she dressed accordingly. Looking into the full-length mirror, she felt pleased with her ensemble. Pleased also with how she looked. The tight-fitting riding breeches defined the female form far better than full, ankle-length dresses. Women's fashion had changed little since the turn of the century. Murphy saw this as another expression of subjugating women by obscuring female sexuality.

Next came outfitting herself with the revolver. The riding breeches she purchased required a belt that provided the ability to secure the revolver holster at her lower back. Back in New York, she tested the suitability of concealing the revolver. The bulky loose-fitting sweater covered it nicely. Took some getting used to sitting with the revolver poking into her lower back, but manageable. The holster attached to the belt held the butt end of the revolver at an angle affording easy extraction. Once in place she practiced withdrawing it several times. Should she come under threat, she must react soon enough to give her a couple of seconds. According to Alan Burke, she must never let a threat get too close.

Satisfied, she loaded the revolver then closed the cylinder into place. Inserting it into the holster, she did a turn in front of the mirror. It was not visible. Also secure from accidental discharge. As a double action revolver, the .38 special did not have a safety mechanism as did a semi-automatic. In an emergency, this prevented losing precious seconds fumbling to release a safety switch. Double action meant she could pull back the hammer and fire a round using minimum trigger pressure resistance as with a single action revolver, or simply pull the trigger exerting more force without first pulling back the hammer. Her father's instructions in the basics of handling firearms allowed her to feel confident should the need arise to use her weapon under actual circumstances. For accuracy, it is best to pull back the hammer and aim. To unleash multiple rounds quickly, just pull the trigger repeatedly.

In a sturdy shoulder bag, she carried her Kodak VPK camera with plenty of film and her notebook.

After having breakfast in the dining room, she inquired at the desk about arranging how best to secure transportation for today and likely for extended use during her stay.

"Where you headed, Miss Murphy?" the desk clerk asked.

"For today up to Walsenburg and back. I'm a writer for magazines. Here to see firsthand and report my observations on the troubles in the coalfields. Want to visit the mines and the striking miner camps. Interview people and take photographs."

"Mind you be very careful. This ain't exactly New York. There may be those that do not like someone taking pictures. Heard stories about some newspaper reporters given a rough time. You don't want to get in the middle of any shooting. Lot of that going on from both sides."

"Thank you for your concern. I'm aware of what's going on. Covered much the same sort of conflict in the West Virginia coalfields a year ago. Can you recommend where I might hire a car and driver?"

The desk clerk nodded. "Perhaps the taxi service can spare one of their two taxis for the whole day. Might cost you but then again, their business is slow with everything that's going on. Want me to inquire?"

"Please do. I appreciate your help."

She sat in the lobby as the desk clerk spoke to someone at length on the telephone. When he hung up, he motioned for her. "I arranged for the use of a taxi all day. It'll cost ten dollars. They said the road up to Walsenburg was passible given the winter weather. The driver is the same young man that brought you from the train station. His name is Charlie. Spoke to his father. Told him you're a reporter from New York. Charlie will be here shortly. I'll have the kitchen prepare sandwiches and a couple of sodas for lunch later on. Where you're goin' might be hard to find a place to eat."

"Thank you. That's very thoughtful."

The young taxi driver entered the hotel twenty minutes later with a big grin on his face. A special event spending all day driving around a pretty New York City lady. Climbing into the aging taxi, he arranged the blanket to cover her lap and legs. It was a clear sunny day but only about twenty-five degrees. "Understand you're a reporter from New York. Plenty of stuff goin' on to write about."

"Seems so. Are things as bad as what I read in the newspapers?"

Charlie replied, "Well, I'd say it's real bad. My Pa says he's never seen so much shooting. People getting killed regularly. Mine guards shooting striking miners, miners ambushing guards. Which side you goin' to be talking to?"

"Both. I want to understand the facts. Hear what each side has to say." Reasonably true, but she clearly wanted to understand the plight of the miners how they justified resorting to killing those working for the mining companies.

Armed with a map of striking miner tent colonies cut from the *Trinidad Chronicle-News*, she told Charlie, "I want to visit the tent encampment outside of Forbes first then the one at Ludlow next. I understand Ludlow is the largest tent colony of striking miners."

"That's what I hear."

The road going north was passible, but modest snow accumulation still slowed the speed of the Model T. There was little vehicle traffic on the unpaved road given the circumstances. Although bundled in a heavy sheep skin hooded overcoat with a scarf about her neck, she welcomed the added warmth afforded by the blanket.

It took forty minutes to make the ten-mile drive to reach the Forbes striker colony. The tent encampment was set back not far from the road. A couple of dilapidated trucks were the only visible vehicles. Two long lines of white tents stretched for a couple of hundred yards. Smoke curled from stovepipes. A few people could be seen moving about. Murphy exited the Model T and extracted her camera.

She and her driver began walking among the tents. The first people she approached were a group of four women. They were standing around a large cast iron pot suspended over a fire of coal contained in a shallow pit. Bundled in heavy overcoats they were tending to some sort of communal food preparation with boiling water giving off a cloud of steam into the cold air. Stepping closer, Murphy introduced herself then asked, "Would you allow me to take your photographs?"

The four women looked at each other for a moment then nodded agreement.

"What are you cooking? Smells good."

One woman replied in a thick Italian accent, "Stew. Mostly potatoes and beans. One of our men shot a jackrabbit this morning so we have a little meat added for flavor."

Another woman said, "We live mostly on potatoes and beans. That's all we can afford. The Union gives us a little money each week for food, but it doesn't go far."

"How much?"

"Three dollars for a man, one dollar for a woman, fifty cents for each child. Not enough to buy meat. The menfolk do what they can to hunt game, but it's mostly jackrabbits. The occasional deer is a rare treat."

"There's no town nearby. Where do you buy the food?"

A different woman with a Greek accent responded, "The Union contracts with those that are willing to bring food to us. Over there is such a wagon." Pointing, she added, "Not enough money to buy much food."

Walking through the tent colony, Murphy speculated out loud to Charlie, "Can't image living in tents in cold weather like this."

Charlie intently surveyed the scene as they walked. When he finally spoke, she could hear the emotion in his voice. "Goddamn! How do they keep warm enough? Been living like this for months. Spring is still weeks away. First time I've seen this. Something awful!"

"Know how you feel, Charlie. Reading about it isn't the same as being out here seeing what it looks like up close. These are tough people. Desperate people. Coal mining is hellish work. Ever think what it's like spending your days underground in the dark doing the most dangerous kind of work?"

Charlie just shook his head and bit his lip.

After taking photographs, Murphy said, "Let's move on. I'd like to see one of the mines and the company's coal camp nearby where the miners lived before the mining companies evicted them. There's a string of them a few miles west of here." Showing Charlie the map published by the *Trinidad Chronicle-News*, "I want to try the CF&I-operated Berwind El Moro No. 2 mine not far from Ludlow."

Somewhat apprehensively he replied, "Okay. But that'll be mining company land. Goin' to be protected by armed guards. Those Baldwin-Felts fellas can be a mean bunch. Probably not willing to let reporters onto company land. Certainly don't want pictures taken."

"All the same, I'd like to see where all this fuss started and get some pictures if possible. You game, Charlie?"

"Alright, Miss Murphy. At least with a woman the guards might be less inclined to do anything violent."

"I just want to get photos so the readers can appreciate what the Colorado coalfields look like. What the mines look like from above ground. What the miners' housing looked like before eviction for comparison to now living in tents during winter in the Rocky Mountains. Don't need to spend much time there. I want to spend most of the afternoon at the Ludlow strikers' encampment. After leaving the mine we can have lunch. I brought along some sandwiches and sodas from the hotel."

—

Charlie found the road leading to the Berwind Mine. It wound through some low hills for a couple of miles. They passed a sign reading *Property of Colorado Fuel & Iron.* As the road came over a slight rise, they could see the mine camp in the distance and a large two-story building Murphy assumed to be the mine offices. Traveling another few hundred yards, they came to a gate blocking the road. Next to the gate two men stood guard. One man stood behind the gate holding a rifle with the butt of the rifle stock resting on the gate. The second man stood in front of the gate with a holstered sidearm visible on his hip.

Holding up his hand, the guard approached the driver's side of the Model T taxi after Charlie stopped the taxi. "What's your business here?"

Murphy leaned over and said, "My name is Keara Murphy. I'm a journalist from New York. Was hoping to speak with the mine superintendent about the strike. Take some photographs if possible."

"You're trespassing. Didn't you see the sign?"

"Yes, I know this is CF&I property. That's why I came here. We're not trespassing."

"Get out of the car!" the guard demanded.

Murphy nodded to Charlie and they both stepped out of the vehicle.

Grabbing Charlie by the arm, the guard checked him for any firearms. "You're both under arrest for trespassing. Get back in the car. I'm taking you to the mine office under custody."

Frightened, Charlie pulled his arm free from the guard who suddenly slapped him hard across the cheek. "Listen you fuckin' kid, you'll do as I say or get a lot worse than that."

Murphy could see this getting out of hand. She suspected these were arrogant Baldwin-Felts thugs that she observed in West Virginia. Not about to allow them to take her and Charlie anywhere. The audacious assumption they had legal authority to make arrests incensed her.

Reaching inside her overcoat she extracted her revolver from under her sweater. Stepping close to the guard, she pointed the weapon in his face.

"We're not going anywhere with you, asshole!"

The surprised guard behind the gate raised his rifle pointing it at her.

Seeing the movement, she stepped to one side placing the guard in front of her between the line of sight of his colleague with the rifle. "Tell your partner to put down his rifle."

The guard glared at her saying nothing.

"Listen carefully. We're going to drive back the way we came. You're coming with us. Don't want your partner getting any ideas about using that rifle."

Defiantly, the guard shook his head. Murphy stepped closer to him suddenly punching him in the nose as hard as she could using her gloved left hand. "I'm not kidding!"

As the guard held his bleeding nose, Murphy grabbed hold of the arm of his coat pulling him toward the taxi. "Charlie, get in the car. This guy will sit in the front, and I'll hold my gun on him from the backseat." To the guard trying to stem his bleeding nose with a handkerchief, she said. "Now get moving." To the guard behind the fence, she shouted, "Put down the rifle. You shoot, your partner dies. We'll drop him off up the road after we're out of firing range."

After making it back to the main road, Murphy told Charlie to stop the car. To the mine guard seated in the passenger seat she said, "Are you with Baldwin-Felts?" The man made no response causing Murphy to push the barrel of her revolver into his neck. "Well?"

He spit out, "Yes. I'm with Baldwin-Felts."

"Thought so. Now get out. Enjoy your walk back."

Standing in the road holding his nose with the front of his coat now soaked in blood, he said, "You'll pay for this. I know your name, bitch."

Charlie put the car in gear and drove off. From the backseat Murphy said, "Are you okay?"

Shaken, he answered, "Yes. Don't want to go through that again though. You carry a gun?"

Murphy chuckled. "Not usually. You see I was in West Virginia a year ago during that coalminers' strike. Newspaper accounts portrayed an even more dangerous environment here in Colorado. Someone I trust recommended I protect myself."

Charlie nodded. "Glad you took that advice. Those Baldwin-Felts fellas are a nasty bunch. Their headquarters are in Trinidad. Two of them murdered a union organizer last summer right on the street. The sheriff never arrested them that I ever heard."

"Listen, Charlie, I know this was an unsettling experience. Would you rather just return to Trinidad?"

"I'm alright, Miss Murphy. Where do you want to go now?"

"Tell you what, let's go the tent colony at Ludlow since we're so close. We'll eat our lunch when we get there. Afterwards, I just want to do a walk about and take more photographs. Then we head back to Trinidad and call it a day."

Charlie smiled, relieved by the prospect of getting back to familiar surroundings. "Sounds good."

Murphy doubted that Charlie would volunteer for another such outing into the coalfields.

Only a few miles away, the Ludlow miners' tent colony looked the same as the one at Forbes although much larger. This encampment housed 1,200 miners and their families. Perhaps as many as 2,000 people total. In deference to Ludlow's importance as the principal union stronghold, another tent enclave sat on the opposite side of the railroad tracks only a quarter mile away. The khaki-colored tents housed a company of Colorado National Guard troops according to a military unit flag waving from a pole. Strategically placed to present a visible deterrent to armed striking miners.

Murphy took another series of photographs before entering the large tent marked with a painted wooden sign on a post reading *United Mine Workers of America District 15*. Inside there were several women and one man seated at tables arranged close to a potbelly stove providing some warmth. After a brief conversation with Louis Tikas the main UMW organizer at Ludlow, Murphy learned that District President John Lawson made his office in Trinidad.

That made her immediate plans easier. Not much more to gain by visiting more tent colonies. The Berwind experience ruled out trying to photograph former company owned mining communities, much less getting photographs of the mines themselves. In Trinidad, she had access to UMW district leaders, Adjutant General Chase of the Colorado National Guard, and as the county seat, the Sheriff of Las Animas County. To attempt an audience with CF&I meant traveling to Pueblo. To interview Governor Elias Ammons required journeying further north to Denver. Pueblo was only 90 miles north and Denver another 100 miles along the same rail route. A heated rail carriage preferable to the unheated interior of an old Model T Ford on poor roads.

Arriving back in Trinidad, Charlie said, "Let me show you something. Get your camera ready. Something interesting but I can only stop for a few seconds. It's the local headquarters for Baldwin-Felts."

Instead of driving to the hotel, Charlie drove a short distance east out Elm Street. An automotive service garage with several service bays stood next to a two-story building. The door of one service bay was open with a long-wheelbase vehicle parked outside. Unusual looking given that it was surrounded by what appeared to be steel plating.

As he slowed, Charlie said, "See that thing toward the back end? That's a machine gun. I'll stop for just a couple of seconds so you can get some camera shots."

Murphy took several photos before Charlie drove on. "Strikers call it the *Death Special*. An armored car. Miners say Baldwin-Felts uses it to harass strikers by shooting up tent encampments. Rumor has it that it was constructed at CF&I's steel mill in Pueblo."

—

Following the confrontation at the gated entrance to the Berwind Mine, the guard struck by Keara Murphy entered the office building. Walking the distance in the cold had reduced the profuse bleeding that now darkened his overcoat and shirtfront.

Baldwin-Felts regional supervisor Leland Atwood happened to be at the mine that day following his own surveillance of the Ludlow striker's tent colony. He was the first to see the injured man. "What the hell happened to you!"

Seething with anger, the man said, "Stopped a man and a woman at the gate. We tried to take them into custody when the woman pulled a gun on Belcher and me. The fuckin' bitch then hit me with the barrel of her gun."

"The woman hit you with the barrel of her gun?" Atwood looked at the man's nose. It was skewed to one side. Obviously broken. No laceration though. To a clerk seated at a desk, he said, "Fetch me a wet towel."

Once the clerk returned from the toilet with a dripping towel, Atwood took it and wiped the injured man's face clear of blood. "She did this with her gun? What kind of gun?"

"A short-barreled revolver."

"Really. Your nose is broken but there are no marks." Atwood suspected the woman hit him with her fist not her gun. "Hold still. I'm going to straighten out your nose. Going to hurt like hell."

Atwood put the towel over the man's nose and jerked it back into place. The man cried out in pain and his nose began bleeding again.

"Hold this in place until the bleed stops. Did you get their names?"

"The woman's name is Keara Murphy. Said she was a reporter from New York."

"The man?"

"A young fella. The car was a Model T taxi with markings of the *Trinidad Taxi Company*."

"Very well. Once the bleeding stops, get your ass back out to the gate and finished your shift. What's your name?"

"Clyde Maddox, Sir."

—

Baldwin-Felts made their regional headquarters in Trinidad for operations in the coalfields of Las Animas and Huerfano Counties. The following day Leland Atwood began his investigation into Keara Murphy. He knew her name from magazine articles published in *McClure's, Colliers,* and attribution in articles appearing in the pro-union *New York Times* newspaper. Atwood served as regional supervisor in West Virginia during the coalfield strike in Kanawha County. When that strike was settled earlier this year, Baldwin-Felts chief Thomas Felts reassigned him to Colorado.

While Thomas Felts employed his two brothers Albert and Lee in senior positions, it was Leland Atwood that he relied on for organizational management in field operations. Atwood was a natural leader. Smart and ruthless, his inclination to use violence for achieving objectives fit well for the activities of Baldwin-Felts. He was good with a revolver and quick to use it, having killed several men. Baldwin-Felts provided him a well-paid career with prestige by characterizing his duties as a law enforcement professional.

Having come from humble rural beginnings in Virginia as the son of a tobacco farmer, Atwood however held disdain for coal miners. He viewed the mountain people of West Virginia and the foreign immigrant majority working in the Colorado coalfields as backward and inclined toward violence. Good for nothing better than digging coal. Alignment as security for the mining corporations gave Atwood a sense of superiority. Given wide-ranging latitude, he relished his power commanding a body of well-armed mercenaries.

Feared by striking miners and union organizers, any opposition to the authority of Baldwin-Felts was met with a harsh response. Murphy's derogatory portrayal of the Baldwin-Felts Detective Agency during the 1912-1913 Paint Creek & Cabin Creek strike in West Virginia angered Atwood professionally. Murphy even praised the exploits of that foul-mouthed grandmother Mother Jones returning to Colorado to incite the miners to revolt as she did previously in Colorado during the 1903-1904 Cripple Creek strike. Fortunately, Jones was being held in custody in Trinidad's San Rafael Hospital under orders from General Chase exercising his authority under martial law. Perhaps Atwood might also find a way to remove Murphy from producing further pro-union publicity and negatively portraying Baldwin-Felts in national publications.

CHAPTER 8

Las Animas County, Colorado | April 1914

The incident at the Berwind Mine had an unsettling impact on Keara Murphy. The aggressive confrontation by the Baldwin-Felts mine guards was unexpected. Instead of just refusing her entry at the gate to the mine, they resorted to armed intimidation by threatening to detain her. Alan Burke did not exaggerate the dangers of the Colorado coalfield environment. That she handled the situation by her own aggressive response left her confident yet disturbed.

That night having dinner at the hotel she again saw General Chase taking his dinner. This time alone without staff officers.

After waiting until Chase finished his dinner and was enjoying a coffee, she approached his table. "General, excuse me for interrupting. My name is Keara Murphy. I'm a freelance journalist here to prepare a series of articles on the Colorado coalfield labor strife. That it has escalated to requiring National Guard troops to maintain order attests to the seriousness of the violence. Might it be possible for you to sit for an interview tomorrow, or some better time for your schedule?"

Chase looked up and smiled. The same pretty woman he admired the previous night. He stood and extended his hand. "Well, how about now? We've both finished our dinners."

"Oh, that is very kind of you, General. I have my notebook right here."

"Excellent. Please take a seat. Care for coffee?"

"Why thank you."

Murphy launched into her interview immediately. "Today I had a disturbing incident when I attempted to visit one of the CF&I mines. The Berwind El Moro No. 2. A couple of Baldwin-Felts hired guns stopped me at the gate. They refused entry, which was their legal prerogative since this was private property. However, they attempted to detain me and my driver. Claimed we were under arrest. Have they been given such authority under the martial law declaration?"

"Good heavens no," Chase answered noticeably surprised. "What happened?"

"Well, I talked my way out of the situation. Made my own persuasive threat. You see, I am also a lawyer. They backed down and I left. Glad to hear the situation has not deteriorated in Colorado to such a degree that private security is allowed law enforcement stature. I was in West Virginia during that recent coal mining strike and Baldwin-Felts routinely exceeded their authority."

"Certainly not here in Colorado. Under the Governor's declaration of martial law, the Colorado Militia assumes responsibility for law enforcement. Local law enforcement is subordinate to my command as adjutant general."

"There have been many reports of violent excesses perpetrated by guards working for the mining corporations. Whether they are contracted Baldwin-Felts employees or colliery employees, how do you deal with tamping down the violence?" Murphy understood that Chase was notoriously anti-union as evidenced during his earlier tenure commanding the Colorado National Guard during the violent Colorado Labor Wars of 1903-1904 involving striking gold and silver mine workers. She wanted to provide him with the opportunity to reveal his bias with comments suitable for appearing in print.

"Unfortunately, Colorado miners all too often resort to armed violence. I believe much of that is the influence of so many foreign workers. Immigrants from places prone to violent rebellion. These striking miners often resort to destroying company property. Harassing and even murdering replacement workers cannot be tolerated. The mining companies have no choice but to provide armed security. Local law enforcement does not have sufficient manpower to contend with illegal acts of widespread violence."

"Baldwin-Felts seems to go beyond security. How do you explain an armored vehicle with a machine gun at the Baldwin-Felts headquarters here in Trinidad?"

Chase responded, "Necessary for maintaining security. Specifically created by CF&I at their Pueblo steel works. Striking miners number in the thousands. A sizeable number are militant and represent an armed threat to civil law and order. That's why the Governor ordered in the National Guard. Even so, the insurrectionists outnumber my available troops. Baldwin-Felts has offered my troops the services of their armored vehicle if necessary."

Murphy noted Chase's telling use of the term *insurrectionists* to define the striking miners as something other than fighting over economic issues and working conditions.

"How do you characterize your position in this conflict, General?"

"Simply to preserve order. Stand between the opposing forces. Use the powers I'm given to arrest those responsible for instigating violence."

"By that do you mean striking miners and union officials?"

"Well, they're the ones chiefly responsible for starting violence. They have set up their tent colonies near the entrance to the canyons where most of the mines are located. The purpose is to harass and attack replacement non-union workers coming in by rail. The mining companies are only reacting by protecting their property and the right to continue doing business."

"The mining corporations do more than that. They create an environment making their workforce little more than indentured serfs. Coalmining is difficult, dangerous, poorly paid work. The mining corporations refuse to bargain over wages and working conditions. By establishing living conditions that breed despair, a natural outcome becomes violence."

"Well, be that as it may, the only thing that can be done after months of violence is to restore civil order."

Murphy moved on. "Newspapers report that the labor activist Mary Jones, known as Mother Jones, is being held under arrest. What are the charges?"

Chase's expression soured. "That old lady is the single most dangerous agitator for inciting violence against the mining companies. Whips striking miners to a frenzy by her speeches. She is charged with insurrection under Colorado law. In deference to her age and health, she is incarcerated at the San Rafael Hospital here in Trinidad."

"Can I be allowed to interview her?"

"Afraid I can't allow that. She'll just spout more inflammatory rhetoric that will find its way into print. Not about to give her a public platform."

Murphy continued to press Chase to obtain comments conveying his anti-union bias that she could quote for publication. Chase seemed to enjoy the experience and Murphy avoided purposely antagonizing him. Better to save her more confrontational interview questions for the principal corporate antagonist in the Colorado coalfield conflict, Colorado Fuel & Iron. The evening ended with Murphy saying, "Thank you for allowing me the opportunity to get your views, General."

Chase stood and extended his hand to Murphy. Puffing on his cigar, he replied, "A most enjoyable evening, Miss Murphy. Please do not hesitate to call on me should you experience any further difficulties."

A couple of days later, Murphy obtained an interview appointment with CF&I President Jesse Welborn at company headquarters in Pueblo, Colorado. Her research into CF&I before leaving New York suggested Welborn was largely a figurehead. The real person that directed corporate operations was Lamont Montgomery Bowers.

In 1907, John D. Rockefeller Jr. assumed control of CF&I when financier and the other major stockholder George Gould suffered severe financial losses in the Panic of 1907 and sold his interest in the corporation. Inheriting Welborn, Rockefeller placed Bowers on the CF&I board with the unofficial mandate to improve financial performance of the large steel conglomerate. Operations included not only coal mines but iron ore mines, steel mills, limestone quarries, coking mills, and the Colorado & Wyoming Railway.

Welborn had risen from within CF&I to the top post and was well-liked by the staff. Rockefeller chose to keep him on as president. In contrast, Bowers possessed little sensitivity for anything other than improving financial performance. Systematically he began reducing employment levels, closing marginally profitable operations, and reducing improvements. As for the workforce, he eliminated previously introduced progressive company sociological and medical programs while maintaining work practices that continued to hold down labor costs per ton of mined product. Profits increased and stockholder dividends paid. These retrograde practices contributed to repeated disastrous accidents in Colorado coalmines with the industry following CF&I's lead.

Murphy was unable to even get a response from Bowers office in Denver. Therefore, the best she could do was confront Welborn with uncomfortable questions based on Bowers' public comments.

It was a two-hour journey by train to Pueblo. Along the route she passed by the tent encampment at Ludlow that stood less than a hundred yards from the train tracks with the National Guard tent encampment across the tracks. Further north as the train travelled north, other tent colonies became visible.

As the train entered Pueblo it passed a vast industrial complex on the east side of the tracks. Murphy assumed this was her destination, the Minnequa Steel Works where CF&I made its headquarters. The train traveled on for a couple of miles before pulling into the station. A taxi then deposited her in front of a large buff colored two-story office building. In the background were many other similarly colored buildings. To the east across the train tracks stood the massive steel mill complex.

After a short wait, a secretary ushered Murphy into Jesse Welborn's office. A large expanse populated with matching wood appointments befitting a president of a large corporation.

Welborn came around from behind his desk and extended his hand. "Please take a seat over here, Miss Murphy," he said motioning to an informal area with comfortable chairs.

Once seated, Welborn said, "Before agreeing to an interview I had one of my staff check on your background. Seems you are a New York attorney. Some sources refer to you as a women's rights activist lawyer. Known for defending women suffrage defendants in court. You are also a freelance journalist published in several magazines. I read your articles concerning the West Virginia strike that crippled coal mining production. Ultimately the violence there required repeatedly instituting martial law and deployment of that state's militia to quell the violence. Somewhat the same situation we find ourselves in Southern Colorado."

"That is why I came to Colorado, Mr. Welborn. The situation in Colorado has proven even more violent than in West Virginia. Are there different underlying causes, or are the same fundamentals in play? I'll be candid, Mr. Welborn. From my research, there exists more similarities than differences. I borrowed the phrase corporate feudalism which is far more than a metaphor for how coal is mined in West Virginia and Colorado. CF&I controls every aspect of the lives of your workforce. Wages, working conditions, housing because the mines are remote, and virtual control over the purchase of necessities of life."

"Unfortunately, that is the nature of coal mining."

"Critics of coal mining corporations, especially large conglomerates like Colorado Fuel & Iron, find the circumstances of governing every aspect of the lives of miners excessively oppressive. Some accuse CF&I of exerting excessive control of Colorado's state and local governments. Governor Ammons is frequently seen as favoring the mining companies. Without an organization such as a union, coal miners have no collective voice with which to lobby for their political interests."

"I disagree with your characterization. Miners can vote for public officials. Unions are not the solution."

"Is that why you have publicly refused to negotiate with the United Mine Workers?"

"Most definitely. The UMW is not there for the miners. The number of workers they get to join and pay dues gives them power. The union leadership then uses that power to negotiate for their own benefit, becoming nothing more than a third party in the relationship. The rank and file are then made to suffer during a strike."

"A member of CF&I's board of directors named Mr. Lamont Bowers has been publicly vocal on the subject of labor unions. Specifically addressing the situation in Colorado, he typified unions ideologically as anarchists. Willing to incite the workforce to armed violence and destruction of property."

Welborn's expression turned dour, regretting having agreed to this interview. He disagreed with Bowers' wholesale disregard for workers' wellbeing in pursuit of profits. John D. Rockefeller Jr.'s subverting of Welborn's authority as president by forcing him to support Bowers' disagreeable management decisions was a constant source of irritation. "As I just stated, I have my own reasons for disliking labor unions. However, I do not see them as anarchists."

"How do you feel about Bowers' comments about a worker's right to work where he chooses without the requirement of belonging to a union? What is called an *open shop*."

"I fully agree with that position. It is the union that resists that idea. They take an all or nothing approach that results in a strike. More economically damaging to the workers than the company."

"I read that more than thirty nationalities are represented among the miners of Colorado. Language sometimes being a barrier to communication. Does that play into the level of violence in this conflict?"

Welborn jumped at the opportunity to inject his own theory that was just as unfounded as Bowers asserting an anarchist conspiracy. "I believe it to be a significant factor. Most of these foreign immigrants come from unstable places where violence is commonplace. Union agitators and people like Mother Jones incite them to take up arms to force their demands Their inherent cultural differences and lack of appreciation for American values are replaced by a common response to resort to violence to achieve what they want."

Murphy held in check her instinct to accuse Welborn of an ideological position even more bizarre than Bowers' anarchist nonsense. "That is surely an unusual theory. Moving on to my more pressing question, how do you see this strike ending?"

"Exhaustion on the part of the striking miners living under deplorable privations without work. The UMW's strike fund is running out causing even meager supplemental pay for necessities to soon cease. I predict destruction of the UMW's influence in Colorado. The same failure they encountered after the West Virginia coal strike."

Murphy responded with emotion now in her voice, "Conditions then are expected to return to those before the strike? The same subsistence wage level for miners? Making little investment in safety improvements? Satisfied for Colorado coal mines to remain the most dangerous in the country?"

Welborn did not rise to her provocation, choosing to respond only to her safety criticism. "We continually invest greatly in adopting best practices in mining safety. Nonetheless, coal mining is inherently a dangerous occupation. The prevalence of combustible gases in Colorado mines have disproportionately affected our record of safety."

Switching topics, Murphy asked, "What do you know about an armored car commonly referred to as the *Death Special*?"

Welborn's expression abruptly changed. "I'm not sure what you are referring to?"

"It's an armored car with a mounted machine gun. Presently sitting at the local headquarters of Baldwin-Felts in Trinadad. The private security firm that CF&I employs as mine guards. The vehicle was constructed right here at your steel mill. Used by Baldwin-Felts to overwhelm poorly armed striking miners."

Welborn shook his head. "Afraid I know nothing about that. We contract mine security with the Baldwin-Felts Detective Agency. I am not familiar with their operational specifics."

Murphy backed off from confronting Welborn with further contentious questions. His tone and equivocations suggesting that perhaps much of what made CF&I practices so egregious came from Lamont Bowers. She elicited further less controversial material from Welborn to augment her articles. Interviewing those like Chase and Welborn proved as frustrating as interviewing politicians. Best to consider their actions and ignore the self-serving rhetoric. After interviewing Welborn as CF&I's president, Bowers refusal to speak publicly about CF&I's practices became less essential to Murphy's project. The same held true for interviewing Governor Ammons.

Her journalistic endeavor was to explain the socio-political aspects of corporate feudalism applicable in the extreme to coal mining in West Virginia and Colorado. Descriptive accounts of the plight of coal miners served to illustrate in real terms the consequences of the repressive environment she wanted to communicate in her published material. Murphy's work was not to take the side of labor over business interests in labor relations specifics. Her intent was to expose the grossly unbalanced socio-economic environment described as corporate feudalism. Circumstances that allowed the coal mining industry control of local government thereby denying constitutionally protected rights to the workforce. This institutionalized oppression afforded corporate mining interests the ability to resist changes for improving worker welfare that would negatively impacted profits. In the coalfields of both Colorado and West Virginia, mining companies did not recognize the right of labor unions to bargain on behalf of coal miners. That stance ensured no direct contact between the warring sides.

—

Following the incident at the Berwind Mine, Leland Atwood assigned a Baldwin-Felts agent to follow Murphy. The agent followed her on the same train to Pueblo then by taxi to CF&I headquarters at the Minnequa Steel Works. He waited outside the hour she was inside then returned by the same train taking them back to Trinidad. After the agent made his report, Atwood telephoned Jesse Welborn.

Welborn said, "She asked me about that armored car. Said she saw it at your headquarters in Trinidad. Don't you keep the damn thing out of sight somewhere?"

Atwood disliked the spineless Welborn but kept his calm. "Needed some work and refitting. Being returned soon to Berwind. What did you and Murphy talk about, Sir?"

"She's clearly on the side of the strikers. Asked all sorts of confrontational questions. Besides being a journalist, she's a New York lawyer. Accused CF&I of some intellectual nonsense she calls corporate feudalism. She might be more articulate than the parade of newspaper reporters covering the strike but she's nothing more than an audacious female. An Easterner no less. Whatever she publishes won't change anything."

Atwood held a different view. Murphy was a threat to Baldwin-Felts. Her nationally published articles made the agency look more of a villain than the mine owners. Not only does she represent a threat to Baldwin-Felts, but Atwood also considered the incident at Berwind a personal challenge. He was not about to wait to read of a female New York lawyer facing down one of his agents armed with a revolver then breaking the idiot's nose.

His simple solution was to provide that idiot Clyde Maddox with the opportunity to take revenge on his humiliation. Let him give Murphy a reason to leave Colorado.

The following morning, Atwood telephoned the mine office ordering Maddox to report to headquarters in Trinidad that afternoon.

—

The following night, Keara Murphy went down to dinner at the hotel restaurant. She had been working all day at her typewriter. Pleased with what she had accomplished, she could see she had enough material to complete a sequence of articles for publication. Linking her observations from West Virginia with the same circumstances in Colorado provided enough material to write a scholarly monograph on corporate feudalism in America.

A deeper societal study of human rebellion going beyond labor discord turning violent.

A couple of glasses of wine helped relax her mind. A hot soak in her own bathroom with running hot water within her room might make sleep easier. The Columbian Hotel was a great find in what otherwise was a western frontier town. The armed violence surrounding Trinidad making it seem even more so.

After starting to run her bath, she made sure the door to her room was locked. As she began undressing, she realized she was still wearing her holstered revolver. Following the incident at Berwind, the security of having the weapon handy allowed for better focusing on her work. Down to her undergarments and a hotel bathrobe, she held the holstered gun in her hand debating about bringing it into the bathroom. Thinking that might be a bit paranoid, logic dictated she should continue to keep the weapon close at hand at all times. Naked inside the bathroom presented an even more vulnerable situation.

Before entering the tub, she placed her robe on a stool that she moved to the backside of the clawfoot bathtub and laid the .38 revolver on it within easy reach.

The hot water with the effects of the wine at dinner relaxed her after soaking for a time. She felt her eyelids fluttering with doziness. Perhaps having dozed off momentarily, she jerked fully alert to what sounded like a key turning in the hallway room door. With the bathroom door closed, it might be nothing more than a sound from the hallway, yet her heart began to race. She reached for the reassurance of holding the revolver.

A moment later the floorboards creaked. Seconds later the bathroom door burst open. Holding a revolver, Clyde Maddox took a step toward her. For a fraction of a second Maddox displayed a leering grin as Murphy stood in the tub naked dripping water. His expression immediately turned to shock as Murphy pointed her revolver. Anticipating an intruder, Murphy had already prepared the revolver by pulling back the hammer before the bathroom door opened.

Without hesitation she fired hitting Maddox in the midsection, followed by a second shot also finding its target.

Maddox dropped his weapon and fell to the floor. Grabbing her robe, Murphy ran from the bathroom then out into the hallway. Yelling for help, two men were standing in the hallway having heard the gunshots. From the far end of the hallway came General Chase, moving quickly in stocking feet dressed only in his uniform trousers and suspenders, brandishing a revolver.

With Murphy holding her robe around herself with one hand while holding her revolver at her side, Chase barked, "What's going on!"

Murphy motioned with her head. "An armed intruder entered my bathroom."

Chase hurried inside. Murphy and the other two male hotel guests in the hall heard his loud exclamation, "Holy shit!" Chase emerged moments later holding a revolver. To the two men in the hall, "Get downstairs and send up the guardsmen on duty in the lobby on the double. Have the night clerk fetch a doctor. There's a badly wounded man in there."

Chase stuck his revolver and Maddox's weapon retrieved from the bathroom floor into his waist band. "Let me have your gun, Miss Murphy. I take it you shot him?"

Murphy nodded.

"Do you know who he is?"

"Yes. He was one of the Baldwin-Felts guards that tried to arrest me and my taxi driver at the Berwind Mine."

"What happened at the mine?"

"Two guards threatened my driver and I with guns. They didn't plan on me being armed. The guy in there tried making it difficult for us to leave. I hit him with my fist. Made a godawful mess with all the blood. By the tape over his nose, I apparently broke it. I suspect he came here looking for revenge." Turning angry, she blurted at Chase, "Somehow, he got a key to my room. Came into my bathroom brandishing a gun. What do you imagine he intended? I clearly have need of protection. Others must be involved. Somebody on the hotel staff provided him a key to my room. Perhaps someone at Baldwin-Felts sent him. Someone unhappy about what I publish."

"I will direct my staff to look into what happened."

"I appreciate the gesture, General. Unlikely that you will uncover anything in this charged environment. You also don't have the resources to protect me. Obviously, I can defend myself if you will be so kind as to return my revolver. I clearly have need to protect myself."

Chase hesitated for a moment before nodding and handing her the .38.

"Thank you, General. How bad is the man I shot?"

"Don't know. One shot in the gut, one higher up in the chest. Lot of blood pooling on the floor."

Three guardsmen came bounding up the stairs with drawn weapons. Chase said, "Sergeant, take charge here. There's a wounded man in the bathroom. A doctor should be on the way. Place him under arrest with a guard. If he survives, I want to question him." To the other guardsmen, "One of you help Miss Murphy gather her belongings while I find her another room."

Settled in another room with a guardsman posted outside her door, Murphy dressed. Sleep was out of the question. She instead set up her typewriter and began documenting the details of the incident while fresh in her mind. Although shaken, anger dominated her thoughts. What happened to her was indicative of the central part Baldwin-Felts played in the coalfield violence. The private army of the mining interests in Colorado and West Virginia served to exacerbate the already charged environment. Her venomous written account alleged the incident was retaliation by Baldwin-Felts management.

Hours later, General Chase knocked on her door. Now well after midnight, Chase looked tired. He sat down in the only chair in the room while Murphy sat on the bed.

"We transported the man that entered your room to San Rafael Hospital. He died while in surgery. According to identification on his person, his name is Clyde Maddox, a Baldwin-Felts employee. Tomorrow one of my officers will investigate further how he might have gotten a key to your room. I will personally confront the Baldwin-Felts operations supervisor and deliver a sharp warning about his operatives exceeding their authority."

115

"Exceeding their authority? That's not how I will portray it in print. Am I in any legal trouble?" Murphy asked. Consumed by rage, the shock of having killed the intruder did not engender any real emotional distress.

Chase shook his head. "No, certainly not. Clearly you acted in self-defense. Maddox entered your room carrying a firearm with the obvious intention of doing you harm." Pausing a moment, Chase asked, "After what has happened, do you intend to return to New York soon?"

"Not yet. The war going on here doesn't seem settled. I've more to see before leaving."

"Afraid you'd say that. I'd rather you left for your own safety, but you are a journalist with a right to be here. I sincerely regret what happened to you. Miss Murphy." Pausing a moment, he continued, "I see you have a typewriter. I will dictate an authorization pass over my signature that you may use to move freely without interference by the National Guard or anyone else."

—

Murphy occupied the following day interviewing United Mine Workers District 15 President John Lawson at length. A veteran of the earlier Cripple Creek Strike of 1903-1904, Lawson proved a wealth of information. Having worked in the mines from an early age he understood what miners endured. In that earlier strike his house was dynamited. Only months ago, he was seriously wounded in a shotgun attack.

Poised and articulate, Lawson provided a well-stated account of the issues that brought about the violence that characterized this current strike. According to Lawson, since the start of this strike going back to September of the previous year, the mine owners intentionally provoked the striking miners to react violently.

Lawson explained. "The strategy has been to justify the use of force by their hired guns in the form of Baldwin-Felts. They continually provoked armed incidents by the striking miners that forced the Governor to declare martial law and bring in military forces. They have accomplished that in part. The Colorado National Guard is ostensibly here to maintain order. They do not represent a neutral party in this conflict. Adjutant General Chase commanding the National Guard has a long record of anti-labor bias. He commanded the National Guard during the Cripple Creek Strike ten years ago.

"As you can see, the National Guard has not even been successful in quelling the back-and-forth violence. They of course only arrest striking miners and UMW organizers. I believe Governor Ammons and the mining corporations would welcome intervention by federal troops. They hold an imbalance of power in both Denver and Washington. Even I would project a settlement brokered by President Wilson would probably result in the mining corporations retaining the right to conduct business with little change."

—

Just days following Murphy's interview with John Lawson, a singular incident would transform the coal mine strike of 1913-1914 into the Colorado Coalfield War. What instantly became known as the *Ludlow Massacre* reverberated across America.

It was Monday April 20, 1914. The location was the tent colony of evicted striking coal miners situated close to the Colorado & Southern Railroad tracks a half mile south of the small village of Ludlow.

That morning before sunrise a Colorado National Guard troop under the command of Lieutenant Karl Linderfelt set up a machine gun next to the railroad water tank. A total of about 200 militiamen took up positions along the railroad tracks directly across from the miners' tent colony. The intention of Linderfelt's deployment remains unclear. However, Linderfelt was known as a particularly brutal soldier that regularly exceeded his authority by acting independently. Armed miners began taking up defensive positions anticipating some sort of aggressive action by the National Guard.

An intense firefight erupted when guardsmen detonated dynamite explosions as a signal for additional militia troops at Berwind and Cedar Hill to come in support of Linderfelt's planned operation. The exchange of gunfire continued all day. Late in the afternoon, Baldwin-Felts mine guards joined the National Guard in mounting an attack. As the sun set, a passing train stopped on the tracks blocking the militia's machine gun emplacement allowing miners and their families to escape to some low hills to the east. However, not all escaped.

By 7:00pm the National Guard prevailed with the encampment now in flames. The tents with their wooden flooring and combustible belongings soon reduced the entire camp to smoldering rubble. Militiamen began searching and looting for anything of value.

Linderfelt captured UMW organizer Louis Takis and two other men that stayed behind. Linderfelt recognized Tikas from earlier confrontations. With troopers holding Tikas, Linderfelt smashed a rifle butt into his head. The following day, the bodies of Tikas and the other two men were discovered. Shot in the back.

During the engagement, four women and eleven children hid in a pit dug under one of the tents created as a secure place from gunfire. In this instance, they died terribly by the flames and smoke. Later accounts would put the total death toll at Ludlow at 20. Only one National Guardsman died in the lopsided battle.

The deaths at Ludlow shocked the nation. The Colorado National Guardsmen causing the most horrific deaths of women and children, then committing outright murder made the Ludlow Massacre a byword for officially sanctioned oppression of workers.

—

News of the Ludlow Massacre reached the other tent colonies by early the following morning. It created a spontaneous response from large numbers of striking miners that set about on a decentralized armed campaign against their oppressors. Departing from his previous stance of attempting to suppress violence on the part of miners, UMW District President John Lawson now called for armed response. Widespread violence erupted throughout the Southern Colorado coalfield region with large numbers of armed miners making repeated attacks against the militia, local law enforcement, and particularly Baldwin-Felts mine guards. This conflict became a departure from the isolated small acts of violence and sabotage occurring in the canyons close to the coal mines in the earlier months of the strike.

The elevated conflict became known as the *Ten Days War.* On April 28, President Woodrow Wilson invoked the Insurrection Act of 1807 ultimately deploying 1,700 federal regular U.S. Army troops to Colorado. Only after the intervention of federal troops did the conflict subside. During the *Ten Days War,* as many as 54 people were killed following the Ludlow Massacre. Disproportionally, most were coal miners.

—

Regardless of her travel authorization from General Chase, Keara Murphy wisely stayed put in Trinidad. Her journalistic subject did not include detailed reporting on the many short battles fought throughout the coalfields. Photographs were not worth the risk of being shot. Her sojourn to Colorado had already exposed her to enough danger. She spent her time during the *Ten Days War* following the Ludlow incident with the office of the managing editor of the *Trinidad Chronicle-News.* This allowed remaining current with daily happenings but out of harm's way. Interacting with the newspaper staff added to her body of useful material for use in her expansive work describing the larger sociological implications of life in the coalfields.

In early May she boarded a train taking her back to New York. Anxious to leave Colorado and return home to civilized Brooklyn. She collected more than enough material needed to complete a lengthy article for publication.

Looking forward to renewing her correspondence and relating with Noreen Hannigan and her brother Alan Burke. Anxious to share her harrowing experiences, she was just as interested in sharing her insights of the social conditions associated with coal mining in these remote regions. She would include in her letters the opening paragraphs of her work titled, *Digging Coal in America*.

> *While there are many occupations that are physically arduous and some very dangerous, coal mining adds other elements that affect the very spirit of coal miners. To descend each workday deep underground to face a myriad of hazards in an environment devoid of natural light while breathing bad air containing unhealthy contaminants, requires either uncommon resolve, or desperation. Freeing coal from seams surrounded by layered sedimentary rock requires the use of explosives. There is a constant risk of releasing combustible gas igniting an explosion from odorless lethal gas or breaking into an underground source of water and drowning. It always risks bringing down the roof of the excavation tunnels. Each miner must experience a moment of terrible uncertainty each time the cry of fire in the hole warns of an impending dynamite explosion.*
>
> *Mining coal in Southern Colorado on the edge of the Rocky Mountains or West Virginia in the Appalachian Mountains means working and living in remote canyons where seams of coal are most often found. It is this condition of remoteness that adds another burden to those that work in coal mines. The mining companies own large tracts of land that force the workforce to live close to the mine. This in turn demands suitable housing not only for miners but also their families. Having to provide worker housing and the ability to purchase goods close by, mine owners often cannot resist the opportunity to offset these added costs of doing business by overcharging their employees for these necessities.*
>
> *The concept has immediate parallels with circumstances of tenant farmers working for landed aristocracy where everything about the peasant worker's life comes under direct control of the landowner. Hence the label of corporate feudalism. In labor disputes, the ultimate*

recourse for workers to pressure for better compensation or improved working conditions is to strike. With the mining companies controlling housing, going out on strike means losing your place of residence. Surviving while un-employed in these remote areas adds further immeasurable hardships for those already living at the margins.

For those working underground in dangerous conditions for low pay there develops comradery frequently transcending ethnic differences. Faced with exploitation by employers supported by governmental institutions biased to business interests, coal miners have understandably responded to corporate oppression with organized violence.

In Colorado and West Virginia, large business interests led by coal mining have corrupted state and local government. A condition of institutionalized oppression exists where fundamental rights defined in the United States Constitution, and further codified in state and local statues, are blatantly ignored in both states. For a coal miner and his family, these places do not look like America.

The oppression of coal miners in America is the most vivid example of the dark effects on workers in an unregulated market economy. Business interests are further shielded by the structure of the American republic where individual states exercise authority not found in other democratic republics. In the coalfields of Colorado and West Virginia the denial of many basic rights expressed in the U.S. Constitution has become institutionalized in the service of profits and political power. Washington has yet to come to grips with this reality.

When the Colorado Coalfield War ended in May of this year it was the bloodiest labor dispute in American history.

CHAPTER 9

Veracruz, Mexico | May 1914

Alan Burke was now in the port city of Veracruz, Mexico on a new deployment when a letter posted weeks earlier from Keara Murphy in New York caught up to him. With a break from duties, he sat alone under a shade tree in the Parque Zamora square near the docks of Veracruz to read Keara's letter undisturbed. Burke's battalion was now quietly sitting out the occupation of the city.

A pleasant sunny day with a gentle onshore breeze blowing from the Gulf of Mexico. Burke was still on duty dressed in his summer cotton field uniform and full combat gear. For Sergeant Major Burke that consisted of his tunic shoulder insignia of rank with three up and three down chevrons, the new *Montana Peak* broadbrimmed field hat, canvas leggings over his boots, with a cartridge belt at his waist.

Given his rank as the most senior NCO rank, Burke exercised some uniform liberties. Because of his extraordinary marksmanship skills with a sidearm, Burke was allowed to carry a sidearm like a commissioned officer. His M7 leather holster had a shoulder strap that he looped over his right shoulder with a second strap wrapping about his midsection then secured to his cartridge belt under his left arm. The holster contained his Colt M1911 .45

caliber semiautomatic service pistol. Since he did not typically carry a rifle, instead of a bayonet, a Bowie knife in a leather scabbard hung from his cartridge belt.

The large heavy knife had a nine-inch blade with an overall length of fourteen inches. The main body of the blade was one and a half inches in width, a quarter-inch thick at the spine with a clip point sharpened on the reverse edge. Weighing 24 ounces, it possessed some of the attributes of a short sword making it a versatile lethal weapon.

The weapon was given to him by a senior sergeant lying next to Burke in the jungle struck down by sniper bullet in the Philippine-American War. The sergeant and Burke became close friends having both come from West Virginia. "I'm not going to make it, Alan. Take my Bowie knife. Better than a fuckin' bayonet in close quarters. Make good use of it." Moments later he died.

Often short on firearms, the Philippine insurgents regularly armed themselves with *bolos*, a traditional long curve blade machete-like weapon. Similar in length, the hefty Bowie knife wielded by a trained professional like the sergeant could compete against a bolo in a knife fight.

It had been March since Burke last heard from Keara Murphy. Nothing since she announced her intention to travel to Colorado to cover the labor conflict in the southern coalfields. He read in the newspapers about the Ludlow Massacre. Wondered if Murphy was alright. Caused him to realize how much he anticipated hearing from her and how anxious he felt knowing where she was going. People were dying in the Colorado violence. Keara poking about as a journalist given her stance against oppression of any kind would make her unwelcome among those of the Colorado power structure.

Keara's opening of her letter brought a rush of feelings as he pictured her in his mind.

Dear Alan,

Colorado proved more of an adventure than I anticipated. Could have used you by my side. By the time I arrived in

Trinidad, the coal mines strike was six months old. The violence had worsened. The Colorado National Guard already present under the Governor's declaration of martial law when I arrived. Their presence not only failed to quell the violence, but they alone are also guilty of perpetrating the horrors at the miners' tent colony the newspapers dubbed the Ludlow Massacre. I'm sure you have read about that. The attacking militiamen were under the command of a psychopath named Lieutenant Karl Linderfelt.

As a result of the Ludlow incident there occurred another spasm of violence instigated by the most militant miners bent on retribution that became known as the Ten Days War. It was simply too dangerous to venture out into the coalfields, so I spent that time working in Trinidad with the staff of the local newspaper. I had toured the Ludlow tent encampment before the killings. Newspapers already published photographs of the aftermath. I already had an unpleasant personal confrontation with those same thugs from Baldwin-Felts employed by the coal mines in West Virginia. Thanks to your advice that I should go into this war zone armed, I survived unscathed. A frightening story in its retelling. Yet if you engage in investigative journalism, you must assume a risk of retaliation.

The episode started when I hired a driver to take me to see the striking miner tent colonies north of Trinidad that including Ludlow. Wanted to interview a mine official at one of the mines. Chose a Colorado Fuel & Iron coal mine since they were the biggest operator in the region. Wasn't surprised when two armed guards stopped us at a gate closing off the road leading to the mine office. They were Baldwin-Felts men. For some reason they chose to take the matter further by pronouncing we were under arrest for trespassing by just driving up their road. In short, I thought it a bad idea to allow them to take me and my driver into custody. Nobody knew we were coming here. Therefore, from behind my back, I pulled my .38 you told me to purchase and stuck it into the face of the closest guard. After the fool wouldn't back down, I broke his nose with my fist and took him hostage until we retreated a mile back up the road.

Days later this same guy broke into my hotel room with a gun in his hand while I'm taking a bath. I recognized the bandaged nose and knew what he intended. Being vulnerable, I didn't hesitate. Shot him twice. He died undergoing surgery. The general commanding the Colorado National Guard declared it self-defense. Maybe sufficient while under the declaration of martial law, but later the local prosecutor might feel different. Likely in the pocket of CF&I. I had no intention to hang around this hellhole until that happened to face charges before a corrupt judge with a jury bought off by CF&I.

I promise to expand with more details when I see you again in person. When might you be getting leave and returning to the States? Would love to show you around New York. Maybe entice your sister to come as well. Noreen and I have become fast friends. We correspond regularly. From when we first met in Charleston, she seems recovered from her personal tragedies. She and your mother appear to be managing their amicable estrangement remarkably well. From her letters, Noreen's emotional wellbeing has vastly improved.

My experiences while in West Virginia came at a time when I also needed to recover from a personal loss. Professionally, it has led to a journalistic pursuit exposing the threat of corporate feudalism to the future of our republic. Colorado only reinforced the scope of the threat of how the unregulated power of capital in our market economy can destroy the fundamental fabric of America.

Sorry to ramble with my socio-political views. I should instead be asking what is going on with you. Are you still in Panama? The newspapers report that we invaded Mexico. The Marines of course leading the occupation of Veracruz. Were you perhaps among those Marines? Are you in Mexico?

126

Somewhere else? Please write as soon as you receive this letter. American forces are reported as suffering casualties at Veracruz. I know you are a soldier, but I think of you whenever reading about some foreign land where Washington has sent the U.S. Marines. Take very good care of yourself, Alan Burke.

Yours affectionately,
Keara

Burke was aghast. He reread the letter trying to grasp the meaning of Keara's shocking statement, *I shot him twice. He died.* Without details, he could only try to envision her traumatic encounter. For a New Yorker, Keara Murphy was a woman to be reckoned with. That evening he penned a letter in reply.

Dearest Keara,

Was aghast to learn of your violent experiences in Colorado. Reading newspaper accounts of the Ludlow Massacre raised even more concerns over your safety. Greatly relieved that you are okay. You sound as if the experience did not leave you permanently traumatized. Remarkable for someone unaccustomed to such extreme physical dangers. Don't let the incident pray on you. The fellow deserved to be put down.

I waited anxiously for you to write knowing you were occupied in Colorado. Your letter only just arrived. Delayed for weeks until the mail caught up to me in Veracruz, Mexico. I am doing fine. We encountered armed resistance from Mexican federal troops only briefly after landing from a naval vessel.

Not at all certain why we are in Mexico. Seems another example of the United States extending control beyond its borders. It's becoming a pattern with each succeeding administration. As a soldier, I resent being used as an instrument to further American business interests. However, as a soldier I am dutybound to obey orders. I tell myself that the Marine Corps serves to ensure America's security by demonstrating our unique capabilities and naval mobility. Mexico on our southern border must be considered vital to U.S. security. Not sure though how Washington's meddling in Mexico's political affairs can remake something so badly broken.

Glad to hear about you and Noreen. I believe you are an invaluable influence on her. As for visiting you in New York, I promise to do just that. The first opportunity I can get extended leave and make it stateside. Not sure how long I'll be in

Mexico. After that, hard to say. Depends on the next trouble spot. At least the climate here is better than Panama.

Once your observations on the Colorado Coal Wars are published, please send me a copy. Let me also ask another favor. As a lonely Marine perpetually stuck in alien places, I would love to have a photograph of you.

I'm still troubled hearing about your Colorado incident. Forced to shoot someone intent on doing you harm can be difficult to process emotionally. I speak from experience. Glad you are back in New York. Stay put there. That's where I'll see you when next I am stateside on leave. Stay strong, Keara.

With much affection,

Alan

—

Burke arrived in the Gulf of Mexico waters on April 21. At 11:00am, along with his battalion commander Major Butler, he disembarked from the U.S. naval auxiliary vessel, *USS Prairie*. In whaleboats, they were the first wave of 500 U.S. Marines to land, accompanied by several Naval rifle companies. The military objective was to prevent an expected arrival of arms aboard a German-register cargo vessel reaching the Mexican Army. With the Mexican Revolution still rendering Mexico politically unstable,

U.S. President Woodrow Wilson was actively supporting Mexican rebels to oust the unpopular military dictatorship of General Victoriano Huerta.

Naval riflemen captured the custom warehouse and telegraph office. The Marines led by Burke's battalion secured the railroad yard and power plant. The brief combat mission against the garrisoned Mexican Army lasted only a couple days but not without significant casualties. U.S. forces suffered nearly 100 killed and wounded with Mexican casualties estimated at 500.

Burke thought this incursion into Mexico was ill-conceived. Even European allies of the United States criticized the action of President Woodrow Wilson as imperialistic as he began the second year of his administration. In the weeks that followed, Burke reflected on perhaps wider implications of American foreign policy. Apart from participating in the brief Spanish-American War in his early military career, Burke also concluded his various foreign deployments resulted more from imperialistic ambitions of the United States rather than national security. China during McKinley's administration. The Philippines, Honduras, and Panama under Roosevelt's. Nicaragua under Taft's. Now Mexico under Wilson's. Burke did not see any of these actions as vital to U.S. security. They seemed primarily issues of specific U.S. business interests rather than national security.

Former governor of the Mexican State of Coahuila, José Venustiano Carranza, assumed control of the Constitutionalist faction rebelling against Dictator Huerta. With the alliance of the populist rebel leaders Francisco Villa and Emiliano Zapata, Carranza became the de facto Mexican head of state. The Mexican Revolution by no means ended, however the situation stabilized sufficiently for U.S. military forces to leave Veracruz in November.

Burke's regiment returned to Panama. The Veracruz climate was more welcoming than the year-round hot and oppressive climate of Panama. Even considering why they deployed to Veracruz, at least it was a city of substance compared to remote Camp Elliott. Like most of his unit, Burke was disheartened by the recurring deployments of Central America. Garrisoned in hot humid remote places like Panama and Guantanamo, Cuba during deployment intervals only added to discontentment.

Burke's commanding officer Major Butler also was unhappy. Soon after returning to Camp Elliott Burke was sharing a beer with the Major. "Do you know they handed out 56 Medal of Honors for our brief military action in Mexico. Ordered by that idiot Secretary of the Navy Daniels. I received one. For doing nothing that would warrant our highest citation for valor." Butler took out the small case from drawer and slapped it on his desk in disgust.

"Such a wholesale distribution for a minor military engagement diminishes the accomplishments of those more deserving. I was on a reconnaissance mission to Mexico City. Traveling undercover as a railroad official. Sent to develop a plan for a military expedition. Modestly dangerous but not worthy of the medal of honor. That was about six weeks before we deployed to Veracruz after our equally unsuited President found an excuse to send us to occupy Veracruz without a strategic objective. Tried to return the medal but I was ordered to wear it."

Burke replied. "What's your guess where we might be headed next, Sir?"

"Well, for the moment the United States has not been drawn into the war consuming Europe. That could change. The assassination of that Austrian archduke heir to the throne by a Serb revealed an entanglement of mutual defense treaties of all the major European powers. Within months, they lined up on two sides and began fighting. The Germans achieved initial success but their offensive into France eventually stalled. Reports say they have begun establishing strong defensive positions in preparation for settling in for the coming winter. This war could go on for some time. No telling what that might mean for the United States."

—

The boredom of Camp Elliott in Panama ended the following summer with a new deployment to Haiti. Burke landed with Major Butler and 340 U.S. Marines in Port-au-Prince on the battleship *USS Connecticut* on July 15, 1915. Neither Butler nor Burke understood the real reason for yet another occupation. All they knew was that Haiti had fallen into violent chaos. Years of socio-economic instability collapsed the small country into anarchy when a mob lynched Haitian President Vilbrun Guillaume Sam following his ordering the execution of 167 political prisoners, including a former president. Sam's presidency lasted only five months with those of his two predecessors also lasting only months. Haiti is a pesthole of the worst sort.

The real reason for U.S. intervention came from pressure by the National City Bank of New York who had become the dominate source of Haitian financing. Haitian debt had risen to a level that threatened default. The Bank used growing regional security concerns as war broke out in Europe to lobby Washington for U.S. military occupation of Haiti. A small but influential number of German businessmen controlled eighty percent of Haitian international trade. These factors combined with a threat fear of German influence so near to the newly completed Panama Canal provided justification for the latest American foreign military occupation.

The landing of the first Marine units went unopposed. The country had no central leadership. Peasant militias called *Cacos*, consisting of poor Afro-Haitians who spoke Haitian Creole, operated independently throughout the country.

The first substantial military confrontation by the Haitian rebels occurred months later. At the time, Major Butler's command was headquartered in the port town of Cap-Haïtien on Haiti's northern coast. A location close to where Christopher Columbus founded the first European settlement in the Americas on his first voyage in 1492. Many abandoned fortifications erected by the Spanish and French during periods of occupation now occupied northern Haiti.

Toward the end of October Major Butler took a company of Marines on horseback southeast to make a reconnaissance of rebel-held Fort Dipitie located close to the border with the Dominican Republic occupying the largest portion of the island of Hispaniola. As the Marines began crossing the Grande River, 400 rifle-armed indigenous Cacos attacked. Outnumbered, the Marines retreated to a position on higher ground. The Cacos followed up their ambush with repeated attacks throughout the night.

The Cacos were notoriously bad marksmen, untrained in the use of a rifle gunsight. In close quarters they often resorted to attacking with machetes. With their superior numbers, many were able to get close to the defensively positioned Marines. Burke killed two Cacos with his heavy Bowie knife.

In the morning, Major Butler ordered a counterattack telling his men to charge as fast as they could and shoot every rebel in sight. The ill-trained Cacos fled at the sight of the charging Marines, some even dropping their weapons. The Marines captured Fort Dipitie after killing 75 Haitian rebels while sustaining only one wounded Marine casualty. The remaining rebels fled into the underbrush.

Less than a month later, Burke found himself again in battle. With 76 Marines this time facing an estimated 200 Cacos holding another stronghold named Fort Rivière. Located on a steep escarpment in the Montagne Noire, these highlands served as strongholds of Haitian independence fighters for over a century.

After an exhausting climb of the 3,600-foot elevation mountain through the night through thick vegetation, the Marines reached the top. They looked at the thick masonry walls of the 18th century French star-shaped fortification. Vegetation around the walls was cleared to create a defensive killing zone. Butler's force surrounded the fortification remaining under cover without alerting the Cacos of their presence.

At 7:50am the next morning, Butler blew his whistle signaling the assault. Although outnumbered, the Marines possessed three M1909 machine guns lugged up the mountain by mules. As they rushed across the open ground, the Cacos returned heavy rifle fire but the rate of fire from the Marines' machine guns suppressed the defender's effectivity.

Standing at Major Butler's side, Burke spotted what appeared to be a storm drain opening coming from under the fort's wall. Large enough for a man to walk through in a low crouch. He pointed saying to Butler, "Look there, Major. Maybe a way inside!"

It proved to be just that. Butler, Burke, and another Marine made their way fifteen feet to the fort's interior. Coming into open air, several Cacos saw them and charged forward yelling kill them in creole. Burke in the lead dropped three charging Cacos with his .45 pistol. As more Marines poured out from the drain the fighting quickly became vicious hand to hand combat. The Cacos dropped their rifles and resorted to machetes. The Marines countered with bayonets fixed to their Springfield rifles. Burke drew his Bowie knife and switched his .45 to his left hand.

The battle raged for less than ten minutes. A fight to the death contest with no means of escape for either side surrounded by the walls of the fortification. Blood turned the soil to mud. As the battle drew to a close, Burke looked up toward the parapets seeing many Cacos leaping to the outside from the fortification walls. Machine guns immediately opened up and kept firing for several minutes. The intensity of the fighting resulted in 71 Cacos killed with dozens more wounded.

It was two days before Christmas at Marine headquarters in a commandeered hotel in Cap-Haïtien, when Major Butler summoned Burke to his office.

Got a couple of pieces of good news for you, Sergeant Major. The first is approval of my recommendation for awarding you the silver star for your actions at Fort Rivière. The second you will likely see as welcomed news although I regret losing the best fighting man I ever served with. You're being reassigned to Port Royal, South Carolina. Marine training center Camp Parris Island."

Surprised, Burke asked, "Why Parris Island, Sir?"

Read for yourself," Butler said handing Burke his orders.

The substance of his orders read, 'Sergeant Major Burke is to assume supervision as senior NCO of recruit training in close quarter combat given his history of demonstrated proficiency in multiple theaters of military engagement under fire. Sergeant Major Burke is to report for duty 2 April 1916 following personal leave of 60 days beginning 1 February 1916.'

Butler brought out a bottle of whiskey and the two spent the next couple of hours in candid conversation as two veteran soldiers regardless of their separation in rank.

"Does what we've been doing here in Haiti and places such as Nicaragua and Panama ever trouble you, Sir?"

"What do you mean?"

"These poor Haitians live little better than slaves. Once they gained independence from France over a hundred years ago, their situation didn't improve. Now they are enslaved by a succession of petty Haitian dictators that serve only until assassinated. There is no government here. Haiti has become nothing more than an ungovernable American colony. We hunt the *Cacos* like wild pigs. They can't fight worth a damn, yet we chase them across these accursed mountains. I can see no good end to this, Sir."

Butler nodded replying, "Haiti is demoralizing duty. A terrible place where civilization has broken down. I envy you going to South Carolina. I've been given command of the Haitian Gendarmerie. An unpleasant assignment but a soldier follows orders. Soldiering is an honorable profession, but it also has its dark side. We follow orders and do the best we can to keep our morality intact. These *Banana Wars* also bother me, Sergeant Major. The places we've been sent these past years don't strategically threaten the United States. Mexico might be an exception, but certainly not Haiti."

Major Butler knew full well the reputation for brutality of the Haitian Gendarmerie. A collection of hardened holdovers of former Haitian regimes. Used to operating with little oversight, they evolved into a rogue police force using the most brutal of means including torture and murder. Now they would serve as American's surrogate police force. They would provide American military leadership with a feared organization of undisciplined thugs as the only means for maintaining civil order. But at what cost? Burke was glad to be leaving Haiti.

Burke said, "We're in these places for economic interests of American private corporations. Not sure that's worth risking your life over. I've told you of the circumstances in the West Virginia coalfields where I came from. The mining companies run West

Virginia like one of these banana republics. The same situation exists in the coalfields of Southern Colorado. Private industry hires their own law enforcement and even control the courts. They've become no better than colonies of American business interests."

Butler replied, "I can see why that must affect how you feel about what we've been doing these past years. Maybe a stint stateside will prove therapeutic. You can do something meaningful by teaching recruits your many combat skills. Help these young men become America's best soldiers while teaching them how to stay alive."

"Maybe. I'm coming up on my twenty years in the Marine Corps next year. Been thinking what else I might do with the rest of my life other than soldiering."

That caught Butler by surprise. He thought of Burke as the ultimate warrior. "I hope you don't leave the Corps, Sergeant Major. It's not often that someone lands in a profession where they are so uniquely qualified. Think about that before you make a decision. At least talk to me first."

Burke smiled and nodded. "Aye, aye Sir. I appreciate your advice." Butler was more than just his commanding officer.

Butler added, "Since the sinking of the passenger liner *Lusitania* in May, the Commandant is anticipating the possibility of the United States becoming actively involved in the war in Europe. Sending you to Parris Island may be part of that. You will note your orders are signed by the Commandant's chief of staff."

—

Alan Burke was not particularly enthused about the prospects involved with his new posting. Yet he welcomed leaving Haiti to return stateside. More than that, the idea of visiting family and hopefully spending some time in New York visiting Kears Murphy was something to look forward to. Selfishly, he would go first to New York to visit Kear Murphy. She was never far from his thoughts.

Dearest Keara,

My posting to Haiti is finally coming to an end. I shall not dwell on how difficult this has been. Haiti is beyond depressing. Will tell you details another time. Which brings me to my news. I am being reassigned to training duties in South Carolina in April. Before reporting, I have a 60-day leave starting around the first of February. Is that a good time to visit you in Brooklyn? I've never been to New York but mostly I want to see you. Doesn't matter that it is still winter.

After visiting you in New York I will journey to West Virginia to visit my mother and Noreen before reporting to Port Royal in South Carolina.

I am so very anxious to hear from you, Keara. Given my remoteness and the mail taking weeks, would you wire me? 5th U.S. Marine Corps Regiment Headquarters, Cap-Haïtien, Haiti. I certainly don't want to intrude on your personal life, but you have become my lifeline to civilized discourse while being stuck in some of the worst possible places under difficult circumstances. You have become important in my life much as you have to my dear sister.

Hope everything is well with you and fully recovered from your traumatic experiences in Colorado. In my career, I have become practiced in doing just that therefore I can imagine how exposure to a violent threat for the first time must feel. That you reacted with such courage is what you must fix in your memory. How you reacted was justified. Put it behind you. Do not harbor any regrets about what happened to the person intending to do you harm.

Will anxiously await hearing from you about meeting in Brooklyn in February.

Alan

CHAPTER 10

Brooklyn, New York | February 1916

Two weeks later, Burke received a telegram from Keara Murphy. *Cannot wait to see you. Leaving month of February open. Wire arrival details when departing Haiti. Much to talk about. Love Keara.*

He stared at the closing. *Love Keara.* Did that hold greater meaning?

Burke's remaining weeks in Haiti passed slowly thinking only of getting stateside. Rebel hostilities abated following the battle at Fort Rivière. The U.S. Marines had the distasteful task of backing up the brutal Haitian Gendarmerie in suppressing insurgent action. Major Butler, now commanding the Gendarmerie, and Colonel Littleton Waller ruled the country under martial law while Washington attempted to draft a new Haitian constitution. For Burke, this was blatant American imperialism. Morally indefensible leaving him deeply conflicted about continuing his military career.

Burke eventually left Cap-Haïtien on a Navy supply vessel returning to the Philadelphia Naval Shipyard on January 21, 1916. From there it was less than three hours by train to New York's Penn Station in Manhattan. He wired Keara his estimated arrival in Philadelphia. Told her he would take the first available train to Manhattan then take the subway to Brooklyn. He would telephone her before his train departed from Philadelphia.

At Penn Station he disembarked the train at 11:00am making his way across the magnificent Beaux-Arts masterpiece opened in 1910 to check subway connections for Brooklyn. He had walked only a short distance before looking in surprise at Keara Murphy waving and hurrying toward him. She looked marvelous bundled in a fur-trimmed overcoat with a matching Cossack-style fur hat.

As she approached, she exclaimed, "Oh my God, it's so good to see you, Alan!" She then threw her arms around him as he dropped his duffle bag and embraced her. To his pleasant surprise she gave him a quick kiss on the lips. "You look so handsome."

"And you look beautiful, Keara," he replied as she disengaged the embrace yet remained holding close by his upper arms. "Didn't expect for you to come meet me here in Manhattan."

"Didn't want you trying to figure out how to make your way to my place in Brooklyn using the transit system. We shall take a taxi instead." Grabbing him tightly by the arm, "Then off we go. I've been so looking forward to your visit, Alan."

As they made their way from the platforms, Burke was captivated by the size and the magnificent glass ceiling supported by a delicate latticework of metal arches. Penn Station occupied two city blocks from Seventh Avenue to Eighth Avenue and from 31st to 33rd Streets in Midtown Manhattan. As they walked outside to find a taxi, he looked back at the Doric columns surrounding the exterior. "This is an extraordinary building. Rivals the skyscrapers by its sheer beauty."

"Penn Station is a work of art. Brooklyn does not have the same grand architecture as Manhattan, but it's quieter. Easy enough though to get into and out of Manhattan with the subway system. This must be some change from Haiti."

"That it is. A most welcome change. But seeing you is the best part."

She squeezed his arm. "I want to hear everything about your adventures these past years. Can't image how it must be living from place to place in different foreign lands. Do you ever miss having a place to call home?"

He smiled. "Oh, yes. Military life has its drawbacks. Especially being a Marine, you become a nomad. It can be a lonely existence.

Been doing this since I was eighteen though, so it's become a habit. Life would be more comfortable if I had a place stateside to call home and return to for extended periods of duty. But I joined the Marines to experience the world so I can't complain."

Settled into a taxi, they drove south on 8th Avenue to Hudson, eventually turning southeast past City Hall. Murphy said, "We'll cross the East River on the Brooklyn Bridge. From there it's just a couple of miles to my home."

Before leaving Manhattan, Murphy pointed to the right, "Down toward the tip of Manhattan is the Financial District and Wall Street. The real seat of power in America. We'll have lots of time to do the grand tour of the sights of New York."

Burke replied, "Photographs do not do New York justice. The sheer size of the city can only be appreciated by being here."

"Unfortunately, it's still winter, but New York can be equally appreciated indoors," Murphy replied." Arriving at a row of brownstone rowhouses in Brooklyn's Cobble Hill District, the taxi pulled to a stop. Murphy pointed, "That's my home there."

Murphy paid the taxi driver while Burke extracted his duffle bag. A beautiful three-story building. A staircase led to ornate double-doors on the second level with the lower down a short flight of stairs from the sidewalk. To either side of the main entry stairs the exterior of each brownstone on her block protruded in a semicircular façade with ornate moldings.

Murphy unlocked the large front door opening into a well-decorated foyer with marble floors. Large double doors opened to a formal living area to the left with matching doors on the right opening to a library and sitting room.

"Oh my. This is quite a house."

"Awfully large but it feels like home. I'm not entirely alone though. I have a wonderful woman that lives in the downstairs level apartment who cooks and maintains the house. She also looks after me. Couldn't take care of a place this size without her help. Angelia is a widow with a teenage daughter. Lost her police officer husband in the line of duty to a Black Hand killer. Angie's been with me for many years. I helped her get through his death. She's a good friend that got me through my own difficult time when I lost Robert. Her daughter Gianna, who I call Ginny, calls me Aunt Keara."

Robert? That must have been her husband she spoke to Noreen about when they first met years earlier in West Virginia.

Burke set his duffle bag on the marble titled floor. Unable to contain himself, he stepped into the library. "This is marvelous."

Bookshelves in dark walnut rose to the eleven-foot-high ceiling on three walls with a moveable access ladder. The front wall held two tall windows with heavy cream-colored curtains that contrasted with the dark walnut paneling. Yet it was not the richly decorated room that captured his interest. It was the books.

Ignoring the full legal library occupying most of the lower wall next to the doorway, he found the section holding classical literature. All in expensive leather bindings. Murphy watched him pass over the titles on the spines, fascinated by his absorption.

Realizing he was perhaps being rude, Burke turned with a guilty expression, "Sorry. Got carried away. Books are my weakness and my passion. Reading is how I survive being stuck in go-dawful places."

"What sort of books do you like to read? Fiction or non-fiction?"

"Both. Tend toward the classics. Will borrow anything of interest and devour it because I usually have only limited time before giving it back. When going on deployment, I must travel light, so I limit myself to carrying a well-used volume of Shakespeare's plays and Homer's Iliad."

"Very interesting. An academic warrior. We have much to discuss, Alan. You are a most unusual man. Robert also loved books as do I. We were together only a few years. When we bought this house, Robert set about immediately creating this library."

Burke nodded. "Noreen mentioned you were widowed but never said what happened."

"Robert died in a train accident in upstate New York. A business trip in 1912. The same year you lost your father and brother. I shall explain more fully later. Right now, let me show you around the house."

They took the staircase opening to an open loft area with comfortable chairs. Three bedrooms on this floor." She opened a door to a pleasant room at the rear of the house with a large window. "This is the larger of two guest bedrooms." Walking to another door toward the back of the bedroom, "A good size water closet in here with a tub. It shares with the other guest bedroom but you're the only guest."

Leaving the bedroom, she opened the door opposite. "This is my bedroom."

Burke looked at the large room with its impressive windows of the second level of the semicircular protrusions extending outward on the front of the building. With the bed in the center, to left was a sitting area with reading chairs and to the right a small writing table.

"A large in-suite water closet but let me show you my favorite feature." Opening the door, she pointed toward the far end where an overhead appliance hung above a sloping tiled area. "The latest thing in indoor plumbing. A shower. Much more efficient than running a tub full of hot water."

Walking back downstairs, Keara said, "With Angie to look after us, I thought this a more comfortable arrangement than putting you up in a hotel don't you think?"

He beamed a wide grin. "I should say so. This is wonderful, Keara. Hope having me as a house guest for weeks is not disruptive."

She stopped on the stairs and turned toward him touching his arm. "I've been so looking forward to having you here ever since you wrote, Alan. Since the first time I met you in West Virginia, I find myself trying to imagine what you are doing and in what faraway land."

She stood there looking at him for several moments before saying, "How about I fix some tea and we spend the afternoon in the library telling each other about our lives. From our letters and my friendship with your sister, I feel like we're old friends, yet we know so little about each other."

"I feel the same, Keara. Nothing I'd enjoy more than spending relaxing time with you in this magnificent room."

"Angelia is making us one of her fabulous Italian diners. She'll come in soon to start preparing everything. She lives downstairs. I told her about you. We usually have dinner together. Hope you don't mind."

"Certainly not. I'd very much enjoy that. Angelia and her daughter sound like part of your family. I feel honored to be included."

While Keara prepared tea, Burke examined the library. Although not specifically labeled by category, he quickly discovered the organizational pattern. The walls occupying the smaller spaces on either side of the double entry doors contained law volumes and associated legal books. On the larger shelving expanse on the rear wall, the lower shelves were devoted to reference volumes. Extending upward within manageable reach were classics from all ages. Going higher was fiction organized alphabetically by author. On the opposite side of the room from the entrance door the shelves contained non-fiction on an endless range of subjects. History, geography, politics, religion, science, and war all well represented.

Burke stepped onto the moveable ladder to view the titles above his reach. He discovered works from all eras and cultures. Ancient empires of from Greece and Rome to the Middle Ages and the Renaissance. Literature to philosophy to scientific works. Discovering works he never heard of made him feel like a boy in a candy shop.

Keara entered with a tray carrying a tea service. "You do love books don't you. Find anything interesting?"

"Interesting? That's an understatement. Everything here is interesting. You possess the best documented works of civilization in this room. I've read a good many classics from earlier times. Especially devoted to Shakespeare and literature mostly from the modern era. Melville's *Moby Dick*, Cooper's *Last of the Mohicans*, Hugo's *Hunchback of Notre Dame*, Dumas' the *Count of Monte Cristo* are among my favorites. What you have on these shelves included many other works by these great writers that I have not read. Impressive. Did you collect all these?"

144

"I helped with the organization, but Robert was the collector. A bibliophile like you, Alan. Spent much of his time reading and frequenting booksellers. Couldn't resist a first edition in excellent shape. Robert's investing in books was more than just collecting though. He was an eclectic reader who enjoyed the personal satisfaction of acquiring knowledge."

Burke climbed down as Keara handed him a cup of tea. Seated, he asked, "What was Robert's profession?"

"Robert was a lawyer. Business law. Specialized in international trade agreements. Said his voracious reading habit was professionally useful. Robert's father and my father are senior partners in an important New York City law firm. That's how I met Robert.

"I was already practicing law when we met. I leaned to more activist endeavors, particularly those involving women's rights. That led to doing work combating conditions in sweatshops and the use of child labor. Made for some interesting discussions with someone that represented business interests of major corporations."

"When did you and Robert marry?"

Keara lowered her teacup and set it on the table between them. "We never formally married. That was my doing, but Robert understood my feelings fully. Both our families disliked the social implications if we cohabitated unmarried. But they had no choice in the matter. My mother especially supported my decision. As a journalist and women's rights advocate, she could hardly argue against my wishes.

"In society and even enforced by many legal statues, women are relegated to second class status in relation to men. Excluded from many occupations, property ownership, and of course the right to vote. As a widow, I continue some societal prerogatives of a married woman with more freedom deemed acceptable than those afforded to a single woman. For example, it gives some latitude for allowing a man to reside in my home. Not that I care what people think about my personal life, but there is no need to make difficulties for my family. Both sets of parents agreed to the subterfuge we created that Robert and I eloped and married abroad on a business trip to London."

Burke said, "I admire the conviction of both of you to forge your lives the way you chose. You managed remarkably well when I met you in West Virginia so soon after losing Robert. Then you went to Colorado. Avoided a violent assault that does not appear to have caused any lasting distress. You are an exceptionally strong woman, Keara. Care to tell me the details of the unfortunate Colorado incident?"

She described the full sequence of the circumstances that led to the failed assault by the Baldwin-Felts agent in her bathroom at the Trinidad hotel. More as a journalist than a personal trauma, she finished with, "Mentally prepared by the violent encounter earlier that day, the shock of an intruder while taking a bath came as less of a shock. Once I saw he held a gun, I just instinctively reacted."

"How about afterwards? How did you cope having just shot a man?"

"Surprised when the door opened but angry at the same time. That's why I shot twice. Furious that someone wanted to harm me. I remained angry even with him lying bleeding on the floor. Sometime later the enormity of what happened set in, but I remained more angry than distraught. That that the man died surprisingly carried little emotional effect."

He had never met a woman like Keara Murphy. Then again, his experiences with women were limited. "Amazing how you came through that ordeal. I can see why Noreen admires you. She is also a strong-willed woman. Probably shaped my view toward women. "I also understand perfectly why you chose to avoid marriage. Marriage did work out well for my sister. Stifled her ambitions. Unlike your loss of Robert, the death of her husband freed Noreen to pursue a different life."

"What about you, Alan? Ever wish for a different life than soldiering?"

Smiling, he replied with no hesitation, "Many times. However, not for reasons you might imagine. Never felt the attraction for a conventional life of family and children. Wanted to pursue wider experiences. A bit self-absorbed. Unhappy about my circumstances being stuck in remote West Virginia made me obsessed with escaping life in the coalfields. Joining the Marine Corps promised travel to foreign lands and a career. The Marines served on naval vessels and guarded our foreign embassies along with spearheading military missions. I set out to excel in my chosen profession. Not just as a soldier but developing the necessary skills to be a modern warrior."

"A warrior? Besides your intelligence, what sort of martial skills make you a warrior?"

"I grew up around guns. Found early on that I was more than just a good shot. Was also a pretty good scrapper in fist fights as a youngster. In the Marines, I took those natural abilities to higher levels of proficiency through study and practice. I learned the Asian martial art judo from a Philippine-Japanese master that ran a *dojo* in Manilla. Defensive in nature, I adapted the judo form of fighting with lethal offensive moves that condense an encounter into just a couple of seconds. Putting it crudely, I'm an expert in instructing other Marines in how to kill efficiently and stay alive in combat."

Murphy grimaced. "Wow! Considering you've proven that in battle by your many ribbons, I guess that qualifies you as a warrior. But even warriors have other human needs. What about romance in your life?"

With an expression of embarrassment he replied, "Romance for a career Marine is always difficult. Recurring deployments to trouble spots provides little opportunity. Unlike some, I never succumbed to the temptations of the flesh among the native peoples. Yet I possessed those normal needs you refer to. Two different affairs with Navy nurses. One became a serious relationship during my lengthy stretch of time stationed at the U.S. Naval base in Guantanamo, Cuba. Together for two years, I lost Dorthy to yellow fever. From the onset of the first symptoms, death arrived in only eight days. That was many years ago, yet still a painful memory."

The front door then opened diverting their candid exchange of personal histories. "That must be Angie," Keara said. A good place to pause this first day. With several relaxing weeks before Alan must leave New York, no need to rush.

A woman several years older than Murphy stepped into the library. "Ah, this must be the handsome soldier you talk so much about, Keara?"

Keara blushed slightly. "Yes. This is Sergeant Major Alan Burke of the United States Marine Corps. And this is Angelia Roselli, Alan. Angie is like the sister I never had and my dearest companion."

Burke extended his hand. "Keara speaks of you in the most affectionate of terms, Angie. Please call me Alan."

The three chatted for a longtime over tea before Angie said, "Well I must begin preparing dinner. Ginny will be along in a while to help. She is at the library doing research on a subject she selected for her graduation term paper."

Murphy said to Burke, "Ginny is graduating high school this year. Attending college in the fall. Wants to eventually become an attorney."

Angie added, "Just like her Aunt Keara."

—

The house was pleasantly warm throughout from a hot water central heating system with radiators in each room supplied from a boiler in the cellar fired by natural gas. Burke awoke refreshed with a feeling of contentment. He enjoyed the prior evening immensely. Felt like being part of a real family.

The following day, Keara took him on a tour of New York City. That meant the sights of the borough of Manhattan. The first segment on her itinerary was a ninety-minute sightseeing boat ride aboard *The Tourist* leaving from Pier 83 on the Hudson River on West 43rd Street. A cold windy day made colder being on the water, but they dressed accordingly. The boat first traveled north as far as Harlem before turning south, passing by Ellis Island just to the west off the tip of Manhattan.

Murphy pointed out, "That's Ellis Island. Where my paternal grandparents arrived from Ireland fleeing the Great Famine in 1848."

Burke reflected on its personal meaning for him. "Where I also arrived at the age of five in 1883 with my parents, my brother Liam, and Noreen. Father and Liam were fleeing British law for their participation in violent Fenian acts of rebellion."

Keara did not respond to his revelation. A conversation for another time as Burke looked at the Statue of Liberty looming large just ahead in silence. The symbol of America to all arriving foreigners. The thought struck him of the reverse reaction when American Marines landed on foreign shores. The American ideal was reserved for Americans, not those in foreign lands.

The rest of the day they spent touring Manhattan starting from the Financial District and Wall Street. Going north on Broadway they passed by the massive Equitable Building just completed the prior year. Just a short distance further on Broadway was the neo-Gothic design Woolworth Building, the tallest in the world at 55 floors, not far from City Hall.

Using the trolley system, they made their way north through midtown Manhattan to Columbus Circle. There they took a tour through Central Park in a taxi. Exiting the Park on Fifth Avenue, Keara said, "Had enough winter weather? I'm feeling chilled and you're certainly not accustomed to this kind of cold."

Burke replied, "I could use some coffee and hot soup for lunch. Know a good place?"

"Yes. My place. Shall we catch a train back to Brooklyn? A couple of logs in the fireplace sounds like a nice afternoon."

"Sounds perfect. Lead the way."

To the taxi driver, she said, "Drop us at the public library." Turning to Burke, "One last stop before we catch the subway. From the interior, the public library is the grandest building in New York. A must see for someone that likes books. We can walk from there to Grand Central Terminal to catch the subway."

Besides its endless volumes of books, Burke was enthralled by the grandeur of the library's interior. Grand Central Station proved an equally impressive building. Onboard the subway, they traveled from mid-town to lower Manhattan to then cross the East River on the Manhattan Bridge. Opened just the previous year, the Manhattan Bridge afforded a view of the Brooklyn Bridge in profile off to the right causing Burke to remark, "Look at that! The Brooklyn Bridge with the Statue of Liberty in the distance. The most recognizable symbols of New York. A magnificent tour. A wonderful experience, Keara."

Taking his gloved hand in hers, "Yes it was. Now I'm hungry and need some warming up."

—

They spent the afternoon together talking seated together on a sofa in front of the fireplace. Two people with developing deeper feelings for each other established largely through sporadic letters over years. Each topic of conversation proved a revelatory discovery.

Dinner consisted of Angie's leftovers from the prior night that Kerara served in the library. The combined effects of spending time outside in the cold, the warmth of the fire, and sharing of a bottle of French wine, left them both beginning to feel drowsy.

"This has been a marvelous day, Alan. Don't want it to end but I am fading fast. We have weeks to share many such days before you must leave. You ready to retire?"

Burke smiled broadly. "I believe so. As much as I just want to sit here with you, I don't recall the last time I felt this relaxed."

They climbed the stairs arm in arm. Reaching the area outside their bedrooms, Keara embraced him. Pulling back slightly, she kissed him quickly on the lips. "Sleep well, Alan." With that, she hurriedly entered her bedroom closing the door.

Burke experienced a twinge of disappointment after Keara's kiss, hoping that it might lead to something more. But like she said, they had weeks together. They were strongly attracted yet knew so little of each other than the indefinable chemistry that bound them.

Sleep illuded Alan Burke. While relaxed, thoughts about Keara kept his mind overactive. From discipline established from years of soldiering, he turned to reading to exclude competing thoughts. His alternative to meditating.

He sat in bed in only his underwear, warmed by a down comforter, reading his well-worn copy of Homer's Iliad. A gentle knock on his bedroom door caught his attention.

Not waiting for a response, Keara entered. Bare foot and dressed in a nightgown, she said, "I couldn't sleep after all. Seems the same for you. What are you reading?"

He closed the book and laid it on the end table under the lamp transfixed by Keara's boldness. "Homer's Iliad."

"Yes of course. The Trojan War with the greatest of all Greek warriors, Achilles. A warrior like you, Alan. Can you make love as tenderly as you make war?" With that she lifted the nightgown over her head revealing her nakedness and climbed into bed as Burke made room for her.

She touched his bare chest with her breasts as he pulled the comforter over her back. Neither uttered any words letting their hands explore and excite them both to increasingly greater arousal.

Their lovemaking lasted until both became fully sated and could not hold back from falling into deep sleep. Burke was the first to wake when Keara stirred with the first light of dawn breaking through the curtains.

After kissing, Keara said, "I've been fantasizing about making love with you since you arrived."

"I was hoping that as well. Disappointed after you kissed me last night then went off to bed. That's why I couldn't sleep."

"Cold feet. Fear of the unknown but I built up my courage. As a warrior, you can understand that. And remarkably, for a warrior, you are an exceptionally attentive lover. Made me feel you enjoyed giving me pleasure as your way of enhancing your desire."

"Lovemaking works best that way," he said unable to resist caressing her breasts.

Keara kissed him and moved her hand to stroke his growing erection. "Let's take a shower together and pick up where we left off last night."

PART TWO

Town of Matewan in Mingo County, WV 1920

CHAPTER 11

Port Royal, SC /Parris Island Marine Base | Spring 1916

B urke spent the best weeks of his life in New York with Keara Murphy. Both recognized this as a serious relationship. They made no definitive plans other than agreeing that he would leave the Marine Corps once his current enlistment expired in October of this year. He was disillusioned about continuing his military career. The rapid deployment capabilities of the Marines became a necessary component for protecting American business interests in foreign lands. America's imperialistic expansion endeavors were about extracting wealth from this modern colonial empire. Justified by security interests often just a cover. The decision to resign from the Marine Corps became easier by finding Keara Murphy.

Keara agreed that with his military background, a civilian career in law enforcement or a management role in private security might be an option.

Burke responded, "Depends on who I'm working for. Organizations like Baldwin-Felts or the Pinkerton Detective Agencies are out of the question. They're just hired strikebreaking thugs armed against miners or workers in steel mills or railroads."

"I understand. Your background qualifies you for something far more than your combat skills as a warrior. In those areas you identify with Achilles from the *Iliad*. I enjoy Homer's sequel the

Odyssey more. I see you more like the cerebral and clever warrior Odysseus."

"Difficult to change careers after twenty years of being a soldier. Yet I cannot see continuing to serve. The world has changed and so have I. My enlistment is up in October. I'll serve out my remaining six months in South Carolina. Training young men how to stay alive rather than killing insurgents in other lands trying to overthrow tyrants. Sometimes the tyrant becomes America."

"While you serve out your enlistment, I'll research possible employment options. Shall I focus on New York City?" Keara said with a coy smile.

"Specifically, Brooklyn," Burke replied returning her smile.

—

Parting was wrenchingly difficult. Keara saw him off as his train departed Penn Station for the trip south. They had spent every day of his extended leave together. Learning more about each other only reinforced their bond. Knowing that separation was for only a manageable period stationed stateside rather than overseas in danger, made their separation easier.

Port Royal Island lies off the coast of South Carolina between Charleston and Savannah, Georgia. Best noted for the quaint town of Beaufort with its collection of antebellum mansions, the U.S. Navy occupied the isolated seaward tip of the island. The area was captured by the Union Army in 1861 in the early months of the Civil War remained a coaling station for fueling naval vessels following the ending of the war. The former Port Royal Naval Station converted to the Parris Island Marine Recruit Depot the previous October in anticipation of expanding Marine Corps strength for possible United States intervention in the war in Europe. Parris Island supported some farming and the small fishing village of Port Royal.

When Alan Burke arrived, there were less than 900 Marine recruits. Burke understood if the United States went to war in Europe the Marine Corps must quickly produce great numbers of newly trained recruits. In 1916, the United States Army had a strength of only 109,000 men, the Marines just 11,000. Recent history suggested if America joined France and Britain in the European conflict, the Marines would be in the vanguard. The Marines were America's elite military strike force. Its strength had changed little over the last ten years. A surge in new recruits meant limited time to transform farm hands and clerks into combat effective soldiers.

Burke's new commanding officer at Parris Island, laid out Burke's task when he reported for duty the first week of April. "All indications are we might be going into service in this war in Europe. It's already the biggest conflict ever. If called on, the Marines will be the first to see action. I requested the best fighting sergeant major in the Corps. They sent you. Reading your record, I can see why. Medal of Honor recipient, two Silver Stars, a Bronze Star, and three purple hearts. Doesn't get more impressive than that.

"Your job is to develop an NCO training staff to handle the expected volume of recruits. In recent years, recruit training has been scattered among four training installations, two on each coast. It will be up to us to provide the bulk of new Marines for Europe."

"Aye, aye Sir. I understand. Is there a core staff of qualified NCOs already on board?"

"On paper perhaps. That's your first job. Qualify the half dozen NCOs already assigned to combat skills training. The entire NCO training staff are now your responsibility. Build a training program. Teach them your combat skills. Several written reports from your commanding officer in various combat theaters claim you are the deadliest Marine he has ever served with. States you far exceed expert-rating with the M1911 .45 pistol, the M1903 Springfield rifle, and hand-to-hand combat. Says you developed a hybrid fighting technique employing Japanese judo combined with use of a trench knife. Except in your case, you use a heavy Bowie knife. Is all this true, Sergeant Major?"

"Yes, Sir."

"Well tomorrow, I want you to demonstrate. A couple of your sergeants are supposedly tough seasoned Marines, so you'll have a real challenge. Not a test. Just an opportunity for you to establish your qualifications to the officer and NCO staff. You okay with that, Sergeant Major."

"Not a problem, Sir."

The following morning, Burke joined the officers and NCOs at breakfast mess. The major greeted him and returned his salute then introduced him to the commissioned and non-commissioned officers in the mess hall. "As you all know, Sergeant Major Burke will be taking control of close quarter combat training. He possesses unique fighting skills that he has agreed to demonstrate. Gunnery Sergeants Todd and McKenzie, and Lieutenant White have volunteered to participate."

The demonstration started on the shooting range. All the officers and NCOs gathered in a semicircle to observe. What distance, Sergeant Major?" the major asked.

"15 yards, Sir. Slow fire using the M1911 standard service sidearm." Burke wore a shoulder holster under his left arm while the others used holsters fixed to a web belt at the waist. In combat, Burke favored the quicker access afforded by locating the weapon under his opposite arm.

Several privates set up four human silhouette targets at the designated range.

Each Marine took their turn emptying their seven-round magazines. Burke won hands down with all his rounds grouped in the forehead of the silhouette. He commented, "Head shots of course are not recommended for a moving target, especially if the fellow is running toward you with a bayonet or machete." To illustrate his prowess, he loaded a fresh magazine into the weapon. "Move my target out to 25 yards." He fired off another seven rounds this time with a tight grouping well-centered in the upper abdomen. "That of course is the proper combat way. You that are rated expert in sidearm proficiency have already developed important key techniques that you need to impart to your trainees."

Moving to a grassy area, Burke asked Gunnery Sergeant Philipps to bring out two rubber practice trench knives. "Gunny

Philipps is not only bigger than me, but I'm sure he volunteered because he's one Marine that few mess with." Philipps grinned. "Now, Gunny, attack me with the trench knife." Philipps asked, "Slashing attack or thrusting?" Burke responded, "Your choice."

Philipps began to circle around Burke who did nothing more than turn to keep his eyes fixed on him. When Philipps moved quickly on the attack making a motion to slice at Burke's abdomen, Burke moved in deftly to grab the larger man now slightly off balance as he lunged forward and sent him to the ground, followed with a straight downward blow of his fist that he pulled just short of smashing into Philipps throat. "The blow would certainly disable your enemy, perhaps even kill him. However, to ensure a kill, using your trench knife is more efficient. Would you like to attack me next Gunny McKenzie?"

McKenzie was more Burke's size. "I would guess Gunny McKenzie is fast as rattlesnake. So go at me with the knife and I will defend with my knife."

McKenzie's attack focused on trying to deflect Burke's weapon to make his thrust with his knife to the midsection.

Burke allowed McKenzie to deflect his right arm holding his own knife upward and used the position to lift his opponent upward off balance then easily topple him to the ground while deflecting McKenzie's knife-hand. In the split second of McKenzie falling then hitting the ground, Burke's knife arm freed allowing him to bring the rubber trench knife to McKenzie's throat.

"Shit!" McKenzie said.

"The throat becomes the best target for killing your opponent decisively and quickly with a knife." Having stood up, Burke pointed to his throat region. "Unlike the abdominal area, the throat is unprotected. The carotid artery here and the subclavian arteries going to the right and left are tucked just under the collarbones here. Severing any of these will cause loss of consciousness in a few seconds. A quiet kill with death occurring in less than 15 seconds."

McKenzie got up and dusted off his uniform. "You're a right quick one, Sergeant Major. Word has it you favor a bigass Bowie knife rather than the standard issue trench knife. That true?"

"Yeah, I do. The Bowie knife is like a short sword with good heft. A fellow Marine gave it to me just before he died of wounds in the Philippines.

"Ever use it combat?" McKenzie asked.

"Nearly decapitated an insurgent in Haiti with it. Weighs 24 ounces. But the trench knife will do the trick for dispatching your enemy if used properly, Gunny."

The demonstration established Burke's fighting credentials. The purpose intended to gain the respect of seasoned Marines tasked with training green recruits. Part of imparting esprit de corps so important for an elite fighting force. Should they deploy to Europe everyone would face a war like no other in history.

—

Spring passed into summer. The disastrous war in Europe would soon enter its third year of human carnage. Millions of fighting men faced each other from defensive trenches stretching along a front hundreds of miles long in northeast France. The failed German invasion through Belgium and Luxemburg in 1914 stalled in its objective to capture Paris attempting to repeat their success in the Franco-Prussian War of 1870. The result was a hopeless military stalemate stretching hundreds of miles of a stationary front from the English Channel to the Swiss Alps. Nonetheless, these defensive trenches still generated staggering numbers of casualties through artillery bombardment and periodic offensive attacks using massed infantry formations.

On June 3, President Wilson signed the National Defense Act in preparation for the likely entry of America into the war in Europe on the side of the Entente powers. On Aug. 29, 1916, Congress authorized an increase in strength of the United States Army, the National Guard, and the Marine Corps by over 50%. Little doubt where this was headed.

During his five months at Parris Island, Burke made great strides in constructing a training program for individual combat skills. He was particularly proud of his staff of a dozen accomplished non-commissioned officers. Raw Marine recruits would at least possess basic combat skills superior to those provided in the U.S. Army recruits.

The Marines would be fighting an enemy with equal capabilities. Equal in numbers. Equally trained. Equally equipped in armaments. Not the impoverished poorly armed indigenous enemy that marked their combat experience of the last twenty years. The Marines would face artillery, poison gas, and the scourge of the modern battlefield, the machine gun. These advances transformed modern warfare. Unfortunately, the general staff of both warring factions still applied nineteenth century infantry tactics without regard for the changed dynamics of twentieth century technology. Reading the daily accounts of the war in the newspapers, Burke was aghast by the unimaginative leadership of the general staff of both sides in over two years of this war. Each new battle repeated the same tactics that previously failed to achieve material results. Only more casualties. Would American military leadership be different?

Burke felt he did all he could to prepare young American men should they be called to fight. In less than two months his final enlistment would conclude. Twenty years in the service of his country was sufficient. Achieving success in what he believed an honorable career no longer held the same interest. Time to leave and take up a new career. One that did not involve killing people in foreign lands for ethically dubious reasons. Time to live in his own country. With brightened expectations that included Keara Murphy, it was the first time he experienced real happiness.

A week after submitting his retirement papers, those plans were dashed when called into the base commander's office late one afternoon. The major handed him a letter. "Just received this, Sergeant Major. Your new Orders. By order of the Commandant of the Marine Corps no less."

```
Date: 7 September 1916
To: Sergeant Major Alan Burke

Subject: Resignation and discharge from the
United States Marine Corps.
```

Your current enlistment is scheduled to expire
25 October 1916. Your distinguished service to
the country and the Marine Corps has been ex-
emplary attested by the remarkable number of
citations for valor in different foreign theaters of conflict. Your leadership and demonstrated fighting skills are vital to the Marine Corps during this exceptional time of national need. Based on my request, the Secretary of the Navy has hereby extended your term
of military service by one year to 25 October
1917.

By order of Major General George Barnett
     United States Marine Corps

George Barnett

Major General Commandant

"Sorry about this, Sergeant Major. As much as I need you here with the wave of expected new recruits, I did not make the request. Best I can promise you is a week's leave at Christmas. That'll be all."

Consumed with disappointment, Burke stood and saluted, "Aye, aye Sir."

—

Burke arrived at Penn Station the day after Christmas. Keara Murphy had taken the news in stride when he telephoned her weeks earlier after learning of his new orders. At the time he chose not to distress her further by speculating that he might be sent to France if the United States formally entered the war in Europe. Better to discuss that in person.

She beat him to it on the taxi ride to Brooklyn after he arrived. "We shall make the best of our week together. You realize of course that you are too valuable to leave the Marines if we go to war?"

"The very thought weighs on my mind, Keara."

"We're both accustomed to dealing with difficult circumstances outside our control. We cope and move forward. We live life on our terms. Having found each other transcends everything else."

"He kissed her. You're an extraordinary woman and I love you dearly."

She returned his kiss. "Angie made sure we had leftovers from Christmas dinner. Ham and one of her pies. She also baked us some fresh bread. I've stocked up on wine and your favorite whiskey. Since you've arrived again in winter, we can just stay warm inside by a fire. I'm sure we can keep each other suitably entertained."

—

Once Burke returned to Parris Island the first week of January of the new year 1917, events moved quickly. On April 2, 1917, President Woodrow Wilson addressed a joint session of Congress to ask for a declaration of war on Imperial Germany. Wilson cited repeated submarine attacks on U.S. passenger and merchant shipping and Germany's attempt to entice Mexico into an alliance with the Central Powers. The U.S. Senate passed the measure on April 4 and the House of Representatives on April 6. The United States officially entered what was already being called the Great War.

Burke received new orders a week later by telegram. *'Report to Philadelphia Naval Shipyard headquarters of 5th Marine Regiment to assume position as regimental sergeant major no later than April 20. By order of Col. Charles Doyen commanding.'*

Burke's commanding officer at Parris Island informed him that the 5th was a newly formed Marine regiment. That meant it was headed for France. Burke had a few extra free days before reporting to Philadelphia if he left South Carolina promptly. The major obliged commenting, "You've earned it. Outstanding job you did here, Burke. You created a solid training staff to carry on your work. Good luck in France." The major then snapped to attention and delivered a sharp salute to Burke. "Semper Fi, Sergeant Major."

Burke returned the salute. "Thank you, Sir."

Immediately Burke went to the communications room and placed a call to Keara Murphy. After telling her what happen, he asked if she could meet him in Philadelphia for a couple of days. "Of course. I'll book us a room at the Bellevue-Stratford Hotel in the city center for the day after tomorrow. Stayed there once when my father attended a business conference."

At the hotel, Murphy outwardly took the news of his likely deployment to France calmly. However, she could not quell the rising anxiety. She read the newspaper accounts of the staggering numbers of French and British casualties. No matter Alan's military skills, surviving this war was largely a matter of chance.

They spent two days mostly in a spacious suite. Between episodes of lovemaking and going downstairs for meals, they spent their time just being together and talking of the future. They avoided discussing the disturbing change from isolationism of a large segment of the American populace's growing enthusiasm for entering the war. In the seats of power, the Great War would serve to demonstrate America's might. For young men, a chance to experience the glory of war. The country ignored the fact that militarily, the United States was grossly ill prepared. A small standing army of no more than 120,000, including the Marines, required transformation eventually to a force of several million.

Burke avoided discussing details of what he expected in France. His military background provided only a pessimistic view. The United States did not have an experienced military general staff or officer corps in leading large formations in combat. No experience in massed warfare against equally sized enemy forces since the American Civil War over fifty years ago. America must field an army consisting almost entirely of inexperienced infantry led by equally combat inexperienced officers.

Their few days passed all too quickly. Keara accompanied Burke in a taxi driving south six miles down 15th Street to the Philadelphia Naval Shipyard on the Delaware River. As Burke walked to the well-guarded gate dressed in uniform, Keara broke down in tears after a final wave of her hand as her taxi pulled away.

A month later on May 27, President Wilson ordered the 5th Marine Regiment to sail to France. They boarded three U.S. naval vessels a week later. Burke traveled aboard the transport ship *USS Hancock* with the regimental headquarters battalion. The 5th Marine Regiment was part of the first American Expeditionary Forces, along with the 28th and 16th U.S. Army Infantry Regiments, to arrive at the French port of St. Nazaire. Originally routed to the major French naval port of Brest on the western tip of the Brittany Peninsula, reports of German U-boat activity in that area caused the convoy to alter course further south to St. Nazaire.

Less than ten days later, Burke relocated with the Regiment's 1st and 2nd battalions to Gondrecourt-le-Chateau in the Meuse Department of northeast France to begin trench warfare training with French battalions. Burke's job was to interact with French NCO instructors using an interpreter. From his first look at the trenches and barbed wire entanglements his heart sank. This was position-warfare at its worst.

Word had it that the commander of the AEF Major General John Pershing was a soldier committed to movement. How would he direct American forces? Burke already questioned Pershing's appointment. His last command leading 10,000 American soldiers in the Punitive Expedition into Mexico to capture or kill the revolutionary leader Poncho Villa ended unsuccessfully after a frustrating ten months. Not the best credentials for prosecuting an entirely different kind of war.

Burke's first letter to Murphy announced his safe arrival and conveyed his affections. His next letter after listening to their French Army allies indoctrinate the Marines with what they learned about surviving trench warfare the past two years, held a different tone. Mindful that correspondence stateside was subject to censorship, he circumvented his criticism of the entire concept of stationary warfare by blaming the French and British. He took the position that the AEF was here to implement a different approach with fresh troops. A position of which he had no confidence would be the case. The AEF might likely find themselves just fed into the meatgrinder replacing decimated units causing gaps in the French and British lines.

Dearest Keara,

We are now located in the east of France, but I'm not allowed to provide specifics. Training with our French allies. Tactics in trench warfare that have framed the war for two years with no success in two years of fighting. More about how to survive rather than how to defeat the enemy. It will be some time before American forces are deemed ready for combat. Most Army recruits received little training before arriving in France. The Marines are better prepared. I am trusting that General Pershing will deploy American troops as an independent fighting force rather than shoring up French and British decimated sectors. According to our colonel, it may require many months of training in France before sufficient numbers of American troops are deemed combat-ready to constitute an independent army. Pershing is also known to favor maneuver rather than defensive entrenchment. How he will navigate the already established character of this war to pursue these objectives remains in question.

As for me, I shall do my best to see that the Marines under my charge have the best chance for battlefield success. It is not realistic to ask you not to worry. However, take comfort in knowing that I am well experienced and know how to use my skills to the best advantage. I intend to return to you, Keara.

For the time being, my regiment is part of the newly formed AEF 2nd Division consisting of the 4th Marine Brigade, which will also include the 6th Marine Regiment, and the 3rd U.S. Army Brigade. Military organizational structure may be confusing. It goes from company to battalion to regiment to brigade to division to corps to army. The U.S. Marines constitute only a small part of the AEF compared to the U.S. Army.

Write often. Letters from home keep a soldier's morale intact. Stay well with a positive spirit. I love you dearly, Keara.

Alan

In a letter from his sister, Burke felt saddened by the strained relationship between her and their mother. Yet, Burke is gratified that Noreen has found a measure of happiness in pursuing life independently since the family deaths five years earlier.

Yet with Alan in France, Noreen feels continual anxiety. She understands the difference between this unprecedented European War compare with the more limited conflicts in which her brother became involved in recent years. The unimaginable casualty numbers and the newspaper photographs made apparent this conflict could rightfully be called apocalyptic. Concealing her concern for Alan, she chose to write in positive terms about *finding herself* as she put it in Bluefield, West Virginia. Noreen said mother was doing less work for the United Mine Workers. Returned to teaching. Mum was in good health, still living in Matewan. We stay in regular touch.

Letters from his mother left little doubt that she remained wholly committed to unionizing efforts of West Virginia coal mines. However, America's entry into the war in Europe changed the circumstances for life in America. Increased demand for coal, steel, railroad transportation services, and other vital industries essential for the war effort meant full employment. Military conscription added labor shortages. While strikes were not uncommon, governmental influences exerted indirect pressure on many business sectors resulting in unions and workers making great strides with compromising economic agreements. This was particularly the case for coal mining and the United Mine Workers. The UMW had little need for the rabblerousing organizing harangues of those like Mother Jones and Maude Burke.

Maude Burke commented in her letters only that union organizing demands had *cooled* since America went to war. *Getting along fine with my return to teaching. Children of miners have a great need for education. Take care of yourself, Alan. Love Mother.*

CHAPTER 12

Belleau Wood, Western Front, France WWI | June 1918

The training location for the Marines was south of Verdon, in the rear of the proposed sector assigned to American forces. In November of 1917, the 5th Marine Regiment was joined by the 6th Marine Regiment to form the 4th Marine Brigade. The Brigade moved south to begin conducting maneuvers with French infantry units. To Burke's dismay, much of this training involved defensive tactics and launching offensives from abandoned trenches. The massive numbers of casualties resulted from futile offensive actions in the open against artillery and machine guns. Was the stalemate of trench warfare to also become the fate of American forces?

Training continued through the winter until March of 1918 when the Marine Brigade relocated to a quiet sector of the front lines. In mid-April a company of the 3rd battalion of the 5th Regiment saw the Marines' first action by successfully repelling a German raid. The engagement proved that the Marines had acquired the tactical skills of fighting in this unfamiliar environment.

In May, the Regiment was reassigned to another sector to engage in open warfare maneuvers northwest of Paris. Tactics more suited to Burke's liking. However, just weeks later, circumstances abruptly changed.

The German Spring Offensive, consisting of five different offensives along a two-hundred-mile front, had begun sixty days earlier. Following American entry into the war, German commander General Ludendorff determined the only chance for defeating the Allies was to drive a wedge between the British Expeditionary Forces in the north and the French in the south. There was a finite window of opportunity before American forces could add their weight of fresh troops. Ludendorff intended to defeat the British then force the French into seeking an armistice. Ludendorff also had the temporary advantage of relocating nearly 50 divisions of German troops from the Eastern Front to the Western Front after the new Russian Bolshevik government signed a peace treaty following the overthrow of Tsar Nicholas.

The German forces comprising the Aisne Offensive now struck the previously quiet sector between Soissons and Reims. German advances soon threatened Paris only 59 miles away to the southwest. To stem the German advance, the American 2nd Division comprised of the 4th Marine Brigade and the 3rd U.S. Army Brigade were ordered into the breach under the command of the French Sixth Army on May 30.

The 5th Regiment traveling by motor transport reached the city of Meaux just 25 miles northeast of Paris before encountering fleeing French soldiers and civilians choking the roads. The Regiment then proceeded by foot with a difficult forced march carrying heavy backpacks through hilly countryside in intolerably hot weather while passing demoralized retreating French soldiers. The Marines arrived three days later to occupy positions north of the Marne River and west of Château-Thierry.

On the night of June 1, the Germans punched a hole in the French lines. After taking the town of Château-Thierry German forces then occupied Bois de Belleau, or Belleau Wood. In response the 5th Marine Regiment and the U.S. Army 23rd Regiment force-marched six miles to plug the breach in the allied line. German forces threatened continued advance westward using their foothold in Belleau Wood.

Burke was standing next to Colonel Neville now commanding the 5th Marines and U.S Army General James Harbord currently commanding the Marine Brigade when a messenger arrived from French Sixth Army headquarters. After reading the message Harbord said to Neville, "The French commander has ordered us to pull back and dig defensive trenches. We'll do no such thing. "Order your Marines to hold where they stand." Turning to Burke, he said, "Is that to your liking Sergeant Major?"

Burke replied without hesitation, "Yes, Sir, it is. That's what we're here for."

He then set off immediately to relay the order to all units. Immediately, the Marines begin digging shallow firing positions with their bayonets. The following day, the Germans attacked from out of the woods crossing a grain field with fixed bayonets where the Marines lay largely concealed. Waiting until the Germans were within one hundred yards, the Marines opened up with deadly rifle fire decimating waves of German infantry. Suffering heavy losses, the Germans pulled back and began digging defensive positions along a defensive line. Over the next two days the Marines beat back repeated German assaults.

The arrival of the 167th French Division allowed the American forces to consolidate a 2,000-yard front. The battle plan called for the French to attack to the left of the American line while the Marines anchoring the northern sector attacked the wooded Belleau Wood that crawled up to a ridgeline.

Burke surveyed the terrain with field glasses. It appeared much like the high ground at Gettysburg during the American Civil War that he saw in old photographs. Tall hardwood trees with heavy secondary underbrush, interspersed with sharply rising knolls populated with large boulders. Surrounding the wooded area was open terrain that the Marines must cross before reaching the woods. The woods afforded the Germans concealed defensive positions from high ground. A well-trained enemy with equivalent weaponry left no doubt that the Marines faced a formidable challenge.

On June 6, the Marines attacked Hill 142 to the west of the larger elevated terrain of Belleau Wood. The 1st Battalion of the 5th Regiment attacked across an open wheat field. The Marines took Hill 142 in ferocious hand-to-hand fighting at the cost of nine commissioned officers and 325 men.

Burke watched from a distance through his field glasses. Realizing this was just the opening engagement to clearing the enemy from the large expanse of Belleau Wood, he turned to Colonel Neville, "Request permission to join the 2nd and 3rd Battalions for the assault on the wooded ridgeline, Sir." Burke felt that he should not remain in the rear while *his* Marines attacked the woods. He trained these young men and accepted that meant he must lead from the front.

Neville hesitated, before replying, "Very well, Sergeant Major."

The French offered only poorly detailed maps of Belleau Wood. French intelligence advised that the woods were only lightly held by the Germans. That proved a gross error. A German infantry regiment was well-entrenched throughout the wood. The natural terrain of varying contours with scattered boulders and a deep ravine cutting through the southern sector made for ideal defense. The Germans had also constructed a great many fortified machine-gun positions strategically arrayed to provide interlocking fire.

On June 6, two battalions, one each from the 5th and 6th Regiments attacked the woods by first having to cross a wheat field. This first wave took terrible casualties from machine gun fire before encountering barbed wire entanglements. The Marines sustained the attack, engaging German infantry in hand-to-hand fighting that eventually gained them a foothold in the woods. This attack cost another 31 officers and 1,056 men as casualties. Burke survived that first attack wave unscathed. The next night the Marines lost more casualties in a German counterattack attempting to dislodge them from their forward position.

The following day Belleau Wood was devastated by an enormous barrage from American and French artillery. The former picturesque hunting preserve was seemingly reduced to a tangle of shattered trees. Yet as with most bombardments, it proved undecisive. The Germans remained in Belleau Wood and began reorganizing.

On June 10, elements from both Marine regiments mounted another attack. Again, they were cut to pieces by machine gun fire.

Sensing the desperate situation of attacking the still well-fortified difficult terrain favoring machine gun emplacements and sharpshooters, Burke approached Colonel Neville, "We must do something to destroy those machine gun positions, Sir. Request permission to mount an assault under cover of darkness. I'll lead a few Marines to try getting close enough to kill as many German machine gun crews as possible."

"How the hell do you expect to accomplish that, Sergeant Major?"

"By stealth. I'll lead three volunteers with proven skills in hand-to-hand fighting and sidearm marksmanship. We'll go out after midnight, hours before the scheduled regimental assault. I'll additionally need three NCOs and three BAR machine gunners to provide support from within our front lines to provide diversionary fire."

Neville regarded Burke's opinions highly when it came to close-in combat. He as much as wrote the training manual. Reluctantly agreeing to Burke's desperate plan, Neville nodded and with a sigh said, "Go ahead. Good luck, Sergeant Major."

Neville did not expect miracles. Burke might be a lethal force in close-quarter combat but getting close enough to take out German machine gun crews would be difficult. To attack separated German positions defied reasonable odds for survival. Yet any attempt was worth silencing as many German machine guns as possible from this natural redoubt.

Burke had only the headquarters company and a company from each of the battalions from which to ask for volunteers. The Regiment had already sustained debilitating losses, and this sounded like a suicide mission for the three Marines that would accompany him into Belleau Wood. He found the three Marines he needed among those he recalled from months of training in France that excelled in close-quarter combat. Each one volunteered without hesitation. As one remarked, "This is no more dangerous work than what every one of us has faced trying to push the Krauts out of that fucking woods, Sergeant Major."

Burke also needed three machine gunners and NCOs as spotters to serve as diversionary fire teams when his strike team attempted sneaking close enough to the German machine gun positions. The Marines came armed with the latest handheld Browning Automatic Rifle, known simply as the BAR. A versatile weapon firing a 30-06 Springfield round that also could be used for accurate targeting at a range of several hundred yards. It was hurried into production with the Marines receiving the first shipment in time to train on the new weapon in France before seeing combat.

Burke split the supporting Marines into three groups consisting of an NCO and BAR machine gunner. The support fire teams would engage the targeted German machine gun position with BAR fire to draw attention away from his team's silent advancing on their position from a different direction.

Burke would lead the kill team consisting of the three volunteering Marines skilled in killing hand-to-hand. What made Burke's plan possible, even as a high-risk venture, was the terrain. Although artillery wreaked destruction on the larger trees, Belleau Wood still retained dense brush, boulders, and natural depressions along with artillery craters that offered concealment. However, even if successfully silencing one machine gun position, repeating attacks on other positions bordered on the foolhardy.

—

Huddled around a bare spot on the ground to the rear of the Marine forward positions at first light the following morning. Burke drew a rough map of the Wood in the dirt. "I've been surveying the objective over the past several days with high magnification field glasses. During yesterday's disaster I identified five likely German machine guns positions as marked roughly by these stones. Not too many landmarks for positioning except for this big boulder outcropping identified by this large stone. Turn around and take turns looking at the wooded ridgeline with the field glasses that you NCOs will carry."

After everyone had their turn. "The kill team shall move under cover of night jumping off at 0300 hours starting from our forward line. Note these German positions in relation to something recognizable as a landmark. Draw your own map to pinpoint each machine gun emplacement." He handed small notebooks and pencils to the three sergeants. "The objective today is to get a closer look during daylight hours. The Regiment will mount another all-out assault tomorrow at 0800. We'll have five hours to accomplish our mission to reduce German machine guns fire. There are more machine gun positions to the north, but we'll concentrate on these five because they seem to represent a sector with obvious interlocking fire capability. If we're successful, it will provide the Regiment the opportunity to punch a wide gap in the German line of defense."

"How are we supposed to support the strike team, Sergeant Major?" one NCO asked.

"Each of your BAR teams will concentrate on one machine gun position. We'll start with the three German emplacements toward the south. If successful, move on to the other two. Coordinate with each other as to dividing up the objectives. Your job is to pour fire into these positions to distract German return of fire away from the strike team. We will attempt to get close enough to surprise and kill the German gun crews. Trench knives if possible, to avoid firing a shot revealing our presence."

The German *Maschinengewehr 08* was a heavy water-cooled, tripod-mounted machine gun weighing 150 pounds manned by a crew of four. Burke and his three other Marines would go armed with two Browning M1911 .45 semi-automatic pistols each and trench knives. Burke carried his .45s in two shoulder holsters and his Bowie knife.

Burke continued explaining details for the planned attack. "At precisely 0430 direct BAR fire on the three most southern machine gun positions from the northwest simultaneously, but at an elevation. Forewarn the officers in charge where you're located to have their men hold their fire until the full assault starting at 0800. My strike team will be out there somewhere approaching concealed from the southeast and we don't want to get shot by friendly fire."

During the next day his team fixed the location of the German positions by provoking German machine gun bursts in response to American sporadic fire. By the afternoon, they compared notes and did their best to outline probable routes of attack by Burke and the strike team. They informed the forward field officers along this sector of the plan for the early hours of the following morning before the planned regimental assault at 0800 hours. Only Burke's fire support team was to engage in any firing before 0800 hours to avoid hitting the Marines making the early morning assault on the machine gun positions.

"Going to be difficult to identify the German positions in the dark," a BAR rifleman commented.

Burke replied, "Good moonlight with hopefully little cloud cover tonight just like last night. Get the location generally right and the enemy muzzle flashes will pinpoint their position."

"How do we know when to open up with the BARs to divert the German gunners?" A sergeant asked.

"If we're successful in sneaking close enough, we'll not need your diverting fire. If any German machine gun opens up, start pouring fire into all three of the identified first locations without waiting until 0430. Any light arms firing might be us or just normal snipping during the hours of darkness. If widespread firing erupts, proceed with your BAR diversion fire as best you can in the general vicinity you believe to be machine guns. Remember it is only to divert attention of those German gunners away from the direction of the strike team. Keep your elevation over the positions. We could be in amongst the German gun crews."

—

Throughout the day, the Marines and Germans engaged in harassing fire. Burke's fire support teams engaged in probing fire to specifically pinpoint the German machine gun positions in relation to certain terrain features that might aid the strike team using only moonlight. They were able to provide Burke with a workable hand drawn map. The difficulty remained in trying to identify terrain features in only moonlight from a different angle.

By sunset, nothing more to be done for the strike team in preparation after cleaning their weapons and sharpening trench knives. They ate a cold meal of canned beef, fruit, and a tin of crackers. Everyone wrote letters of endearment to their loved ones but avoided spelling out details of what they were about to do in a few hours. Burke rationalized that what appeared to be a near suicidal mission was really no more dangerous than what every Marine in the regiment would probably face again tomorrow. All those arrayed to the west of Belleau Wood were already survivors of repeated assaults over the past days. This war left no room for the expectation of survival. That was largely a function of chance or for the religious, divine choice.

At 0300 hours, Burke and his strike team set out following a circuitous route toward their first objective to optimize using available cover given the cloudless night. Slow going after progressing from a low crouch to moving on all fours to eventually reducing to a crawl when within a couple hundred yards from a particular stone outcropping. Out of view, the first German machine gun emplacement objective was only twenty yards further.

Viewed from a distance through field glasses, the area appeared still covered in underbrush. A mixed blessing affording better cover, but also slowing advance. Yet there was enough moonlight for Burke to define a reasonably unobstructed pathway to the objective. A distinctive German helmet protruded from the position shielded by piled rocks pinpointed the objective. Burke could hear speaking in German. At least two of the gun crew were awake.

Ahead of schedule by thirty minutes, Burke positioned his team using hand signals to communicate silently. Extracting his Bowie knife, he gestured to the two Marine corporals to also attack with their trench knives. He pointed to the side of his throat as the point of attack for a quick kill. If lucky, they might find one or two of the German gun crew asleep making it easy to dispatch all four silently.

The other Marine was Sergeant McKenzie from his instructor team after arriving at Parris Island. As a crack shot with the Browning .45, McKenzie would serve as backup. Burke hoped to dispatch several machine gun crews in silence before resorting to sidearms. The interlocking fields of fire put them at great risk if another machine gun turned on them should they fail to maintain surprise before crawling close enough to mount a success attack.

Burke led first followed by the two corporals crawling noise-lessly through the damp grass. Within feet of the exposed German, he moved quickly, the sharpened double-edged point of the Bowie knife plunged into the right side of the man's neck several inches. No scream, just a reflex stiffening of the man's body and collapse within seconds. Without hesitation before the first victim hit the ground, Burke saw the other German from the corner of his eye just feet away. In almost a continuous move, he pulled out the Bowie knife from the dead German then took a step swinging the heavy knife violently causing the blade to catch the kneeling German in the throat with enough force to penetrate deeply. Another silent kill.

Simultaneously to Burke dispatching the second German, both Marine corporals pounced on the sleeping gun crew. Trench knives to the throats. Only seconds transpired for the silent attack to kill the Germans gun crew.

Burke looked at the hand-drawn map in the direction of their next objective. Perhaps fifty yards away above another large boulder. With the time approaching 0430 designated for his fire support teams to commence BAR automatic fire over the German positions, Burke silently motioned their route of approach to the team. Pointing to his watch, he communicated that once closer, they would wait for the BARs to commence firing then make their assault with sidearms.

Burke again took the lead as they crawled closer to the German emplacement. Next to him was Sergeant McKenzie. Reaching the prescribed point, they waited ten minutes.

At 0430, the BARs opened fire on the three German positions. Within less than a minute, the German machine gunners in these and other positions began returning fire toward the muzzle flashes from the American line. Given the limitation of the 20-round detachable box magazine, the BAR fired in only short bursts with the accuracy of a rifle before changing magazines. For the purpose Burke intended, that was sufficient to divert attention of the German machine gun crew with their continuous belt-fed rate of fire.

Moving rapidly crawling with their elbows while holding a .45 semi-automatic pistol in each hand, Burke and McKenzie surmounted the German machine gun dugout breastworks and shot all four crew.

With the BARs keeping up steady distracting fire, the third German machine gun position fell in the same manner as the second.

Burke's BAR teams ceased firing for over thirty minutes. Likely relocating to take on the remaining two German machine guns targeted for this night's attack. Burke's plan now ran into difficulties. The first rays of daylight began illuminating Belleau Wood. Once the BARs opened up on the remaining designated German positions, it became obvious to the enemy that something was wrong. The three companion machine gun positions toward the south did not participate in firing into the American lines. Also, there was no largescale firing coming from the American front. Only sporadic BAR fire. This was just probing fire.

Burke signaled for the team to reload their sidearms with fresh magazines while enough noise existed to conceal the sound of jamming a magazine into place in the Browning.45 pistols. Under cover of brush, they approached the fourth objective reaching a point within twenty yards. Burke assessed their line of assault to be from slightly below the German dugout emplacement. That meant, if discovered, the Germans could not depress the angle of the machine gun to turn it against them. If executed quickly enough they could overwhelm the German gunners crew at a disadvantage by resorting to defense using awkward Mauser rifles with mounted bayonets.

As with any combat situation, the first casualty is the battle plan. In this case, it was encroaching daylight, an enemy alert for an unknown threat, and the unknowable information that this gun emplacement held not only a four-man machine gun crew but also an officer and another NCO.

Burke understood that current circumstances compromised his advantage of surprise. Trying to get closer before launching the assault might only add risk. Therefore, he spread the team for a combined assault to hit the position simultaneously.

Burke abruptly got to his feet signaling the start of the attack. As they closed the distance, a German soldier spotted them giving enough time to fire two rounds from his Mauser. Although a bolt action weapon, the Gewehr 98 Mauser could still put out a rate of fire of 15 rounds per minute. A round struck one of the Marine corporals in the chest. Burke put a .45 round into the face of the German.

As Burke and his two remaining Marines climbed over the slight embankment breastwork defining the machine gun dugout position, they realized their predicament as they faced five more Germans. The immediate threat came from the officer holding a Lugar pistol and a sergeant holding a Mauser with fixed bayonet.

The sergeant lunged at Burke with the rifle-mounted bayonet. Sidestepping the thrust, Burke shot the German pointblank twice in the chest. However, the German officer shot Burke in the chest with his Lugar before Sergeant McKenzie put him down. The fight raged on in the confined area. The three remaining Germans engaged with Sergeant McKenzie, the remaining corporal, and a badly wounded Burke in hand-to-hand fighting. The fight lasted only seconds.

The other Marine corporal took a Mauser round to the mid-section. Burke shot the German with the remaining rounds from one of his pistols. Sergeant McKenzie shot another German. Burke pushed close into the remaining German deflecting the bayonet and throwing him to the ground. With his last gasp of energy, Burke dropped his pistol from his right hand, withdrew his Bowie knife and drove it into the German's neck.

Sergeant McKenzie checked the corporal. Dead from a bullet to the heart. Kneeling next to Burke, Burke said, "You okay?"

"Yeah. Jefferson's dead though. Don't know about Rodgers who got hit first. How bad you hit, Sergeant Major?" Blood escaped from Burke's mouth as he struggled for breath. McKenzie took out a field dressing and pressed it against the entry wound to stem the bleeding. He knew it was bad. Burke probably wasn't going to make it.

"Bad enough, Sergeant. Get yourself back to our lines. I'm in no shape to make the attempt. We did good today. If I'm still alive, find me here after today's offensive. Even if the Regiment doesn't take the woods," Burke paused coughing up blood, "we saved the lives of a lot of Marines."

"Right you are 'bout that. But quit talking. Keep pressure on the dressing. I'm going to drag you down off this fucking hill. Give you a fighting chance to live."

"Don't do that, Sergeant. That's an order," Burke said, gurgling more blood from his mouth."

"Fuck that! Can't understand a damn word you're saying, Sergeant Major. Not going to leave a wounded Marine behind."

Before dragging Burke away from the German machine gun position, Sergeant McKenzie took one of the two coin-like dog tags from the dead corporal, leaving the second one to identify the body. As McKenzie began easing Burke down the slope, he confirmed the other corporal shot first in the assault was also dead. Eventually McKenzie sat down next to Burke shielded by the large boulder used as a landmark. This was as far as he could go without sunrise exposing them in the open area before reaching the American lines. Dragging Burke was not possible. As much as Burke required medical attention, better to wait for the American offensive scheduled to begin in two hours. Rescue depended on the Regiment advancing further than the failed attempts over the past several days to take Belleau Wood. For Burke, it also depended on surviving loss of blood.

McKenzie sliced open Burke's tunic to expose the bullet entry wound. There was no exit wound from the German Lugar 7.65mm round so it was still inside of him. McKenzie covered the wound with a fresh field dressing. He could do nothing for Burke's pain. Only medial staff had the ability to inject wounded personnel with morphine.

CHAPTER 13

Reims, France WWI | June 1918

A n hour after the start of the coordinated offensive of the 5th and the 6th Marines Regimes in the southern sector of Belleau Wood commenced, Sergeant McKenzie waved a white handkerchief to draw attention to several Marines scrabbling toward his position. Not far behind, they hailed a medical corpsman who secured a better dressing over Burke's wound, wrapping him tightly to maintain compression. An injection of morphine relieved Burke's pain and eased his labored breathing.

However, the medic had to press forward to treat other wounded. McKenzie was forced to drag Burke alone using a makeshift sling of web belts looped around Burke's ankles. That slow progress improved as they came across another wounded Marine. With one arm disabled and suffering distress, the Marine nonetheless provided enough help to eventually get Burke to a forward aid station manned by a surgeon.

—

Burke survived the arduous rescue and subsequent transport to a U.S. military hospital in Reims where him underwent surgery. The doctors were guardedly optimistic after removing the bullet and repairing the tissue damage. The remaining concern was the threat of infection. It was days after being wounded before he was weaned off morphine except for overwhelming bouts of pain. Once able to remain alert finally allowed for writing a letter to Keara.

My Dearest Keara,

Since my last letter, the Regiment moved to the front. The German offensive launched in the spring forced General Pershing to send in American troops to reinforce French lines under dire pressure. We have been in the thick of battle for weeks. I received a wound but am now recovering in a military hospital. Took a bullet in the chest. The prognosis is for a full recovery, but it will take some weeks to fully heal. Means I will not be returning to the front for an indefinite period, so you need not worry. The worst is behind me. Got out of bed yesterday for the first time. The German offensive appears blunted. The AEF now entering the conflict may mean the war is reaching a tipping point in favor of the Allies.

I could use some reading material to pass the time. Have not read many European novels. Having wound up in Europe, seems only fitting that I should experience European culture through their literature.

This finishes my military career. Keep writing often until I see you in New York. Anxious to begin the next chapter of my life with you, Darling.

Love, Alan

Burke's recovery progressed over the following weeks. In September he returned to the 4th Marine Brigade at the headquarters of the 2nd AEF Division to the east of Reims. The Division fresh from three days of battle at San Mihiel was now deployed just west of the Argonne Forest and Blanc Mont as part of the French 4th Army. Yet further action remained with the Germans expected to bitterly defend this sector close to the German border. Critical rail junctions essential for the German forces to retreat back into their homeland made this the last line of defense against the Allies. For Germany, the war was lost. Positioning for an armistice remained their only option.

Burke arrived at headquarters in a truck full of Marines. Showing his orders to a Marine sergeant seated at a table checking new arrivals. The sergeant looked up at Burke then abruptly stood. "You're to report to General Neville, Sergeant Major. The Colonel just got his star. He now commands the Brigade. Says to be on the lookout for your arrival. All of us heard what you did at Belleau Wood. Glad to hear you survived your wounds."

General Neville was effusive as he greeted Burke in the large tent. As a colonel, Neville commanded Burke's 5th Regiment at Belleau Wood. "At ease. Take a seat." As Burke sat down in a canvas field chair, Neville said, "Damn glad to see you up and around, Sergeant Major. Extraordinary what you accomplished at Belleau Wood. You're being promoted from sergeant major of not just the 5th Regiment, but the entire 4th Brigade. Effective immediately, you now become part of my staff. No more combat exploits as much as I find them inspirational. Been wounded in your career, what four times now? Christ, can't have a two-time recipient of the Medal of Honor and hero of France getting killed when this war is about over."

182

Burke looked puzzled for a moment before Neville clarified what he just said. "That's right, Sergeant Major, day after tomorrow. General Pershing will personally make the presentation of your second Medal of Honor. Major General Lejeune commanding the AEF 2nd Division will present you with another purple heart. French General Henri Gouraud commanding the French 4th Army will present you with the Croix de Guerre."

Alan Burke did not participate in further combat during the Great War. On November 11, 1918, Germany agreed to cease hostilities. Having decidedly lost the war, Germany will sign an Armistice and be made to suffer punitive terms. The 4th Marine Brigade will remain in Europe as part of the Allied occupation of the demilitarized Rhineland. As for Burke, he is presented with his discharge papers in March of the new year.

Following the Armistice, Burke wrote to his former commander Smedley Butler. Although of different ranks and backgrounds, both men shared a mutual respect as battle-hardened soldiers. Unfortunately for Butler, when the United States entered the war in Europe his organizational skills caused him to remain in Haiti commanding the Haitian Gendarmerie under U.S. military occupation. Eventually sent to Quantico, Virginia, he was promoted to colonel in command of a Marine regiment. Sent to France in September of 1918, neither Butler nor his regiment saw combat in the Great War. Although a decorated soldier, rumor had it that Butler was considered something of a maverick which may have accounted for not receiving a combat unit command in Europe.

However, Butler's proven organizational abilities, commanding Camp Pontanezen, the disembarkation location for arriving AEF forces in Brest, France, turned out to be invaluable to the AEF. A model of efficiency, Butler reacted with great ingenuity in the management of medical treatment presented by the unprecedented challenge of the influenza pandemic. All the warring parties suffered staggering losses of battle-ready troops caused by the deadly virus. Colonel Butler was immediately promoted to brigadier general in recognition of his contributions while commanding this critical non-combat installation.

In regular correspondence during Burke's convalescence, Butler candidly shared his disenchantment with American foreign policy. He admitted to having guilt over killing peasants to support dictatorial regimes for the sole purpose of defending American business interests wrapped in the cloak of national interests. He cynically remarked to Burke, *"I believe that Wilson, a pacifist that vowed to keep the United States out of the conflict may have caved to pressure since we had been funding Britain and France incurring enormous debt. It was important that we join in the fight to ensure defeat of Germany to protect our investment. Wall Street's investment. American imperialism writ large. The United States is now the most powerful nation in the world."*

Butler was also a close friend with General Neville and heard the details of Burke's exploits at Belleau Wood. Burke wrote to Butler that he was leaving the Marine Corps. Making known his interest in pursuing a career in law enforcement or security given his military background, Butler responded in a letter:

You are certainly suited for law enforcement. Got a taste of that myself commanding the Haitian police. Can't say I found it satisfying, but then again it wasn't real policing, just making sure the ever-present threat of insurrection didn't take hold. Found that effective policing is about acquiring good intelligence.

You mention in your letter about returning to West Virginia to take care of your mother and sister. From what you told me when you went back there years ago, state and local law enforcement are corrupt. Paid for by the mining corporations. Hired guns for crooked elected officials. Even the courts oppress the poor miners. That's how Washington's been using the Marines to protect American business interests in foreign countries, Sergeant Major.

If its law enforcement you looking to join, I suggest you do so at the federal level. That just about leaves only the U.S. Marshal Service or the Federal Bureau of Investigation. I don't know much about either one, but I'll write to my father who might be of assistance. Pennsylvania Congressman Thomas Butler has been in Congress for over twenty years. Carries a lot of influence. Knows Washington. Currently a member of the United States

House Committee on Naval Affairs. Makes him a friend of the Marine Corps.

With your service record and skills as a leader, you should be a natural for either law enforcement organization. I will send my father a letter. You are an extraordinary Marine and I would get immense satisfaction if I can help you find a suitable civilian career.

You said you were shipping out sometime in January from the Rhineland occupation to return to the United States. That means coming through Camp Pontanezen in Brest. Stop and see me for a visit before you sail for home. I would consider it an honor, Sergeant Major.

Regards, BGen Smedley Butler

Alan Burke took up his former commander's invitation. He arrived at Camp Pontanezen by train in a crowded rail carriage full of celebratory U.S. Army soldiers, many drunk, all overjoyed at having survived hell in one piece. Most were in their early twenties. Burke felt relief but more reserved while absorbed in his thoughts. His wound now completely healed, he suffered no aftereffects other than ugly scars front and back on his upper torso from surgery. In field uniform he chose not to display his impressive service citations that would raise all manner of inquisitive questions. They left the older Marine sergeant major in peace, which suited him fine.

Arriving in Brest the mood of thousands of departing American doughboys was markedly different than his arrival with the first wave of American forces in Saint-Nazaire in 1917. Then the young men joked with bravado eager to experience battle. A great adventure holding the false prospect of glory. The combat-experienced Marines knew this war was to be something much different. Now returning home, the horrors of the Western Front changed every one of them in some profound way. The laughter of joy of going home tempered by the sobering sight of arriving wounded awaiting loading onto a hospital ship. Broken men being comforted by women volunteers of the American Red Cross. A good many with life-changing disabilities.

Burke's orders put him on a transport ship scheduled to sail the following day for New York. Among the chaos of transit Camp Pontanezen with the AEF demobilization, Burke made his way to the commanding general's headquarters.

Presenting himself before the gunnery sergeant manning the large lobby of the commanding general's office. "I'm Sergeant Major Alan Burke. General Butler requested I report to him before I ship out to New York tomorrow. I served with the General in various theaters of war."

The gunnery sergeant looked up at Burke. "Very well, let me check with the General."

Moments later short the slightly built Brigadier General Smedley Butler walked out from his office. "Sergeant Major Burke! Delighted to see you. Come into my office."

Stepping into the office, "Butler said to two officers seated in front of his desk. If you'll excuse us gentlemen, this is an old friend. The toughest Marine I ever served with. Winner of the Medal of Honor in China during the Boxer rebellion than again last year at Belleau Wood."

In the presence of someone awarded the Medal of Honor twice, both officers stood and a delivered a sharp salute that Burke returned. "An honor, Sergeant Major," one officer said as they left.

Burke and General Butler chatted for over an hour. Where Butler one time tried to discourage Burke from leaving the Marines, he now felt differently. "You and I've been through lots of tough assignments during our military careers. In hindsight, not all of it for reasons we find morally defensible. For me, I'm disappointed at not being given a field command during this war. Due to my organizational abilities commanding the Haitian gendarmerie, I ended up putting together Camp Pontanezen. Possibly being considered for assuming command of the Marine Base at Quantico, Virginia after demobilization moves further along.

"As for me, I'm kind of stuck with continuing my military career. At least until I get a second star. However, with your illustrious military record and your intention to pursue a different career, law enforcement makes sense. Better yet, you might have a shot at becoming a U.S. Marshal, in West Virginia. I wrote to my

186

father. He became enthusiastically impressed by your exceptional military record."

Butler reached into a desk drawer and extracted a folder and handed it to Burke. "In there is a letter to you from my father. Seems he's been lobbying some of his cronies in the House. Specifically, the new House Judiciary Committee Chairman Andrew Volstead. His committee carries a lot of influence with the Department of Justice. New to the chairmanship after the Republicans took control of both houses of Congress in last year's election. Don't be put off by Volstead supporting this new constitutional amendment campaign to prohibit the sale of liquor. He doesn't know you like your whiskey.

"There's a position opening up this fall in the Southern District of West Virginia. Based out of Charleston, the seat of the federal district court. A marshal is appointed by the President for a four-year term for each federal district in the country. The Department of Justice usually makes recommendations to the President with the appointments requiring Senate confirmation. The Marshal Service attempts to appoint marshals familiar with local culture. As a native of West Virginian, you are a perfect fit. Should you get the appointment, your war record should ensure confirmation. Means going to Washington and interviewing for the appointment. There's a letter of invitation from the Department of Justice, a letter of recommendation from Volstead, one from my father, and my own letter of recommendation relating to our service together."

Burke replied, "I'm overwhelmed, General. I have no way of thanking you enough for all this effort on my behalf."

"Thanks are not necessary, Sergeant Major. Your years of extraordinary service under my command are thanks enough. Glad I could be of assistance. Promise to stay in touch. Remember not to shoot any badmen in West Virginia. From what you've told me over the years, plenty that might deserve it though."

Burke was surprised by the offer of immediate employment in law enforcement. Even though he joined the Marines to leave West Virginia over twenty years ago returning taking a position as U.S. marshal might be a good beginning of a new career. He knew the place, knew the culture. Intimately knew the violent la-bor unrest of the coalfields. The underlying issues never resolved. American war-interests only suspended the discord between coalminers and mine operators. With the ending of the Great War, no reason that past antagonisms would not erupt in new violence.

However, if he got the position, as a federal law enforcement officer he would be outside the local corruption bred of the cor-porate feudalism that Keara Murphy labelled as the oppressed cir-cumstances of coalmining communities. Not sure where U.S. mar-shals fit into this environment. Most policing matters came under state laws with state and local law enforcement having jurisdic-tion. This was not the old west territories of forty or fifty years ago when U.S. marshals represented the only law. On balance, it was a still a start. Something to build on that might lead to better op-portunities. The principal concern was Keara. Not sure she would accept living in Charleston. How would she continue her own ca-reer that seemed centered in New York? Keara was far more im-portant than this job.

—

As the ship passed by the Statue of Liberty, Burke's eyes teared up. He survived so many years of fighting in foreign lands. Mostly small wars but nonetheless dangerous. Attested to by a chest full of medals with combat wounds to prove it. Then the Great War where he made it out alive by chance rather than his soldiering skills. The prospects of a different life ahead of him with a woman he deeply loved. Hopefully his letter posted from France preceded his arrival in New York and Keara would be on the dock waiting.

As the ship pulled into the dock on the Hudson River, Burke joined the other mostly Army soldiers standing at the railings searching the crowd below for relatives awaiting the ship's arri-val. A sunny but chilly day in early April. Scanning the crowd, his eyes watered with sheer joy as he spotted Keara. Pulling off his cap, he waved until getting her attention.

Burke descended the gangway in dress uniform carrying his duffle bag. He wanted to show his best when meeting Keara. Among the mostly U.S. Army soldiers in drab field uniform, Burke stood out. His uniform consisted of a dark blue tunic with brass buttons and high collar displaying the Marine Corps emblem with the distinctive matching Marine cap. Lighter blue trousers with a red stripe down the outside. The tunic was a riot of color starting with his sergeant major insignia of rank of yellow chevrons trimmed in red, three up, three down on each upper arm with matching yellow stripes at each wrist denoting years of service. On his chest he sported an impressive display of meritorious valor citations, campaign ribbons, and other insignia of accomplishment. As a member of the 5th Marine Regiment, he wore the French unit distinction emblem the fourragère, a braided cord with brass fob from shoulder under the left arm awarded to members of the two Marine regiments that fought at Belleau Wood. Around his collar his two Medals of Honor hung from light blue ribbons.

Keara rushed up to him embracing and giving him a kiss. "Welcome home, Darling. These gentlemen are from the New York Times to document the return of a true American hero."

A photographer took several shots, several including Keara. The reporter then asked a series of questions, making notes of Burke's reply. Keara had already briefed the reporter about Burke's illustrious military background. The episode lasted ten minutes before Keara dismissed the newspaper men and slipped some bills into their hands.

"What was that about?" Burke asked as they made their way out of the throng.

"Public relations. Getting your photograph in the *New York Times* is good for your resume. Lots of war heroes returning so an opportunity to differentiate yourself when looking for a new career. Glad you wore your dress uniform. You stand out from those drab Army soldiers with all your medals. Saw them looking with envy."

"Of course they were. Because they're looking this beautiful woman and thinking what a lucky guy I am. Can't begin to express how good it is to see you, Keara."

Homecoming could not have been better. Soon after arriving at Keara's townhouse in Brooklyn, they were in bed. After lovemaking, Keara leaned over to examine the scars of the surgery of his wound from Belleau Wood. "Does this still hurt?"

"No."

"It certainly did not affect your performance. Now what?"

With a puzzled look, he replied, "Well looking at you naked while stroking me might lead to more of the same."

She grinned, "Maybe later. I meant what are you planning to do about employment?"

He hoped to get into that discussion later but said, "I have a possible opportunity of joining the U.S. Marshal Service."

"Really? That's wonderful. How did you come by that?"

"Through the efforts of my former commander. We served for years together in many deployments. His father is an influential congressman. Problem is, the job is in Charleston, West Virginia?"

Keara raised her eyebrows. "Why is that a problem?"

"Because of you. I intend to remain with you. Not going to take you away from New York and your work. That's of course if you want me around."

She thumped him in the chest with the heel of her fist, "Of course I want you with me, silly. Charleston's not such a bad place. Furthermore, I've developed a professional interest in the labor and political situation in West Virginia. Unlike the Colorado coalfields labor conflict since I was there years ago, circumstances have only gotten worse in West Virginia. Been closely following things there while corresponding regularly with your sister. We'll work it out how to be together."

Relieved, he sat up and embraced her. Kissing turned into renewed arousal and more lovemaking.

CHAPTER 14

Washington D.C. & West Virginia | Summer 1919

Burke's news about the prospects for appointment as U.S. marshal in West Virginia did not come as an unwelcomed surprise for Keara Murphy. Since he left for France, she became invested with the distorted social-political circumstances associated with coal mining. Already an activist for social justice for women's rights and anti-child labor, the plight of those involved in coal mining took on added meaning after her experience in Colorado. It provided a basis for journalistic success that reinforced her sense of accomplishing more than with her legal efforts.

The following morning as they enjoyed a late breakfast, Keara remarked, "To ease your mind about your considering this marshal position in West Virginia, let me explain what I've been doing the last couple of years. I chose not to burden you with details since they involve your mother and sister. Didn't wish to add what might have been further distress while fighting this dreadful war in France."

Burke looked at her with an expression of concern.

"My interest started of course when I first went to West Virginia years ago. That exposed me to the extreme circumstances of living the life of a coalminer. Dangerous, low paid work, exploited by big business through corrupted local governing institutions. That led to my journey to Colorado over a year later. Experienced firsthand the violent grip on the area when I had to shoot one of the Baldwin-Felts hired thugs. Stayed on to cover the dreadful Ludlow Massacre perpetrator by state militiamen. That entire experience became a larger endeavor that turned much of my attention toward journalism. Not about the issues behind the labor discord but rather the broader social implications. The ethical and legal issues of the exercise of economic power in direct defiance of constitutional rights. The uniquely un-American conditions that prevail in the West Virginia coalfields.

"After Colorado, the subject consumed my interest. My research took me back several decades to the labor violence in the anthracite coalfields of Schuylkill County in northeastern Pennsylvania. The unfounded accusations against a secret Irish organization, the Molly Maguires. The infiltration of the coal miners by agents of the Pinkerton Detective Agency. The subsequent trials and executions in the late 1870s of numerous Irish miners. Here we are with the same indentured labor servitude in the coal mines over forty years later. Mining companies oppressing miners by corrupting government. Using hired guns, Baldwin-Felts, to enforce their will.

"All this time I kept up a regular correspondence with your sister. Noreen is an exceptional person. Since everything that happened to your family several years ago, she has changed."

Burke nodded, "I agree. I see it in the tone of her letters. She has a keen mind. Knew that even when I was a youngster.

Keara added, "She has an exceptional mind. Intellectually inclined with talents that might surprise you. A solid moral compass."

He added, "Helped that she moved some distance away from Mum. Not burdened by Mum's devotion to unionizing efforts."

Keara replied, "Don't be too quick to dismiss either Noreen's views or even your mother's. They are not as estranged as you might think. Here, let me show you what the three women in your life have been up to these last couple of years."

Kera went into her study and returned with several folders. "First of all, let me explain what your mother has been doing. She prefers to live in Matewan. The Tug Fork Valley has become the center for the same confrontational conditions that prevailed in the Paint Creek & Cabin Creek Strike in Kanawha County in 1912 and 1913. The shameful *Hatfield Contract* never settled anything."

Keara was referring to the union settlement with newly elected West Virginia Governor Henry Hatfield in 1913 following repeated imposition of martial law by his predecessor. The back-to -work agreement Governor offered striking miners certain favorable terms for returning to work but with the alternative threat of deportation from the state if the strike continued. His settlement did nothing to change the oppressive practices exercised by the mining companies.

"Among those practices was the use of hired armed security in the form of the Baldwin-Felts Detective Agency. During the strike, no Baldwin-Felts agents were arrested whereas scores were arrested on the labor side of the confrontation for various serious criminal offenses. Union organizing militant agitator Mother Jones being among those. Violence continued for several months in Kanawha before subsiding. The labor situation remained stable throughout the war years following entry of the United States into the Great War. Wartime restrictions imposed by the Wilson Administration controlled mine wages and prohibited work stoppages under emergency presidential executive order along with suspending many constitutional rights across America. All that ended with the signing of the Treaty of Versailles formally ending hostilities of the Great war but not labor hostilities."

"I'm impressed with your grasp of the details contributing to the situation. But where do Mum and Noreen play into this?"

"Your mother has not forsaken her dedication to unionization. Just changed tactics with the changed circumstances. District 17 of the United Mine Workers has new leadership. Young militants by the name of Frank Keeney, the new district president, Fred Mooney, and William Blizzard. Much of the confrontational posturing is now centered in the southern counties along the Tug Fork River Valley. Particularly Mingo County where your mother chose to relocate. Your mother remains close to the new UMW leadership. She's a longtime friend of Blizzard's mother Sarah. Her insider information passed along to Noreen indicates the probability of another major coal strike. The mine operators refuse to negotiate with the UMW. Noreen speaks of a tense atmosphere in the southern coal counties. Noreen is quick to pick up fragments of information that suggests the mine operators are gearing up for confrontation. That will lead to another strike. Renewed evictions. Strikebreakers. Militant miners will counter with armed violence. 1912 all over again."

"Christ! With my mother right in the worst of it."

"True, but she has taken a different tact. Her letters do not mention delivering inflammatory speeches. Still on the payroll of the UMW. Says her duties now are teaching school for miner's children. Less visible activism. However, Maude Burke has not shied from more active rebellion. She's instead turned into something of a subversive."

With a look of surprise, Burke said, "Subversive?"

"Yes. A spy. Your mother produces candid photographs. Here, look at these clippings from newspapers and magazines. Note the captions."

Keara pushed a stack of clippings in front of him while explaining the subject matter and where it appeared in print.

Burke examined the images remaining speechless as Keara narrated.

"She uses a Kodak VPK just like I did in West Virginia and Colorado. The same camera you told Noreen to get through Sears & Roebuck."

"So, Mum sends you these photographs?"

"Not directly. Through your sister. Noreen bought your mother a camera. It was Noreen that convinced your mother to resist by turning her energies toward publicizing the social injustices suffered by those working the coal mines."

"Let me understand this. The three of you are in this together?"

"You might characterize it that way. More nuanced though. Let me start by explaining Noreen's motivation. At least my interpretation. Noreen is every bit as appalled by the oppressive conditions in the West Virginia coalfields as you, me, or your mother. She lived much of her life under those conditions. Lost her father,

her brother, and her husband because of the violent environment. In a way, she also lost her mother when Maude turned her grief into labor activism as her means of coping.

"During the years you were away in the Marine Corps, Noreen lost hope in achieving the kind of life she envisioned. Inability to bear children followed by the death of her husband, then the responsibility of looking after your mother. Stuck in this rural environment when her mind yearned for something more.

"Noreen is as tough as you or your mother. She took charge of her life yet did not abandon your mother, nor her conscience. Turned her energies to teaching in a more prosperous location became both refuge and cover. Never capitulating to the distressed circumstances of life for working people in this place, she turned her intellect toward confronting this social condition I call corporate feudalism through subverting the enemy.

"Noreen cleverly sold your mother on this as a more effective way to attack the mining companies, while keeping her less conspicuous. Your mother bought into the logic and became a spy. Noreen became the spy master. She annotates the photographs, defining the location and circumstances then passes the material to me. I became the instrument for using the material to invoke the power of the press. Nothing in my published material reveals either Noreen or your mother as sources. Your mother sends her undeveloped film with explanatory notes to Noreen by mail disguised in packages of cookies. Noreen replies by sending her packages of books and fresh undeveloped film."

Burke commented, "Noreen then becomes the conduit for you to keep the plight of the miners in the public eye."

"Yes. However, Noreen goes further than just passing on photographs and local information from your mother showing what it is like to live the life of a coal mining family. Noreen has a uniquely placed deep-cover source. Someone within the headquarters of Baldwin-Felts."

"What! How on earth is that possible?"

"A quirk of circumstances that just came together. You see, Noreen has suffered silently since the losses in your family. She understood your mother's reaction but did not emotionally embrace unionizing as her means of coping. Noreen possesses a strong social consciousness having lived under the hopeless circumstances for those working the mines. Yet she blames the deaths of her family members on your father. Baldwin-Felts may have killed them, but Noreen says it was your father's irrational act that resulted in the tragedy."

"Sadly, I share those same feelings," Burke commented. "Doesn't change my disgust toward Baldwin-Felts. Hired assassins with no morals. Your experience in Colorado confirms that."

"What I'm saying is that Noreen dealt with her grief by condemning the social injustices perpetrated by the mining companies and the complicit corruption of local officials as the fundamental cause. The use of a hired militia-like armed force represented by Baldwin-Felts is just the visible manifestation of the illicit use of power in West Virginia. The crudest example of corruption exits in Logan County, ruled over by a virtual dictator in the form of Sheriff Don Chafin.

"Noreen has found a new life but has not forsaken some inner compulsion to resist the injustice. Taking this path of subverting the corrupting corporate power structure is her way of confronting the fundamental source of the problem."

Burke let out a long sigh. "Go back to your earlier comment about Noreen spying directly on Baldwin-Felts. How is that possible? Doesn't that put her in danger?"

"Possibly. However, she is too invested to turn back. Knowing you would see me upon your return to New York, Noreen told me to explain what I'm about to tell you.

"Months ago, Noreen befriended a young woman employed at Baldwin-Felts headquarters in Bluefield where Noreen lives. She met twenty-year-old Francis Duncan at a community event where they struck up a conversation, as both were unattached females. The young woman is the daughter of the Bluefield chief of police who is a personally friendly with Thomas Felts the managing partner of Baldwin-Felts. According to Noreen, Francis is exceptionally intelligent but plain in appearance. Poor prospects for marriage and little chance for a career being stuck in Appalachia. She tells Noreen about working to save enough money to leave

Bluefield and West Virginia. As part of the clerical staff, she reports to Baldwin-Felts chief of operations, Leland Atwood. As the most accomplished with taking shorthand from both Atwood and Thomas Felts, Francis has access to all manner of confidential material.

"Francis eventually confided to Noreen about being troubled by reading newspaper accounts of the deadly labor violence that is part of her daily work-life. She is appalled by how those at Baldwin-Felts regard the mine workers as something little better than cattle. Experiences guilt over her employment with Baldwin-Felts who she becomes convinced is the instrument of violence and intimidation of the miners and their families.

"Francis found in Noreen an outlet to express her disgust. She looks up to Noreen as a role model and mentor. Encouraged by Noreen's success given the struggles of your family after coming to West Virginia as an immigrant at an early age. The sacrifice of parents eking out a hard scrabble existence to offer a better life for their youngest children. Noreen was able to finish high school then attend college for a couple of years before becoming a teacher, while her younger brother made a career in the military.

"Francis began regularly sharing sensitive information with Noreen to express her feelings. Information that disgusts Francis for its callous disregard for the miners. Noreen eventually coached Francis in looking for the most telling confidential information as a way to damage Baldwin-Felts. Noreen told Francis that doing so would absolve her feelings of guilt for working there. Noreen told Francis she has the means of getting this confidential information to influential people outside of West Virginia using the power of the press. She assured Francis that they will only transact information that cannot be traced back to her as the source."

Burke smiled. "I'll be damned. You and Noreen create quite a team. Can't wait to see her. Spent most of my adult life interacting with her only through letters. We both missed so much being separated for long periods. Noreen as my connection to family."

Keara said, "Then let's set the trip to Washington D.C. to do your interviews then continue from there to West Virginia. See your mother and Noreen before visiting Charleston. I'll be going with you."

"I would like that," Burke said. With a measure of anxiety, "If I were to get this job in Charleston, would you be willing to split your time living between Brooklyn and Charleston?"

Keara came to him and held his face with her hands. "Of course. Already thought about that. I intend to be with you, Alan Burke. We're right for each other. Easy enough to maintain residences in both places. It's only a day's travel by train between Charleston and New York. I can also work in Charleston or Brooklyn."

"Since we'll be living together, I want you to meet my parents. They understand my views on the legal limitations of marriage for women so they will not exert pressure. They already know my feelings for you and are used to my ways. We'll make our life together on our terms. To the wider world, we shall be husband and wife. I'll retain my family name for professional reasons."

—

Keara took over making the appointments for Burke's interviews in Washington D.C. scheduled for July before Congress left for summer recess in August. Burke took the opportunity to call Congressman Thomas Butler personally to thank him for securing the opportunity to interview for the appointment.

"My pleasure, Sergeant Major. My son has great respect for your soldiering while under his command. Your commendations attest to that. We need men like you in federal law enforcement. Coming from West Virginia makes you eminently qualified. You realize that being a federal marshal is largely administrative. Not the sort of armed violence when marshals represented the only law on the western frontier decades ago."

"I understand that, Sir. I've seen enough combat for a lifetime. Look forward to continuing service to my country in this new capacity. Good to be back in the United States permanently with prospects for a rewarding career that is a natural continuation of my military service."

"Excellent. When I see you on Wednesday July 9 according to my calendar, I've reserved time to walk you over to the Senate chambers and introduce you to both senators from West Virginia. Howard Sutherland is a former businessman involved with railroads and mining. Newly elected Davis Elkins served as an officer in the U. S. Army during the Great War. He's also an industrialist involved in railroads and mining. Both his father and grandfather previously served in the Senate from West Virginia. If the President approves your appointment for a four-year term starting in January, confirmation by the Senate is required. With your background that should be just a perfunctory process. Yet some lobbying is always good politics.

"You first need to secure the appointment which in this case will probably come from the Chief of the Marshal Service for the Department of Justice, George Trenton. He will take into account recommendations already made by myself and Congressman Volstead as Chairman of the House Judiciary Committee which carries weight as the congressional oversight body for the DOJ and federal courts.

"Might suggest you get down to West Virginia and speak with the outgoing U.S. Marshal who is retiring early in the fall from his second term early for personal reasons. His name is William Osborne. Based in Charleston. He can brief you on the situation in southern West Virginia. Things are quite unsettled in the coal fields there as you well know. The restrictions imposed during the Great War tamped down the labor violence but there is talk in the newspapers about the possibility of renewed coalmine strikes throughout the country. Be wise for you to access the situation firsthand to understand how this might affect the duties of the U.S. marshal."

Burke and Keara left New York by train for Washington D.C. Coached in advance by Keara, she also prepared a resume that she forwarded to those Burke would be seeing. He spent two days making the rounds selling himself for a job that he knew very little about. From the onset, Congressman Butler did most of the selling, treating him as a war hero celebrity. The congressmen and senators seemed more interested in hearing of his military exploits rather than ascertaining his abilities to discharge the duties of a U.S. marshal. He left with the impression that other than Trenton at the DOJ, none had specific knowledge of the duties of a U.S. marshal. As Congressman Butler characterized the job, it sounded more administrative than dealing with law enforcement requiring the use of firearms. That suited him fine.

Both West Virginia senators were delighted to have a candidate of his stature with ties to West Virginia. Following Keara's counsel, Burke modified his family history accordingly.

"You can't very well be forthcoming about your family's background. The death of your father and brother on the side of striking coalminers and your mother's union advocacy will not endear you to the West Virginia senators. Both are businessmen with backgrounds involving mining and railroads. Better not to put your heritage on the side of militant miners in a labor war. Instead, you immigrated from Ireland at the age of five with your older sister. No mention of an older brother. Your father was a railroad man and your mother a teacher. Your father died in an industrial accident at the Chesapeake & Ohio Railroad's Huntington Works years ago. No mention of living in Kanawha County or the strike of 1912-1913. Your mother and sister are schoolteachers and currently reside in West Virginia."

—

Before leaving Washington, Burke telephoned his sister in Bluefield to tell her he and Keara Murphy would be arriving the following afternoon by train. By his letters, Noreen Hannigan understood that her brother had left the Marine Corps and arrived in New York from France. Knowing the romantic connection he and Keara developed over years of separation through letters, spending time with Keara first was understandable.

Burke said, "Don't tell mother until we get there. We want to spend a few days with you before going to Matewan to visit her. After that, I have business in Charleston before Keara and I return to New York. Got some interesting news to share with you. Can you get us a room at a hotel in Bluefield?"

"Of course. We have a fine hotel in town. I'll probably be at school when you arrive, but I'll show up at the hotel in the afternoon. Can't wait to see you, Alan. So happy for you and Keara. You are right for each other. You know I'm indebted to Keara for helping me through those difficult times."

"Keara thinks the world of you, Sis. She credits your intellect and strength of will for surviving to achieve a better life. Is school out for the summer?"

"Oh yes. I'll spend the summer working at the local library. Discovered some books you might find interesting."

"Can you get away for a few days? Come with us to visit Mother, then all of us go up to Charleston for a couple of days. I'll take you ladies shopping. What do you say?"

"That can be arranged. Sounds wonderful, Alan."

—

That first day back in West Virginia was another experience for Alan Burke's transition to civilian life. Bluefield was a city of 15,000 people in 1919. The area prospered from the coal boom that began in the latter nineteenth century. It then become a major railroad center for transporting coal from the southern West Virginia coalfields. Just eight miles north of Bluefield was the small town of Bramwell known for its concentration of numerous large homes of wealthy coal mine owners.

Noreen greeted them at the train station. Burke happily observed the affection she felt for Keara. His sister's demeanor had changed for the better. Gone was her emotional self-restraint replaced with a sense of confidence and purpose evidenced in last couple of years.

After embraces and kisses on the train platform with tears of joy in the eyes of everyone, Noreen said. "I booked a very nice room in the Altamont Hotel just across Princeton Street once we walk out the passenger station."

At the hotel desk, Noreen took charge saying to the desk clerk. "I made a reservation for my brother Alan Burke and his wife

Keara." Turning to Alan and Keara, Noreen winked and smiled conspiratorially.

"Yes, of course. Welcome to the Altamont Hotel. You have one of our best rooms on the top floor. Three nights. Is that correct?"

Keara replied, "That is correct. Where is your restaurant?"

"Right through there, Mrs. Burke"

Keara and Noreen marched off to the restaurant arm-in-arm while Burke registered and tipped a young man to carry their luggage to the room.

Seated in the well-appointed lobby, Keara arranged for the restaurant to serve a pot of coffee in the lobby allowing them to visit before returning to the dining room for dinner an hour later.

After exhausting the pleasantries, Burke jumped into the question foremost on his mind. "Keara filled me in on your secretive activities with Mum. Never thought you felt so strongly about the distressing circumstances of those mining coal."

Noreen replied, "Neither did I. It got hold of me when dealing with how Mother reacted after losing Dad, Liam, and Fergus. I was angry at Dad for causing us such grief with his irresponsible actions. Eventually I came to realize that Mum's committing herself to unionizing was more than just her way of coping with the tragedy. It had substance. Her way of confronting the enemy at the source of this oppression.

"Mum and Dad knew something about oppression. They left Ireland because of their activism against the British. Their early efforts, even the violence perpetrated by Dad and Liam, eventually led to something. The Irish rebellion of 1916 failed but the current rebellion is fully involved throughout much of Ireland. Backed by the entire Irish population, this time might prove successful. You might say rebellion is in my Irish blood.

"While I do not embrace the United Mine Workers Union as the sole remedy for what ails coal mining, I recognize the enemy clearly. The mining companies that rule West Virginia are just like those British plantation owners with their foot on the neck of Ireland for hundreds of years. The idea struck me about redirecting Mum's activities to something less hazardous than rabble rousing for the UMW. Never liked Mother Jones or Mum inflaming miners to take violent action. Rather than argue with her, I found the opportunity to convince her of a more effective method of resisting."

Alan nodded with an expression conveying not only understanding but recognition of his sister's new demeanor. Looking at Keara he could see her expression of *see what I mean about your sister*. "The way you express yourself with such confidence is extraordinary. I could see how you have changed by reading your letters. Being here together with family is a wonderful experience."

"Well, you'll also be surprised when you see Mum. She's changed too. With the signing of the labor agreement that ended martial law years ago, like many others, she was unhappy that it did nothing to change the abusive practices of the mine operators. When the war curtailed any union threat of strike she returned to teaching. With my own sense of social responsibility weighing on my mind, it provided a perfect way to mend the rift between us with something productive."

"That you and Mum have found a new relationship makes this a special homecoming."

"We'll see where things are heading. The local UMW has new leadership. A new confrontation with the mining companies is brewing. But enough about labor strife. What's this news you want to tell me about?"

"Well, there's no secret about Keara and me. What is new is the possibility that we may be coming to West Virginia."

Visibly surprised, Noreen looked at Keara. "You're leaving Brooklyn?"

Keara replied, "Not entirely. Should Alan get this position he's applied for, I will split my time between Charleston and Brooklyn. A good deal of my time is spent on writing articles exposing the conditions and corruption associated with mining coal. Helpful to spend time working close to the source. But I will not leave Alan's side for any extended period." Alan reached over and grasped Keara hand.

"Wonderful. What sort of position is this?"

Alan answered, "United States Marshal for Southern West Virginia. Based out of Charleston."

For a moment, Noreen was speechless. "Oh my. Sounds important. What does a federal marshal do?"

Alan explained, "Supports the federal courts and U.S. attorneys. Arrests suspects for federal crimes. Provides security for the federal courts. The southern district has four court locations, in Charleston, Beckley, Huntington, and here in Bluefield."

"As federal law enforcement, will you become involved should renewed violence erupt should there be a new strike? The current climate suggests that is inevitable."

"Not necessarily. Law enforcement response for most of the violence involves state laws. I can officially act only where federal laws are broken. Usually then only when the federal court issues a warrant requested by the U.S. attorney. A lot of what the marshal does is administrative. The marshal service is quite small. I'll only have four deputies to cover twenty-three counties."

"What made you consider this as your next career?"

"When I decided to leave the Marines, law enforcement seemed a suitable profession with my military experience. Something at the federal level avoided the political corruption of local law enforcement. My former commander of many years offered the assistance of his influential father in Congress in Washington. My service record and being from West Virginia helped. It's a prestigious position. Requires appointment by the President and confirmation from the Senate. A stroke of good fortune should I make it. I'll know in a couple of months."

Noreen said, "Well I hope you get the appointment. It'll be wonderful to have you close. How about you Keara? You prepared to live in Charleston at least part of the time?'

Keara replied, "Oh yes. Be good to be close to you and in the thick of what's happening in West Virginia. To tell you the truth, it's rewarding to be participating in a meaningful way with something I feel strongly about. What goes on here is far beyond the injustices associated with a labor dispute. I'm more interested in exploring the broader implications of life under these oppressive conditions. The collective oppression of big business with the complicity of corrupt local government. Besides, living with your brother already has changed my life and I choose to remain at his side."

CHAPTER 15

West Virginia | Summer 1919

It proved a remarkably enlightening few days in Bluefield for Alan Burke. A wonderful reunion with Noreen. Impressed far beyond what he already gathered from her letters over the last couple of years with her emotional emancipation. No longer stifled by a loveless marriage living a dead-end life teaching school in a remote backwater. Yet faced with the responsibility of looking after her mother. Difficult with the natural grief faced by both, her mother's embrace of militant union organizing strained their relationship. Changes in circumstances and the passage of time led Noreen to take stock and make the wrenching decision to live separately from her mother. According to Noreen, choices made under stress now appeared to make a positive difference. Mother was doing well. He was now going to find out for himself if that was the case.

"Mum, this is Alan. How are you?" he said over the party telephone line.

"Alan, so good to hear your voice. Good visit with Noreen?"

"Very good. We'll be in Matewan on the eleven o'clock train tomorrow. Can't wait to see you. Keara's with me you know."

"Yes, Noreen told me. Keara's a wonderful woman. So glad you are together. We'll have a grand reunion."

When the train pulled into Matewan Maude Burke was there waving as she saw her son in the train carriage window. From the onset, it was a happy reunion for the Burke family. From the long absence of seeing her only son fighting in France to his wounding, Maude was in tears as he stepped from the train. Maude looked older. Gone was the fiery union crusader yet her strength was still evident. Burke was pleased by his mother's display of affection for Noreen. The estrangement now replaced with that of mother and daughter with mutual recognition of equality rising above past differences.

They made their way to the Urias Hotel a short distance on Mate Street. After reserving two rooms, they walked to a restaurant down the street to enjoy lunch. Alan broke the news of his possible appointment as U.S. marshal. "I'd be based in Charleston, but my region of responsibility included all the southern counties of West Virginia. I'll be able to make regular visits to see both you and Noreen."

The joyous news brought more tears of joy to Maude as she grasped her son's hand. "More good news. That's wonderful. When will you know if you have the position?"

"Probably in the next couple of months. Can you image that it needs the President of the United States to nominate me then the Senate to confirm my appointment?"

"After all you've done serving your country, that's only fitting."

"We're heading to Charleston after leaving Matewan. I'm meeting with federal officials there. Hoping that you can come with us for a couple of days and extend our reunion. What do you say, Mum?"

Maude nodded. "I'd like that, Alan. What about we walk over to my boarding house? It's just a short walk. "There's a large parlor there where we can sit and visit some more. Only the landlady and her daughter will be there with the other tenants away at work for most of the afternoon. We can have the place to ourselves."

Settled in the parlor of Maude's boarding house on McCoy Street after lunch, Keara Murphy extracted a folder from her narrow leather briefcase and said, "Take a look at your handywork, Maude. These are your photographs. From your notes, I wrote the captions. Along with your insider information about the troubles, readers get insights of what's it's like living under these conditions. Some of these were published in *McClure's* and *Colliers*. Major national magazines. Some in newspapers, including the prestigious *New York Times*. No matter the strength of the written word, when accompanied by illustrative photos, the impact becomes much greater."

Maude leafed through the clippings, pausing occasionally to linger over an image.

"Do these pictures make a difference, Keara?" Maude asked.

"I believe so. No real way to measure the impact of a given photograph. It's the broader impact that comes from sustaining attention on an issue. In the larger context of the coalfield conflict, your photographs make for a compelling visualization that cannot be conveyed by words alone."

Maude nodded. "If it contributes to showing what it's like here then it's worth the effort. Things are only getting worse. Nothing much has changed since the great strike of 1912 in Kanawha County. Only difference here in Mingo County and Pike County, Kentucky across the river is a higher percentage of union membership among miners. Makes no real difference though. All the coal mine operators along the Tug Valley refuse to negotiate with the UMW. With the ending of the war in Europe, all the problems between the mining companies and the miners have returned. You can be sure, there'll be another strike coming soon."

After two nights in Matewan, all four left by train for Charleston by way of Huntington. They took rooms at the Kanawha Hotel in the Arcade Building on Virginia Street. The same hotel where Alan stayed in 1912. The following day, Keara called Angelina her housekeeper in Brooklyn to tell her she would be in Charleston for a few days before returning home.

Angelina said, "Glad you called. A telegram was delivered yesterday for Mr. Burke. Sounds important. From Washington."

"Please read it to me, Angie."

'Informing you that Attorney General Palmer has approved submitting your name to the White House as the DOJ recommended candidate for U.S. Marshal Southern District of West Virginia. Will keep you advised of status regarding formal presidential nomination to the Senate for confirmation. Good luck. Signed George Trenton, Chief of U.S. Marshal Service.'

Keara turned to Burke and gave him the news. "Looks like you'll get the appointment unless there's some political snag. Presidential appointments sometimes have little to do with the qualifications of the candidate. At least your position should not be high enough profile in Washington to prompt anything but Senate confirmation without debate."

With selection as the Department of Justice candidate recommended for the position, Burke had good reason to meet with local federal officials. Important to better understand the specific duties of a U.S. marshal. In broadest terms, he understood the principal function of the U.S. marshal's office consisted of ensuring the functioning of the federal courts in the district. This included providing security, acting as paymaster for staff and court expenses, serving summons, and executing warrants executed by the U.S. attorney's office. District Judge Benjamin Keller was therefore foremost on his list.

A busy man, the soonest possible time Judge Keller's clerk could offer was the day after tomorrow. Burke would then start by speaking with the outgoing marshal.

William Osbourne was retiring early from his second four-year term. His office was in the same building as the federal court in Charleston. Staffed with a female clerk, Burke gave his name and only that he was sent by Washington to see Marshal Osbourne. The woman returned with a man in shirtsleeves. "I'm Deputy Marshal Richardson. Can I help you? Marshal Osbourne is out of town today. Should return tomorrow."

"Perhaps if I might have a little of your time, Deputy Richardson. I understand Marshal Osbourne is resigning before the ending of his term. Is that correct?"

The deputy looked at him suspiciously. "Well, I cannot comment on that."

"I'm here at the suggestion of Mr. Trenton in Washington. The Department of Justice has submitted my name to the White House for nomination as the new marshal for this district. Thought I would call on Marshal Osbourne and get a better understanding of circumstances here."

The surprised deputy realizing this might be his new boss responded, "Yes, Sir. Please come in. Be glad to offer my comments."

Deputy marshals are hired by the district marshal and often are replaced when a new marshal takes office. Best to make a good impression in hopes of retaining his job.

Richardson did make a good impression on Burke. While avoiding any direct pronouncement of his feelings concerning the political conflicts raging in the coalfields, he did not disparage coalminers. "I come from north of here. Clarksburg. Served as a deputy in the Harrison County Sheriff's Department before getting this position with Marshal Osburne when he began his first term in 1914. Sorry to see him leaving early. I can tell you, with these hostilities we're often treated like the enemy by many people."

"Enemy? By what people?"

"Coal miners and their families. They consider us somehow the same as some of those in the local sheriff's departments. Those counties where the conflict has begun heating up since the end of the war. The legal issues mostly involve only state laws. The mining companies hiring outside armed security makes matters worse. Those Baldwin-Felts detectives are a mean bunch. They're not lawmen. Outside of serving summons and now policing moonshining under this new Prohibition law, the troubles in West Virginia usually do not involve violation of federal law. You might want to talk to U.S. Attorney Kenna. He's a fair man. He'll give you a better explanation of the situation in West Virginia as it affects us on the federal side of law enforcement."

"I appreciate your observations, Deputy Richardson. I'm also from West Virginia. But I've been in the Marine Corps for over twenty years making me somewhat of an outsider. My mother's a teacher. My father worked for the railroad. I have followed the coalfield labor conflicts from afar. A sad state of affairs."

Richardson said, "Did you go to France during the war?"

"Yes. Fought at Belleau Wood."

"Oh my! Read about that in the newspaper. Was it as bad as they say?"

"Far worse. Been a professional soldier all my life. As a Marine, I saw my share of combat in foreign lands. Belleau Wood was as bad as it gets. Lot of Marines never returned from weeks of bloody fighting trying to dislodge the Germans dug in on wooded high ground."

Burke found Assistant U.S. Attorney Joseph Kenna more vocal about the labor conflict. He was acting as U.S. attorney for the district until the President filled the vacancy. Kenna was decidedly sympathetic to the plight of coalminers. He welcomed Burke as the likely replacement to Marshal Osborne.

"Bill Osborne is a fine man. Came into office in 1913 when things settled down after the conflict surrounding the Paint Creek & Cabin Creek Strike. Background as a teacher and superintendent of schools. Not sure that's the best preparation for law enforcement. Told me he regrets accepting a second appointment as marshal in 1917. Your background as a career soldier sounds more relevant to the turmoil in West Virginia.

"Mark my words, they'll be another strike. Just like in 1912 here in Kanawha. This time it'll be in Mingo County. The Tug Fork River Valley is the next hot spot. The mining companies refuse to negotiate with the Union. The UMW will have no choice but to call a strike. The violence will likely escalate beyond the ability of local law enforcement to maintain order. Then they'll be a repeat of 1912 with a declaration of martial law. If that happens the coalfields will run with blood.

"The West Virginia National Guard exists largely on paper. Nationalized and sent to France, they are now demobilized. That leaves the West Virginia State Police, newly created just months ago. Should widespread violence erupt, state and local law enforcement might not be able to maintain civil order under a declaration of martial law. Should the situation get out of hand that will result in a call for intervention of federal troops. That means you and your deputies could be thrust directly into the conflict."

Burke found District Judge Benjamin Keller not particularly friendly. Escorted into the judge's chambers by his secretary, the short, stocky Keller leaned across his desk and shook Burke's hand. Keller was in his sixties but looked older. He had a gray pallor and seemed to breathe heavily. Burke knew Keller had been on the bench since 1901. That meant he experienced many labor conflicts in the West Virginia coalfields. "Please have a seat, Mr. Burke. My secretary said you are the DOJ's recommended candidate to replace Marshal Osborne. Has the White House submitted your nomination to the Senate?"

"Not yet, your honor?"

"Very well, what can I do for you?"

"Nothing specific, your honor. Just wanted to introduce myself since my responsibilities entail making sure your courts function efficiently and safely."

"What's your background, Mr. Burke?"

"Professional soldier for twenty-three years. Served in the United States Marine Corps. My last deployment was to France as part of the AEF. Served many years as Sergeant Major of the 5th Marine Regiment then as Sergeant Major of the 4th Marine Brigade. Saw action at Belleau Wood."

"Decorated?"

"Yes, your honor. For service in many war zones."

"What medals did you receive?"

"The Congressional Medal of Honor, twice. Silver star, bronze star, French Croix de Guerre, four purple hearts."

That got Keller's attention. "Good lord. That is impressive. However, the responsibilities of the U.S. marshal's office extend more to administration. How does your background qualify you for that?"

"As Sergeant Major, I was the most senior non-commissioned officer of the regiment. Part of the commanding colonel's staff. Responsible for the welfare and training of 4,800 Marines. Organizational and administrative responsibilities dominated my duties."

"Well, I'll take your word for that, Mr. Burke. Been satisfied with Marshal Osborne's discharge of his responsibilities over his years of service. Should the Senate confirm your nomination, I just expect a continuation of a smooth running of my court.

"A difficult job for all of us on the federal side of all that is going on here in West Virginia. The legal ramifications of the labor conflict with the coal mines are a state issue. My docket overwhelming deals with illegal liquor violations. Before this stupid Volstead Act prohibiting the production and sale of alcohol spirits, it was about moonshining in the mountains to avoid taxation."

The following day, Marshal Osborne returned to Charleston. Burke's immediate impression was someone you would not recognize as a law enforcement officer. Instead of displaying his badge, he kept it in a leather wallet in his pocket. In their conversation, he said he rarely went armed. "I leave that sort of work better done by my deputies." Burke could see the distress Osborne felt with the escalating tensions. He too predicted an impending miners' strike accompanied by renewed violence.

Osborne said he was resigning before his term expired for personal reasons involving his wife's health. The limiting of his required traveling through the southern counties comprising his region hampered discharging his responsibilities. He was cordial to Burke wishing him success should he get the appointment. However, Osborne provided little insight into the challenges of the job except for expressing frustrating bureaucratic difficulties over funding with Washington.

—

Burke, Keara, and his family spent important time together. Reuniting after many difficult years, each of them held the promise of new beginnings. While Alan Burke harbored doubts about his prospective new position, it did not lessen the positive aspects of returning to West Virginia.

"What do you think about the job, Alan?" Keara said on their last night in Charleston before they took the train back to New York.

"Hard to tell. More apprehensive about the many administrative functions."

"Apprehensive? You'll master all that within a short time."

"I agree. It's not that. After a life filled with more intense challenges, not sure I'll like becoming a pencil-pusher in an environment with so much going on. Everyone I spoke to, including Mum, says the labor situation with the coal mines will only get worse. That means a return to the violence of the past. That's the nature of mountain culture. The infamous Hatfield-McCoy feud was not an isolated example. A couple of generations ago, this was the American frontier.

"As a federal law enforcement officer, I'll be officially outside much of the conflict unless federal laws become involved. Not sure I like being a spectator to the oppression that you describe. Your journalistic actions put you in the fight."

"You'll just have to see how things develop. Should new violence erupt, don't assume there won't be a role for you to play. Unlike enlisting in the Marines, you can always resign and move on if the job doesn't suit you."

"Not sure I'd do that. I finish what I start. Now how about you? Can you see yourself living in Charleston? At least part of the time?"

Keara embraced him. "Of course. Not part of the time, most of the time. New York is not that far away to visit mother and father. I've Angie and her daughter to look after the house in Brooklyn. I'll be here with you, doing my work. Journalistic and legal work. Right in the middle of something important. When you were off meeting with the local federal officials, I explored many areas of the city with Noreen and your mother. Charleston's not New York but a comfortable enough city as long as I'm close to you."

—

Burke and Keara returned to Brooklyn in late September 1919. A couple of weeks later, Keara answered the door. A Western Union messenger handed her a message for Mr. Alan Burke. She hurried into the study and gave the envelope to Burke. The telegram read, '*U.S. Senate confirmed your appointment as U.S. Marshal for the Southern District of West Virginia for a four-year term commencing December 1, 1919. Congratulations, George Trenton, Chief of U.S. Marshal Service, Department of Justice.*'

"Well, there it is. A new beginning full of all manner of unknowns."

Keara kissed him. "A great new adventure. We should start packing right away. Get to Charleston in time to enjoy the beauty of the leaves turning fall colors. Get settled in before winter arrives and you begin your official duties. We'll both be busy. How exciting!"

Keara supervised the packing. They would carry clothing for a couple weeks with the bulk of their personal goods coming in steamer trunks shipped later after finding a residence in Charleston.

Making their farewells to Keara's parents, Angelina, and her daughter Gianna, Burke and Keara departed Brooklyn the last week of October. Keara insisted they stay at the Kanawha Hotel until they found a permanent place of residence. That was Keara's task while Burke began formally making introductions to those he would be working with closely. All federal officials of the Southern Federal District of West Virginia were officially informed by Washington of Burke's appointment.

Burke's welcoming took a decided different tone now that his appointment was official. Along with the federal judge, and the U.S. attorney's office, the U.S. Marshal Service represented the legal authority of the federal government in southern West Virginia. His appointment may have little direct impact on the labor unrest, but it was of significance to the region's power structure.

Burke's four deputy marshals were located one each in Charleston, Huntington, Beckley, and Bluefield. Important that he got a sense of their capabilities and how the satellite court locations functioned. Making the journey by train, he started first in Huntington then followed down the Tug Fork River Valley. He stopped for a day in Matewan to visit his mother before journeying east to Bluefield to spend a couple of days with Noreen before making his way back to Charleston to the north by passing through Beckley.

The United Mine Workers called a nationwide coal mining strike on the first day of November. Affecting bituminous coal mining in many states, 394,000 coal miners out of a total nationwide workforce of 615,000 walked out. 40,000 of those were West Virginia coalminers.

Under the wartime *Lever Act* regulating food and fuel costs, the UMW consented to a wage agreement to run until the end of the Great War. The demand for coal during the war was high, keeping coal mining employment high and wages based on tons produced at an acceptable level. With demand dropping off sharply following the ending of hostilities, the UMW sought to recoup a portion of coalmining profits earned during the war.

Noreen said, "Everyone knew this was coming. My source at Baldwin-Felts said the mine operators along the Tug have been gearing up for months anticipating a possible walkout. Baldwin-Felts has been bringing in more agents. Mostly for the mines along the Tug Fork River Valley. Here's a packet of intelligence to pass on to Keara."

"This young woman at Baldwin-Felts is quite the spy," Burke said.

"That she is. Her father is the chief of police for Bluefield. Her relationship with him is strained. Apparently, he drinks too much. When drunk, Francis says he abuses her mother. Francis has two older brothers. Both have good paying jobs with some of the wealthy mine owners that live in Bramwell just a few miles north of here. Needless to say, Bluefield with Baldwin-Felts headquarters and the area populated with coal mine owners makes for an environment decidedly anti-union, anti-miners."

Burke returned to Charleston temporarily satisfied with his current four deputies. They knew their jobs. Judge Keller praised their efficiency in keeping all the court locations running. While unsure of their political leanings regarding the labor conflicts, Burke put that aside. Those issues were outside the scope of federal law. He was mostly concerned with how they discharged their responsibilities. All the deputies were West Virginians.

None of them held much interest in pursuing enforcement of federal Prohibition laws. Making moonshine was a tradition going back well over a hundred years in Appalachia. Avoiding taxes on liquor part of that way of life. Burke felt the same. Gave his deputies the impression that their new boss was not some crusader stuck here by Washington. His office would enforce blatant violations of the new law but without any vigor. Turning a blind eye to smalltime operators of stills just trying to get by. A bushel and a half of corn could produce a gallon of whiskey. More profitable than the corn it took to make the liquor. Easier to transport. A source of much needed money in this dirt-poor place.

On December 1, 1919, Alan Burke was sworn in as the United States Marshal for the Southern District of West Virginia by Judge Benjamin Keller. The brief low-key ceremony held in Keller's chambers. The only people attending were retiring Marshal Osborne, Deputy Richardson, Acting U.S. Attorney Joseph Kenna, Keara Murphy, and reporters for the *Charleston Gazette* and *Charleston Daily Mail*.

As Burke and Keara left the courthouse, he said, "I need to stop at the hotel before heading over to the office. On meeting all four of my deputies, I was encouraged that they all carried sidearms. This is a rough place. Culturally, disagreements are tall too often settled with guns down here. Doubly true for criminals. Osborne said he did not go armed unless the situation called for it. A foolish practice in this hostile environment. I need to pick up my service issue Browning .45. Conceal it in my shoulder holster under my suit jacket while displaying my badge prominently."

—

The national coal mine strike lasted for forty days. United Mine Workers National President John L. Lewis eventually signed a new labor agreement in December that included a 14% wage increase. However, it did not address other work-related issues. The oppressive conditions of mining coal that Keara Murphy labelled corporate feudalism continued to remain unchanged in West Virginia with the approaching new year of 1920. Mine operators continued to refuse meeting with UMW representatives.

Even with the nationwide coal mining labor agreement, labor relations remained so hostile that West Virginia Governor Cornwell requested intervention by federal troops. While 50% of the West Virginia coal mines were unionized, these were predominately in the northern counties of the state. The focus of UMW District 17's renewed organizing activities centered on a threat to organize a march of thousands of miners into Logan County. A move surely to result in violence. Logan County was ruled by Sheriff Don "Boss" Chafin with his own private army of deputies paid by the mining companies. Chafin was a violence-prone local despot that ruled most everything in Logan County with an iron fist under the color of the law.

The Wilson Administration turned down requests for federal intervention prevalent during the Great War. Washington followed the pre-war policy of limiting use of federal forces in labor disputes only to those situations where state national guard units were unable to maintain public safety.

The UMW wisely rethought their plans for Logan County by moving organizing efforts instead to Mingo County. Burke learned this from his mother who remained very much connected with the UMW. Living in the town of Matewan therefore placed her in the center of the next flashpoint.

CHAPTER 16

West Virginia | December 1919

B urke had the use of a government model T Ford. While useful in the cities, the remoteness of much of southern West Virginia rendered the poorly maintained dirt roads impassable during periods of rain or snow. In early December the weather was cold but too early for snow. His first exploration was to revisit Paint Creek. The coal mine near Mucklow where his father and brother were killed by Baldwin-Felts mine guards eight years earlier in the Battle of Mucklow. This time with a badge he would not be put off.

His first stop, however, was to visit his high school friend Camero Shaw in Pratt. As he drove the 25 miles on the satisfactory road paralleling the Kanawha River, Burke's thoughts strayed to his youth. Sent to Pratt to get an education while his father, brother, and brother-in-law worked in the mines was not a happy period in his life. At the time, he did not recognize his good fortune. His parents sacrifice allowed escaping a life in the mines for a career in the United States Marine Corps. That career now brought him back to West Virginia in a prestigious position. Appointed by the President and confirmed by the Senate no less. Yet West Virginia regrettably resembled a war zone.

Cameron Shaw was delighted to see his old friend. He had read newspaper accounts of Burke's exploits during the Great

219

War in France. Shaw congratulated him on his appointment as U.S. marshal. "Too bad you're coming back again to another coal-field battleground, Alan."

"Such is life, I guess. I want to visit Holly Grove. See if anything is left of where the miners' tent colony was. Thought I'd try this time to get another look where my dad and brother died."

"Can't say if there's much to see about the tent encampment. Mind your step going near the mine though. Everyone's on edge. The settling of this latest nationwide strike hasn't calmed hostilities. Those Baldwin-Felts boys maintain an aggressive profile."

"Well, this time's a little different. I'm the federal law now."

"Just be careful. Those fellas operate outside the law."

Burke left Shaw after lunch and drove the short distance down the road to Mucklow paralleling the railroad tracks. He never lived in the Holly Grove tent encampment, so he was not sure where his family lived following eviction from their mine-owned housing. Driving slowly, he came to a wide clear expanse surrounded by a low hill with trees. Scattered evidence of overturned rusting potbelly stoves and miscellaneous household debris littered the area.

He got out of the car and walked around for several minutes. A disturbing place. The scene of another infamous event that Noreen related in disturbing detail.

Following another provocative incident, striking miners from Holy Grove attacked Mucklow. In retaliation, Kanawha County Sheriff Bonner Hill and bunch of Baldwin-Felts agents then attacked Holly Grove that same night, killing one person and wounding many. They arrived in an armored train called the *Bull Moose Special*, spraying the tent encampment with machine gun fire. The train consisted of a locomotive, passenger car, and iron-plated baggage car outfitted with two machine guns. Financed by the coal companies and constructed at the C&O Railroad workshops in Huntington, Baldwin-Felts used it to escort replacement workers to the mines.

Burke wanted to see the Paint Creek Mine where the gunfight that took the lives of his father and brother that took place. With his official position, he could not be denied as he was when visiting in 1912.

Driving a mile further, a closed gate blocked the road. The sign read, *No Trespassing. Private Property. Residents Only.*

Burke stopped and exited his car. Two armed men stood guard at the gate. Approaching the gate, Burke opened his coat to reveal his badge and said, "I am a United States Marshal. Open the gate."

"Jesus, he's armed!" one of the guards said. The other guard raised his Winchester rifle and pointed it toward Burke.

"Lower your weapon. I'm a federal law enforcement officer."

The other guard said, "What's your business?"

"My business here is none of your concern. Now open the fucking gate!"

Both guards took a step back. One still pointed the rifle at Burke and the other drew a revolver from his hip. "Can't let you do that. Orders."

"You fellas Baldwin-Felts?"

One answered, "Yeah. We work for the mine. This is their property."

Burke said, "They don't own the town of Mucklow. Now, you've one more chance to put down your guns and open the gate." Burke drew his .45 Browning from his shoulder holster.

Both guards looked uncertain as Burke held his gun pointed down to avoid provoking a sudden response from the guards.

"Just leave here, Marshal before there's more trouble."

"I'm not leaving. Drop your guns or I'll shoot both of you. Don't even move a muscle. You'll both be dead before you get off a shot. Killed lots of men with this .45 during the war. Head shots."

After a tense silence, the guard with the revolver said, "Okay. Listen, we'll lower our guns. Frank, lower that rifle. Still can't let you through."

"Gentlemen, you're making this worse. Step over here to the gate. Need to explain how things are."

The guard with the revolver stepped to the gate while his colleague stayed back with his rifle at the ready. Burke smiled and smashed the guard across the side of his head with the Browning, dropping the man to the ground. He then pointed the Browning at the other guard holding the rifle. "Drop the rifle or you're dead."

The guard stood frozen uncertain what to do. "Throw the rifle in the ditch beside the road." The guard complied. "Now unlock the gate then pick up your friend and help him to my car." At the car, Burke handcuffed the injured man. "Help him into the passenger seat then you get behind the wheel. You're both under arrest for threatening a federal officer with a firearm. You're going to drive us to Charleston so I can turn you over to the Sheriff."

The guard said, "We can't leave our post with the gate unlocked."

"Sure you can, unless you want to get the same as your friend."

It took an hour to make the drive back to Charleston. At the sheriff's office, Burke presented his credentials to the startled sheriff's deputy at the desk. "These two gentlemen are under arrest. Charged with threatening a federal law enforcement officer with firearms. You'll be hearing from the U.S. attorney's office for the filing of charges tomorrow."

A stocky man in shirt sleeves came out from an office, "What's going on? Who're these people?"

"I'm the new U.S. Marshal. Name's Burke. And you are?"

"Sheriff Jarrett. Who are these fellows? What happened to that one?"

"They're Baldwin-Felts. The one bleeding resisted arrest. Both pointed weapons at me blocking the road down at Mucklow."

"Christ. They're licensed to carry firearms as private security."

"Doesn't matter. Showed 'em my badge. Can't be threatening people much less a federal officer."

"Sonofabitch. Not a particularly good way to start off, Marshal. Baldwin-Felts employs a lot of security for the coal mines. They're an important part of things here abouts."

"That's what I hear. The folks down in Paint Creek think they're just thugs. They remember the evictions years ago. The shooting up of the miner's tent colony at Holly Grove. Seems I read that was Baldwin-Felts men led by your predecessor Sheriff Hill. They need to understand their place though. They're not law enforcement. You might pass that word around, Sheriff."

Burke immediately went to the federal building to submit the arrest details to Assistant U.S. Attorney Kenna.

Kenna was dumbstruck. Burke had been on the job less than two weeks and was already making waves. "You want me to pursue this?" Kenna asks. "Judge Keller will probably just dismiss the charges if for no reason than to keep the peace. Tensions are already too high. He won't want to involve the feds unnecessarily."

Burke smiled and replied. "No need, Mr. Kenna. It's too small an affair. I made my point. The Marshal Service is not part of this anti-union conspiracy of mining companies and local law enforcement. Call the sheriff's office tomorrow morning. Tell them the Marshal says the incident is too insignificant a matter to prosecute. But let this be a warning against further challenges to federal authority."

———

Burke was certainly not neutral in his feelings about what was going on in West Virginia. Yet he cautioned himself to conserve the use of his authority for serious issues when it involved local government officials. The confrontation at Paint Creek involving Baldwin-Felts agents, however, was a different matter. The private security firm held no official status. His resentment toward Baldwin-Felts ran deep. Little better than hired thugs, there was no reason to shy from confrontation with them regardless of their cozy status with local law enforcement.

Burke's territory spanned twenty-three counties. Although his official duties did not directly involve the coalfields wars, several counties were at the center of the violence. Kanawha County where he was based was clearly one of those. Heading south by train he would cross into Boone County. From there he would head to Logan County then to Mingo County on the Tug Fork River. After a visit with his mother, he would follow the river route southeast to McDowell County, then from there to Mercer County to visit with Noreen.

Burke had never been to the county named for frontiersman Daniel Boone who lived here 125 years earlier. The meeting in the small town of Madison, population 600 with Sheriff John Hill was cordial. Burke was surprised to learn that Hill had only four deputies to cover 500 square miles. The population of the county was 15,000, of which the overwhelming majority were miners and their families. Any violent uprising by striking miners could only be contained by state or federal troops.

His next stop was the town of Logan in Logan County. With the same geographic area as Boone County, it held a population of 41,000 with the majority also involved with coal mining. Yet Logan County stuck out as unique. It was the poster image for Keara Murphy's term corporate feudalism as practiced in West Virginia. The county was virtually ruled by an Appalachian despot by the name of Sheriff Don Chafin.

When Burke arrived in Logan, he began walking toward the train station after disembarking. Two men approached him almost immediately. Coming closer, Burke could see badges on their suit jackets as they stopped in front of him baring his way. "What's your business in Logan?"

Burke opened his coat and suit jacket to reveal his badge which also exposed his .45 in a shoulder holster. "I'm U.S. Marshal Burke. Came here to see Sheriff Chafin."

Seeing Burke's weapon, the larger of the two deputies reacted by pulling his revolver from a holster on his hip while attempting to disarm Burke by reaching for the .45 with his left hand. Bad move against someone practiced in unarmed combat techniques.

Burke reacted by reaching up with his left arm, lifting the deputy's extended arm going for Burke's pistol. Using a classic judo takedown, Burke dropped the man to the ground using his leg for leverage while simultaneously extracting his .45 Browning pistol. With the downed deputy turned toward Burke he mistakenly attempted to raise his right hand holding his revolver. Burke smash him across the side of his head with the .45. The blow was hard enough to knock the man back to the ground and drop his revolver.

The other deputy stunned by Burke's assault fumbled to draw his revolver. In a fluid motion after striking the larger deputy, Burke extended his arm pointing his .45 just a couple of feet from the deputy's face.

"Don't do it! Ease your weapon from the holster."

The uninjured deputy complied, handing his revolver to Burke who stuck it into his waist. The injured deputy remained on the ground but had shakily risen to his knees. Blood seeped through his fingers soaking his shirt from a nasty gash to the side of his forehead. Burke picked up the injured deputy's revolver.

Burke holstered his .45 Browning and emptied the cartridges from both deputies' revolvers. Pocketing the cartridges, he handed the empty revolvers to the standing deputy.

Several people on the station platform witnessing the altercation stood transfixed. Physically confronting the law in Logan County was unthinkable.

Burke yelled, "What the hell did you idiots think you were doing! I announced myself as a federal marshal. I'm here to see Sheriff Chafin. Now you're going to look stupid standing disarmed in front of your boss. How far is it to the sheriff's office?"

The uninjured deputy replied, "Three blocks."

"Give your colleague a hand. He doesn't look so good. Now get moving."

As they entered the sheriff's office another deputy jumped from behind the desk to assist the bloodied deputy. Burke barked at the deputy, "I'm Marshal Burke from Charleston. Get Sheriff Chafin so I can explain what's going on!"

Moments later two men in shirtsleeves with holstered revolvers on their hip emerged from a back office.

"I'm Sheriff Hurst," the taller of the two said.

Interrupting, the shorter man said to the deputies, "What the fuck happened?"

The uninjured deputy said, "Just enforcing the ordinance against carrying weapons when this fellow pulls a weapon and smashed Elmer in the face, Boss."

225

Boss? Burke said to the man, "And you are?"

"I'm Don Chafin. Former sheriff. Right now, I'm officially clerk of the county court while also serving as a deputy sheriff. Running again for sheriff in this fall's election. Frank here's my brother-in-law. He's keeping my desk warm until I get back in the saddle. Now what's this all about, Marshal?"

"These deputies stopped me as I got off the train. Asked about my business in Logan. I announced who I was. Showed them my badge. Said I was here to see you. Regrettably the big fellow got carried away after seeing I was armed. Pulled his weapon on me. Attempted to disarm me. They have no legal authority to do that. I resolved the situation without bloodshed. Well, at least not deadly bloodshed."

Chafin stood there glaring at Burke uncertain what to say. He ran things in Logan. Did not abide anyone challenging his authority. Deciding not to press the matter since this was a federal official, Chafin said, "Regrettable for sure. Now what, Marshal?"

"I could file charges for assaulting a federal officer, possibly citing obstruction. Considering everything going on in southern West Virginia, I'll just caulk this up to poor judgement and let it pass. The big fellow already learned his lesson."

"Very well. Since you came down here to see me, let's go down the street and I'll buy you dinner. Tell you how I see things. Logan County ain't like Kanawha where you're from, or those pestholes of Mingo and McDowell down on the river. "

Burke already knew that Logan County was different. Keara's research painted Don Chafin as something like a southern antebellum plantation owner with slaves. West Virginia might be remote, arguably backward, but this was still the United States. To say the least, Burke's dinner with Chafin was interesting. Chafin did most of the talking allowing Burke to avoid revealing anything as to his feelings concerning the mine wars. He admitted only being born in West Virginia while spending his adult life elsewhere as a soldier. More of an outsider which was true.

—

Burke returned to Charleston after traveling the first week following his swearing in. Recalling the incidents in Paint Creek and Logan, Burke said to Kera, "What I experienced this last week makes everything you write about of parts of West Virginia being foreign to America real in all its ugliness. Baldwin-Felts is a private army of thugs hired by coal mine operators to enforce their pursuit of profits using violence. Then you have this twisted little shit Chafin ruling an entire county like some banana republic dictator."

Keara's research previously determined that Chafin supported the mining companies for his own economic interests. To enhance his iron grip on the County, Chafin replaced the need for the mining companies to pay Baldwin-Felts for muscle by instead paying an unofficial *tax*. The rate was from half a cent to one cent per ton of coal produced to fund a bloated department of county sheriff's deputies. This was serious money. The arrangement was legal under state law and the amounts concealed since no one in the county government ever conducted an audit.

Keara said, "Corruption is rampant across much of West Virginia, but Don Chafin and Logan County stand out as a stark example. Did you know that Chafin is related to the extended Hatfield clan?"

Burke replied, "Not surprising. The Hatfield legacy permeates West Virginia. On this trip when visiting my mother, I learned the chief of police of Matewan is Sid Hatfield and the sheriff of McDowell County is William Hatfield. Then there was Henry Hatfield that became governor during the Paint Creek & Cabin Creek strike. As far as I know, none of these are closely related. Hatfields are spread everywhere across West Virginia.

"According to Noreen, the famous Hatfield-McCoy feud started back during the Civil War. The time West Virginia split off from Virginia to become a border state in 1863 when Virginia being a Confederate State. The Hatfields came from Logan and Mingo Counties in West Virginia, the McCoys from Pike County in Kentucky across the river. Noreen says stories and myths surrounding the feud reflect something fundamental about Appalachian Mountain culture."

To lighten the conversation Keara asked, "Is that your reason for resorting to violence against these characters you recently encountered?"

Burke laughed. "I'd rather think that comes from military training, but who knows."

"What about local law enforcement in the other counties you visited? Keara asked.

"Pleasantly surprised by Sheriff Blankenship of Mingo. Seems a real law enforcement officer caught in an impossible situation. No question that he is not friendly toward Baldwin-Felts. When I visited Mum in Matewan, she also told me the town's chief of police Sid Hatfield openly sides with the miners. A popular guy amongst the locals.

"Different story in McDowell County. Sheriff Hatfield, no relation of the Hatfield guy in Matewan, is probably aligned to the infrastructure controlled by the mine operators. At least that's what I suspect although he avoided discussing specifics. McDowell County experiences fewer violent labor incidents than Mingo.

"Now in Mercer County there is no question where Sheriff Elliott stands. Then again, the entire county is heavily biased toward the interests of the coalmining companies. Baldwin-Felts with their headquarters in Bluefield just ten miles from the county seat in Princeton is an important part of the local power structure according to Noreen."

"How's Noreen's doing?"

"Good, except she's worried about Mother. The UMW has refocused organizing efforts to Mingo County. The town of Matewan is in the center of that. Once again Mother Jones has joined the battle along the Tug Fork. Once school resumes after Christmas, Noreen fears Mother might abandon teaching to resume organizing efforts again.

"I told Noreen I didn't think Mother would do that. When I spoke with her, she seemed more concerned about being of service to the mining community by teaching the children. Mother also embraces the subversive activities encouraged by Noreen as her means of rebellion. Takes pride in the photographs she sends that you publish. I think she likes the idea of being a spy. Yet she and Sheriff Blankenship tell me the mine operators are not backing down. Threatening miners that sign on with the UMW with termination. Things do not look good. Mum is an old war house that doesn't shy from a battle."

Just two days after returning to Charleston, Acting U.S. Attorney Kenna telephoned. "Have you heard the news about Judge Keller, Marshal?"

"No. What's happened?"

"The Judge suffered a severe stroke yesterday. Doctor said it is debilitating. Bedridden, he's now resting at home."

"What's this mean as far as the functioning of the court?"

"Don't know. I've spoken to the Attorney General. He doesn't know either. I suspect cases will be transferred to neighboring federal districts until Keller either recovers or retires. If he can't continue serving on the bench, then it'll mean an appointment to seat a replacement. I'll keep you posted. You might want to consult with your superior at the Department of Justice. Welcome to West Virginia."

—

A week later, Keara received a communication from Noreen. Keara has disguised her identity as the crusading journalist Keara Murphy. Her articles are frequently reprinted or cited in influential publications about West Virginia corruption and the oppression of coalminers. Baldwin-Felts features prominently as the sinister private army taking on the role of law enforcement hired by the mining companies. At the hotel where she has decided they will temporarily reside in a suite, she is known as Mrs. Burke. To receive information from Noreen, she has secured a post office box under the name K. S. Reynolds. Reynolds being her mother's maiden name. The correspondence from Noreen coming from Maude Burke and Francis Duncan is typed without identification or return address should the material fall into the wrong hands.

Opening Noreen's first communication since she and Alan arrived in Charleston, she handed it to Burke. Looks like you got yourself noticed. Read what Noreen just sent from her source inside Baldwin-Felts headquarters. *'Baldwin-Felts chief Thomas Felts and operations supervisor Leland Atwood discussed recent confrontations with the new U.S. Marshal from Charleston. Marshal arrested two Baldwin-Felts agents at Paint Creek then had a violent confrontation in Logan with deputy sheriffs. Baldwin-Felts sources inform them Boss Chafin was sent into a rage over the marshal assaulting one deputy then had the audacity to drag them before Chafin. Atwood ordered Baldwin-Felts operatives to monitor the marshal closely.'*

CHAPTER 17

Matewan, Mingo County, West Virginia | Spring 1920

Since the ending of the national coal mining strike in December the prior year, the longstanding conflict between mining companies and miners deteriorated. Tensions continued to grow in the Williamson Coalfield that spanned the southern half of Mingo County along the north side of the Tug Fork River and across the river in Pike County, Kentucky. The United Mine Workers of America chose this as the new organizing front in southern West Virginia. In a two-day period in April of 1920, close to 300 miners joined the UMW. The Burnwell Coal and Coke Company was among the first mines to retaliate by firing all those miners that joined the UMW. Along with termination, the miners were given three days eviction notice to vacate company-owned housing.

Burnwell Coal & Coke turned to their contracted security force of Baldwin-Felts agents to carry out the evictions. Mingo County and the town of Matewan were however an anomaly in the mine company-dominated southern counties of West Virginia. Mingo County Sheriff George Blankenship, Matewan Police Chief Sid Hatfield, and Matewan Mayor Cabell Testerman openly sided with the coal miners in the longstanding labor dispute of the region. They served as a buffer to the otherwise unrestrained power exercised by the mine owners in most other counties.

A large contingent of Baldwin-Felts agents proceeded with executing evictions from the Burnwell Mining Camp. Sheriff Blankenship backed by a couple of deputies called a halt to action then placed 27 Baldwin-Felts personnel under arrest. Albert Felts, brother to Baldwin-Felts cofounder and managing partner Thomas Felts supervising the eviction process, was among those arrested. After agreeing to provide adequate notifications of evictions and to allow only county law enforcement to supervise those evictions, charges were dropped. Sheriff Blankenship made further progress by negotiating with UMW officials to restrain striking miners from taking violent action if evictions were supervised by county officials.

In early May, Fred Mooney and William Blizzard arrived from the state headquarters of the United Mine Workers to supervise organizing activities in Mingo County. In a steady rain downpour, they addressed an outdoor rally of 3,000 miners. Following the rally, most of the attendees signed memberships in the UMW union. The achievement appeared even more significant with the mining companies universally forcing miners to sign restrictive employment contracts that became known as *Yellow Dog* contracts as a condition for employment.

These notorious employment agreements stated the miner understood that joining a labor union would result in immediate termination. The agreements first came into use in West Virginia coal mining by the Hitchman Coal Company in Wheeling in 1907. Numerous injunctions filed by mining companies in the West Virginia courts over the years resulted in injunctions allowing enforcement of the agreements. While the UMW pursued redress in the state appellate court, the coal mining companies in southern West Virginia now widely adopted using *Yellow Dog* contracts as another instrument to impede organizing efforts by the United Mine Workers.

In Mingo County after reaching agreement with Baldwin-Felts, Sheriff Blankenship ignored his pledge to supervise evictions of the residences of striking miners using the excuse that he was awaiting circuit court rulings. The tactic worked temporarily after the UMW's Mooney and Blizzard admonished the unionized miners to obey the law and await the courts to deliver a ruling. Several Mingo County mine companies were of no mind to delay. Striking miners could not continue to occupy company-owned housing. They turned to Baldwin-Felts to implement evictions forthwith.

U.S. Senate hearings brought public attention to the brutal excesses of Baldwin-Felts operatives during the Paint Creek-Cabon Creek Strike seven years earlier. As a result, the West Virginia legislature enacted legislation intended to curb the use of force by Baldwin-Felts. However, the language of the statute failed to provide any penalty for violations rendering it meaningless. Critics claimed the glaring failure of the statute was intentional to present a fig leaf of reform with no power of enforcement. As quieter years of labor unrest in the coalfields passed during the United States participation in the war in Europe, the legislation was ignored. This emboldened the mining companies and Baldwin-Felts to proceed forcefully against this new threat of union penetration.

The Stone Mountain Coal Company mining camp just outside the town of Matewan became Baldwin-Felts first target following the strike that ended the previous December. On the morning of May 19, 1920, Albert Felts and a contingent of Baldwin-Felts agents, including another brother Lee Felts, arrived in Matewan on a morning train from headquarters in Bluefield. Stepping down from the train, the group of seven made their way to the Urias Hotel on Mate Street. The day overcast with sporadic light rain.

Matewan had a population of only 800. The sight of a several men in working clothes milling about in the middle of the day foretold of a possible confrontation with what Baldwin-Felts came to do. Before proceeding to the mining camp to execute evictions, Albert Felts understood that he might face armed resistance from miners. Regardless, he expected to carry out the evictions within the day then leave before County Sheriff Blankenship could interfere by bringing in deputies from Williamson. Matewan had only a police chief and one regular deputy.

After eating lunch at the Urias Hotel, the Baldwin-Felts agents exited the hotel carrying rifles to await the next train bringing five additional Baldwin-Felts agents. To hedge his bets, Albert Felts attempted to bribe Matewan Mayor Testerman to allow for strategic placement of machine guns in the town should circumstances turn ugly. Testerman refused.

By prior arrangement made by the sympathetic hotel owner, the agents then piled into three waiting automobiles. Onlookers watched as the vehicles drove out of town along the road up Mate Creek. Everyone knew their destination was likely the Stone Mountain Coal Company mine camp just a quarter mile from town. Word spread warning of the arrival of the reviled Baldwin-Felts thugs.

A short time later, word came that the agents had begun evicting remaining miner families occupying company-owned housing. The process included unnecessarily ransacking the small houses and throwing all the belongings outside onto the muddy ground.

Maude Burke had spent the night with one of the striking miner families still occupying one of the company-owned weatherboard cabins. She volunteered to help remaining families move their belongings to a tent encampment erected by the UMW off mining company-owned property. Maude also arranged for a wagon with a team of horses to transport miner's household goods to the tent community. The relocation began the day before. Today was the deadline imposed by the eviction notice. With assurances from Sheriff Blankenship, no one expected the arrival of armed Baldwin-Felts agents to forcibly evict those remaining tenants.

Maude and the woman residing in the house were in the process of carrying goods to the wagon when two Baldwin-Felts agents pushed past them entering the house. A moment later, they pushed the man of the house outside at gunpoint. Without saying anything, the agents began smashing dishes followed by throwing goods outside with deliberate destructive intent.

Maude stepped outside and withdrew her camera from a pocket in her apron. As she snapped repeated photographs, one of the agents saw what she was doing as he stepped from the doorway and heaved a sack of flour that ruptured when hitting the ground. Reaching back inside the house, he grabbed his rifle and quickly approached Maude.

"What the fuck you doin' you old bitch!" the large man yelled. Without warning he smashed Maude in the head with the butt of his Winchester rifle. The blow delivered with full force made evident the malicious disregard for life held by Baldwin-Felts.

A group of miners and family members witnessing the assault moved in closer. Albert Felts motioned for several of his agents to force back the miners with their weapons. Several women rushed to attend to Maude Burke lying unconscious. The woman whose house was ransacked said to her husband, "Frank, we must get Mrs. Burke to the doctor. She's in a bad way. I'll fetch a mattress to make her comfortable in the wagon so we can get her to Matewan."

As the wagon left with Maude still unconscious, Matewan Mayor Cabell Testerman and Police Chief Sid Hatfield arrived and confronted Albert Felts. Hatfield said, "What the hell you boys think you're doin'?"

Albert Felts understood that Sid Hatfield sided with the miners. He also knew Hatfield could be a threat. He was known not only as "Smiling Sid", but also "Two- gun Sid" for the two revolvers he carried.

Felts said, "The circuit judge in Williamson gave approval to remove these people from mining company property. These miners are on strike. Can't be living here while not paying rent."

Hatfield replied, "Show me the court order."

Felts said, "Wasn't time to get it in writing. You can call the court clerk."

Outnumbered, Hatfield and Testerman returned to Matewan. Felts and his agents resumed the evictions.

By 1:30pm, Hatfield and Testerman made contact by telephone with the county sheriff's office then county prosecutor Wade Bronson. Bronson told them, "The evictions are illegal. I'll get the judge to sign arrest warrants. I'll have them ready by the time you get someone up here to pick them up. In the meantime, proceed with arresting these Baldwin-Felts individuals."

The situation was primed to ignite. One of the telephone operators warned the Urias Hotel owner who informed Felts and his agents later in the afternoon after returning from the evictions at the Stone Mountain camp. Mayor Testerman and police Chief Sid Hatfield awaited the arrival of the 5:15 train from Williamson for formal arrest warrants before moving against Baldwin-Felts.

The arriving train with the warrants was the same train the Baldwin-Felts would take to return to Bluefield. By now, the entire town knew the situation as miners began filtering in from the Stone Mountain camp. They spread word of mine guards evicting six families and clubbing an old woman trying to help the mining families. As the Baldwin-Felts agents waited in the Urias Hotel, Mayor Testerman said to UMW loyalist Hugh Combs, "Gather a dozen sober-minded men to back up Chief Hatfield as special police officers."

Forewarned of what Hatfield was up to, the Baldwin-Felts agents broke down their Winchester rifles and packed them in suitcases. Albert Felts and his two top deputies Lee Felts and C. B. Cunningham stuck revolvers in their belts since they were the only detectives licensed to carry firearms in Matewan. They did not want to give Chief Hatfield a reason for their arrest.

As the Baldwin-Felts contingent left the hotel to walk to the train station, they were stopped by Sid Hatfield who said to Albert Felts. "I have warrants to arrest all of you. Issued by County Prosecutor Branson and signed by the court."

Felts chuckled. "Well, ain't that somethin'. I've got a warrant right here to arrest you."

Both Hatfield and Felts continued walking while both seemed to make light of the standoff until joined by Mayor Testerman. Standing in front of Chambers Hardware Store across from the train station Felts said, "I have an arrest warrant for Sid Hatfield. He'll be coming with me back to Bluefield."

Testerman said, "That's bullshit. You have no authority to make arrests. Let me see that warrant." Felts extracted a folded paper from his jacket and handed it to Testerman. After reading the document, Testerman declared, "This is a bogus warrant."

They all stood in the doorway to the hardware store out of the light drizzle. Details are unclear as to what followed. Witnesses would provide conflicting observations as to who fired the first shot. What is clear is that during the opening moments of what developed into a raging gunfight, Albert Felts fell dead and Matewan Mayor Cabell Testerman was mortally wounded. Sid Hatfield would claim that Felts fired first shooting Testerman causing Hatfield to then shoot Felts.

Enraged miners led by Hugh Combs and his deputized group of armed miners proceeded to gun down the Baldwin-Felts agents. It was a one-sided slaughter with only two remaining Baldwin-Felts armed with revolvers able to return fire. Having dismantled their weapons earlier, the other Baldwin-Felts agents were executed. The death toll ran to seven dead among the Baldwin-Felts contingent with six miraculously escaping. The dead included brothers Albert and Lee Felts. The dead on the opposing side included Matewan Major Cabell Testerman and two miners.

Sid Hatfield became a heroic figure to coal miners. The first successful defeat of the mining company hired thugs. For Baldwin-Felts chief Thomas Felts, the conflict turned personal with the death of his two brothers. For many others in positions of official power, it gave license for them to violently exercise their anti-miner bias.

America in 1920 was also suffering other anxieties. Following the Russian Revolution and the creation of the Bolshevik Communist Soviet Union, the Red Scare made populist organizations such as labor unions politically suspect. Many in the labor movement espoused socialism that many people equated to communism. This was also the era of *Jim Crow* laws. West Virginia with its large number of African American coal miners' population was no stranger to this latent attempt to segregate blacks from white society. Congress was politically now conservative republican. The forthcoming presidential election favored whoever would be the republican candidate. All this meant a decided turn in Washington favoring business interests over labor.

What would become known as the *Battle of Matewan* became a defining event that would ignite continued violence for the next eighteen months in the bloodiest labor war in American history.

—

The miners delivered Maude Burke to a large house in Matewan, the home of the only doctor in the area. The large parlor served as a medical office. It was only modestly equipped, suitable largely for treating minor accidents and stabilizing patients requiring hospital treatment with the closest hospital in Williamson fifteen miles away.

When Maude arrived, she was conscious but required help from the miners transporting her to get her into the doctor's office onto an examining bed. The laceration required suturing. However, the doctor was more concerned with the dramatic swelling and the likelihood of concussion. Possibly even a cranial fracture. He did not have x-ray equipment. His examination and her responses to his questions showed symptoms of concussion. She must be transported to Williamson for urgent treatment.

The miners delivering Maude to the doctor returned to the Stone Mountain Miners camp. The Baldwin-Felts agents were just leaving to return to Matewan. One of the miners approached a man in a suit speaking with the families sifting through damaged belongings piled on the ground outside their former dwellings.

"You from the Union?"

William Blizzard replied, "Yes. I'm Bill Blizzard."

"Those bastards clubbed an old woman a while ago. She's in a bad way. Just took her to the doctor in town. She wasn't even one of us. Stayed with us last night to help us move out today. Then these Baldwin-Felts bastards came. Maude Burke's a fine lady. No call to do that to her."

"Maude Burke? I know her," Blizzard said. "Is she badly injured?"

"Could be. She's with the doctor now."

"Where's that?"

"Take the road to town. Big white house on your left with a sign on a post. Can't miss it."

Bill Blizzard knew of Maude Burke who was close to his mother during the Paint Creek & Cabin Creek Strike eight years ago. Worked alongside Mother Jones. Blizzard arrived at the doctor's house much to the relief of the doctor. "Mrs. Burke's taken a turn for the worst. Can you drive her to the hospital in Williamson? Blizzard replied, "Certainly."

The doctor's wife fixed blankets and pillows in the back seat of Blizzard's four-door Chevrolet sedan to make her comfortable. All three situated Maude laying down in the backseat.

The fifteen-mile drive to Williamson on the road parallelling the Tug Fork River took close to an hour driving slowly to minimize jarring from potholes. The doctor telephoned ahead to the hospital to explain the patient's condition.

While waiting to hear of Maude Burke's condition, Blizzard overheard an emotional conversation at the reception desk. The receptionist was obviously distressed by what the caller told her. Hanging up, she excitedly summoned another hospital staffer to relate news of a massive shooting in Matewan. The hospital should prepare for possible casualties.

Blizzard learned that the hospital reached Maude's daughter by telephone. She would arrive in Williamson early the next tomorrow morning. With nothing more to be done for Maude, Blizzard returned to Matewan to investigate what happened after he left just several hours earlier.

—

The following afternoon, Alan Burke arrived at the hospital from Charleston. Noreen was there speaking to a Catholic priest in the visitor waiting area.

"How is she?" Alan asked his sister.

"The doctor says she's stable. She has a skull fracture and a severe concussion. This is Father Geary who was here making rounds of patients when mother was brought in."

Occupied with other thoughts, Alan nodded and shook the priest's offered hand.

Father Geary said, "A United Mine Workers official by the name of Bill Blizzard drove your mother here from Matewan yesterday afternoon. Told me a mine guard struck her in the head with the butt of a Winchester. Seems your mother was helping mining families being evicted by Baldwin-Felts. You may have heard that some justice was done after that when the murderous bastards tried to leave Matewan. Seven reported killed."

"Yes. I heard the news before leaving Charleston."

"Your sister said you are the new United States marshal. Such a terrible beginning for your new job."

"Right you are, Father. Another war zone. Please excuse me now. I must see my mother. Can you lead the way, Noreen?"

Maude Burke was asleep. Noreen whispered to Alan, "They have her sedated for the pain. When she is conscious, she doesn't seem to remember what happened. Maybe a good thing. Seems confused. Speech is blurred. Has bouts of nausea. The doctor says the seriousness of the skull fracture is possible bruising of the brain which can cause swelling. Internal bleeding becomes a more serious possibility. Nothing much can be done for treatment. Just keeping her still and comfortable. Closely monitor her condition. Recovery may take time."

Returning to the waiting room, Father Geary was still there speaking to staff. Seeing Alan and Noreen, he said. "Let me drive you to a hotel. Are you both staying on in Williamson until you know more about your mother's condition?"

Alan answered, "Yes."

"Perhaps I might see you here tomorrow. Good to chat with an Irishman with a heritage from Ireland's rebel county?"

Alan looked puzzled. Geary clarified, "Noreen said your family emigrated from County Cork like mine. Known as a rebel county for a hundred years of rebellion against the British. The Irish War of Independence going on as we speak is being waged most vigorously in County Cork. The oppression of coal miners in West Virginia shares much with British oppression. I'd like to learn your views as a federal law enforcement officer. Maybe we can talk when I make my rounds tomorrow to my infirmed parishioners."

"I'll be here all day tomorrow. Waiting for my wife coming down from Charleston to help my sister look after my mother. The day after tomorrow I must go to Matewan. Although what happened in Matewan is a state and local matter, the implications may be far reaching. I need to get a better understanding of the current state of law and order."

"Thought I should do the same. Lots of Catholics in Matewan. I try to get down there at least every other Sunday to say mass in the afternoon. I have a car. Care to ride down with me?"

"Thank you. I'll take you up on your offer."

CHAPTER 18

Mingo County, West Virginia | Summer 1920

Father Geary drove an old Model T Ford that was showing signs of use from traveling the poor roads of Mingo County. With Burke settled in the passenger seat, they left Williamson early the next morning.

"Before you arrived, your sister told me about your mother. How she became active in unionizing efforts of the coal miners since the troubles during the strike of 1912 in Kanawha County. Told about losing your father, your brother, and her husband. She also recounted a couple of incidents since you became marshal for southern West Virginia. Is it fair to say you are sympathetic to the plight of the coal miners?"

"You could say that. Can't abide this situation where mining companies exert control of the workforce in every aspect of their lives. Critics call it corporate feudalism."

"Corporate feudalism? Yes, your sister used that term. A most appropriate label. Miss Hannigan is a most astute woman. She also told me something of your illustrious military background. Seems you don't shy away from a fight."

Geary continued minutes later. "Sheriff Blankenship is a fine fellow. Follows the law. Not in the pay of the mining companies. Not much he can do though against the likes of Baldwin-Felts. He only has two regular deputies. After what happened in Matewan, what do you suppose the governor will do? "

"Can't say. Suspect he'll likely use the state police force established months ago after the strike settled last December. West Virginia no longer has a National Guard. They mobilized for the Great War but disbanded after the Armistice and never reinstated. Then again, he might declare martial law and ask for federal troops."

"Since you represent federal law enforcement, is there anything you can do?"

"Unfortunately, no. All this violence violates only state law. I'm going to Matewan for the purpose of assessing the situation to keep Washington apprised should the governor declare martial law and request federal troops. The problem with past martial law declarations is that it does not resolve anything. Just temporally halts the violence. Suspends most civil rights that punishes striking miners without affecting mining companies or their hired guards."

Geary said, "Last evening, I mentioned the war going on in Ireland. Lots of parallels with the plight of the coal miners. I blessed the local boys of the West Virginia National Guard that went off to France in the Great War. In this world filled with oppression I think about the biblical warriors of the Old Testament like Joshua and Gideon. They did God's work. I believe God favors the just in times of war. I pray for those IRA lads fighting the security forces of the British Empire. Someone needs to fight the cause of these West Virginia coal miners who suffer under similar oppression enforced by the gun."

Father Geary then gave Burke a brief accounting of his background. "I come from a long line of Fenian rebels. My parents emigrated from Ireland in 1870 as part of a general British amnesty. They settled in the Bronx in New York City. At the time my father was a fellow prisoner of Irish revolutionary Jeremiah O'Donovan Rossa. Both agreed to leave Ireland under the conditions of the amnesty. Father made a good life here blacksmithing. Rossa continued his fight against the British from exile in New York City.

"Being a bright student while attending Catholic school, the parish priest was instrumental in securing me a position to attend St. John's Seminary in Boston. Of course, Boston is heavily Irish with anti-British sentiments firmly ingrained from descendants of the exodus of the Great Famine in the late 1840s. Upon ordination as a priest in 1896, the seminary rector secured me a position in the heavily Irish Catholic southern West Virginia coalfields. I served in the Cathedral in Charleston for a time before becoming **pastor** of Sacred Heart Catholic Church in Williamson almost twenty years ago. Given my background, I cannot ignore the oppression suffered by my parishioners. My journey from Boston to West Virginia is God calling me to action."

Burke knew of Jeremiah O'Donovan Rossa. After exile from Ireland, it was Rossa that organized a bombing campaign against infrastructure targets in Great Britain. Participation by Burke's father and older brother led to their flight to America to escape British justice. No need to relate that personal information to Father Patrick Geary. However, the priest could become a useful source of information into the miners' community.

"Yet how to confront a particular injustice in a meaningful way is often unclear. As a priest you are in the business of confronting evil. Do you not feel the futility of your efforts?"

"Very much so. As a priest, I turn to prayer. Yet to avoid discouragement, I believe I must do something more tangible. Something that may have material effect even if only in some small way. For example, speaking of these things to you."

"How should that help oppressed coal miners?" Burke responded.

"Couldn't say exactly. But I believe you to be a good man. A man of courage that deplores injustice. A soldier that has turned to enforcing the law. Someone holding a unique position of authority in this violent land of divided loyalties. As the saying goes, the Lord moves in mysterious ways."

Burke had no idea how Father Geary thought he might help the coal miners. For a man of God, Geary seemed to harbor a distinctively secular militancy. Listening to his support for the Irish Republican Army rebels involved in the current Irish rebellion,

Geary never left behind his Fenian heritage. As for Burke, although born a Catholic and baptized, neither he nor his family attended mass. His religious feelings at best described as ambivalent. Nonetheless, he liked Father Geary.

As they pulled onto Mate Street running parallel to the railroad tracks with the Tug Fork River on the other side of the railroad tracks, Matewan buzzed with activity. Causing the commotion was a group of over a dozen men in working clothes holding rifles at the ready. They surrounded a wheeled freight trolley holding two caskets.

With Father Geary at his side, Burke approached one of the men holding a rifle. Burke pulled open his jacket to display his badge. "What's going on here?"

The man looked at Burke's badge then registered an instant of surprise noticing the .45 pistol in his shoulder holster. "Two dead Baldwin-Felts fellas in those coffins. Brothers of that fella in the fancy suit standing next to the coffins I'm told. Waitin' for the train heading south to take them for burial."

"Who are you guys?" Burke asked.

"Special deputies. Sheriff Blankenship came into town just hours after the shootout on Wednesday and deputized a dozen of us. Afraid an army of Baldwin-Felts might descend on Matewan and start a real war."

"Where's Sheriff Blankenship?"

"He's with the local police chief Sid Hatfield. That building over there next to the post office."

Inside Chambers Hardware Store, Sheriff Blankenship sat with Sid Hatfield. Burke shook hands with Blankenship who he had previously met then Sid Hatfield. Ushered outside, Blankenship said, "Sid Hatfield shot Albert Felts. Felts shot Matewan Mayor Testerman and maybe Ed Chambers. Who fired first depends on who you ask. It'll be a long time sorting out this mess. I rushed here from Williamson and deputized a bunch of men that I hope can be trusted to not get out of hand. Afraid that Baldwin-Felts chief Thomas Felts might overreact. He's that fella in a suit standing outside the train depot supervising the return of the bodies of his brothers Albert and Lee Felts."

"How you going to maintain order, Sheriff?" Burke asked. "These miners you deputized aren't exactly neutral."

"Governor is sending down a contingent of state police. Should be here sometime today. For the time being, I'm still the law in Mingo. Mark my words there's goin' to be hell to pay for what happened here. Several witnesses say Sid Hatfield shot Albert Felts in self-defense. Seems certain though that Albert Felts shot and killed Mayor Testerman."

Burke and Father Geary went about Mingo asking questions of individuals that were in town at the time of the shootout. Burke got the distinct impression that the miners gunned down some of Baldwin-Felts agents that were unarmed at the time while trying to escape. A couple of miners even proudly displayed a suitcase containing a disassembled Winchester Model 1886 rifle, standard-issue for Baldwin-Felts detectives.

Finished in town, Burke located his mother's apartment, and with the help of Father Geary, they packed her meager belongings. Unlikely she would be returning anytime soon.

As Father Geary drove back to Williamson, he said to Burke, "Apart from telling me about your wartime exploits, your sister said you possessed certain unusual combat skills. She remarked that you once told her, *my job is not only to teach soldiers how to kill the enemy but how to survive.* What skills was she referring to?"

Rarely did Burke speak of his deadly skills. No way to convey delicately, it was better to avoid detail. Geary seemed to have a reason for asking, so he'd make an exception.

"Close quarter combat. How to strike first and immediately kill or disable your opponent. How to prevail if unarmed, armed with a knife, or with a sidearm. In close combat, death is measured in seconds."

"How did you come by these skills?"

"Partly from my older brother then later in the Marines from a sergeant in the Philippines that was proficient in the Japanese martial art of judo. He modified the defensive moves of judo by incorporating deadly blows after disabling your opponent. The sergeant understood about vulnerable points of the body and how to kill silently.

"As for my firearms proficiency, seems I was born with some special eye-hand skill that allowed shooting a handgun with exceptional accuracy. Unlike a rifle, shooting a handgun accurately is more difficult. At twenty-five feet I can put repeated rounds through a playing card."

"Besides knowing how to kill efficiently, does that mean you know how to defend just as effectively?"

Burke looked over at Geary. "No. My comment about keeping my men form getting killed relied on killing the enemy first. Not truly what I'd call defensive tactics. What's this about, Father?"

"Again, I don't have anything specific to suggest. The miners are not soldiers yet they're fighting a real shooting war against an enemy experienced using firearms. Seems they could benefit from some military training. Defensive tactics when coming under attack. What better person than a proven expert in a range of combat skills?"

"You can't be serious, Father. I'm a U.S. marshal. What you're suggesting must be illegal."

"Possibly. I don't know the law all that well, but I'd think it an arguable distinction between instructing in self-defense and abetting a crime. If your participation remains clandestine, that becomes academic."

"How would I hide my identity." Burke was intrigued by a Catholic priest advocating violent resistance.

"Gave that some thought. You're new to West Virginia. Your face is not known to miners. Change your appearance slightly. You've still got a touch of Irish accent. With a cover story that you've been involved with Irish rebels and had to flee Ireland makes for a credible reason for helping Irish coal miners. All of us fighting the same type of enemy."

"You are serious," Burke said. Not sure that he bought into Geary's crazy idea, but he couldn't deny a kernel of interest.

"Make this an Irish thing. You train some trusted Irish miners. Fellas already bent on resisting beyond just striking back. Question is, do you think a small number of trained men can make a difference?"

"They can make an impact. What kind of impact might be hard to predict. Could have unintended consequences. How broad an impact depends on a great number of variables. Not the least of which is determining who they'll be up against. Baldwin-Felts certainly, but what about law enforcement? State police? Federal troops? Taking up arms against Baldwin-Felts thugs might be argued as self-defense given the circumstances, but not law enforcement. Even those like Don Chafin's deputies in Logan County. Any violence against law officers becomes a criminal offense. I personally will not be any part of that. Question becomes does providing technical assistance become a criminal offense?"

"That you're even discussing this further means you have an interest in helping, my son."

Burke remained silent. There did exist an interest. Already he was thinking how he might contribute to Noreen's subversive conspiracy. Her network involving Mum, Keara, and a spy inside Baldwin-Felts. He felt just as strongly about the miners' struggle. Thoughts of those many places in which he fought for the wrong side remained a constant source of guilt. There was no such question as to the right side in this fight.

There must be some meaningful way for him to contribute. While his position as a federal law enforcement officer offered no official capacity in which to participate, it still provided reason for intruding into the conflict. Since federal forces might become involved, he held the status of an official observer. He regularly reported to the Department of Justice. Newsworthy events such as the details of the Matewan incident he communicated by telegram, more confidential intelligence with observations sent by mail at least weekly.

When Burke returned to the Appalachian Hotel in Williamson, he said to Geary, "Thank you for your kindness in watching over my mother and helping me gather her belongings. I'll consider our discussion. "We'll talk again, Father." Keara had arrived earlier. A message at the desk said she was at the hospital.

After kissing Keara and his sister sitting in the waiting room, Burke asked, "How is Mother?"

Noreen said, "According to the doctor, better. Actually, he said hopeful. There doesn't seem to be signs of excessive pressure on the brain that would indicate intercranial bleeding. She still experiences severe headache pain, so they regularly administer sedatives. She's asleep right now."

Burke nodded. "How long must she stay in the hospital?"

"They're not sure. Depends on progress. Doctor says she can leave in a couple of days if she continues making progress."

Keara said, "The doctor showed us the x-ray. The fracture to her skull is clearly evident. Must have been a terrible blow she received. Even when she leaves, she'll be needing looking after for some time."

"I've already made arrangements with Olivia Snyder my boardinghouse landlady. Mother can share my bedroom. There's room to squeeze another single bed into the room. Olivia and the housekeeper are there all day to attend to any of Mum's needs while I'm at the school."

"Wonderful. Father Geary was kind enough to help me gather Mum's belongings from Matewan. They're at the hotel."

Keara said, "When they brought your mother in, she was clutching her camera. The UMW fellow that drove her to Williamson told Father Geary that a miner said she was taking pictures when one of the Baldwin-Felts struck her with a rifle. Geary gave me the camera. I took out a roll of exposed film. Maybe she captured images before being injured. Such photographs will add clarity to what newspapers are labelling the *Battle of Matewan* or the *Massacre of Matewan*. Since Baldwin-Felts' so-called detectives suffered more casualties, some newspapers are suggesting they were victims. Photos showing the provocative incident that precipitated the shootings might go toward countermanding that depiction of events."

Before accompanying Keara and Noreen to relocate his mother to Bluefield by train, Burke paid a visit to Father Geary. After again expressing his thanks for helping with his mother, he told Geary, "In my opinion it is ill advised to attempt to train miners in combat techniques to defend against Baldwin-Felts. The mining companies have the weight of most local law enforcement on their side. The governor cannot allow a total breakdown of society. If the miners attempt wholesale confrontation there will be no alternative but to turn to the federal government to restore order by using the U.S. Army. If that happens there could be dire consequences. The miners can't win. Should they try, it would damage their position with the public."

—

In the wake of the carnage in Matewan Governor Cornwell was under pressure from the mining companies to request federal assistance and declare martial law. Had there been a reconstituted West Virginia National Guard after the Great War, Cornwell might have done that. Seriously ill President Woodrow Wilson still suffering the effects of a stroke in October of 1919 resisted a declaration of martial law that required use of regular U.S. Army troops in the absence of a West Virginia National Guard. Governor Cornwell was therefore forced to rely solely on his small state police force.

The officially named Department of Public Safety created the prior year in the wake of labor unrest consisted of only 121 troopers. Cornwell appointed Jackson Arnold, a combat veteran and grandnephew of Confederate General 'Stonewall' Jackson, as superintendent. The best Cornwell could do was send a company of state troopers to Mingo County to augment Sheriff Blankenship's meager police force.

For a brief interlude, violence abated in Mingo. That changed in July when the UMW called a new strike. Baldwin-Felts resumed evictions of miners from mine-owned housing. Miners countered by harassing arriving strikebreakers. Railroad coal gondolas were destroyed along with mine equipment, particularly tipples, the equipment that conveyed extracted coal into an apparatus for loading into railroad gondolas. Tipples were the most exposed equipment and easily disabled with readily available dynamite. Random acts of sniper fire on both sides left enough dead and wounded to create a climate of terror for mining families. The state police with insufficient manpower failed to maintain order in Mingo County.

—

Once in Bluefield, Burke was even more impressed with Noreen's commanding fortitude in overcoming continual setbacks. Surviving made her stronger. She had everything concerning the care of their mother well planned. That included finding a doctor in Bluefield after satisfied with his competence in treating her mother's injury. Noreen brought along the medical file with the x-rays and comments by the attending physician in Williamson. Alan and Keara would spend two nights in Bluefield in a vacant room at Olivia Snyder's boarding house. Burke was comforted by the close friendship between Noreen and the landlady, Olivia Snyder.

That first night, Alan, Keara, and Noreen went to a restaurant in Bluefield to talk alone. Not about their mother but better that she be left out of what was on his mind. He needed their input on what they thought he should or could do to contribute toward helping the plight of West Virginia coal miners.

After explaining Father Geary's attempt to recruit his services to train miners in tactics and using weapons, Keara said, "This guy's a Catholic priest? Sounds more like an IRA recruiter."

"More like an IRA rebel ready to pick up a gun," Alan replied.

Noreen smiled. "He's one of those affable Irish characters that has a dark side. Hope I didn't tell him too much about your background, Alan."

"Not to worry. What you told the good father is already public knowledge. He'll become a good source of information within the miners' community. So will this young fellow Bill Blizzard with the Union. But the Union doesn't always represent the views of all miners. Miner's wives might hold views different from their husbands."

"How true. Women's voices are often lost, Keara said. "It's their more nuanced outlook that often see issues portrayed in black and white terms as gray."

Alan said, "That's why I'd like your opinions. I want to do more. Contribute to the efforts you, Noreen, and Mother have put together to make a difference. However, instructing miners in combat skills doesn't seem a good idea. I'm a known government official. Besides, I fear it might embolden them to engage in even more violent confrontations. That gets into dangerous ground. Ever read the Gothic novel *Frankenstein*? Talk about unintended consequences."

Noreen said, "Yes. Backed by politicians and even the courts, Baldwin-Felts will always enjoy an unfair advantage."

Burke said, "Speaking of Baldwin-Felts, tell us more about this young woman Francis Duncan. According to Keara, Duncan's insider material gives her articles a sense of how invaluable Baldwin-Felts is by providing mine operators the physical means of intimidating the coal miners."

"Francis possesses strong convictions. I agonize over what I can tell Keara that is safe to publish without incriminating her as the source. Baldwin-Felts infiltrates spies into the UMW, so they must be sensitive to securing their own confidential information. If they should suspect a spy in their midst, Francis would be in real danger. Yet her material is also an example of unintended consequences. The reason Mother was at the Stone Mountain Mine Camp where she was injured came from Francis' advance information about the forced eviction."

CHAPTER 19

Mercer & McDowell Counties, West Virginia | Summer 1920

Noreen Burke Hannigan came to Bluefield in 1913 following the rift with her mother. Since that time, she had made a new life. Freed from a life directly involved with coalmining proved transformative. Her relationship with her mother even improved. Circumstances caused both to settle into independent lives. They remained close enough to feel a sense of family yet separated by ninety miles forced interaction mostly by letters with occasional visits. Maude Burke had also lost much of her activist zeal in union organizing. Returning to teaching children of mining families with a modest wage from the UMW replaced more active militancy.

For Noreen, Bluefield in Mercer County was still coal mining territory but a town of 15,000 inhabitants. More prosperous with less labor strife than small Matewan in Mingo County where her mother chose to live to continue working with the United Mine Workers. Bluefield was removed from the worst of labor violence. Perhaps influenced by being the headquarters of the Baldwin-Felts Detective Agency. It was comparatively more cosmopolitan than other towns its size in southern West Virginia. The Norfolk & Western Railroad made its Pocahontas Division headquarters here. Just six miles north of Bluefield was the small town of Bramwell. In the late 1800s Bramwell acquired some notoriety for having the largest number of millionaires per capita in the United States. Numerous large homes were built in the town by wealthy coal operators. The area provided much better teaching opportunities for Noreen while remaining within manageable distance to her mother.

Although Mercer County was heavily in the pocket of the mining companies, that did not directly affect Noreen. Living in a place with less labor strife was welcoming. Finding a rewarding teaching position allowed for transforming her life at age thirty-nine. Settled into a new life alone, Noreen however did not become a recluse. With a sharp mind and engaging nature, she made friends easily. Her chosen environment proved a life-altering decision.

—

Noreen first met Francis Duncan when she was a high school senior in Noreen's history class in 1915. The daughter of the Bluefield chief of police is 22 years old in 1920. Exceptionally intelligent but plain in appearance enough to limit good prospects for marriage with little chance for developing a real career in Appalachia. Graduating from Concorde State Normal College in Athens, West Virginia the prior year, she did not want to teach school. The small teachers' college was the best she could do with limited funds and only 20 miles from Bluefield. Duncan wanted to save enough money to eventually leave Bluefield and attend a regular university in a larger urban environment. As much as anything, she yearned to be on her own in a larger city offering greater career opportunities for a smart woman.

Her father's connections secured her a clerical position with Baldwin-Felts Detectives Agency headquartered in Bluefield. She quickly stood out among the clerical staff and began handling all manner of confidential material, including taking shorthand for managing partner Thomas Felts and Operations Supervisor Leland Atwood.

At the annual community Fourth of July celebration in Bluefield in 1920, Duncan sat with Noreen discussing the renewed labor hostilities in Mingo County with the calling of a new strike. Duncan valued Noreen's counsel as a person she admired. Noreen is everything Duncan aspires to achieve. A single woman making her own way using her intellect. Long ago Duncan abandoned the idea of marriage. Without the physical appearance to attract a suitable suitor, prospects were non-existent in rural West Virginia.

On a sunny Saturday, Duncan and Noreen were sitting alone on a blanket under a large shade tree sharing a picnic lunch of fried chicken and bottles of coca cola. They were out of earshot by other picnickers. Duncan invited Noreen as an opportunity to relate firsthand news from inside Baldwin-Felts. Normally her communications with Noreen are carefully restricted to maintain security. She must meet Noreen only occasionally, concealing their close friendship. Living with her parents, Duncan refers to Noreen as her former high school teacher that gives her advice about furthering her education.

This was a fortuitous opportunity to meet with Noreen for an extended time under explainable circumstances. Duncan normally relayed her confidential information in typewritten form with no markings. She used an old typewriter her father brought home for her to use in her preoccupation with attempting her hand at writing fiction. This allowed her to type information she acquired from the office.

As an avid reader of Arthur Conan Doyle's Sherlock Holmes stories, she developed a sense of detail and criminal forensics that served to heighten her sense of secrecy. The boarding house where Noreen resided was on the outskirts of town. Not far away was an ancient collapsed barn. The barn's foundation was constructed from field rocks secured in place by mortar. Duncan discovered a large rock loosened from the mortar offering a space behind it. When lifted back into place, it looked secure and perfectly normal. As a teacher of history, Noreen made references to the spy technique used during the American revolution. It became a perfect dead drop.

Duncan said, "It has been weeks since the Matewan Massacre. Been an awful uproar at the office. Mr. Felts is always angry.

Never a kind word to anyone since the deaths of his brothers in Matewan. Everybody is always upset. Mr. Atwood's worse than normal. He's a real nasty piece of work. Never polite. In normal times, Mr. Felts is nice to the staff. Not Mr. Atwood. A real bully. He and Mr. Felts frequently discuss things behind closed doors. The other girls and I think they're talking about how to avenge the killing of Mr. Felts' brothers. It's clear they blame their deaths on Matewan police chief Sid Hatfield. Didn't you say your mother lives there?"

"She used to live near there in the town of Williamson. Mother's getting along in age. Not in the best of health. Just retired from her teaching job. Staying here in Bluefield now where I can look after her."

"That's nice she'll be taking it easy and staying close to you. Not easy what happened to your family years ago."

Noreen only told Duncan that they lived in the small town of Pratt on the Kanawha River. Her Father, brother, and husband all dying in the same mining accident of a collapsed shaft. She did not want to get into the phycological ramifications of the actual circumstances of their deaths. Difficult to explain her conflicting emotions of blaming her father for his foolish act and the disgust of the mining companies employing hired killers.

As teachers, she and her mother sought to leave those memories behind and seek jobs elsewhere. Mother went to Williamson, and she came to Bluefield. Noreen never revealed her maiden name as Burke to avoid association with her mother's public unionizing activities. She explained her anti-mine company political views using similar rhetoric that Keara Murphy might use. Noreen never revealed her brother was the new U.S. Marshal for Southern West Virginia.

Duncan said, "Here's some new information that sounds important. Just learned this yesterday. Baldwin-Felts will be supervising another eviction. Very confidential for some reason, but I saw the duty schedule. Unusual because it's to take place in McDowell County at the Mohawk Coal & Coke Company's mine in Mohawk. Apparently, a significant number of miners there have secretly joined the UMW. Mohawk is close to Mingo County where so much of the hostilities are originating. Involves twenty detectives. Atwood will personally oversee the operation. Scheduled for this coming Wednesday.

"I also overheard Mr. Felts discussing this with the McDowell sheriff on the telephone. He told the sheriff his role was only to provide legal cover for the eviction. Mr. Felts told the sheriff not to worry. Baldwin-Felts will handle any trouble with the miners. The Sheriff just needs to provide a single deputy to make the eviction legal. This just isn't right, Noreen. People in America shouldn't be treated like this."

"No, they shouldn't, Francis. That's why you and I take risks to get the story out. I have some contacts within the miners' community. If I warn them, will that put you at risk?"

"I don't think so. Others in the office know and the detectives that will be going to Mohawk must know in advance."

"When the miners find out will there be more trouble like what happened in Matewan?"

Noreen nodded and sighed. "Maybe. Probably even likely. Better that they are prepared though. They must have already received eviction notices so they must know this is coming soon. Knowing the day when Baldwin-Felts agents move in to enforce the evictions by force at least allows time to get families out of harm's way."

"Here's a bit of other news. Months ago, I passed you information concerning the new United States marshal. Seems he had a run in with Baldwin-Felts detectives up in Kanawha County. Then another incident in Logan County with that tough sheriff there. Mr. Atwood views the marshal as a threat. They've been looking into his background. He comes from West Virginia. Something of a war hero. Got all sorts of medals serving with the U.S. Marines. Atwood seems to think he has important friends in Washington. Thinks he should be considered hostile to mining company interests. Warned Mr. Felts that he may try to use his position as a federal law enforcement officer to work against Baldwin-Felts."

—

Thomas Felts expected trouble at the Mohawk mine. In fact, he made sure that was the case. Mohawk Coal & Coke sent out eviction notices giving a week's notice for evacuation to be completed by Friday. This would give the appearance of ample notice while allowing for striking miners to prepare for resistance. Felts' intention was to provoke a firefight. With the limited manpower of the West Virginia State Police occupied with trying to maintain order in Mingo County, a major incident widening the violence to neighboring McDowell County might just force the Governor to request federal assistance.

With the time-sensitive intelligence provided by Francis Duncan regarding events in Mohawk to happen on Wednesday Noreen could not wait to communicate by mail to Keara as was her usual practice. The following morning being Monday, Noreen placed a telephone call to Alan at his office in Charleston. Safer than telephoning him through the hotel desk that might not be secure. When he answered, she just said, "Just wanted to ask if you could come down this week, Alan. Wanted to share some important news. Kind of personal so I'd rather not discuss it on the telephone. Could you come to Bluefield tomorrow?" Realizing his sister had something urgently important, and did not even give her name, he replied, "Of course. I will be there this afternoon."

Burke visited Bluefield regularly since the town represented the federal district court's division for Mercer, McDowell, and Monroe Counties therefore one of his four deputy marshals was stationed in Bluefield. Yet he chose not to alert his deputy marshal this trip until he understood the reason for Noreen's summons. He was not sure how much to trust this deputy. Over the past months since Burke's arrival, the man made several unguarded comments convincing Burke he was unsympathetic to coal miners.

Arriving late Monday afternoon in Bluefield, Burke met Noreen at her boardinghouse where she shared Francis Duncan's latest information about Mohawk.

He was uncertain what he could do to avoid what appeared to be deliberate provocation for violent confrontation at Mohawk by Baldwin-Felts. Should he alert the miners? If he conveyed the information to either Bill Blizzard of the United Mine Workers or Father Geary, what might that accomplish? Undoubtedly with the current heated climate, the miners would come out in force. They were not equipped or trained in military-style combat. Baldwin-Felts would undoubtedly come prepared with superior firepower. That could mean machine guns. A bloodbath. Whatever was to happen was already in motion. The best he could do is present himself as a neutral party with the implicit weight of the federal government. For this he would take along his Bluefield deputy marshal if for nothing more than a witness should events turn violent.

Burke stayed in Bluefield that night. Without explanation or forewarning, Burke would order his Bluefield deputy to drive them late the following night to survey the situation at the mining camp in the darken early hours of Wednesday morning. Better not to give him any opportunity to forewarn anyone of Burke's presence. Burke wanted to reconnoiter the area before daylight. Where and how might either side deploy for expecting armed conflict? Were the mining families already departing in accordance with the eviction notice? Were armed miners assembling for a confrontation? Since this was Mohawk Coal & Coke property, were Baldwin-Felts agents already on hand? How many?

—

Burke spent the next day with Noreen and his mother. That at least was a pleasant experience with his mother largely recovered from the assault seven weeks earlier. The laceration having healed nicely, also showed the attending physician's skill for minimizing scarring with his suture technique. Burke placed a call to Deputy Abner Pritchard at his home from the boarding house.

"Sorry to call this late Abner. Had your dinner yet?"

"Yes, Sir. Just finished. What's up?"

"Somthin' unexpected. I just arrived in town on the train. Need you to return to the office. Need to investigate something that might occupy both of us all night so come prepared. Rather not discuss details over the telephone. I'll meet you at the office in thirty minutes." Burke disconnected the call.

Sitting alone with Alan in the boarding house parlor, "Noreen asked, "This is about what's going to happen tomorrow isn't it, Alan? What are you going to do?"

"Don't actually know. I have no jurisdictional authority. Afraid of making the situation worse if I attempt to pass the information to the UMW. Might just ensure a violent confrontation. Emotions are already running out of control in Mingo County since Matewan. Another incident could ignite all the southern coalfields. Not only those in the Tug Valley but counties like Logan, Boone, Raleigh, and Kanawha."

"But that's where your going isn't it?"

"Yeah. Might just be an observer, but maybe a federal badge can help avoid a bloodbath like Matewan."

"From what Francis told me, Baldwin-Felts already takes unwelcomed notice of you. Think it wise to go to Mohawk?"

"I am their enemy. Not likely they would attack a federal official with so many witnesses. I'll also be taking along Deputy Pritchard."

Noreen nodded her understanding, but it did nothing to allay her fears. Yet Alan having survived war all over the globe with a chest full of medals for valor, dealing with violence was in his nature.

Having brought just a small overnight bag, she silently watched her brother check his Browning .45 then check two loaded spare magazines in a leather pouch on his belt. Preparing for war. As he left the boarding house to walk the several blocks to meet his deputy, she kissed him on the cheek. "Take care, Alan. Come back safe and sound ya hear? I love you dearly."

Burke showed up at the small marshal's office in the same building housing the Bluefield division court and judicial chambers. It was eight o'clock, the door unlocked when Burke arrived. Deputy Pritchard sitting on the edge of his desk, greeted him, "What's up, Boss?"

"Got some intelligence that something might be going on to-morrow morning at the Mohawk mining camp in McDowell. Another eviction of striking miners. Might be trouble."

"Not much we can do. We've no legal jurisdiction. That's a problem for the McDowell County Sheriff."

"I'm aware of that, Abner. However, we have a vested interest in monitoring this labor violence and keeping Washington informed. Quite possible federal troops might be called on to maintain order. The West Virginia State Police can't even maintain order in Mingo. Let's get going. It'll take us a couple of hours to get there by car. Want to use the dark to reconnoiter what's going on. Are Baldwin-Felts and a bunch of armed miners going to square off? I don't like surprises. Sorry to take you from your bed tonight. Let's get going."

A none-to-happy Aber Pritchard got behind the wheel then headed out of Bluefield. At least this was summer with a balmy evening. A clear sky with a nearly full moon favored them with good light to survey the area before dawn.

Pritchard said, "Brought along a thermos jug of coffee my wife made to get us through the night. How'd you come by this information?"

"Somebody that knows somebody that knows another somebody. It's reliable though."

They arrived in Mohawk around ten o'clock that night. Mohawk was nothing more than an unincorporated community existing only because of the Mohak Coal & Coke Company mine. It was six miles upriver from the hamlet of Iaeger, population 500. Nothing more than a spot on the map. Important only as a junction for the Norfolk & Western Railroad carrying coal from the mines along the Tug Fork River.

They pulled off the main road paralleling the river onto a service road marked for the mine. A gate on the road stood open. No mine guards were visible. The mining camp comprised what was known as the unincorporated community of Mohawk.

"Park over there off the road. We'll walk from here," Burke said.

The miners' housing consisted of two facing rows of weather-beaten unpainted clapboard small houses with woods sloping up gentle rises on either side. A couple of wagons stood outside with loads covered by canvas tarps. Presumably household goods ready for transport in the morning. The eviction notice expired at midnight. No one was about at this hour. No smoke from chimneys since this was summer and too early for making breakfast.

Burke and Pritchard began walking the perimeter in silence. If there were armed miners hidden in trees on the high ground, they did not want to be taken as Baldwin-Felts guards. After a thorough surveillance of the grounds covering many acres, Burke had a good sense of the terrain. If the intelligence proved accurate and Baldwin-Felts agents were already here, then Burke thought it most likely they would descend on the houses after dawn to carry out evictions. Considering the hostilities further along the Tug, the chances were good that some miners would use these evictions as a pretext to mount an armed attack. If they had sufficient resources, their best strategy was to entrap the Baldwin-Felts guards in a crossfire from firing positions in the wooded areas on high ground of either side of the camp.

Burke and Pritchard returned to their car to pass the early morning hours drinking coffee while awaiting sunrise.

At the first rays of dawn a car came up the road and stopped next to their vehicle. A large badge painted on the side on the side read *McDowell County Sheriff Department*. Pritchard's official car had a similar painted logo on the sides reading *United States Marshal*.

The driver exited the car as did Pritchard and Burke and said, "What are you fellas doin' here?"

Burke replied, "Probably the same as you. Monitoring the eviction. Keeping the peace."

"This ain't your jurisdiction," the deputy sheriff said.

Burke replied harshly, "The whole fuckin' county is my jurisdiction, Deputy. You out here alone?"

"Yeah."

"Guess the sheriff isn't expecting any trouble," Burke said. "What do you think, Deputy?"

The McDowell County deputy sheriff just shrugged.

"Well, tell you what. Let's all three of us take a stroll and check things out."

Without waiting for the deputy sheriff, Burke and Pritchard headed towards the miners' camp. As they got closer, a small truck pulled close to the end of the row of houses. Something raised in the truck bed was covered with a tarp. Following behind were twenty Baldwin-Felts guards all carrying Winchester rifles. Seeing Burke, Pritchard, and the sheriff deputy standing on a slight rise overlooking the camp, the person leading the guards held up his hand halting those behind him. Turning to his armed squad, the leader motioned with his arm directing their deployment. He and several of his men then briskly walked up the rise toward Burke and the other two officers.

Coming to a halt in front of Burke. Leland Atwood said, "What's this about, Marshal?"

"Just here observing. Who are you?"

"Name is Atwood. I represent Mohawk Coal & Coke security. Here to enforce an eviction notice. The deadline expired yesterday. Seems many of the miners chose not to vacate company-owned housing. I have a court order making it legal for us to enforce the evictions. I appreciate the county sheriff sending a deputy to supervise things since this is a local matter. Why are federal marshals involved?"

"Like I said, observing. Assessing the situation. Seems local law enforcement is having difficulty maintaining order around mines all along the river. If things become worse, federal intervention will become necessary. Then what goes on will directly involve my office."

"Very well, Marshal. We'll go about our lawful business while you observe," Atwood replied sarcastically then began barking orders for his men to begin going through every house."

Several miners came out of some of the houses carrying rifles. It appeared to Burke women and child had previously vacated the area. The miners were expecting trouble, which meant there were undoubtedly more riflemen concealed in the tree lines ready to bring down fire on the Baldwin-Felts mine guards.

Atwood assumed the same and came prepared. He waved to the two men standing in the bed of the stopped truck. They pulled away the tarp to reveal what Burke recognized as a tripod mounted Model M1917 Browning water-cooled machine gun. Developed for U.S. troops for the Great War. The weapon fired 30-06 caliber rounds at a rate of fire of over 400 rounds per minute from a belt fed system with a two-man crew. Adding to the Baldwin-Felts' fire power, Burke could see at least two other agents carrying Browning automatic rifles. The heavy hand-held rifles added serious firepower.

Within a minute of revealing the mounted machine gun in the truck bed, gunfire erupted from multiple positions from the trees directed against the machine crew on the truck. However, Burke kept his attention on Atwood who obviously expected an armed response from the miners. Yet Atwood was concentrating his attention instead on the three law enforcement officers standing in front of him.

Burke was shocked when several Baldwin-Felts agents standing behind Atwood leveled their rifles toward him and the other two law enforcement officers. The closest agent fired his rifle mortally wounding the shocked deputy sheriff. Abner Pritchard fumbled trying to extract his revolver from the holster on his hip but was struck with a round before he could fire a shot. The couple of seconds with Baldwin-Felts directing fire at the deputies allowed Burke time to drop to one knee into a firing position. With his skill with the .45 Browning pistol, he dropped both of the Baldwin-Felts gunmen with shots to their head.

Atwood had moved away as his agents opened fire on the law enforcement officers. Having seen his two agents fall, the other agents and Atwood tried to distance themselves from Burke while returning fire as they run away. Burke emptied his .45 at the fleeing Baldwin-Felts.

At the first cracks of the rifle fire from miners concealed in the tree line, Baldwin-Felts agents opened up with fire from the mounted machine gun. The battle recalled the bloody days at Belleau Wood for Burke. All he could do was remain lying flat on the ground.

After reloading a fresh magazine into his. 45, Burke crawled sideways to examine the deputy sheriff. Dead with a shot through the heart. Pritchard a little further away was in great agony. Burke examined the wound causing excessive bleeding soaking from his lower abdomen. He'd seen many wounds to the gut. Most were fatal. Pritchard probably wouldn't last long enough to make it to a hospital.

Pritchard grunted out through the pain, "Why'd they shoot us? Am I goin' to make it?"

"Just hang in there. I'll get our car over here and get you to a doctor."

Not only was that impossible with the battle still raging but Pritchard was rapidly bleeding out. Burke surveyed the battle scene. The machine gun and Browning automatic rifles kept up a steady rate of fire while miners maintaining cover among the trees returned fire.

Sporadic firing continued for another twenty minutes before tapering off. Then silence. Several miners near the camp housing lay on the ground.

Since Baldwin-Felts had unsuccessfully attempted to murder law enforcement officers at the scene, Burke chose not to approach remaining Baldwin-Felts agents. They lost at least two of their own on the hill firing on the lawmen and maybe more to miner gunfire.

Pritchard was now unconscious. Feeling for a pulse at his neck. Burke confirmed he was dead. Adding to his firepower, Burke picked up one of the Winchester rifles and began retreating toward the car in a crouch. He'd drive to the village of Iaeger, find a telephone, then make a report of what happened and request assistance from McDowell County Sheriff Bill Hatfield.

From a telephone at a service station in Iaeger, Burke reached the sheriff. "There's an ongoing gun battle going on at the Mohawk mine. Need you to send more deputies. Also contact the state police headquarters and request backup."

"How bad is it?" Sheriff Hatfield said.

"Baldwin-Felts is using machine guns. Miners are returning fire from positions among the trees. Baldwin-Felts just killed your deputy, Sheriff. This is a major engagement."

Burke understood this may be the beginning of something larger. Armed violence would not end here. Spilling over the border from troubled Mingo County meant the coal war was widening. He needed to call Keara and Noreen and tell them he was uninjured since news would spread immediately. Call his other three deputies next. Inform U.S. Attorney Kenna in Charleston that federal criminal laws now applied. The murder of a U.S. deputy marshal and another count of attempted murder on him. Once back in Bluefield he would call Washington to make an official report by telephone to be transcribed by a DOJ stenographer.

His first obligation upon arriving in Bluefield was to visit Abner Pritchard's widow and give her the tragic news. See that someone she knew stayed with her. He then went to the McDowell County seat of Welch to prepare an official report and give depositions to local authorities.

—

The largest newspaper in the region, the *Bluefield Daily Telegraph*, was the first to publish an account of the incident at Mohawk.

BATTLE OF MOHAWK KILLS 9

On the morning of Wednesday July 7, security personnel for the Mohawk Coal & Coke Mining Company in McDowell County attempted to enforce evictions of striking miners from company-owned housing. The evictions were authorized by West Virginia Circuit Judge Delbert Zimmerman. The deadline for striking miners to vacate company property expired the previous day and mine security personnel were there to force removal of any remaining tenants.

According to a Mohawk Coal & Coke spokesman, before operations even began, an undetermined number of armed striking miners opened fire from concealed positions from adjacent wooded low hills.

With the continuing labor violence raging in Mingo County currently being policed by West Virginia State Police, Mohawk Coal & Coke security personnel came prepared to counter possible armed resistance in the absence of sufficient county law enforcement resources.

Regrettably, McDowell County Sheriff Deputy Lyle Davenport was killed by sniper fire from striking miners in the first moments of the conflict. Sheriff Hatfield lamented the death of Davenport who was only there to supervise the execution of a court order. "McDowell County like Mingo County does not have law enforcement resources sufficient to maintain law and order for violence on this scale. The death of Deputy Davenport attests to that. Governor Cornwell must provide state police or request federal assistance."

Standing next to Deputy Davenport was U.S. Deputy Marshal Abner Pritchard who also died from gunfire from the concealed miner firing positions. The death toll then rose with four Baldwin-Felts detectives killed and three others wounded by striking miners. Casualties among the attacking miners remains uncertain except for three dead left at the site of the gunbattle.

U.S. Marshal Alan Burke was also present that morning. Marshal Burke said only that he and Deputy Marshal Pritchard based in Bluefield were at Mohawk to observe the eviction process which held the possibility of violence given recent labor hostilities along the Tug River. Burke has accused the Baldwin-Felts Detective Agency under contract with Mohawk Coal & Coke to maintain security at the mine of provoking the armed confrontation. Burke went on to allege that Baldwin-Felts even used machine guns that morning. Burke declined to provide further details citing an ongoing investigation by the U.S. attorney's office for criminal charges of murder and attempted murder of federal law enforcement officers. Burke also declined further comment related to his involvement during the gunbattle.

McDowell County Sheriff Hatfield stated that he has already filed an official request with Governor Cornwell for immediate assistance by state or federal law enforcement resources necessary for maintaining civil order in the county.

Thomas Felts, the managing partner of Baldwin-Felts who provides security throughout most mines in the West Virginia coalfields with headquarters based here in Bluefield, commented, "In May the massacre in Matewan resulted in the killing of seven of our employees. Now another four in Mohawk. This unlawful carnage will continue until Governor Cornwell declares martial law and requests federal troops for West Virginia to establish order that now appears better defined as insurrection rather than solely labor violence."

CHAPTER 20

West Virginia | Summer 1920

After explaining the details of what took place in Mohawk to his sister and concluding official business in Welch, Burke returned to Charleston. He declined making any further comments to the *Bluefield Telegram* reporter before consulting with Keara and U.S. Attorney Kenna. Over the hours following the battle, Burke reflected on what truly happened at Mohawk.

Baldwin-Felts intended this to be a violent confrontation. Francis Duncan's intelligence and the arming of his agents with machine guns confirmed that. The murders of Deputy Sheriff Davenport, Deputy Marshal Pritchard, and the attempt to kill him were not spontaneous. No question that was Atwood's intent. His agents opened up on us without hesitation or even a command from Atwood. Pritchard and I were not expected to be there. Killing the deputy sheriff probably part of Atwood's plan. Blamed on a striking miner sniper explained as the start of the larger firefight. His and Pritchard's deaths only added weight to the fabrication that the attack was instigated by striking miners. Since he survived as a witness to the murders, that created a problem for Atwood.

Other than the Baldwin-Felts perpetrators, there were no witnesses to the murders of the deputy sheriff and Pritchard. If Burke made an official claim of premeditated murder, he did not have any source of corroboration. In fact, Atwood could claim that Burke killed two of his agents first in an unprovoked attack. As the situation stood, Atwood had no reason to accuse Burke of shooting his agents unless Burke pursued the matter officially. Both Atwood and Burke would therefore remain silent avoiding making any accusations. A Mexican standoff.

Back in Charleston, Burke related details of the incident to U.S. Attorney Kenna. After giving a deposition, Kenna agreed that there existed insufficient evidence to bring federal charges against Leland Atwood or Baldwin-Felts for the murder of Abner Pritchard and attempted murder of Burke. Kenna commented, "At least some measure of justice was done by your killing of the two assailants."

After processing Burke's reciting of the events at Mohawk, Keara said, "As your lawyer, you're on firm legal grounds. You gave a deposition to the U.S. Attorney who agreed there was insufficient evidence to pursue filing criminal charges. Baldwin-Felts has yet to make any allegations. Probably won't. Regardless, there's no evidence that you acted other than in self-defense."

Keara Murphy let out a long sigh then remarked, "Hoped all that violence was long over for you once you left the Marine Corps. Guess I was being naïve. Law enforcement can be a risky profession. Seems being U.S. marshal involves far more than administration. Guess that's why you carry a gun. You and Atwood might be at impasse, but you must know how dangerous he now becomes to you personally."

"That I do. Gives me concern about your safety, my love. "You also shot a Baldwin-Felts agent in Colorado. For all you know, Leland Atwood may have been involved in that incident. What about considering returning to New York for a couple of months?"

She shook her head, "Not a chance. Not going to go through worrying about you again as I did when you were in France. You almost died there. I'm staying. You can issue me a concealed firearms permit. Then figure out a way that I can conceal it yet within easy reach. Little more of a challenge with women's attire rather than the rough clothing I wore in Colorado. Got any ideas?"

Keara put her arms around his neck and kissed him leaving no doubt what she had on her mind. He obliged by playing along. "You have no pockets in your dresses. Nowhere to hide a holster. Perhaps somewhere among your undergarments. Shall we explore?"

"By all means," she said pulling him into the hotel bedroom.

—

Neither Burke nor Murphy knew just how dangerous Atwood would become. For Leland Atwood, Mohawk was a personal catastrophe. Burke was unaware that one of his shots fired at the retreating Atwood following the murders of the deputy sheriff and Pritchard found its mark. The large .45 caliber round struck Atwood in the left elbow shattering the joint. Following surgery in Bluefield, the surgeon told Atwood, "Got some bad news. The elbow joint is effectively gone with irreversible damage sustained to both the humerus and radius. Had to remove a good deal of bone fragments but able to save the lower arm. However, the damage is extensive enough that it will severely limit the mobility of your arm for life. Will also affect the use of your left hand, but to what extent won't be known until all the soft tissue heals."

—

The encounter at Mohawk prompted Burke to take more direct action. This now became a personal matter for him. Baldwin-Felts targeted him even knowing he was a federal officer. There is much of West Virginian-mountain culture and militant Irish in Burke's makeup that calls for revenge as the only means of achieving justice. The mining companies are responsible for oppressing the coal miners, but Baldwin-Felts is the instrument of that oppression. Therefore, they should become the target of something more effective than just disorganized random counter attacks by striking miners.

Within a couple of weeks of the battle at Mohawk, Burke stopped in Williamson on his regular tour of the federal divisions located outside Charleston. Sitting in Father Geary's study at the parish rectory, they talked while sharing a bottle of Irish whiskey.

Burke began explaining the reason for his visit. "I'm not a practicing Catholic, Father, but if I tell you something that I wish to remain absolutely confidential, are you bound by Canon Law to observe the seal of the confessional?"

Geary looked at Burke with a puzzled expression. "Yes, my son. I am bound by the absolute sanctity of a penitent's confession. What is troubling you?"

"Lots of things, but not guilt regarding what I am about to tell you. You suggested to me that my background could be valuable by helping striking coal miners protect themselves from Baldwin-Felts mine guards."

"Yes. What is that to do with what is troubling you?"

"I have an idea that might be useful in defending against violence directed at miners. First let me tell you what has brought me to do something directly. You have read the newspaper accounts of the incident at Mohawk a couple of weeks ago."

"Of course. Your name is mentioned at being there as an observer, but little more. The reporting says that miners killed your deputy marshal and a sheriff's deputy."

"Miners didn't kill those deputies. Baldwin-Felts agents shot them dead as they stood next to me on a rise overlooking the miners' housing camp. No misunderstanding. Not killed by striking miners. Just cold-blooded murder with a purpose."

Geary registered surprise but did not interrupt Burke.

"The newspapers said that the miners also killed four Baldwin-Felts agents. However, I killed the two sonsofbitches that murdered the deputies. I put a bullet to the head of each. The Baldwin-Felts guy in charge got away. I chose not to publicly explain what happened. Claiming self-defense with the only witnesses being Baldwin-Felts killers seemed a bad idea. Nor can they accuse me of murdering two of their own after claiming the deputies were shot by miners.

"Baldwin-Felts staged the evictions to intentionally provoke an armed incident. Came prepared to use machine guns against the miners. I believe their objective is to force the Governor to

273

request federal intervention. They will likely leave the details of the confrontation as reported in the newspapers."

Geary nodded, "And why are you telling me this?"

"To provide the reason for my giving help to the striking miners."

Finished, Geary asked, "Do you wish for me to give you absolution for the killing of those men?"

Burke shook his head. "Don't feel the need. I'm already doing penance by being stuck in this war zone. My whole life has been fighting wars. My fate just won't let me shake that jinx."

"Perhaps it's God's hand directing events."

"Don't start with that philosophical argument, Father. Now let me tell you what I'm proposing. First of all, I have sources of information willing to indirectly provide me with confidential information on the enemy. I am offering to provide you that intelligence for use as you choose. All I need is someone you trust in Charleston to pass the information to you. A fellow priest perhaps? I'd feel better if the conduit was also bound by the seal of the confessional."

Geary said, "You realize that the miners may use that intelligence for violent purpose?"

"Of course."

"There is a priest at the Sacred Heart Cathedral in Charleston that shares my ... unorthodox views."

Burke nodded. "Some time ago you attempted to recruit my services to provide military training to some of your more militant miner parishioners. Not possible to turn miners into an army. Even if they could learn to fight in military fashion it would end in a bloodbath for them. They cannot confront mine guards on equal footing. Local law enforcement is also on the side of the mining companies. At some level, labor violence begins to look like insurrection against the government. That brings down the weight of well-armed trained militia or federal troops.

"The only successful form of armed resistance is guerrilla warfare. Warfare like the IRA is waging against the British in Ireland. Considering striking West Virginia coal miners are armed only with an odd assortment of antique weapons, squirrel rifles, and shotguns, sheer numbers cannot overcome inferiority in ordinance. That's why forces like the IRA must resort to different tactics.

"Guerilla warfare means using sudden immediate harassing engagements than opportune disengagement. Steal weapons from the enemy. Disappear back into the countryside. Become unrecognizable. That requires having support among the population. Coal miners constitute much of the population, so the support circumstances exist. They need intelligence on the enemy and the means of inflicting damage. I just offered access to intelligence. Guerrilla units are small in number. Disciplined. Committed. As to the means of threat to the enemy, I have a suggestion that might multiply the effects of a bunch of mountain men armed with antique weapons."

Geary said, "Will you help to organize these guerrilla units?"

"Not directly. I'll offer my services to train a handful of former soldiers that served in France. Such men already possess the necessary discipline and will be familiar with the Springfield rifle. These men will become snipers to conduct guerrilla operations. For that they'll need weapons to fire accurately from long distances. Sniper rifles outfitted with optical sights."

"How can we obtain such weapons?"

"There I cannot help you. But surplus weapons from the Great War should be available for sale in gun shops. These rifles are probably still even being manufactured for civilian hunting use."

"You are familiar with these weapons?"

"The Marine Corps used them in France. I'm not an expert sniper tactics, but I fired the rifles on the training range and understand the principles of long-distance shooting. Selected Marine marksmen were trained with them when I supervised training at Parris Island before the war. You need to obtain Springfield M1903 rifles fitted with a Winchester A5 optical scope. Some might be mounted with a Warner & Swasey scope, but I prefer the Winchester scope. If you can't find rifles already fitted with scopes, scopes can be purchased separately. They can be fitted to Springfield rifles by a competent gunsmith. The Springfields are bolt action 30-06 caliber rifles with an effective range of several hundred yards. It's a suitably accurate weapon that gives a sniper aided by a spotter with field glasses the ability to disrupt enemy operations. The weapon gives a small armed unit the remarkable ability to harass a larger force and limit the enemy's maneuverability.

"Each sniper teams up with a spotter. Someone with binoculars to help locate targets and provide required adjustments to place the round on target. Firing from a couple of hundred yards is not the same as bringing down a deer at fifty yards."

"Would you be willing to instruct these former soldiers in the use of these weapons?"

"Provided you can ensure they cannot divulge my identity."

Geary smiled, "You are a most unusual man, Marshal. Seems you also possess something of a Fenian militancy in your soul."

"How do you suggest keeping my identity a secret?"

"Let me see. How 'bout first of all playing up being Irish. You still have a slight accent. Maybe exaggerate that. Give yourself an Irish rebel background. Do you follow the war in Ireland?"

"Of course. "

"Close enough to fabricate a cover story of why you left Ireland to come here?"

"I think so. Something about being arrested by the British. Escaped and forced to flee to America. Problem is someone is sure to recognize me as the U.S. Marshal. How do I deal with that?"

"Your face is not widely known as far as I know. Not that it's difficult to alter your appearance just enough to become a different person. Perhaps a theatrical mustache and clear eyeglasses. Simple but makes a whole different face. Consider a medical knee brace that stiffens one leg making it easy to fake a limp. Wear an Irish flat cap. Can you get your hands on a British Army revolver? Disguise your military background as serving in one of the Irish Regiments of the British Army rather than the American Marines."

"Seems you were born to this sort of intrigue. Let's see how much of a creative Irish rebel you are, Father. Think you can find the means of getting your hands on these sniper rifles?"

"I have many connections in Boston where I attended seminary. Friends of the Irish Republican Brotherhood. Good lads sending money and smuggling arms to the IRA fighting the British. I'm sure I can find support in Boston to help fellow oppressed Irish miners in West Virginia."

"Very good. I'll portray the Boston IRB as those that sent this Irish rebel to West Virginia to train striking coal miners in how to kill the enemy. Mind that you create an intermediary so procuring the weapons does not lead back to you, Father. Don't suppose your Bishop would look with favor on one of his priests taking up arms."

—

The West Virginia State Police, having taken over local law enforcement in Mingo County, did little to quell random attacks by striking miners. Unlike previous labor-friendly Sheriff Blankenship, Captain James Brokus commanding Company B of the state police in Mingo was a no-nonsense police officer. Brokus soon became a reviled figure in the West Virginia coal wars, earning him the epithet *the meanest sonofabitch in West Virginia* for his aggressive tactics directed at striking miners. However, Brokus had only 45 state police to support a handful of sheriff deputies, making evident the inability to adequately police Mingo County.

Thomas Felts' strategy to expand the coal war beyond Mingo County by creating another bloody confrontation proved successful. Led by the Red Jacket Coal Company, the largest operator in Mingo County covering 11,000 acres with 1,000 employees, the mining companies along the Tug Fork River brought pressure to bear on Governor Cornwell to request federal military assistance. The inability for state resources to suppress the conflict in Mingo County now expanded to into McDowell County, prompted fear of further widening violence.

Beleaguered Governor Cornwell now had little choice other than to request federal intervention fearing virtual revolt in southern West Virginia. He made his request to the new commander of the U.S. Army's Central Department, Major General George A.

Read, for a battalion of troops to guard the mines of southern West Virginia. General Read responded by forwarding orders to the 2nd and 40th Infantry Regiments stationed at Camp Sherman, Ohio to move into West Virginia.

Federal intervention meant a conditional declaration of martial law whereby Governor Cornwell retained overall civilian control. 500 regular U.S. Army troops under command of Colonel Samuel Burkhardt arrived by train in Williamson on August 29. The next day, the troops deployed to maintain peace using squad-size patrols near Mingo County coal mines.

—

Federal troops could only ensure civil order for the duration of deployment. The fundamental issues of labor discord remained unchanged. Once federal troops left, violence would return until there was an end to this collective oppression of coal miners. However, the mining companies stood to gain in the short term during martial law. Protected by federal troops allowed for maintaining production by bringing in replacement miners. Striking miners therefore risked permanent loss of employment.

As long as Baldwin-Felts remained free to function with legal impunity, Burke found no reason to abandon his planned subversive efforts. Might Leland Atwood's failure to kill him at Mohawk make him a personal threat? Did that also put Keara at greater risk? Burke drew a measure of comfort when Keara showed what she created to conceal her .38 special revolver to always go about armed.

"What do'ya think of this," she said not long after their discussion following the Mohawk incident. She showed off a lightweight leather suede jacket by taking a turn for him to see all angles.

"I think you look beautiful. Very stylish."

"See anything unusual?"

Looking puzzled, "Just the alluring figure of a grand-looking woman."

She unbuttoned the jacket and opened it to the left. Inside was a holster stitched securely into the lining. She reached in and extracted her .38 special revolver.

"Amazing. I couldn't detect the bulge."

"Yes, it tucks nicely just under my left breast. Got the idea from how you carry your gun. Now with winter approaching, let me show this."

Returning from the bedroom, she now wore a longer wool overcoat. Inside, this garment a similar holster was fitted in the same position. "No matter where I go, I'll be armed. Either in a coat or my handbag. My incident with Baldwin-Felts in Colorado convinced me never to take threats of violence lightly."

It made Burke feel only somewhat less concerned about Keara's safety, but he must live with her resolve to stay with him in West Virginia. Had Burke known that it was his shot that maimed Atwood, Keara going about armed would hardly be enough protection.

Keara knew what Alan was offering to Father Geary. An extreme venture that flirted violating the law, especially for a law enforcement officer. Yet she understood that established law enforcement in West Virginia was often corrupt or at least unevenly applied. In such cases, extrajudicial means becomes the only recourse.

After returning from making his offer to Father Geary, Burke took stock of what he, Keara, and Noreen were undertaking. "Besides helping some miners harass Baldwin-Felts we only have Noreen's source within Baldwin-Felts with which to confront this climate of oppression. Frustrating not to be able to do more."

Keara said, "Intelligence can be a decisive weapon. You have said that yourself. Your mother's work taking candid photographs has helped to keep the violence in West Virginia continually in the news. The only way things will change is for the public to demand justice. That will happen only through new legislation, state and federal. There must be a change in law prohibiting private armed cadres like Baldwin-Felts enforcing the interests of corporations by force of firearms. That includes private enterprise funding local law enforcement such as in Logan County. That disgusting homespun despot Don Chafin should not exist any-where in America."

Burke said, "Well I've got something in store for Chafin. Running Logan County like his personal fiefdom includes a lucrative trade in making moonshine. Although Prohibition is a stupid federal law, my office is expected to go after those trafficking in liquor. Logan County is therefore high on my list."

Burke then added, "Not everyone in West Virginia is corrupted by coal mining interests. Acting U.S. Attorney Kenna is a good example. He also has a close friend in the West Virginia legal community. A former U.S. Attorney for the Southern District of West Virginia over ten years ago by the name of Elliot Northcott. Currently in private practice after serving in foreign diplomatic posts. Kenna says Northcott is in line for appointed as U.S. Attorney again. Northcott probably has connections in Washington. Might be a useful conduit for channeling information to those with influence in state and federal government. West Virginia can only change with legislative action to break the mining interest stranglehold."

"I have another idea. Something more immediate," Keara said. "Father Geary could be of further service. A more conventional form of subversion than organizing bands of guerrilla fighters. He could enlist all sorts of people in Mingo County armed with cameras to take photos. Just like what your mother was doing. They give him the exposed film, which he then gives to you."

Burke said, "That puts you even more at risk."

"No, it doesn't. Those photographs appear in publications attributed to Keara Murphy. I'm known hereabouts as Mrs. Burke. Remember we did that for a reason. Didn't want my muckraking articles to lead back to your mother, Noreen, or Francis Duncan. Feel out Father Geary. I'll even buy the cameras. It's important to keep up public pressure. Once federal troops withdraw, circumstances will likely revert to widespread violence."

CHAPTER 21

West Virginia | Autumn 1920

By mid-September the efforts of coal operators to import strike-breakers to the region moved forward with federal troops now protecting strikebreakers. As they arrived at the Williamson train station, soldiers escorted them to the mines among taunts by angry striking miners. The presence of federal troops allowed coal operators to reopen several mines. In protest, rioting broke out in Williamson.

Soon after arriving in Mingo County, federal troops deployed infantry tactics in confronting determined miners. In separate engagements, sizeable groups of armed miners fired on the troops at the Howard Colliery in Chattaroy and another mine in Thacker. After being dispersed under heavy response by the military, miners continued random armed harassment.

To press their advantage for continued federal intervention, the Red Jacket Coal Company filed a suit in the federal court of Eastern District of Virginia against United Mine Workers leadership for the strike called in July. The filing took place in Virginia rather than Southern District of West Virginia because of the absence of a sitting federal district judge in Charleston. The court ultimately awarded a preliminary injunction to Red Jacket for virtually all they sought. The ruling effectively precluded the UMW from interfering with mining operations. This included not only organizing but even inducing existing non-union miners to strike. As U.S. Marshal for West Virginia, Burke had no choice other than to serve the injunction on UMW District 17 headquarters. With the presence of federal troops enforcing the federal injunction, strikes subsided. However, sporadic violence continued unabated.

—

One morning in October, Father Geary showed up unannounced at Burke's office in Charleston. "I have some interesting news to report. My friends in Boston found those Springfield rifles with optical scopes you specified. Eight weapons in all plus a thousand rounds of 30-06 ammunition."

Burke nodded. "Where did you get the money?"

"Not sure. Didn't ask the six Irish lads that served in the U.S. Army in France. My parishioners. These lads are volunteering for your training on how to raise organized havoc on the mine operators and Baldwin-Felts. They found the means for raising the money. I suspect they passed the hat for donations among their more militant brethren. The rifles are in a wooden crate in the basement of the rectory."

"Very well, Father. Know a place where I can train these former soldiers?"

"One of the fellas suggested a place called Buffalo Mountain in Mingo County. East of Williamson, a thirty-minute drive over some poor logging roads into the hills. Rugged country without coal mines."

Burke nodded. "Fix a date two weeks from today. I'll meet you at the rectory on an early train in the morning. We'll leave for the hills after you've said mass."

"I'll have the lads ready. You decided on how to disguise your identity? Prepared your cover story?"

"Yeah. I'm IRA. Arrested by the Royal Irish Constabulary for killing British Black & Tans. Some of my mates broke me out of an RIC barracks in Cork. With a price on my head facing the gallows if recaptured, thought it best to escape Ireland six months ago. I'll be using the name Dillon Quinn. Career in the British Army from 1900 and the Boer War in South Africa. Served with the Royal Dublin Fusiliers at Passchendaele in 1917 where I was wounded. Accounts for my stiff left leg and slight lip. Someone in Boston put me on to Father Geary and some mercenary work needed for the labor troubles in West Virginia."

Geary chuckled, "Very creative. That should impress these former soldiers."

Burke added, "Since you are committed to helping the coal miners, Father, I have another suggestion where you can strike a blow against West Virginia oppression. My mother did her part to subvert the practices of the mine owners and their armed guards by secretly taking photographs. That's what she was doing in Matewan during the eviction when a Baldwin-Felts thug struck her in the head with the butt of his rifle. She had been an activist supporting the United Mine Workers organizing efforts for years. She connected with a New York journalist crusading against child labor and unsafe working conditions. Mining coal is notoriously known among the worse professions on both accounts.

"With my mother now injured, the journalist contacted me looking to replace her source in the ongoing coalfield wars. What if you were to arm a bunch of your parishioners with cameras to take photographs that portray the mining companies and Baldwin-Felts in condemning pictures? The journalist has offered to provide easily operated cameras and film. I can arrange for you to send the exposed film to me and provide new supplies of undeveloped film."

Father Geary enthusiastically embraced the idea. "Excellent idea. Maybe the written word accompanied by pictures will prove more effective than the gun."

—

Arriving in Williamson to meet the former soldier-coal miners, Burke knocked on the front door of the rectory. The housekeeper answered the door. She looked at a man dressed in clean work clothing wearing a flat cap, a common appearance for so many of the church's parishioners. "Yes?"

"I'm here to see Father Geary. Name is Dillon Quinn. He's expecting me."

The housekeeper ushered Burke into Geary's office. "Mr. Quinn is here, Father."

Geary looked up, pausing for a moment trying to place the face. Burke took his advice. Keara had her housekeeper purchase a theatrical mustache with adhesive and clear rimless glasses from a theatrical distributor in Brooklyn. A medical knee brace and British Webley .455 caliber revolver from a firearms dealer fulfilled the disguise. The Webley was tucked in his waist band out of sight at his lower back hidden under his jacket,

Realizing this was Burke, Geary replied, "Thank you, Mary. I've been expecting Mr. Quinn."

After closing the office door, Geary said, "Remarkable how much different you look."

Burke took a couple of steps back and forth showing off his fake limp. "Works like you said if I exaggerate it a bit. Are we ready to meet these Irish lads?"

"We're to meet one of them that will be waiting where we're to leave the main road. The others are concealed so as not to attract attention. The man's name is Frank Donovan. Joined the U.S. Army when war broke out. Promoted to sergeant by the time he demobilized. Returned to join his father digging coal."

—

They departed for Buffalo Mountain in Father Geary's old Model T touring car. The rifles were wrapped in blankets on the rear seats. It was slow going once they left the main road adjacent to the river then began heading into the hills over an unimproved road. Eventually, Geary said, "We should be coming to a logging road turnoff to the left soon. That's where Donovan will be waiting for us with an old truck. He'll have the hood up feigning difficulty with the engine should anyone question why he is on this remote road."

Minutes later, Geary pulled his car well off the road onto the turn off. He and Burke exiting the car. They approached the man standing next to the truck. Geary stuck out his hand, "Hello Frank. This here is Dillon Quinn. The Irishman I told you about. Are the other lads here?"

"Just a ways up this rutted path."

Burke offered his hand to Donovan, "Father Geary said you served in the American Army in France. Where'd you see action?"

"In the Meuse–Argonne. With the U.S. First Army. And you?"

"Royal Dublin Fusiliers from County Kildare. British Army. Been soldiering now 'bout twenty years since I was in South Africa for the Boer War. A sergeant major when I fought the first three years in the Great War until I took shrapnel in my leg at Passchendaele in Flanders in '17."

"Right you are. Sounds like you've been around, Sergeant Major. Just follow my truck, Father. We're goin' only 'bout a mile to where the others are waiting."

Once they arrived, five men emerged from the woods all carrying Winchester lever action rifles. Father Geary announced, "Boys, this here is Sergeant Major Dillon Quinn. Formerly of the British Army, more lately the Irish Republican Army fighting the British in Ireland. I'll let the Sergeant Major give you something of his special background in unconventional warfare. We'll start out with a surprise. In the back seat of my car are some special rifles. Pull 'em out along with a box of ammunition from the floor."

Each of the miners set their Winchesters against a tree and picked up one of the Springfields then sighted through the scope.

One miner said, "Sonofabitch. Saw a couple of these in France but never fired one. They're for sniper work."

Burke said, "That's right. I'm goin' to teach you how to use these to reach out and touch your enemy from considerable range. The British Army used an Enfield rifle firing a .303 round in the Great War. We used the same Winchester A5 optical scopes as did the Americans with the Springfield."

"As Father Geary said, "I've only recently arrived from Ireland a few months ago. I'm in the Irish Republican Army fighting to free Ireland from the fuckin' British. Same kind of shit you blokes put up with here in West Virginia I understand. Guerrilla warfare is what we're doin' in Ireland. What you've been doin' here. What's called irregular military warfare. Ambushes, sabotage. Hit and run tactics then melting back into the civilian population. Harass the enemy in a war of attrition. Avoiding pitched battles.

"Served in the British Army since 1900 to 1917 until wounded in the Great War. Back in County Cork, I took up with the IRA. Know somethin' of soldiering. Not a sniper but I taught weapons use so I know the basics. You lads were selected because of your military background. I expect you know rifles. I've been hired to teach you how to become effective snipers and something of IRA guerrilla tactics. Father Geary convinced certain people in Boston to find someone who knew his business to lend a hand to miners in West Virginia."

Geary asked, "Did you lads bring the targets?"

Donovan replied, "Yes, Father."

Burke said, "Father, please hand out those binoculars. Set the targets out at 100 yards. What say we get to it?"

After setting the targets and loading the rifles, Burke said, "Let me say something before we start. Your targets are human silhouettes with a four-inch painted circle in the center of the torso. When targeting a man, expect that you intend to kill him. This is serious business. This is not conventional warfare. No prisoners of war for those captured. When I was fighting in Ireland, capture for killing a RIC officer or British soldier meant the gallows. I was captured. Escaped to avoid that fate only by my comrades attacking the RIC barracks where I was being held.

"You face the same if arrested for killing someone. Don't admit to anyone your dark deeds. Also, never fire on regular army troops or national guardsmen acting under martial law. That'll only bring in more trained soldiers, better armed than you miners can ever hope to be. It also will turn away public support. Guerrilla units cannot survive without popular support.

"Let's begin. First thing we need to do is sight in everyone's weapon. Here's a ballistic chart for the 165 grain 30-06 rounds you'll be firing." Burke passed out a copy to all six men. "Since we're firing from 100 yards, the bullet doesn't drop. We'll use this as the starting point to adjust the sights of each weapon. Separate into teams of two to start. Find some pieces of wood to fix a rest for the rifle from a prone position. Those not firing become spotters using binoculars. Having a spotter will help to be more effective in the field. Now take your shot aiming with the cross hairs of the scope in the center of the circle. Then take a second shot. If you are a good marksman there should be very little difference between the striking point of both shots.

"Shooter and spotter then compare what you estimate as the amount of deviation right, left, up, or down. With little cross wind today makes for getting your weapon accurately sighted in. For a given shooting situation, you will need to adjust for windage depending on specific conditions by using the graduations on the scope. I'll then show you how to adjust using a coin in the slotted screws and the thumb screw on top. Let's start with you, Sergeant Donovan."

Burke worked with the six men for the next two hours getting their weapons sighted in after repeated shots for incremental adjustment until satisfactory. The makeshift circumstances were not perfect, but the Springfield rifle was an accurate weapon from the factory. Any repeatability deviation was mostly due to the shooter.

All the miners were excited with the prospects of possessing such fine rifles. Breaking for a lunch of sandwiches and warm Coca Cola, Burke had to be cautious about getting too far into his fictious cover story as comradery engaged everyone in conversation.

The afternoon settled into practice at longer distances.

"We'll start with taking the target out to 150 yards. Note on the ballistic chart, the drop of the bullet is about one inch. You need then to adjust your aim on the horizontal reticle line of the scope accordingly. Your spotter should also determine if there is a cross wind. The amount of adjustment for that variable you will have to gauge through practice. 150 yards should be your practice range. This is a good compromise for accuracy and enough distance for good concealment.

"We'll finish up today by taking some shots from 200 yards. That's probably the practical limit for most shots with the bullet dropping almost four inches. Time in the air makes wind a bigger factor. Lastly, work as a team as of shooter and spotter. The spotter helps locating targets, observing shoot placement, and identifying threats.

"We'll meet again in a couple of weeks. Father Geary will give you enough ammunition for practice. Then we'll discuss guerrilla tactics. Now you can show me how good you lads are. Remember, the sniper isn't just about killing people, it's about harassing the enemy. Frightening and disrupting him. The sniper can also disable motor vehicles and damage equipment, particularly electrical equipment."

—

Back in Williamson, Burke handed over eight new cameras and a quantity of unexposed film to Father Geary. He then demonstrated how to operate the camera and extract the exposed film. "Have your photographers note the location and circumstances where the photos were taken. Mail the exposed film to this post office box in Charleston under the name K. S. Reynolds. Do not put a return address on the package. Mail from different post office locations."

Before departing from Buffalo Mountain, Burke said to Geary, "Keep an eye on this guerrilla crew we're creating, Father. Once they begin raising havoc by sniper attacks, it may elevate things from other random shootings. Make sure they never shoot U.S. soldiers. That will look like an insurrection to Washington and bring in more troops. The fallout will be counterproductive. It'll cause loss of popular support for their cause and appear un-American."

"You made that clear to them. I'll keep close to what these lads are doing. Of course, they're not the only ones doing the shooting especially at the Baldwin-felts guards."

Two weeks later, Burke returned to Williamson. He and Father Geary made their way back to Buffalo Mountain for another training session with the coal miner snipers.

As each man showed his proficiency at 150 yards, Burke was impressed. "To all of you, that is some right smart shooting. Now let's discuss tactics. Whether leading a strike team or acting as a sniper, you should understand the basic concepts for conducting this type of warfare. Your objective is to disrupt the enemy. You do that by sabotaging equipment and harassing the mine guards. Taking down a man should be your last resort. Make the enemy always looking around fearing you are out there somewhere ready to put a bullet in them.

"Using the Springfield 30-06 for damaging electrical equipment is the most effective way to sabotage operations. Distribution transformers and switch panels are the best targets. Not only does it put equipment out of operation, it also serves the psychological purpose of demonstrating the enemy's vulnerability. All without putting a mine guard down.

"As a sniper, selecting the firing location is everything. Good concealment, obviously. Higher ground than the target is always helpful. A good rest position for holding the rifle on target. Always determine your path to retreat after the attack. That should be a way that the enemy cannot easily chase after you without risking taking casualties. You're not there to stand your ground. You're there to do a job and survive. You lads are former soldiers, so you know what I mean.

"The spotter's job is to suggest targets and assess range. He also maintains overall situational awareness while the shooter focuses on executing the shot."

The rest of the day they spent running scenarios taking turns with four men acting as the enemy against a sniper and a spotter. By day's end, Burke said to everyone, "You lads are as good as any soldiers I ever served with. Hope I added to your skills. I wish you success."

—

With hundreds of federal U.S. Army troops in Mingo, Logan, and McDowell Counties, violent incidents decreased. Since the federal troops protected strikebreaking non-union miners coming into the region, the United Mine Workers Union threatened Governor Cornwell with a statewide strike if he did not withdraw federal troops. Cornwell acceded and federal forces left West Virginia. On November 4.

Within days of the withdrawal of federal forces, renewed violence erupted. Initially this included harassing threats to discourage strikebreakers. Striking miners in a tent encampment fired on working miners at Nolan. Two men were wounded in a gun battle at Rawl. In Thacker, dynamite destroyed a large tipple. Another dynamite explosion destroyed a railroad trestle. Arson destroyed two mine company buildings. Days later a state trooper was killed in a gunfight with moonshiners. Striking miners fired on non-union workers at two mines and beat up workers at another mine. A union man was killed and another wounded in a gunfight with non-union strikebreakers on a moving train.

Burke learned from Father Geary that none of the shooting deaths came from any of the snipers he trained. However, they participated in violent attacks on the mines as evidenced by widespread reports of sabotage of mining equipment by gunfire predominately directed at disabling electrical equipment.

It soon became evident that a single company of state troopers under command of Captain Brokus and a handful of local Mingo County deputy sheriffs could not contain civil order. More than a hundred businessmen in Mingo County appealed to Governor Cornwell for the return of federal forces to quell unrelenting incidents of violence.

Proclaiming that Mingo County was in a state of insurrection, Cornwell had no choice but to again declare martial law for Mingo County on November 28 and call on the U.S. Army's Fifth Corps Area commander to return troops to West Virginia.

—

As photographs begin coming in from Father Geary, Keara established a reporting arrangement with the *New York Times* managing editor to run a regular column in the Sunday edition titled *West Virginia Coal Wars Latest News*. That would at least provide for continually damaging press keeping the coal wars in West Virginia in the national spotlight.

While Burke was satisfied that he had done all he could to support the cause of the striking coal miners, he understood that was nothing more than personal satisfaction. He did not have the means to materially damage the ingrained corporate oppression that ruled the West Virginia coalfields. With the imposition of martial law and hundreds of regular U.S. Army troops again maintaining order, violence only temporarily decreased.

The thought occurred to him that as a federal law enforcement official he had a least one avenue of legal authority to move against the entrenched local power structure. While Burke disagreed with everything about the new national Prohibition law, it did provide a basis to go after the most corrupt political structure in the state. The Logan County fiefdom of Don Chafin. It was common knowledge that making moonshine was a lucrative business in Logan controlled by Chafin with his army of deputies paid for by a tariff on all coal tonnage extracted from Logan mines. In lieu of hiring Baldwin-Felts as mine guards, this funding arrangement served to provide Chafin with a large armed force that could operate under the color of authority as law enforcement.

As U.S. Marshal, Burke was expected to aggressively enforce the new law prohibiting trafficking in alcoholic spirits. Although miners liked to drink, they universally hated Don Chafin. Burke would have a conversation with UMW official Bill Blizzard, the person who got medical attention for his mother. He would ask Blizzard to use union miners to provide intelligence on who was making illicit alcohol in Logan County, the locations of the stills, and the distribution warehousing.

PART THREE

Blair Mountain, Logan County, West Virginia
Federal troops arriving by train in 1921.

CHAPTER 22

West Virginia | November 1920

Leland Atwood's wounding from a bullet fired by Alan Burke at Mohawk months earlier had now healed. The extent of the permanent disability to his left arm now became apparent. The large .45 caliber slug irreparably destroyed his elbow. Nerves and tendon damage reduced the function of his left hand and fingers. Although in the chaotic gun battle that erupted after his Baldwin-Felts detectives murdered a deputy sheriff and deputy U.S. marshal, Atwood knew it was Burke's bullet that destroyed his arm. For a split-second Atwood locked eyes with Burke when Burke fired directly at him. The simultaneous pain left no doubt as to the source.

U.S. Marshal Burke had no witnesses to corroborate any allegation that Baldwin-Felts murdered the two law enforcement officers. Atwood speculated that Burke's immediate killing of the Baldwin-Felts assailants might be the reason Burke chose to remain silent. Burke had no official reason for being present at the court-ordered eviction of the mining families from company housing. Accusations from either of them could easily be refuted.

Burke was now a dangerous enemy. On various occasions, he had proven hostile to mining company interests and Baldwin-Felts. What happened at Mohawk compelled Atwood to obsess over how he might take revenge.

293

Easy enough to access Burke's documented background as a federal official. A highly decorated United States Marine with over twenty years of service, twice awarded the Congressional Medal of Honor placed him in an exclusive class of soldier. Highly skilled with weapons and deadly with close quarter combat. Obviously has important patrons in Washington. Age forty-two. Born in Cork County Ireland. Emigrated to the United States at the age of five. From there, certain inconsistencies in the reported backgrounds of some of his family members became apparent.

It took diligent investigative work to get a more complete picture of Alan Burke. Yet Baldwin-Felts was a detective agency. Experienced in criminal investigative work, managing partner Thomas Felts eventually found a more lucrative calling in security services, first for the railroads then for coal mining corporations.

From immigration records, Atwood learned Burke's father Joseph was a coal miner in County Cork, Ireland. Joseph Burke did not die in a railroad accident in Huntington as the record states. He died instead of gunshot wounds at Paint Creek in Kanawha County, West Virginia during the strike of 1912. Died by Baldwin-Felts machine gun fire while leading an armed attack of striking miners. The attack resulted in the deaths of twelve miners, one of which was Alan Burke's older brother, and four Baldwin-Felts employees.

Burke's mother, Maude became an outspoken union organizer allied with Mother Jones. She continued those efforts after moving to Matewan in Mingo County. She is the woman injured by a blow to the head from a Baldwin-Felts operative during the eviction of mining families earlier the same day of the Matewan Massacre.

Easy to understand the depth of U.S. Marshal Burke's hatred toward Baldwin-Felts. Atwood next wanted to understand how this career soldier met his wife. The only information was a newspaper clipping saying that Mrs. Burke came from New York. Sources in Charleston could provide only her given name as Keara. While a common ethnic Irish female name, it struck an alarm to Leland Atwood. He knew the name Keara Murphy from years of reading articles attributed to her in national newspapers and respected periodicals. Critical articles of coal mining corporation despotism and virulently condemning of Baldwin-Felts as hired thugs. More than that, it was Keara Murphy that had an altercation at a mine outside Trinidad, Colorado in 1914. Broke the nose of a Baldwin-Felts detective then shot dead the incompetent idiot entering her hotel room after Atwood encouraged him to teach the woman a lesson by assaulting her in her hotel room in Trinidad.

Could Burke's wife Keara be Keara Murphy? Answering that involved bribing sources at the Kanawha Hotel where she and Burke resided. Atwood learned that she always referred to herself as Mrs. Burke, or Keara Burke. Mail addressed to the hotel read *Mrs. Keara Burke*. Yet with modest bribery to a Charleston postal clerk, his source uncovered repeated letters and packages with a return address in Brooklyn from an Angelia Roselli. Atwood hired a private detective agency in New York to determine the connection to this Roselli woman.

The New York detective agency responded within days reporting that *'Angelia Roselli is the live-in housekeeper for an upscale brownstone property owned by one Keara Murphy. Murphy is a practicing attorney specializing in women's rights and frequently publishes articles on political related issues. Keara Murphy is an unmarried widow and the daughter of a prominent New York international business attorney, and her mother is a senior copy editor for the New York Times.'*

With his assembled dossier on U.S. Marshal Alan Burke, Atwood presented his findings to Thomas Felts. "You need to take a look at this, Boss."

Atwood never revealed to Thomas Felts the true sequence of events at Mohawk. It was Atwood's idea, not Thomas Felts, to kill the deputy sheriff to cast blame for the killing on gunfire from concealed striking miners to magnify the threat of unionized violence. Unexpectedly seeing Burke and his deputy U.S. marshal standing next to the deputy sheriff, Atwood decided to make the opportunity far more serious and ensure federal intervention by causing the deaths of federal law enforcement officers. He explained his version of events to Felts as, "One of my men raised his rifle pointing it toward Burke when we stood facing each other close together on a slight rise. Burke reacted as if threatened then drew his .45 from a shoulder holster and shot the detective that raised his rifle. My other detective reacted by trying to shoot Burke but missed and hit either Burke's deputy or the county sheriff deputy. Not sure which. Gunfire erupted from miners positioned in the woods from both sides of the mining camp. I attempted to retreat to find cover and looked straight at Burke who then put a bullet in my arm.

"I was in a bad way losing a lot of blood from my arm. The boys bound my arm with a tourniquet to stop the bleeding then drove me to the nearest doctor an hour away in Welch. After coming out of surgery the next day, I thought it best to let all the deaths be blamed on the miners' ambush. Burke is federal law enforcement with powerful friends. I can't prove he instigated the incident. I can't accuse him. No witnesses close enough to corroborate what happened. Much the same circumstances surrounding the murder of your two brothers in Matewan by Hatfield and Chambers."

Felts read the dossier on Burke. After absorbing every detail, he said to Atwood, "Excellent piece of detective work, Leland. What do you think Burke was doing at Mohawk?"

"No way to know exactly. Burke has no legal jurisdiction over any of this labor strife, yet he apparently has a personal interest in events. Burke has reasons to hate the mining companies and Baldwin-Felts with the deaths of his father and brother. Lately the injury to his mother in Matewan. Somehow, he hooked up with this Murphy woman. Possibly when she first began writing about the coal wars starting with the strike in Kanawha County in 1912. I'd say Burke is pursuing a vendetta. Afterall, he's a native from this region infamous for the celebrated Hatfield-McCoy feud. These mountain people tend to settle disputes with a gun. Whatever his motivations, as U.S. Marshal that makes Burke a dangerous adversary, Sir."

"I agree. Especially if Burke is allied with his wife. It would be beneficial if we could eliminate Murphy's attacks on Baldwin-Felts in the national press. Get some people to put them both under surveillance. For a start, try to identify Murphy's local sources for the information she publishes. Also, the photographs that make her articles more powerful. Appears she has a network of sources armed with cameras working in the southern counties. Make it your objective to find a way to interrupt the flow of damaging press material, Leland."

"I'll get some people on it right away."

Felts said, "Right now I'm more focused on seeing Sid Hatfield and Ed Chambers brought to justice for murdering Albert and Lee. I will not leave their deaths unavenged."

"I understand, Sir. I've got that spy Charles Lively, code named *Number Nine,* we use on confidential internal documents, already working on it. I recruited him to Baldwin-Felts years ago during the Paint Creek & Cabin Creek Strike. Strange fellow. Good with people, makes friends easily among union miners, yet has no qualms about betraying them. He even has a history as a dues-paying UMW member while spying for us. Considers spying as a profession. Gives him a sense of power I imagine. He was useful in Colorado.

"Got Lively working undercover in Matewan. Situated him there since the gunfight in May. Fronted him to set up in the restaurant business. His establishment occupies the first floor of the same building housing the local offices of the UMW on the second floor. He's working on his restaurant patrons trying to identify witnesses willing to give incriminating testimony against Hatfield. We're paying him to put together enough evidence to convince the district attorney to present to a grand jury to seek an indictment against Sid Hatfield and everyone associated with the murder of Albert and Lee."

—

While Thomas Felts was consumed with his own vendetta against Sid Hatfield, Leland Atwood directed his hatred toward Alan Burke. Every minute of every day his severely debilitated arm reminded him of what happened months earlier in Mohawk. Learning more about his nemesis only increased his motivation for eliminating Burke regardless of whatever collateral damage that might involve. Better yet if that collateral damage included should his wife.

Atwood immediately sent four Baldwin-Felts detectives to Charleston. 24-hour surveillance using two teams of two detectives, one to shadow Burke, the other his wife. They were to report in each day by telephone to him personally. Within a week the detectives surveilling Burke produce intelligence following Burke making his rounds by train of the federal court's divisions.

The first piece of information to draw interest was a visit by Burke with a Catholic priest in Williamson. Was Burke a practicing Catholic? What was his relationship with this priest? Atwood assigned a local Baldwin-Felts operative to investigate the priest.

With Bluefield as one of his marshal offices, Burke held interviews with candidates for replacing the deputy he lost at Mohawk. However, before even appearing at the local U.S. marshal office, Burke first paid a visit to a boarding house in the town. Atwood later assigned a detective from headquarters to investigate.

The following day, Atwood received his first telephone reports. The priest in Williamson was the local pastor. Father Patrick Geary. Irish. Large congregation of Irish and Italian mining families. Geary was well known as an activist ministering mostly to a congregation of mine workers. Known to deliver fiery sermons condemning the mining companies. Reportedly using derogatory terms liking slave owners for the mining companies with their murderous overseers Baldwin-Felts. An active supporter for union organizing efforts by the United Mine Workers.

From Charleston, detectives watching Keara Burke observed her picking up mail and a small package from a post office box. Some money changed hands with a postal clerk who provided the name of the postal box holder as K. S. Reynolds. Inquiring as to the sender, the clerk said she did not handle the mail distribution. With the promise of a future bribe for obtaining that information, the clerk agreed to monitor the mailing locations of the mail to the postal box. The detective said he would return periodically.

By observing the comings and goings of the boarding house residents, Atwood learned there was a high school teacher by the name of Noreen Hannigan. Further investigation determined

Hannigan was Burke's older sister. Widowed by the death of her husband in the same incident that took the lives of her father and another brother in 1912. More than that, staying with her was an elderly woman that was soon determined to be her mother, Maude Burke.

This intelligence gave Atwood targets of those close to Burke that might be useful in extracting revenge. However, only personally killing Burke would satisfy Atwood's need for revenge.

—

Since 1917 when the United States entered the war in Europe, Secretary of War Newton Baker initiated a policy of allowing direct access for Governor Cornwell to appeal directly to the Fifth U.S. Army Corps Area commander for federal assistance to quell civil violence. That was a wartime expedient to avoid characteristic delays in seeking presidential authority. This typically involved placing state national guard units under federal military authority to act under a federal declaration of martial law. Since the end of November 1920, federal infantry from Ohio attempted to contain the violence under a mandate of only state-declared limited martial law. Their authority was hampered by the West Virginia State Police force and county law enforcement retaining control of the state-ordered declaration of martial law.

The fact that West Virginia never reconstituted its national guard after demobilization following the Armistice rankled Secretary Baker. Baker instructed the Fifth Corps commander General Reid to plan for the imminent recall of his federal forces from West Virginia. Yet both General Reid and Governor Cornwell feared the potential for serious violence with the forthcoming trial of Sid Hatfield and other defendants charged with the murder of Albert Felts in Matewan the previous May. Cornwell assured Baker that federal troops were needed until the state legislature voted pending legislation to reconstitute the West Virginia national guard. Secretary Baker agreed to delay beginning incrementally withdrawing troops only until January.

Through the efforts of Thomas Felts and Baldwin-Felts operations supervisor Leland Atwood, an indictment for murder was handed down by a grand jury in Williamson, the county seat of Mingo County. The activities of Baldwin-Felts spy Charles Lively proved instrumental in bringing Hatfield to trial. Witness bribery for delivering incriminating testimony produced sufficient testimony produce an indictment from a less than neutral grand jury. This was an intensely personal vendetta for Thomas Felts for the deaths of his two brothers. Illustrative of the corporate authoritarianism prevailing in West Virginia, the presiding judge further allowed Felts to provide and pay a team of four experienced criminal lawyers to assist the local prosecutor.

Following delays after two motions for continuance were granted by the presiding judge, the trial of Sid Hatfield and the other defendants charged in the events of the Battle of Matewan was eventually scheduled to begin January 28, 1921. Hatfield and his codefendants became instant celebrities among the population of coal miners. The community easily raised bonds in the amount of $10,000 for each defendant immediately following indictments.

The trial held all the promise of a spectacle and a referendum on the hold of mining interests in Mingo County. In such an emotionally charged environment, the threat of violence loomed large should the defendants be found guilty. Expected to be a lengthy trial, federal troops would have been withdrawn leaving law enforcement to the inadequate resources of the West Virginia State Police and the Mingo County Sheriff Department.

—

Continued surveillance of Alan Burke and Keara Murphy yielded Atwood only limited information in subsequent weeks. Burke had made repeated contact with Father Geary in Williamson in Mingo County as well as in Charleston. No way to determine the reason for their meetings. Atwood believes that Geary acts as a source of information from within the population of striking miners across the region. It is possible that Geary could be the source of photographs and local intelligence finding its way to Keara Murphy for use in her inflammatory articles.

As a priest, Geary probably enjoys wide access to union miners across the region that could serve as a network of clandestine sources armed with small modern cameras. The information provided by the Charleston postal clerk on material addressed to K. S. Reynolds is postmarked from many different locations across the southern West Virginia Counties. That does not lead to narrowing the source, or multiple sources, of Murphy's surprisingly detailed information of material for constructing her published articles. As for the photographs, that might point to Father Geary who can recruit an unlimited number of spies within the mining community and arm them with cameras. Regardless of a network of sources, eliminating Murphy would close off the most troublesome of the bad press.

Noreen has been careful in disguising the origin of intelligence against Baldwin-Felts and never mails material from Bluefield. Instead, she takes the trouble of mailing Francis Duncan's information to Keara Murphy from the town of Princeton 12 miles away by car, or from Welch 35 miles away by train to avoid postmarks from Bluefield. Somewhat awkward but necessary to protect Francis Duncan and even herself. Father Geary also varies his mailings of candid photographs from different locations.

While the continued surveillance on Burke and Murphy did not yield much new information, it did provide detailed information on the habits and movements of Keara Murphy. Enough information for Leland Atwood to begin planning his revenge on Burke by targeting Murphy with the support of Thomas Felts. He would keep his four assets monitoring them until satisfied that he had a workable operational plan.

—

While Leland Atwood plotted against Burke and Murphy, Burke moved forward on his plan for going after Logan County despot Don Chafin. It was common knowledge that Chafin financially benefited from protecting moonshining operations in the county. Now with Prohibition the law of the land, distributing illicit mountain liquor produced a lucrative market in urban centers outside West Virginia.

Burke turned to Bill Blizzard of the UMW for assistance in producing intelligence. The UMW had thousands of union coal miners in Logan County. While the miners liked their moonshine, they universally hated Don Chafin. The miners might not be keen on turning on fellow mountain moonshiners, but some might be amenable to providing information on Chafin's distribution business.

Blizzard's office was located on Kanawha Boulevard on the river just several blocks from Burke's office in the federal courts building on Capital Street. Since Blizzard rendered assistance to Burke's mother after her assault in Matewan, Burke and Blizzard were on friendly terms. While Blizzard understood Burke's sympathies were with the coal miners, Burke never discussed his clandestine activities with Father Geary.

Over coffee in Blizzard's office one morning, Burke said, "As a federal law enforcement officer, I am responsible for enforcing Prohibition. Stupid as the law is, I have a duty to perform. Thought I might start with Logan County."

Blizzard smiled broadly, "Couldn't happen in a better place. You know that sonofabitch Don Chafin is up to his arse in moonshining."

"That's what I'm told. Would like to avoid coming down on mountain men making whiskey as they've done for generations to help get by. Don't have the manpower to go stompin' around the hills looking for moonshine stills anyway. Thought I'd go after the distribution side of the business instead. Hit the collection sites where they warehouse the liquor for loading onto trucks. Thought maybe some of your rank and file might think that as a good bit of fun to piss on Chafin. Make a few dollars as special deputies."

Blizzard laughed. "I'm sure I can find some boys willing to help out."

"Thanks, Bill."

CHAPTER 23

West Virginia | December 1920

Bill Blizzard came through in short order. He provided four different warehousing locations where moonshine was collected from numerous stills and warehoused. Chafin's enterprise had advanced from distributing moonshine by getting into barrel-aging in 20-gallon oak barrels to make whiskey. The predominately clear raw moonshine product takes on the amber color of aged whiskey as the internally charred oak barrels impart subtle flavors with the liquid absorbing into the wood over time. This product looked and tasted closer to pre-Prohibition commercial whiskeys that commanded higher prices than *white lightning.*

Summoned to Blizzard's office, Blizzard laid out a map of Logan County. Pointing with his finger, "This one outside of Rossmore just south of the town of Logan is said to be the largest of the illegal whiskey aging warehouses. A prosperous working farm with a herd of beef cattle and two barns. One barn houses hay for winter cattle feed, the other is the whiskey warehouse. Whiskey barrels are stacked on racks for aging concealed by surrounded stacks of bailed hay when you enter the barn. The location is well back off this secondary road about here I'm told.

"A couple of other warehouses are located where I've marked on the map. I've noted what my sources had to say about each location. You know of course that Chafin has hundreds of deputies at his disposal, mostly contracted to the mines as guards. They could be serving as security at these locations."

"Well aware of how Boss Chafin operates. Forces the mine operators to contract with him rather than Baldwin-Felts. Has the benefit of controlling the county with his own private army legalized as law enforcement."

"Lots of fellas with a badge toting a gun. How you plan to contend with that?"

"As federal law enforcement pursuing criminal violation of federal law, my authority overrides local law enforcement, legitimate or otherwise. However, I'm mindful of how things are in West Virginia. As U.S. marshal I have the authority to deputize others as necessary to execute my responsibilities. My full-time deputy marshals are spread out covering twenty-three counties. Just three of them after losing one in that firefight in Mohawk a few months back. Can you recommend a couple of good fellas? Must be former soldiers so I can count on men accustomed to discipline. Intelligent. Trusted men of good character."

Blizzard replied, "I'll cast about. Should be able to find some candidates. Might this lead to full-time work as deputy marshals?"

"Possibly. Need at least to replace one opening in Bluefield. These guys I need should not have ties to Logan County. Don't want to put targets on the backs of any locals with the likes of Chafin's army of deputy sheriffs. But none of the candidates are to know anything about what I'm planning to do in Logan."

"I understand. I'm sure I can come up with some names that might be suitable."

Burke had no doubt about finding a few good men willing to take on what he expected might become dangerous work. Accordingly, he telephoned Washington to requisition the necessary weapons to equip extra deputies. With the push to enforce Prohibition, the Department of Justice cooperated immediately.

His regular deputy staff were woefully under armed. Their standard-issue sidearm was the Smith & Weston Model 10 double action .38 caliber revolver with a four-inch barrel. The most popular police weapon of the time. For what Burke had planned he needed greater firepower.

A couple of weeks later a shipment of arms and ammunition arrived in a wooden crate by train. Enough to reequip four full-time deputy marshals and another four for temporary deputies with heavy duty firepower. Springfield 30-06 rifles, Winchester 12-gauge pump shotguns, and reliable Colt Peacemaker .45 caliber revolvers. Heavier caliber with a longer barrel than the Smith & Weston police .38s. As a force multiplier, the shipment also included a Browning automatic rifle.

—

With traffic coming and going in the federal building housing the U.S. district court, U.S. attorney's office, and U.S. marshal's office, it was difficult for Atwood's surveillance positioned outside. Therefore, the handful of candidates for consideration as temporary deputies coming in to see Burke over several days did not produce any names of interest from the Baldwin-Felts watcher.

Blizzard's efforts produced three suitable candidates. Two were coal miners and one was a former coal miner turned union organizer. All fought in the U.S. Army in the Great War as part of the AEF. The union organizer even recalled hearing of the exploits of Marine Sergeant Major Burke at Belleau Wood. Burke planned on striking at one of Chafin's illicit liquor warehouse locations with a team of three plus himself. Instead of using his full-time deputy in Charleston, he would hire all three of these candidates on a temporary basis. He had sufficient budgeted funds specifically allocated for illicit liquor enforcement.

Explaining that the job meant going after bootlegging in violation of the Prohibition law, he made a point of saying he was not going after the proliferation of small still operations endemic to life in Appalachia. "Not going after good ole boys you might know making their shine for local consumption."

One fellow asked, "You expectin' some sort of a firefight with these bootleggers?"

"Could be. That's why I'm recruiting men like you that know what that means. Soldiers that understand discipline and are good with a rifle, shotgun, and revolver."

With the promise of two months' good pay and a chance for permanent employment outside the mines, all three enthusiastically jumped at the opportunity.

—

After the weapons arrived, Burke set off by car for the sixty-mile journey south to the target farm outside Rossmore in Logan County. There was little traffic on these backroads. After getting several miles outside Charleston, he noticed another car that seemed to be following after he purposedly slowed down to a crawl allowing the other vehicle to pass. Instead, the car following at reduced speed to stay behind him.

Pulling off onto what appeared as nothing more than a wagon path climbing over a hill, Burke parked his car. Quickly getting out, he ran into the nearby trees and circled back down toward the road. From concealment, he looked down at the car that had been following, now pulled off the main road.

After watching for several minutes, the car pulled onto the wagon path and climbed to the crest of the slight rise. Seeing Burke's car parked at a distance, the driver likely assumed Burke was relieving himself.

Without waiting Burke came up quickly to the car's driver side with his .45 drawn.

Tapping the .45 on the window, the startled driver rolled down the window. "Thought you might be having car trouble. Not much traffic on this road."

"Out of the car!" Burke said.

"Who are you? What's this about?" the driver stammered.

Frisking the man, Burke felt the revolver at his waist. Pulling open the man's overcoat, Burke removed the revolver then demanded, "Identification."

With a sigh of resignation, the man produced his wallet. Inside a card revealed him as an employee of Baldwin-Felts. Burke said, "Why are you following me?"

"I'm not following you. Just trying to be helpful."

Burke struck him on the forehead with the barrel of his Browning eliciting a sharp exclamation of pain. "Try again."

"Don't know why. Just following orders. I'm with a detective agency."

"You realize I'm a federal marshal?"

The man nodded.

"What am I then to do with you?"

"I'm not breaking any law."

"Well, I don't know about that. Could probably invent some charge to arrest you. The problem then becomes I'm stuck with you. Think I'll just let you go. We're a good many miles from anywhere and it's damn cold today. Suggest you walk briskly to keep warm."

With that, Burke took the man's revolver and shot out all four tires and the spare. As Burke turned his car around and pulled past the man standing there, Burke yelled to him, "You tell Leland Atwood I catch anyone watching me again, they'll end up in the hospital or with the undertaker."

The incident confirmed that Atwood presented a personal threat. That raised concern for Keara's safety as a possible means of getting at him. Burke realized the reason for this trip would make for another powerful enemy. His new career in law enforcement was proving far more than administration of federal courts and the occasional serving of summons and court orders.

—

The reconnaissance foray into Logan County provided a good look at the illicit whiskey storage facility. Burke spent several hours observing the activity at the farm from a distance concealed in a stand of trees using binoculars. He identified a handful of men in the barn that served as storage for aging barrels of whiskey. Others acting as security were likely keeping warm inside the farmhouse. Just in the time spent watching the location, Burke observed several trucks delivering whiskey barrels as well as a couple being loaded for transport.

A week later, Burke was again making the trip south to execute the raid. This time accompanied by his three well-armed temporary deputies. He had no reason to distrust any of his regular deputy marshals, but West Viriginia was a troubled place with divided loyalties. Other than his deputy in Charleston, he did not know the political leanings of the other two posted to Huntington and Beckley all that well. With the unfortunate Bluefield deputy killed at Mohawk, Burke only suspicioned his anti-miner sentiments. Better to tighten security for this raid and leave his regulars to attend to administrative court matters in the various jurisdictional locations.

Before setting out to raid Chafin's bootlegging warehouse, Burke picked up his men at predetermined locations. Sworn in as deputy U.S. marshals, they knew they would be earning their pay this day as they shared space in the four seat Model T with Burke's arsenal. Once outside Charleston, Burke stopped in a secluded rural area. "Step out men. I'll explain what we'll be doin' today."

"You can see by the weapons I'm expecting trouble. Before we get back in the car, each of you strap on the Colt revolvers. Pick a Springfield rifle just like you used in France along with a shotgun. Load all the weapons. When we arrive at our destination after a couple of hours of driving. We'll be making entry into a barn by surprise. Sling the Springfields on your shoulder and put several additional ammo clips in your pockets. You'll be going in with the shotguns. I'll be taking the BAR should we need that kind of firepower."

"What's the objective, Marshal.?" One of the men asked.

"A barn full of barrels of whiskey. You'll be hitting Don Chafin in his wallet where it 'll hurt the most."

Everyone laughed. One said, "Sonofabitch! That'll be like kicking a hornets' nest. What kind of opposition you expectin', Marshal?"

"Hard to tell. A handful of guys working in the barn. Probably security guards in the farmhouse. Don't know if there are armed reserves close nearby. Could turn into quite a firefight. Since you fellas volunteered, y'all still on board?"

They all nodded, with one commenting, "Damn right! Wouldn't miss the chance to kick Don Chafin in the balls."

As they set off, Burke's mind wandered as these former soldiers bantered amongst themselves as a way of dealing with nervousness before going into battle. He realized here again was another December in West Virginia, up to his neck in the recurring violence of the place. First returning home following the death of his father and brother. Then a year ago returning to accept what he feared might prove a boring career in federal law enforcement. Careful what you wish for. During the past year he experiencing the personal violence inflicted on his mother and his own narrow escape of death at Mohawk.

Today he hoped to overpower these bootleggers without resorting to violence. Unknown was what sort of security he might face. For the remainder of the drive, he cleared his mind by surveying the countryside of Appalachia. The trees were barren of leaves, yet a couple of months ago this magnificent land would have been awash with the reds and yellows of autumn color. Unspoiled wild land if not despoiled by coal mining. The soil poorly suited for large scale farming but suited for raising livestock. Now he had come here to make war on moonshining. A way of life for these people for generations.

Reaching the destination, Burke pulled onto a little used track a quarter mile from the farm he found during his reconnaissance trip. Today the track was covered with a light dusting of snow confirming no traffic had passed over it in the last twenty-four hours.

Burke led his team to observe the objective from a stand of trees on a low hill. When everyone had a chance to look through the binoculars, Burke said, "We'll wait down by the road until a truck shows up. Doesn't matter if delivering or taking on a load. It will draw out most of those working there into the open. Maybe any security people that might be in the house.

"We're going to leave our car concealed where it is while we wait close to the turnoff from the main road. You boys will stay hidden in the thicket while I wait for a truck to turn onto the road heading up to the farm. I'll flag it down."

"What if this truck has nothing to do with the whiskey business?"

"Doesn't much matter," Burke said. "It's the vehicle we're after. We'll use it to approach the barn without raising an alarm. We leave the occupants at the road and drive up to the barn. Once there we stop then immediately assault the barn. Delaney and I will make entry from the front. "I'll yell, this is a raid. Lay down any weapons and raise your hands. O'Shea and Taggart, you'll move to the backside of the barn to make entry from there. All three of you go in with the shotguns."

"What happens if any of these fellas shoot at us?"

"Return fire. Put down anyone that doesn't drop their weapon. You're peace officers. Firing at you or even pointing a gun at you is a criminal offense."

Thirty minutes after taking up position at the road, a stake-bed truck proceeding up the main road slowed and turned onto the drive for the farm. Burke stepped out in front of the ruck raising his hand. The heavy Browning automatic rifle supported with the sling over his shoulder was an intimidating sight."

The truck jerked to a stop and the driver stepped down from the cab. "What the fuck's goin' on!"

Burke swung the BAR pointing it at the driver. "Tell your partner to get out and come around here."

As Burke's team emerged from concealment. Burke said to the truckers, "You boys armed?"

They both nodded and handed over revolvers to Burke's deputies.

"What's your business at the farm?" Burke asked.

"Here to pick up a load."

"A load of what? Hay or whiskey?" Burke said sarcastically while smiling.

"Whiskey."

"How many people are at the farm?"

"Usually four in the warehouse."

"Security?"

"Usually two in the house."

"What kind of weapons?"

"All the workmen carry revolvers. The guards have Winchesters."

"You boys are done for the day. Start walking back the way you came. If I see you again it'll cost you prison time. Now git!"

Burke motioned for his deputies to get into the idling truck, O'Shea and Taggart climbed up into the truck bed then crouched behind the cab.

Burke drove the truck past the front barn housing hay to the whiskey barn off to the left and behind the front barn. As he stopped the truck a man swung open the two large barn doors. Turning around he shook his head with an expression of disgust as he walked over to the truck.

As Burke opened the truck door, the man said, "Turn the fuckin' truck around and back into the barn. You new at doin' this?"

Burke drew his .45 semi-automatic from his shoulder holster. Stepping up to the startled man, "Drop that gun on your hip to the ground." The man complied. "How many others inside?"

"Four."

Burke pulled the BAR from the cab with his left hand. "Walk in front of me. You know what this big rifle is?"

The man shook his head.

"It's a machine gun. It'll cut your mates in half. Best if they surrender or they'll die."

Unfortunately, events materialized differently. One workman saw Burke and scurried back out of sight. Someone inside fired a shot. As Oshea and Taggart made entry in the rear, an exchange of gunfire erupted.

The men working the warehouse did not put up an effective fight. One was killed and another wounded within a minute. The other two threw down their weapons and stepped forward. Outside was a different matter. Burke watched as two men armed with rifles came running from the farmhouse and took up positions behind a hay wagon for cover. These were security. However, they did not fire or attempt to approach the barn. Burke closed the large barn doors leaving them open a foot to observe what was going on outside.

Burke's deputies had the three warehouse uninjured workers seated at the base of a multi-layered rack holding oak barrels of whiskey.

Burke said, "We've got two out front with rifles. Positioned behind cover waiting for us to make our move. Delaney, you cover these fellas. O'Shea and Taggart, open up the bung holes of some of these barrels with a puller. One of you climb up to the barrels on the top rows and turn a couple of barrels to allow whiskey to spill over the barrels below."

"What you plan on doin, Boss?" Delaney asked.

"Torch the place."

Taggart said, "Shit! Ain't that kind of dangerous for us with those fellas out there?"

"When the time comes, we'll break out in the truck. That's why I brought along this BAR for firepower. Get to it, lads so we can leave."

Pulling the bung plugs from the side holes of enough barrels to release enough flammable whiskey took some many minutes. Burke eyed the men outside still hunkered down behind the wagon. He guessed that they made a telephone call to summon help.

A short time later, a car arrived coming to a stop near the house. Four men armed with rifles exited then made their way to the hay wagon.

Turning to Delaney, Burke said, "Reinforcements just arrived outside. Goin' to have to shoot our way out. You up to drivin' while the rest of us remain in the truck bed? I'll lay down suppressing fire with the BAR from over the cab while O'Shea and Taggart kneel to fire from the left side as we pass these gunmen."

"Got it, Boss. Where am I to drive to?"

"I'm thinking best to head out over the open ground. Should be frozen solid enough and the truck's unloaded. Make it up to the tree line." Burke pointed through the partially open barn door. "We abandon the truck and make it back to our car on foot. The bad guys may be sending more men.

"Get into the cab and start the engine. When we're ready push the doors open with the truck's bumper. I'll give them a couple of bursts from the BAR then turn to the right and head for the tree line."

Turning to O'Shea and Taggart, Burke yelled, "That'll do it, lads. Get over here." As both gathered next to him, "We're bustin' out here. Delaney is at the wheel. He'll head the truck across the field where we'll jump out and make it on foot to our car. I'll stand over the cab and give covering fire with the BAR as we break out of the barn. Now set this place ablaze."

As they lit puddles of whiskey with matches, the flames quickly licked upward to the soaked barrels on the racks. The warehouse workmen looked wide-eyed as the fire began taking hold. Burke yelled at them, "Get out the back and take your wounded mate with you."

With his deputies in the truck, Burke pounded the top of the cab signaling Dalaney to move out. Immediately as the truck pushed opened the barn doors, rifle rounds began pouring toward them. Delaney eased the truck out and swung the steering wheel to the right as he leaned over to avoid being hit by rifle fire.

The opposing gunmen broke cover to concentrate fire on the emerging truck. It provided Burke with clear shots to multiple targets. The Browning automatic rifle had a withering rate of automatic fire but only a 20-round magazine. Burke had a spare magazine in his coat pocket, but reloading would take valuable seconds while taking fire. He therefore needed to inflict maximum effect while he held the element of surprise before relying on O'Shea and Taggart to sustain firing while he reloaded.

While an automatic weapon, the BAR was exceptionally accurate. Burke used that to sight his target and fire short bursts. Three gunmen went down within seconds from the devastating 30-06 rounds sending the others dropping to the ground. As Delaney turned the truck, Burke riddled the hay wagon with the remaining rounds in the magazine. As he reloaded, O'Shea and Taggart began firing their rifles. The truck bounced across the open ground, both sides exchanged rifle fire. Burke saved his last BAR magazine should they need the firepower to make their escape out of Logan County.

None of Burke's deputies was wounded. Now on foot they looked back toward the barn. Heavy smoke and orange flame poured out the hay door near the barn roof.

Once inside their car, they emerged back onto the main road. With Delaney driving, Burke said, "You lads did a damn fine job today. Got a ways to go before we're out of Logan County. Have your revolvers at the ready should we meet any more of the opposition."

"Shame to see all that good whiskey go up in flames, but it felt good to stick it to Don Chafin," O'Shea commented as they all laughed.

Delaney asked, "How many casualties did we leave back there, Boss?"

"Don't rightly know. Besides the two in the barn, I saw three others go down after being hit with the BAR. Could be others."

CHAPTER 24

Mingo County, West Virginia | Spring-Summer 1921

The incident at Rossmore made all the West Virginia newspapers. Labelled as the Battle of Rossmore, the headline of the *Charleston Gazette-Mail* read '*U.S. MARSHALS INFLICT CASUALTIES ON LOGAN BOOTLEGGERS*'. The article opened with: *Yesterday U.S. Marshal Alan Burke led a raid on an illegal bootlegging warehouse outside the small community of Rossmore in Logan County. Expecting armed resistance by the bootleggers, the federal agents came prepared to enforce the new Prohibition laws. The ensuing gun battle pitted four U.S. marshals against an unknown but superior number of well-armed criminals. Trapped inside a farm barn housing barrels of whiskey aging in oak barrels, the federal agents became trapped inside while in the process of arresting those inside. A force of heavily armed men arrived forcing the federal agents to fight their way out under a hail of bullets. The marshals left behind four dead bootleggers and several others wounded without suffering any of their own casualties. As a former highly decorated U.S. Marine, Marshal Burke demonstrated extraordinary military skill in leading his deputy marshals in what became a fierce gunbattle.*

During the exchange of gunfire, the flammable illicit alcohol ignited. A local eyewitness reported the barn burned so hot that it ignited an adjacent hay barn on the farm burning both to the ground.

With the turning to the new year, the budget allocations for the U. S. marshal service increased with the demands imposed by

315

enforcing Prohibition. Burke had sufficient funding to not only for replace the loss of his Bluefield deputy with Delaney, but to also hire O'Shea and Taggart full-time. After serving in France during the war, returning to the mines for livelihood was a hard blow. These proven men jumped at the opportunity to pursue a career in real law enforcement not the often-corrupted local police working for powerful business or political interests.

In January, Burke used his expanded funding and staff to strike another of Chafin's bootlegging locations. This time he chose a major distribution location near Greenville, a small backwater fourteen miles south of Logan. This location was a sprawling collection of several barns. There was a working agricultural products cooperative with a smaller barn well off the road serving as a distribution center for illicit whiskey. The liquor travelled to Greenville by various means from collection sites and aging warehouses like at Rossmore. From the Greenville cooperative, shipments were regularly transported by truck eastward to Beckley, often concealed under loads of truck produce from the cooperative. In Beckley, Chafin had connections that bottled the aged whiskey. Using numerous ways of concealment as other goods, the whiskey was then shipped out on the C&O Railroad from Beckley to urban locations for distribution to speakeasies.

Burke's intelligence from Bill Blizzard's sources within the mining community fixed Greenville as the best target to damage Chafin's bootlegging distribution infrastructure. This raid would be with a heavier force. With his new three deputies he would add his Charleston and Beckley deputies.

In two cars, Burke and his five deputies hit the *Greenville Agricultural Cooperative* after making the drive from Bluefield where they spent the previous night. With advance intelligence, they knew how many armed guards usually protected the place. Observing the location from a hill, Burke formed an attack plan to avoid a repeat of the Rossmore incident.

Armed with shotguns with Delaney in reserve with the BAR should circumstances turn ugly, they overwhelmed all the guards without firing a shot. After placing them in handcuffs, Burke pulled all the workers together. "If you fellas want to avoid arrest, you'll do as I say. For starters, all this liquor needs destroying. You heard about the fire in Rossmore. Let's not have a fire here. Spill it all onto the ground. Be quick about it. Use axes to the barrels. Don't be stupid and try anything or you'll end up going to prison. Now get at it."

It took a couple of hours to destroy all the barrels of whiskey. There was legitimate activity going on at the cooperative produce barn, but everything stopped after learning what was going on in the liquor barn a short distance away. Everyone at the location knew about the bootlegging. A group of other workers stood at a distance watching the goings on even though it was a bitter cold day.

While his deputies supervised the destruction of the whiskey, Burke came up to a group of men. "I'm U.S. Marshal Burke. You fellas are not in any trouble. In fact, I'm inclined to give your friends working the liquor barn a break by not arresting them. Pass the word that trafficking in alcohol is now illegal. If you know those making moonshine, tell them to keep it here in the mountains. Try shipping it to the cities to make money, they risk arrest or getting shot.

"Right now, I'm arresting those that were armed protected Boss Chafin's liquor. They're goin' to jail. Facing serious time in a federal penitentiary. Got a half dozen that need transport to Beckley. I'll pay good money for someone to drive them in one of those covered delivery trucks parked over there. Anyone interested?"

An older man said, "Me and my sons have two trucks and we're headed for Beckley. We can make room to haul those arrested fellas."

Burke said, "Be ready to leave within the hour." He also suspected that these might be truckers already scheduled to take illicit whiskey into Beckley for bottling, but no matter. Once in Beckley, the county seat of Raleigh County, Burke delivered those arrested at Greenville to the local sheriff for incarceration under federal criminal charges.

Burke was however not done with bloodying Don Chafin. The following morning his team raided the location that bottled the whiskey and prepared shipment by rail disguised as legitimate goods. This raid also avoided violence except for the destruction of a lot of bottled whiskey to the dismay of his Irish marshals. Five more arrestees were delivered to the surprised sheriff who knew this to be Don Chafin's operation. Following the Battle of Rossmore, this new U.S. Marshal was declaring war on Chafin.

—

Atwood was displeased over the failure of his surveillance sources to learn of Burke's raid at Rossmore. Burke's miraculous escape from another fierce gun battle all the more frustrating as a missed opportunity. A tough man to kill. Now a popular hero after a series of other successful raids against illicit liquor trafficking further galled Atwood. Having never learned that Burke and his deputies spent the night in Bluefield before the raids at Greenville and Beckley angered him further.

Don Chafin was universally hated, and common opinion assumed Chafin controlled whiskey making and bootlegging in Logan County. Atwood now understood that someone else with powerful resources had reason for eliminating Burke. Chafin might become useful as an ally.

While Atwood harbored his own need for exacting revenge, his boss Thomas Felts, was about to experience his own frustration at thwarted revenge. The trial of former Matewan Police Chief Sid Hatfield and twenty-two other defendants for the murder of Felts' brother Albert the prior May got underway at the Williamson courthouse in Mingo County on January 28.

The entire city was on edge. Businesses closed. People stayed off the street fearing violence could easily erupt. Fifty state police took strategic positions around the courthouse. The morning of the trial as many as forty Baldwin-Felts mine guards milled about the vicinity, all heavily armed.

On the third day of the trial a union miner told the trial judge that 1,000 armed miners were ready to descend on Williamson should Baldwin-Felts seek revenge by murdering the defendants if they were acquitted. Convinced it was no bluff, a truce was arranged. Baldwin-Felts removed their men from the town and the miners stood down.

Despite Thomas Felts assisting the prosecution by paying the services of four additional attorneys, and bribing witnesses to provide damaging testimony against Hatfield, after nine weeks, the jury acquitted all the defendants on March 19. The proceeding was a judicial farce. Regardless of the truth of what transpired that day setting off the gunfight, the verdict was a foregone certainty. No juror could cast a guilty vote without fear for his or his family's life. This was a community of coalminers. With the acquittal, Sid Hatfield took on even greater stature for again standing against the mine operators and Baldwin-Felts.

Another blow to Thomas Felts that only hardened his resolve to see Sid Hatfield dead. That meant the burden of achieving that objective fell to Leland Atwood.

—

The United Mine Workers launched a concerted campaign to unionize all the southern West Virginia coal mines. Those mine operators in the Tug Fork coalfield took the initiative by increasing use of the most intransigent hostile positions to keep the UMW out. Miners who joined the union were fired resulting in increased evictions from company-owned houses. Non-union replacement workers provoked new rounds of sporadic violence.

In newspaper accounts of the violent encounters, Burke could detect the probable handiwork of those snipers he outfitted and trained. However, the striking miners never deployed guerrilla-style tactics for optimized effect. The low-level warfare seemed to involve ad hoc groups against questionable targets of opportunity, poorly planned.

Father Geary remained active by keeping a continual stream of detailed reports and candid photographs flowing to Keara from his network of sources. The depiction of the hopeless circumstances of thousands of miners and their families stuck in the backcountry of Appalachia made for her powerfully moving pieces appearing in national publications.

Maintaining order in Mingo County fell to newly elected Sheriff Pinson and the state police force under Captain Brokus. Violence held to a manageable level until May. Striking miners on both sides of the tug Fork River then began widespread rifle sniping at houses, trains, cars, mine equipment, and Baldwin-Felts agents.

On Thursday May 12, striking miners organized a more organized assault with gunfire from the hills on a dozen mining communities along the Tug River from Williamson to Matewan. Nonunion miners, Baldwin-Felts mine guards, Mingo County sheriff deputies, the West Virginia State Police and Kentucky National Guardsmen from across the river fired back. The thousands of shots fired created a no man's land. Unfortunately, homes with families of non-combatants lay within reach of the bullets. Bridges and mine tipples were sabotaged with dynamite. Fighting raged for three days before a truce was arranged between the State Police and striking miners with the aid of a courageous physician that made his way into the hills. The engagement became known as the *Three Days Battle of the Tug*. While the exact casualty count was never known, reliable accounts placed the number of casualties in the dozens.

While the battle raged, newly elected Governor Ephraim Morgan having taken office in March, requested President Harding to send federal troops. Washington again declined, claiming this remained a West Virginia problem. Governor Morgan had at his disposal the West Virginia militia that had been reconstituted by the state legislature as a National Guard unit in March.

Left with no alternative, Governor Morgan, declared martial law. Acting Adjutant General of the West Virginia National Guard Major Thomas Davis posted the proclamation in Charleston. On May 21, two companies of the West Virginia National Guard joined Captain Brokus' state police and Mingo County Sheriff A. C. Pinson to maintain order under the limited martial law declaration.

By this time the coal mine operators had the upper hand politically using legally empowered armed resources. With the added manpower of the West Virginia National Guard, State

Police Captain Brokus also organized a *Vigilance Committee* in Mingo County to help enforce the restrictions imposed by martial law. This vigilante group was comprised entirely of middle-class non-union miners.

In late May, trouble erupted at the union subsidized Lick Creek tent encampment of striking miners near the Big Splint Colliery. After the death of a law enforcement officer, hostilities escalated. A report of a car carrying the superintendent of the White Star mining Company as it passed through the tent encampment being fired on prompted a response by authorities. Investigating firsthand, Major Davis, Captain Brokus, and Sheriff Pinson were then fired on. The enraged Brokus returned with state police and vigilantes.

On June 14, these armed forces raided the Lick Creek tent colony. The raid went largely unopposed by the miners. Brokus ordered the tent colony destroyed. They shredded the canvas tents and burned the belongings of the mining families. One miner was killed and another injured. 47 miners were arrested then marched to Williamson and jailed in a single cell. The same day, the state supreme court ruled that under a declaration of martial law only military authorities were empowered to enforce order forcing the release of the Lick Creek arrestees. A rare symbolic win for unionized miners that did nothing to stem the growing tensions in the southern West Virginia coalfields.

—

In July, President Harding appointed George McClintic as the new Federal district judge for the Southern District of West Virginia. A large backlog of cases existed from the months-long vacancy of a sitting district judge resulting from the infirmity of former Judge Keller. Burke's administrative workload immediately increased with reestablishing the functioning of the several court locations within the district.

McClintic was a blunt often abrasive individual. For whatever reason, he enthusiastically embraced his court's responsibility for upholding the Volsted Act and the Eighteenth Amendment to the

U. S. Constitution. His court soon became dominated by criminal cases for Prohibition violations. McClintic therefore took a liking to Burke for what he deemed aggressive pursuit of criminal activity for Burke's publicized bootlegging raids in Logan County.

—

Thomas Felts' rage over the deaths of his brothers Albert and Lee over a year earlier in Matewan became further inflamed with the acquittal of Sid Hatfield in March. Not only the personal loss of his brothers, but further embarrassment to the Baldwin-Felts Detective Agency. With no judicial way to bring Hatfield to the gallows, Felts decided to take extrajudicial action. Immediately after the not guilty verdict in Williamson, Leland Atwood proposed an extreme solution. Anywhere other than in the coalfields of southern West Virginia, his scheme would be deemed inconceivable for its audacity flaunting of the law.

"If you want Sid Hatfield put in a coffin, I have an idea, Boss. I can stage an incident in McDowell County. I'll create another incident at the Mohawk Coal & Coke Company's mine in Mohawk like what happened last July. Shoot up the mining camp now housing mostly non-union workers and a small community nearby with a post office, general store, and not much else. The few people living there mostly work for the mine in supervisory or administrative jobs. Some of our detectives will dress in work clothes and shoot up the place. They won't harm anyone, just raise a general ruckus while threatening mining employees."

"Where does Hatfield come into your scheme?" Felts asked.

"We blame him and his deputy Ed Chambers for leading a bunch of union miners from Mingo County in the attack. A show of force instigated by the UMW to pressure the Mohawk miners into joining the union. Make it out to be Hatfield demonstrating his new influence as a hero of the coal miners. We then build a case with enough witness depositions to get the McDowell district attorney to file charges. If we can get an indictment, Hatfield and Chambers will be required to go on trial in Welch.

"We have a sympathetic sheriff in McDowell County. We make sure that we control the environment when Hatfield and Chambers appear for trial. No sheriff deputies around to interfere. Hatfield is known for bragging about using his gun. We have a couple of men shoot him before he gets to the courthouse claiming self-defense. If he's not carrying a gun, we'll plant one."

Thomas Felts reflected for a moment before replying, "Do whatever you need to do, Leland. I want Sid Hatfield dead. Nobody ever killed a Baldwin-Felts man and lived very long to brag about it. Especially can't allow Hatfield getting off scot-free after murdered my brothers."

The confrontation where Atwood suffered injury resulted in Mohawk Coal & Coke now operating with a non-union workforce. That offered a plausible cause for staging an alleged UMW incident. Atwood began working to build enough evidence against Hatfield to force criminal charges for his alleged participation in violence in McDowell County and bring him to trial.

In mine operator-friendly McDowell County, Atwood's efforts proved successful with a grand jury returning an indictment against Sid Hatfield and Ed Chambers for attempted murder. A trial date was set for August in the county seat town of Welch. According to sworn depositions by numerous Baldwin-Felts mine guards and anti-union white collar mine employees living in the area, Sid Hatfield and his deputy Ed Chambers led Mingo County strikers in the armed assault.

Sid Hatfield and Ed Chambers arrived in Welch on a morning train from Matewan with their wives and a UMW provided attorney on Monday August 1. McDowell County Sheriff Bill Hatfield, no relationship to Sid Hatfield, assured them and UMW officials that his department would assure their safety. With this assurance, Sid Hatfield and Ed Chambers therefore arrived unarmed. They went to a hotel and secured rooms before setting off to the courthouse for arraignment.

Unknown to them, Sheriff Hatfield had left the county the day before to take the waters at Craig Healing Springs in Virginia. Furthermore, Sheriff Hatfield had deputized several Baldwin-Felts agents. All part of a deal struck with Leland Atwood.

Sid Hatfield and Ed Chambers accompanied by their wives left the hotel and walked through downtown Welch to the courthouse. The UMW attorney stayed behind at the hotel to answer a long-distance telephone call.

As all four climbed the steep steps up to the courthouse sitting atop a hill, Charles Lively stood on the stairs in front of Sid Hatfield and his wife. This was the restaurant owner and Baldwin-Felts spy from Matewan. "Hello, Sid, glad to see you." With that, he withdrew a revolver and shot Hatfield.

With Lively's first shot, other Baldwin-Felts, now deputized as sheriff deputies, began firing. Bill Salter, a survivor from the Matewan Massacre, was among the Baldwin-Felts agents firing at Sid Hatfield and Ed Chambers a few steps on the stairway behind Hatfield.

Hatfield was shot four times. Mrs. Hatfield turned to run toward the courthouse for help. Chambers was hit three times and fell backwards down the steps. Mrs. Chambers threw her body on top of her husband to protect him. Immediately a dozen Baldwin-Felts surrounded the fallen victims. Charles Lively ignored her pleas to stop shooting and placed the barrel of his revolver behind Chambers' ear and fired twice. Two Baldwin-Felts dragged a hysterical Mrs. Chambers away.

Since Hatfield and Chambers came unarmed, another Baldwin-Felts man, Buster Pence, placed guns in the hands of both victims to claim self-defense. Baldwin-Felts agents then repeatedly shot the bodies to make a statement of contempt. Hatfield's body was shot seventeen times, Chambers thirteen times.

Aware of the plot, Welch Chief of Police Mitchell watched the murders of Hatfield and Chambers from a safe distance across the street. There was also a detachment of West Virginia State Police in Welch at the time. With even the Governor aware of the high-profile legal proceedings in Welch accompanied by implicit rumors of possible violence, there was no order issued to afford protection of the defendants.

No attempt was made to conceal the blatant conspiracy behind the public assassinations of Sid Hatfield and Ed Chambers. The assassins were all employees of Baldwin-Felts. While the

Governor did not see fit to provide state police resources in Welch, he however assigned Captain Brokus to command a large contingent of state police armed with shotguns to prevent trouble for the funerals in Matewan. Thousands of miners gathered in the rain to pay their respects. No violence occurred yet the funeral marked a beginning of worsening violence rather than an ending.

The murders of Sid Hatfield and Ed Chambers became a watershed event that would push West Virginia coal miners into organized widespread confrontation against coal mine operators aided by corrupt government institutions under their influence.

CHAPTER 25

Mercer & Kanawha Counties, West Virginia | Summer 1921

Francis Duncan gathered a wealth of confidential intelligence from inside Baldwin-Felts headquarters following the murders of Sid Hatfield and Ed Chambers. Thomas Felts reveled in exacting his revenge. Sid Hatfield was one of few people to have stood against Baldwin-Felts. That it was public knowledge that Baldwin-Felts was responsible for the assassinations in Welch only bolstered their feared reputation.

Atwood took the opportunity to again suggest taking action to silence the journalist Keara Murphy and her husband U.S. Marshal Burke. The day after the successful killings in Welch, Atwood was unguarded in his comments with Felts.

"We need to silence Keara Murphy, Boss. Even if we don't move directly against her husband the U.S. Marshal, it will put him off from attacking us directly."

"What are you suggesting, Leland?"

"No need to kill her. Just damage her enough to stop her from publishing. Physically and emotionally damaging. Something explainable as just a sexual assault on an attractive woman. Nothing to point to us. I'll have a chat with Don Chafin. His name has appeared often in Murphy's articles. Chafin's pissed off and crazy enough to arrange going after Murphy as a way of indirectly getting even with Burke for disrupting his bootlegging trade. I'll offer to provide him with surveillance intelligence but let him do the dirty work."

Felts said, "Very well, go ahead. Just be careful to keep our name out of it."

—

Going about her duties, the trusted Francis Duncan picked up enough of this conversation between Felts and Atwood to understand the immediate threat to Murphy. That evening she typed up everything she overheard. Late that night, she slipped out to place an envelope in the dead drop of the old collapsed barn. In the morning, she would drop an unsigned letter addressed to Miss Noreen Hannigan in the mailbox at her boarding house reading *urgent information in the usual location.*

It was a warm summer night. Unknown to Francis, her father was outside their house sitting in a lawn chair drinking whiskey. She did not see him hidden from her view by the large oak tree in the backyard.

Clarence Duncan heard the back screen door creak then leaned forward to look around the tree. Expecting to see his wife in a flannel nightgown coming out to give him hell for sneaking out to get drunk, he was surprised instead see his daughter. Not only fully dressed, but looking about furtively as a neighbor's dog began barking.

Francis quickly made her way around the side of the house into the night. Her father followed her as she walked briskly down the street. He was able to keep at a distance without her seeing him while able to keep her in sight with a near full moon on this clear night.

It was over a quarter mile to the edge of Bluefield when Francis left the road and began walking through a field toward an old barn fallen into ruin. As she disappeared behind the collapsed pile of rotting roof timbers, he circled to observe her. All he could she was her doing something with what looked like a rock. After five minutes, she looked around then left in a hurry.

Clarence Duncan waited several minutes before approaching the spot where he saw his daughter doing something with a rock. With closer inspection then poking about the deteriorated field rock foundation of the barn, he eventually discovered the loose rock that concealed Francis' dead drop. Inside he found an envelope. What the hell was she doing?

There was enough moonlight to read the typed sheets inside the envelope. Under his breath, he said, "Sonofabitch!" Walking at a brisk pace back to his house while taking swigs of whiskey from the bottle he brought along only intensified his anger.

Arriving back home, Clarence Duncan made no attempt to conceal his rage. He slammed the door and made for his daughter's bedroom. Opening her bedroom door violently caused the doorknob to crash into the wall plaster. His daughter in a state of undress having removed her dress to slip into her nightgown, shrieked in surprise.

Her father pulled off his belt and began lashing his daughter's bare back. "You stupid bitch, what the fuck you been doin'?" Not stopping the beating, "You've been spyin' on your employer! Who you been givin' this to?"

Francis' mother came into the room and took hold of her husband's arm to stop his blows with the belt. "No more, Clarence! I won't stand for you touching Francis when you're drunk."

He thrust the typed pages toward his wife. "Look at this. The stupid girl's been spying on Baldwin-Felts. God knows who she's working for."

Francis' mother scanned the typed pages. "Good lord, Francis, What's this?"

Francis remained silent only sobbing as she got dressed.

His anger spent, Clarence Duncan said to both daughter and wife, "You know what this means? It means if Thomas Felts finds out about this, we'll all have hell to pay. He just had two men killed in Welch. Might send his right-hand man Atwood to take care of Francis. God knows Atwood's one mean sonofabitch. Francis knows too much. No telling what might happen to her. Thomas Felts will see that I lose my job as Bluefield police chief.

"What are we to do, Clarence?" his wife asked, her voice displaying anxiety.

Clarence Duncan let out a long sigh and sat down hard on the edge of the bed as Francis huddled at the other end of the bed without speaking. After several moments with everyone silent, he said, "She needs to leave. I'll drive her tonight to stay with your sister in Roanoke until we figure out what to do. Don't call your sister. Can't trust an operator listening in on the line. I'll explain when we arrive in Roanoke."

"Then what?"

"You call the Baldwin-Felts office. Tell 'em Francis went out of town to visit relatives and took sick. Too ill to come in today. The next day you'll call again saying she is seriously ill. In a hospital in Virginia. Might be some time before she can return to work according to the doctor. Eventually, I'll go in and explain that Francis is dying. Make up some serious illness. Maybe cancer. We all stick to that story. Agreed?"

Looking at Francis, "Agreed?"

Francis nodded.

Clarence Duncan added, "You can't ever come back here, Francis."

Francis' mother hung her head and began to weep.

—

With Thomas Felts' approval to silence Keara Murphy, Leland Atwood immediately went to Logan City for a meeting with Don Chafin. Atwood outlined his plan to Chafin for eliminating Murphy, telling him she was actually Burke's wife currently residing in Charleston."

Murphy's bad press often mentioned Don Chafin as the signature depiction of her crusade against corporate feudalism. Yet U.S. Marshal Burke was of more immediate interest for Chafin.

"Why doesn't Baldwin-Felts deal with this woman?"

"Not a good time to raise another controversial issue involving Baldwin-Felts after what went down in Welch."

329

"Why should I stick my neck out?" Chafin said. "It's her fucking husband that I want dead. He's hurting my business interests. His wife is just a pain in the ass. Don't give a rat's ass what she prints in those communist newspapers and magazines."

Atwood responded, "You know as well as I do that killing a U.S. marshal is unwise. We need to keep our feud contained to West Virginia, Sheriff. I want Burke dead maybe even more than you do. It was his shot that did this to my arm." Atwood said lifting his impaired left arm. "If we assault his wife, Burke will be consumed with rage but unable to go after Baldwin-Felts or you for that matter if you're careful who you put on this job.

"Burke will be preoccupied with caring for his wife. Distracted from presenting a challenge to any of us. Maybe discouraged enough to even resign and leave West Virginia."

Chafin considered the proposal before responding. "What do 'ya have in mind?"

"A sexual assault on Murphy. Do enough physical and emotional damage to put her in the hospital. She's a beautiful woman. Maybe not so beautiful after this. I have people watching Murphy and Burke round the clock. I'll put whoever you send to Charleston in touch with them."

Chafin said, "I'll think this over, Atwood. I'll let you know by telephone in a couple of days."

Chafin agreed and within a few days, two trusted Logan sheriff deputies involved with Chafin's illicit liquor enterprise arrived in Charleston. For a couple of days, they followed Keara Murphy with the assistance of the Baldwin-Felts detective assigned to watch Murphy. Told of Murphy's regular trips every other day walking to the post office, they settled on a plan to abduct Murphy then drive north out of town to a rural location previously determined. Here they could commit the assault without interference. Leave a damaged Murphy stranded to make her way to find help giving them ample time to get miles away.

On the second day after arriving in Charleston, Ernest Spivak and Grady Chalmers stood with the Baldwin-Felts undercover detective across the street from the Kanawha Hotel. This was August and already a warm day by mid-morning. They watched as

Keara Murphy walked briskly in the direction of the post office. She wore trousers, lace-up boots, a lightweight leather jacket over a form-fitting blouse and carried a shoulder bag.

The Baldwin-Felts detective said, "I'll leave her to you fellas," as the Logan men got into their Model T. Allowing Murphy to walk further down the street, they timed their arrival to intersect her at a cross street by driving slowly from well behind her.

Spivak was driving with Chalmers poised in the passenger seat ready to jump out. Coming to an intersection, Spivak abruptly turned right into the cross street bringing the car to a sudden stop in front of Murphy as she stepped off the sidewalk.

Startled, Murphy took a step backwards. Simultaneously, a man stepped from the car clearly holding a knife in his hand. Grady Chalmers was a tall well-built man wearing a floppy wide-brimmed hat to obscure his appearance. Using a knife as a means of threatening disfigurement to a woman's face seemed a better threat than using the revolver stuck into the waist of his trousers. Seeing the large knife might even discourage Murphy from screaming.

Murphy did not scream. She had been attacked before. That terrible ordeal in her bathroom at the hotel in Trinidad, Colorado years ago left a vivid impression. The insistence by Alan that she always go armed caused her to have a winter coat and this warmer weather jacket modified with concealed internal holsters for always having her short-barreled .38 revolver available. The threat to her husband kept her constantly vigilant.

Immediately recognizing what was happening backed away further allowing time to reach inside the jacket left unbuttoned due to the warm weather. As Chalmers yelled at her from not more than six feet away, "Make a sound and I'll slash your face, bitch! Just come quietly," she pulled out the .38 from the holster sewn inside the jacket.

After the violent confrontations experience by Alan, he took her into the hills to practice shooting aided by his expert instruction. He made her to practice the technique of how to place two rounds in quick succession into your adversary as the best way to put him down. His admonition was when threatened with bodily harm, never hesitate.

With the benefit of Murphy's training, Grady Chalmers took two .38 caliber slugs into his chest at point blank range. One struck his heart proving immediately fatal. He dropped like a sack of potatoes to his knees then pitched forward almost touching Murphy's feet had she not backed away another step.

During the encounter between Chalmers and Murphy, Spivak exited the driver side of the car. Coming around the front of the idling vehicle with a revolver in his hand, he looked in shock at his colleague lying face down on the sidewalk. Seeing Murphy pointing her .38, Spivak hurriedly backed away to make his escape. They had no orders to kill Murphy. The attack was a disaster. Doing anything further only endangered him. Spivak jammed the idling car into gear and sped away. Best to make his getaway and make his way back to Logan County.

As the rush of adrenalin subsided, Murphy felt lightheaded. Breathing heavily, she bent down on the sidewalk on one knee trying to ward off fainting. She was in front of a dry goods store where the proprietor and a female customer emerged to render her aid.

Helping her inside, Charleston police soon arrived. Murphy told them who she was. Alan Burke arrived within five minutes, coming to an abrupt stop behind a police car in his official car driven by his deputy. He observed the body on the sidewalk as a Charleston police officer held open the door to the dry goods store.

After hearing what happened from Keara, Burke went outside with the Charleston Police Chief having just arrived on the scene.

"Ever seen this man, Marshal?" the Chief asked as his officers turned over the body.

"No. My wife said she's never seen him before either. Who is he?"

"Don't know yet. He's not carrying any identification. The proprietor here was the first person on the scene after hearing the gunshots. Stuck his head out the door and saw a car driving away fast. Fits with what your wife told the first of my officers to arrive.

She said the fellow lying on the sidewalk got out of this car and threatened her with that knife laying near the body. Also armed with a revolver. Sounds like an attempted abduction. Your wife apparently didn't hesitate. Just shot him twice. Seems she knows her way around firearms."

"That she does. Taught her myself. Because of me, that's why she goes about armed with a concealed weapon permit. Not the first time that she's faced an armed assailant."

"Really?" What happen the other time?"

"Shot and killed that guy too."

"Jesus! Well, looks like she nailed this sonofabitch with one in the heart. According to your wife and the shop keeper, the other fella was armed with a gun who drove off after seeing his partner on the sidewalk. Not just some drunken characters looking to harm a pretty woman. Does she have reason to have enemies?"

"Afraid so. She's a writer. Write's articles about what's going on here in West Virginia with the coalfield wars. Then again, she's married to me, and I've acquired some nasty enemies."

—

Alan Burke was beside himself. His acceptance of the U.S. marshal position propelled him into a prestigious new career but at what cost. Finding the love of his life, happiness is now threatened by becoming a peace officer. All the more frustrating since as a federal law enforcement, there was little he could do officially. Keara's safety may now be threatened by his unorthodox actions to make a difference.

Labor strife in the West Virginia coalfields long ago become a way of life in this corner of Appalachia. The region known for the violent generational feud between the mountain clans of the Hatfields and McCoys evolved into a more virulent form of violence since the Civil War. The circumstances driven by corporate greed in an environment of unregulated capitalism that in many ways was still an American frontier. Mining coal supplied the vital energy source that fueled the industrial revolution that began well before the turn of this century.

Keara's emotional wellbeing now became Burke's overriding concern. Tomorrow he would broach the subject of persuading her to return to Brooklyn. She of course would refuse but he might at least persuade her to get away from here for a few weeks of recuperation. Angie would take good care of her in familiar surroundings back in Brooklyn.

The next day, Keara was hard at work working on her latest article. A first-person account of the thwarted attack to abduct her. Alan agreed to drive her to the post office that afternoon and see if any new material arrived from Noreen or Father Geary at her post box. Before finding the right opportunity to take up the subject the following evening, Burke received a telephone call at his office from Noreen.

"Thought it better to call you at your office. You said the hotel switchboard might have someone at the desk listening in on your conversations. I just received a letter from Francis Duncan our source inside Baldwin-Felts headquarters. Seems she was found out."

"Oh no! Is she alright?"

"If you mean safe, yes. She telephoned me at school. She's staying with her mother's sister in Roanoke. Fortunately, it was her father that caught her in the act of placing some timely information into our dead drop. Just received a letter from her in the mail today. She says her father thrashed her with his belt until stopped by her mother. Once he regained control, he became frightened of what might happen to her if Baldwin-Felts discovered her betrayal. Francis thought him more afraid of losing his job as Bluefield police chief. Thomas Felts held that kind of local power.

"Anyway, Baldwin-Felts believes she is seriously ill. Receiving treatment out of state for cancer. She will not be returning to Baldwin-Felts."

"At least she's safe," Alan said.

"However, what she related her latest intelligence that scares me to my core, Alan. She overheard Thomas Felts and his operations manager Leland Atwood discussing going after Keara. They learned that Keara's last name is Murphy. The journalist giving them grief with her publications. Apparently emboldened by the killings of Hatfield and Chambers in Welch, Felts ordered Atwood to put Keara out of business. Atwood also wanted to go after you, but Felts wouldn't go that far."

"Atwood's a murderous pig. He murdered my deputy and tried killing me at Mohawk. Can't prove that though. Forgetting that, no need for you to worry, Noreen."

"What are talking about? These murderers plan to harm Keara."

"Take it easy, Noreen. Two men tried to abduct Keara yesterday. Keara shot one of them dead. The other escaped in a car. Keara is fine. Uninjured, but upset naturally. She's already writing the incident for publication. More angry than frightened. I'll have her call you."

There was a long silence before Noreen processed this newest violence brought to the family. "I'm so relieved. One more piece of information Francis offered. Atwood's plan was to coerce Logan County Sheriff Don Chafin to find some men to do whatever they intended to do to Keara. Atwood told Felts that Chafin was enraged over you going after his illicit liquor business."

It was Alan's turn to digest this new information. No question about having created some nasty enemies. And now without a spy inside the enemy camp, the danger became even greater.

That evening, over dinner downstairs in the hotel restaurant, Alan tried to convince Keara to take a short vacation by relaxing in Brooklyn for a couple of weeks. She was having none of that. Anger overrode concerns over her safety. Keara used the incident to write a blistering article setting the blame for the failed assault on factions holding the reins of economic and political power in West Virginia. She knew those behind the incident but could not back it by any evidence therefore she would not make uncorroborated allegations.

"As a journalist, this is too important to abandon being at the center of this turmoil which I write about. Besides, we've been over this before, my love. I could not possibly leave you alone in West Virginia while I worry constantly about you from New York. We're partners and we stay together. Besides, I think I've proven myself capable of defending myself. Thanks to your expert instruction. How many women do you know that can say they shot two men bent on doing them harm?"

"Don't know that many women. But right now, I think it's me that needs something to settle my anxiety. Got any suggestions?"

"More than just suggestions, I have some very specific therapy in mind. Shall we adjourn to our room?"

CHAPTER 26

Southern Coalfield Counties, West Virginia | Summer 1921

The funerals for Sid Hatfield and Ed Chambers on August 4 set off a sequence of escalating events, each moving West Virginia closer toward widespread armed revolt. Newly elected Republican Governor Ephraim Morgan supported by the mine operators was to prove no more capable in managing the labor crisis than his predecessor conservative Democratic Governor Cornwell.

United Mine Workers District 17 President Frank Keeney and Fred Mooney met with Governor Morgan. Keeney and Mooney were local men, articulate, and veterans of previous labor disputes in the southern coalfields. They presented a list of miners' demands for legislation they felt could tamp down escalating tensions and possibly avert more violence. Morgan rejected everything proposed by the UMW.

The failed UMW overture caused the miners to begin speaking of marching on *Bloody Mingo* and seize control by force to free hundreds of miners jailed under the declaration of martial law. On August 20, 5,000 militant miners gathered near Lens Creek Mountain outside the town of Marmet not far from Charleston the state capital. All were armed with a diverse range of weapons ranging from small caliber squirrel rifles, shotguns, and old revolvers to 30-06 Springfield rifles from those having served in the

Great War. They even obtained a vintage machine gun with thousands of rounds of ammunition.

Marmet sat on the Kanawha River near where the Paint Creek & Cabin Creek strike of 1912-1913 occurred and where Burke's father and brother died. To march to Mingo County from Kanawha County meant traversing a considerable distance over rugged, mountainous terrain through Boone County then Logan County before entering Mingo County. The miners faced not only the obstacle of distance and terrain but also the opposition they could expect to encounter. Logan County was Sheriff Don Chafin's heavily defended fiefdom. In Logan, they would also have to cross through Blair Gap that separated the twin 1800-foot peaks of Blair Mountain. A natural topographical barrier affording a perfect defensive position by occupying the high ground commanding a natural bottleneck.

Miners near St. Albans, in Kanawha County, commandeered a Chesapeake & Ohio freight train intent on joining the advance column of marchers at Danville in Boone County on their way south to *Bloody Mingo*.

In Logan, Sheriff Don Chafin began setting up defenses on Blair Mountain. With financial support from the Logan County Coal Operators Association, Chafin assembled a private armed force of nearly 2,000. To this were added the resources of the state police under the field command of notorious Captain James Brokus.

On August 23, Governor Morgan made another appeal to Secretary of War John Weeks for federal military assistance as he did the previous spring. However, the result was much the same. President Harding still felt this should remain to West Virginia to resolve the problem. They failed to reconstitute their national guard following demobilization in 1919 following the Great War. Doing nothing to reorganize a state militia for two years, the West Virginia legislature only recently reauthorized the small state militia as a national guard unit.

However, Secretary Weeks was mindful of the escalating situation that could spiral out of control by state resources alone. He again dispatched Major Charles Thompson to Charleston to make an assessment. It was Thompson's previous assessment in the spring that led to denying Governor Morgan's request for federal intervention. At that time, Secretary Weeks wanted to force West Virginia to act by reestablishing a functioning national guard. That may have worked, but the killing of Sid Hatfield and Ed Chambers had moved the charged environment to a new level of antagonism between coal operators and miners.

By August 25, lead elements of striking marchers were within two miles of crossing into Logan County with the bulk of the miners still over fifteen miles away. The first clashes nonetheless began. Chafin's massed private army, supported by Governor Morgan and the state police, fanned the flames by proclaiming, "No armed mob will cross Logan County." The miners' side countered as they marched toward Blair Mountain singing, "We're gonna hang Don Chafin to a sour apple tree," to the Civil War tune of *John Brown's Body*.

Secretary of War Weeks apprised President Harding of the dire situational assessment provided by U.S. Army intelligence officer Major Thompson, a veteran of assessing the labor violence in the West Virginia coalfields. General Read, commander of the U.S. Army's Central Department, promptly received orders to place the Army's 19th Infantry in a state of readiness while Weeks dispatched Brigadier General Harry Bandholtz to Charleston. A veteran of the Spanish-American War, the Philippine War, and the Great War, Bandholtz was both a tough-minded soldier and a skilled negotiator. Banholtz was charged with defusing the situation or making the call for federal assistance under a federal declaration of martial law.

General Bandholtz arrived in Charleston by train at 3:00am in the morning on Saturday August 27 with his aide Colonel Ford. Major Thompson was there to meet him with Alan Burke standing at his side.

As Bandholtz stepped down from the train carriage, Major Thompson saluted, "Welcome to Charleston, General. This is U.S. Marshal Alan Burke. The Marshal has been most useful in assisting my assessment of the situation."

Bandholtz and Ford shook Burke's hand.

Bandholtz said, "I've read about you in the newspapers, Marshal. Thought I recalled your name from my time in France. You're the Marine famous for your action at Belleau Wood. Twice awarded the Medal of Honor I recall. An honor to meet you, Sergeant Major."

Burke nodded. "Thank you, Sir."

"Do we have an insurrection here in West Virginia, Marshal?"

"Not sure I'd call it that, General. A lot of these striking miners also fought in France. Can't see them firing on U.S. regular army troops. Their fight is with the mine operators' mercenary army of mine guards in collusion with corrupt local law enforcement. Sheriff Chafin of Logan County is the most prominent example."

Bandholtz raised his eyebrow, then turned to Major Thompson., "Is the situation worse than when you were here months ago, Major?"

"Yes, Sir. The killings of the Matewan police officers in Welch changed everything. The miners believe the Baldwin-Felts men are assassins guilty of murder. Retribution for killing the brothers of the head of Baldwin-Felts. By the circumstances surrounding the killings, there might be some truth in that."

"Alright, gentlemen. Since I got no sleep and I'm standing out here in the wee hours of the morning, no reason not to roust Governor Morgan out of his bed. This is his goddamn problem that needs fixing. Same goes for the leadership of the United Mine Workers. If they can't find a way to call off what's coming down, then there'll be hell to pay. Can you help us, Marshal? Know where to find the Governor and these union fellas?"

"Yes, Sir. Be glad to fetch them. How 'bout you use my office in the federal courthouse as your headquarters?"

"Thank you, Marshal."

General Bandholtz lived up to his reputation. He met with Governor Morgan at 4:00am and accused Morgan and his predecessor of being out of touch and doing nothing to prepare for what has transpired. At 5:00am he met United Mine Workers Frank Keeney and Fred Mooney ordering them to stop this march that will end in bloodshed which will force him to hold them criminally responsible. Bandholtz, Ford, Thompson, and Burke then accompanied Keeney and Mooney on a train to Madison in Boone County where the lead elements of the miners' march were camped waiting for larger numbers to join them.

Keeney and Mooney held a rally and told the miners the matter had gone too far. If they went into Logan County, there would be full scale conflict. President Harding would consider this insurrection and send in regular U.S. Army troops. They read from a proclamation drafted by Bandholtz. The majority of coal miners were patriotic. A great many had served in the AEF in France. Firing on U.S. soldiers would be out of the question. Many of the marchers wept with relief that this terrible ordeal was over. Special trains were arranged to transport the marchers back to Kanawha. Keeney and Mooney wired Bandholtz that miners were abandoning their march south.

Bandholtz wired Washington that he at least was able to broker a ceasefire. Yet not entirely convinced the peace would hold, he wired General Read to hold the 19th Infantry in readiness for possible immediate deployment.

The following day, Bandholtz and his Army officers left Charleston by automobiles to inspect the front lines of the marchers to assess the cessation of hostilities first-hand. Bandholtz went as far as Marmet in Boone County while Burke accompanied Major Thompson to Paint Creek and Cabin Creek in Kanawha County. Armed miners overwhelmingly expressed relief. Alan Burke welcomed the standing down of a massed confrontation but understood that the underlying issues of animosity would not change.

—

President Harding issued a proclamation for *all persons engaged in insurrection to disperse and retire peaceably in their respective abodes on or before 12 o'clock noon of the first day of September 1921 and hereafter abandon said combinations and submit themselves to the laws and constituted authorities of said State.*

Don Chafin was not however with being denied his war. He hated not only the United Mine Workers Union, but coal miners in general. This was an opportunity to put a stake in the heart of the UMW local by crushing the coal miners' revolt. Provoke the miners to violent confrontation forcing intervention by federal troops. In Logan County he was the constituted legal authority. Martial law meant a return to the status quo enforced by Washington if federal troops became involved.

As Keeney and Mooney stopped the miners' march short of descending into Logan County in mass, Governor Morgan ordered Captain Brokus to move his state police contingent from Mingo County to Logan to reinforce Chafin's forces as a precaution. Chafin saw his opportunity to provoke an armed confrontation.

Earlier that month state police had been humiliated by striking miners near the county line. When Brokus arrived in Logan with seventy state troopers Chafin convinced him into going to Sharples and Clothier to arrest twenty miners that participated in that earlier incident. Chafin added two hundred of his deputies to accompany Brokus state police.

The following morning Brokus' small army entered the Spruce Creek Valley dotted with several mines every half mile. This was union territory. Armed clashes resulted inflicting casualties on both sides. Resistance by armed miners eventually forced Brokus' forces to retreat. Yet the battle achieved Chafin's objective. Word spread throughout Boone and Kanawha Counties.

While gratified with stemming the impending confrontation, Frank Keeney and Fred Mooney learned they had been indicted on criminal charges in Mingo County stemming from the *Three Days Battle of the Tug* in May. They had no intention of facing a rigged trial in West Virginia, choosing instead to flee to Ohio.

Following events at Sharples and Clothier, the enraged miners resumed their march south. Word spread through the mountains swelling the numbers. The miners commandeered every kind of transportation at gunpoint. Automobiles, trucks, and even trains. Fiery Bill Blizzard assumed the role as the recognized UMW leader when in fact the march had no unified structure of command. Blizzard formed the men into columns and began moving south. New recruits joined the march in great numbers until it exceeded well over 10,000 armed men.

Lead elements of marchers crossed into Logan County headed for Blair Mountain the most direct route through the mountains to their objective of invading Mingo County. In Charleston, Governor Morgan designated eight companies of the newly reconstituted West Virginia Guard to deploy to Logan. Morgan appointed William Eubanks, a military veteran of the Mexican border expedition of 1916 and the Great War, as colonel in command.

With the striking miners marching south, opposing forces of the West Virginia National Guard, the West Virginia State Police, and Sheriff Chafin's deputized small army descended on the Blair Mountain area. A violent clash became imminent.

With a special train consisting of a locomotive and a single passenger carriage, Major Thompson and Burke headed to the small community of Blair during the night of Tuesday August 30. Arriving at the Blair train depot, Thompson and Burke descended from the train early the following morning. A large gathering of armed miners moved in closer to Thompson dressed in U.S. Army uniform.

Thompson opened his briefcase and began reading the Presidential proclamation ordering the ending of the rebellion by noon of September 1. Armed miners gathered around him. Many did not understand the legalese. Some began arguing. Some shouted angrily at Thompson. Thompson attempted to yell in response, "This is from the President of the United States. I'm just here to read it."

The crowd of miners remained vocal and increasingly unruly. Disgusted, Thompson tacked the proclamation on a telephone pole and another on a building. While he was doing this the train bring him and Burke pulled away to turned around on a siding. Preparing to take them back to Charleston, the train came to a stop behind Thompson and Burke. Several miners crowded closer. One miner yelled, "Get the hell out of here." Thompson replied, "I'm here representing the President and I'm not yet ready to go." Thompson then began to shout at the miners, "The best thing you men can do is lay down your guns and go home."

As the situation grew heated, Burke sensed things could get out of hand. One miner then mistakenly drew a revolver and push toward the front to get closer to Thompson, Burke saw the threat and drew his .45 as the man emerged from the crowd. Pointing his weapon at the miner's head from only a few feet away, Burke said, "Stand down. You don't want to do somethin' foolish. I'm a U.S. Marshal."

"Don't give a rat's ass who you are. Both of you get the hell back on the train or you'll be getting a bullet the same as that fucker Chafin."

"Not unless you want to be the first to die," Burke said.

Other miners readied their rifles but did not point them at Burke. They pulled back from the man brandishing the revolver.

After realizing he was not going to make any headway, Thompson said, "We're through here. Mind what I said. We'll be leaving now." He stepped up into the train with Burke following while not turning his back on the crowd of angry miners. As their train made its way back to Charleston, they observed at each stop large numbers of armed miners preparing to march to do battle.

That same day, the opposing sides met along a ten-mile front. Bill Blizzard engaged his thousands of miners in a three-pronged attack against the forces of Chafin, state police, and national guard under the unified command of Colonel Eubanks. The first shots of the *Battle of Blair Mountain* began with a fierce exchange of sustained gunfire.

The principal attack occurred at Blair Mountain. The terrain consisted of heavily wooded steep hills. The tangle of underbrush made movement difficult but afforded significant concealment for those on both sides. Yet the tactical advantage heavily favored the defending forces occupying the high ground of the twin peaks of Blair Mountain. By midnight September 1, twelve hours after President Harding's deadline, Bandholtz abandoned his peacekeeping efforts after hearing the depressing assessment from Thompson and Burke. Bandholtz sent for Morgan and told the Governor he is recommending sending in regular U.S. Army infantry to restore order under a federal declaration of martial law.

Burke journeyed by train with Major Thompson, newly promoted to colonel, to meet the first arriving U.S. Army troops arriving in Huntington on the West Virginia border. The train carried an initial compliment of three companies of the Army's 40th
Infantry from Camp Knox, Kentucky.

Thompson introduced Burke to the colonel commanding the
arriving troopers. "Let me introduce U.S. Marshal Burke, Colonel.
Marshal Burke has been invaluable to General Bandholtz and my
efforts in evaluating the circumstances that led to the calling up of
your forces. The Marshal staved off a potential ugly confrontation
in our effort to return to Charleston to report to General Bandholtz
the ignoring of the President's proclamation for the miners to
cease hostile activities. We'll accompany your troops to Logan
County. Reports advise that a major armed confrontation is fully
engaged at Blair Mountain."

As they arrived in Logan on September 3, Colonel Thompson
confronted Colonel Eubanks of the West Virginia National Guard
commanding the defensive state forces at Blair Mountain as the
senior military officer. Thompson said, "Colonel Eubanks, all
forces in the field are now under federal military authority by direction of the President. You will immediately begin to halt any
action by these defenders." However, Eubanks was intoxicated to
the point of being unable to exercise any meaningful control of the
diverse forces defending against the miners. While U.S. army
troops made their presence known on the battlefield, Thompson
and Burke took the initiative to begin ordering anyone appearing
to be in charge to halt further aggressive action and to withdraw
from further engagement.

Burke came upon a machine gun that was still firing bursts
down the hill. He approached the man operating the trigger and
rapped him hard on the head with the barrel of his .45. Stunned,
the man exclaimed, "What the fuck?" Turning around and seeing
the .45 sticking him in the face, "Who the hell are you?"

"I'm a U.S. Marshal. You fellas are to stand down. No more
shooting."

"Fuck off. I'm supposed to kill as many rednecks as I can."

Burke thumbed back the hammer on his Browning. "Fire again and you're a dead man."

The man held a defiant expression for a moment. Burke added, "Try me and I'll blow your head off. All of you stand up. Abandon your weapons and get the hell out of here. The war is over."

For a moment Burke almost lost control. By their badges, these men were nothing more than Chafin's deputized thugs. Mercenary scum. He would like nothing more than for them to make a threatening move. All three men manning the machine gun sensed Burke's resolve and obeyed.

As for the assaulting forces, bullhorns announced the presence of the U.S. Army. The miners quickly understood that the might of the U.S. Army now weighed against them. More importantly, they refused to fire on regular U.S. Army soldiers. The miners did not see this as insurrection against the United States government. This was a rebellion directed specifically at the oppression exercised by the mining companies aided by corrupt institutions of the State of West Virginia.

By the following day, the coalfield war ended as the *Battle of Blair Mountain* abruptly halted with the arrival of regular U.S. Army troops. The brief but intense engagement resulted in an estimated 50 to 100 miners killed with an unknown number of wounded. Chafin's defenders reported 30 dead.

—

The aftermath proved disastrous for the coal miners. During September and October of 1921, grand juries in Logan County returned 1,217 indictments for complicity in the insurrection against the State of West Virginia, 25 indictments for treason against West Virginia, and 325 murder charges. Hundreds of miners were arrested and jailed. Many were transferred to other counties to stand trial. Among those charged was Bill Blizzard, the most visible leadership figure of the United Mine Workers Union District 17. Frank Keeney and Fred Mooney returned from Ohio and surrendered to charges filed in Mingo County. Although federal troops were called upon to quell the rebellion, all criminal charges were dictated by state statutes.

The debacle at Blair Mountain proved a resounding defeat for the United Mine Workers Union in West Virginia. With 50,000 members in West Virginia in 1920, within months of the Blair Mountain confrontation, membership began a precipitous decline. The strike in Mingo County continued but suffered serious weakening. The emboldened mine owners continued refusing to have any dialog with the UMW. Striking mine families would again face the coming winter in union-subsidized tent colonies along the Tug Forks River.

CHAPTER 27

Charleston, West Virginia | September 1921

B urke and Colonel Thompson returned to Charleston to report to General Bandholtz following the cessation of hostilities at Blair Mountain. Exhausted from lack of sleep their meeting was brief. As Burke made to leave, Bandholtz said, "I extend my sincere gratitude for your assisting of Colonel Thompson, Marshal. I shall draft a letter of appreciation to Attorney General Daugherty. You are a credit to the Marshal Service. As a recipient of the medal of honor, I salute you."

Following military protocol, Bandholtz came to attention and snapped a salute. Burke returned the salute replying, "Thank you, General."

Burke returned to Keara at the hotel having called her from his office after first arriving back in Charleston. Hearing what happened at Blair Mountain, she embraced him, holding him for a long time. "Go sit down. We both need a drink. The hotel managed to find me a bottle of good bourbon."

After sitting in one of the easy chairs in their suite, he took a sip of whiskey then said, "I'm amazed that the carnage was not greater. These poor miners were attacking a defended position on high ground while facing machine guns. Reminded me of Belleau Wood. Most had no military training. Poorly armed. No organization to provide tactical direction under fire. Relying solely on their vast numbers. No chance they could have ever gotten all the way to Mingo County. Sickened me to see them reduced to such desperation. Cost too many lives. Achieved nothing."

Keara came over to him and sat on his lap. Stroking his cheek. "You've done all you could to help them. The problem is too entrenched. Only change in laws at the national level will force change in the coalfields."

Burke nodded and took a stiff drink of whiskey. "Won't do this anymore. I've made up my mind to leave West Virginia. I can't make a difference in this miserable place. The murders of Sid Hatfield and Ed Chambers by Baldwin-Felts ignited this open warfare. The audacity of Thomas Felts and Leland Atwood points to the depth of corruption that exists here. There's talk of charging those Baldwin-Felts involved with the murders, but justice will never be served. Felts will spread enough money around to bribe witnesses and jurors in a county that is notoriously anti-union. Acquittal is almost assured.

"Things will now go back to how it's always been. Corporate feudalism at its worse. As for us, we have made powerful enemies intent on doing us physical harm. I can't have us living in constant fear for no tangible purpose. I want us to return to New York, Keara."

Surprised, she said, "Is that what you truly want, Alan?"

He smiled and said, "Yes. I didn't come to West Virginia to become involved in another war. A war that has turned personal. There's no reason to stick out another two years of my term as marshal. When I thought of law enforcement as a new career, I didn't envision becoming drawn into this snake pit. Everything that happened to us had nothing to do with my job enforcing federal laws. Corporate feudalism as practiced here violates every fundamental right defined in the American constitution. Yet I am powerless to do anything.

"Should have known better than to come back to West Virginia. Attracted by the esteem of being offered this job as U.S. marshal. Forgot that I joined the Marines to get away from West Virginia. I'll take this as a learning experience."

Keara said, "Then that's what we'll do. You'll find something much better." She kissed him suggestively. I'm sure you're hungry. We can go down to get dinner or make love and have something brought up later. What's your pleasure?"

"You're my pleasure. I need a bath first."

"Very well, I'll join you in the tub."

—

Burke resumed his duties, staying busy with keeping the courts functioning. The fact that the mine operators began filing petitions for injunctive relief by the United Mine Workers only irritated him further by serving subpoenas on the UMW local.

A week after federal troops withdrew from West Virginia, U.S. Attorney Elliot Northcott came to Burke's office.

"Got a telegram here from Attorney General Daugherty. You should be getting one also. Seems both of us will soon receive congressional subpoenas to appear before Senator Kenyon's labor subcommittee investigating the labor unrest in West Virginia. They want us to testify about the state of affairs existing in West Virginia."

Burke replied sarcastically, "Testify about what? Washington sees the situation here as a West Virginia problem. Congress can't seem to grasp the obvious problem that the rot is so deep that West Virginia is incapable of change. Coal miners here are little better than indentured servants."

"Not sure I can disagree with that assessment, but maybe this is a start for doing something at the national level. Daugherty was pressured to offer our testimony by Kentucky Democratic Senator Augustus Stanley who has a vested interest in the region. Also getting pressure from Progressive California Republican Senator Hiram Johnson who is a member of Iowa Senator Kenyon's Committee on Education and Labor investigating the coal war in West Virginia. They're looking at the implications of large business interests controlling state and local government. The inherent abuses associated with private interests funding local law enforcement. Daugherty submitted our names to the subcommittee as suggested witnesses. They started hearings back in May. Suspended by the recent events but rescheduled to resume September 19.

"Senator Stanley is also a keen observer of the Appalachian coalfield labor wars that also affects Kentucky coalfields over the Tug River from Matewan, the center of much of the violence. During his tenure in the House, Stanley served on the Committee on Mines and Mining and possesses a keen understanding of the abuses of corporate mining interests."

Burke remarked, "Haven't been back to Washington since I interviewed for the marshal position. After this past year, I could use a vacation. I should tell Daugherty that my wife might make a better witness. She's been researching and publishing material for years about the political circumstances that gave rise to these coalfield wars. Not only in West Virginia but in Colorado."

"Good idea. Was the incident where she shot a would-be assailant weeks ago connected?"

"Probably. I suspect either Atwood or Sheriff Chafin of attempting to harm her to get at me. The assailant was a former Chafin deputy. Again, there's no evidence."

"On a related subject, Mr. Keena showed me your deposition you gave after that violent confrontation in Mohawk earlier this year. You claim this Leland Atwood ordered the murder of your deputy and attempted murder of you? This happened while both of you were only a few feet apart?"

"That's correct. Have no proof to corroborate the allegation so we both agreed that an indictment was impossible. It was Baldwin-Felts thugs that did the killing, the same as those that assassinated Hatfield and Chambers in Welch that ignited the march that led to the Battle of Blair Mountain. Atwood could simply claim that I fired the first shots killing two of his detectives. Since he could offer no evidence to support that allegation, he chose to keep quiet. Those deaths he caused at Mohawk ultimately achieved Baldwin-Felts' objective to have the governor declare martial law. Up to that point, the violence was centered in Mingo County whereas this made it appear spreading into McDowell County."

"Yes. That's the same way Kenna framed it. Also told me your wife had a run in with Baldwin-Felts some years ago in Colorado?'

"That's right. Baldwin-Felts is a group of mercenary thugs that enjoy local legal cover since they work for those holding political power. Leland Atwood is the operations superintendent. Without question, he's a murderer. I suggest the same applies to Thomas Felts the head of Baldwin-Felts. Atwood has been with him for years."

Northcott said, "Will your wife be traveling with you when we go to Washington?"

"Definitely. Wouldn't leave her alone in this dangerous environment."

"Excellent. Let's coordinate and take the same train. Lot's we can talk about. I'm from West Virginia. Have a personal interest in seeing things change here. Appropriate federal legislation could give us the power to challenge this endemic corruption."

The following day, Burke received a telephone call instead of a telegram from Attorney General Daugherty. After explaining the reason for Burke's and U.S. Attorney Northcott's appearances before the Senate subcommittee, Daugherty added, "After you testify at the subcommittee hearing, I'd like to meet with you on another matter. Are you familiar with the Bureau of Investigation?"

"Just the name. The federal police agency."

"Right. President Roosevelt created it in 1908. The current director is William Burns. Hell of a detective. Bill's a former secret service agent and a close friend. His appointment was just confirmed in August. Bill became aware of your exploits in West Virginia. That deadly shootout at Mohawk then those raids on bootlegging operations. Then I get a letter from the Army general putting down the confrontation with the striking miners citing your assistance. Of course I told Bill about your military background. To say the least, Bill would like to have you in the BOI. It's a young agency that needs experienced men like you."

Burke was surprised and given his decision to leave West Virginia, decidedly interested. "I still have two years remaining on my term as marshal, Sir. How would that set if I were to resign for a new government position?"

"Happens all the time in Washington, Marshal. Probably would require leaving West Virginia. Would that be a problem?"

"No, but it depends on where I would be relocating though. Yet that is secondary to understanding more about the job and measuring it against my current law enforcement responsibilities. For what it's worth, I'm recently married. My wife is a lawyer and journalist from New York. She has no interest in staying in West Virginia."

"That's exactly what Bill and I thought. We of course know of your wife's background. Can I at least tell Bill you are open to the possibility?"

"Yes, Sir."

Following the call, Burke went to the hotel to share the news with Keara. He asked her to begin researching what she could learn about the Bureau of Investigation and William Burns.

Keara quickly learned that William Burns was a celebrated detective. Newspapers even dubbed him the *American Sherlock Holmes*. Famous for his investigative work on several high-profile cases, Burns' instinct for attracting publicity also made him a celebrity. His exploits made the national newspapers and gossip columns. Not waiting for the whims of interested journalists, for years Burns authored his personal *true crime* stories for detective magazines.

Attorney General Harry Daugherty was also not immune from burnishing his image by seeking favorable publicity. Having helped get Warren Harding elected as President, he became part of Harding's clique of close advisors known by the pejorative the Ohio Gang. The publicity associated with bringing someone of Burke's headline making exploits to the BOI would play well in Washington and his home state of Ohio.

Keara summarized her research on Burns and the Bureau of Investigation to her husband. "Burns seeks publicity. Makes no attempt to hide that. Yet his accomplishments bear out the fact that he is damn good at what he does. His skills fit for an agency engaged with actual police work. Investigation of federal crimes and making arrests."

"You mean not administrative responsibilities of supporting the federal district court?"

"Exactly. Except for going after Chafin's bootlegging business for entirely different reasons, your other exploits have been outside you're the official duties as a U.S. marshal. Sounds like real police work. Heavily focused on investigation. Still federal so not caught up in local corruption like so many police departments. That it could base you in New York City would be wonderful."

"Interesting. I don't have a background in investigation. Why me? Because I got my name in newspapers because of gun battles?"

"No, because you're smart. For the same skills that lead to recommendations for appointment as a U.S marshal. That even required presidential appointment and congressional confirmation. You're a talented guy."

—

Burke received his subpoena to appear before Senator Kenyon's subcommittee to give testimony on September 21 in Washington. That same day, Keara received a similar telegram in Brooklyn. Her housekeeper called her at the hotel. She was also to appear to testify the following day after Burke.

Surprised, Burke said, "Makes sense. You've been writing about this for years. As a lawyer your journalistic work may carry greater credibility. Your position on the political situation in West Virginia will become even more public. That makes you more of a threat to anyone aligned with the coal mining industry. You're a target for more reason than just a way to get at me. Makes the decision for us to leave West Virginia imperative. You cannot stay here, and I won't be separated from you."

After reflecting on his decision for several days, Burke told Keara, "If this possibility of transferring to the Bureau of Investigation turns out to hold no interest, I'm still resigning as U.S. Marshal in West Virginia. Same holds true if the job is not based in

New York. The months I spent with you in Brooklyn after returning from France were the happiest of my life. For someone raised in Appalachia, guess I'm now an urban creature. I liked everything about New York. Coming back to West Virginia was a mistake."

"Are you going to submit your resignation when we're in Washington?"

"Yep. Regardless of whether or not I'm offered a new job. I'll give them two months' notice. That way you can stay in Brooklyn while I tie up my official duties."

"What about asking your mother and Noreen to spend Christmas with us in Brooklyn?"

Burke nodded, "I'd like that. Maybe Mother would like to come to Washington with us to sit in on the hearings."

"Noreen too," Keara said.

"Sure. Depends on her teaching commitments. As a substitute teacher, Mother has more discretionary time."

Keara said, "In case a position with the BOI does not pan out, I shall resume researching suitable job opportunities in New York that I started before the U.S. marshal offer came along. You now have a resume that includes law enforcement. Plus, some impressive press clippings. I'll talk to father and mother and get their thoughts. They are on close terms with a host of influential people in New York."

"Since that's settled, how 'bout we take the train to Bluefield Friday and spend the weekend explaining our plans to Mother and Noreen?"

"Excellent idea."

That weekend was a bittersweet celebration. Maude and Noreen were happy for Alan and Keara to be leaving West Virginia and out of harm's way. They knew full well that both had created powerful enemies here. Those enemies remained a physical threat as evidenced by their willingness to commit conspicuous murders.

Yet Maude and Noreen still felt West Virginia was home. They had reconciled their differences. Age had mellowed Maude while Noreen had forged a successful new life. Teaching was rewarding and she was now fully invested in writing fiction. More importantly, the coal wars seemed over. Not a favorable ending according to their sense of justice for coal miners, but for Maude and Noreen their first taste of living in a peaceful environment in years.

Noreen said, "I feel badly about what happened to Francis Duncan. She's an intelligent, thoughtful young woman. She should have a future. She managed working at Baldwin-Felts into something worthwhile at great personal risk. I hate to think what might have happened to her had someone at the office discovered her spying."

Keara asked, "What is she doing now?"

"Works as a clerk at a small bookkeeping firm. Lives with an aunt and uncle in Roanoke. She wanted to return to a university to study something more rewarding than secretarial skills."

Keara said, "What about after we get settled in back in Brooklyn, I bring her to New York? We've a big house and she can easily commute to colleges in any of the boroughs in New York. She provided me with indispensable confidential information for my articles. I feel I owe Francis something."

Noreen smiled. "That would be grand, Keara."

Alan asked his mother, "Don't you want to see your son testify before Congress, Mum? You can come with Keara and me to Washington. After the hearing we'll train up to Brooklyn. You can spend the holidays with us."

Maude smiled and nodded with moistening eyes. Her first experience of happiness in a very long time.

Alan turned to Noreen, "You're welcome too if you can get away from school. If not, might you at least come up and stay over Christmas week?"

"I would love to celebrate Christmas with the family, Alan."

CHAPTER 28

Bluefield, West Virginia | September 1921

Thomas Felts was delighted with the outcome of the miners' insurrection. The rash and audacious act of murdering Sid Hatfield and Ed Chambers in retribution for killing his brothers became the catalyst for causing the rebellion. The fact that Baldwin-Felts employed the assassins should not prove a problem. With enough manufactured witness testimony in a county sympathetic to mine operator interests, he should be able to engineer an acquittal using the best lawyers. At the least, none of the defendants would dare incriminating anyone higher up in the Baldwin-Felts' organization.

Provoking the striking miners to irrationally react by engaging in a misguided rebellion against the mine operators caused their downfall at Blair Mountain with the intervention of U.S. Army troops. The leadership of the United Mine Workers District 17 now under indictment only added to the successful outcome.

At the national level, public sympathy for striking coal miners fell after the armed assault at Blair Mountain portrayed as insurrection forcing the President to respond with the Army. Time for Baldwin-Felts to press the advantage. Solidify the gains for the mine operators. Felts set out to coordinate with the coal operators' association to hire a fleet of lawyers to assist in the prosecution of those arrested. The same tactic used in the Matewan trial of Sid

Hatfield. The trial of UMW official Bill Blizzard held particular significance. With enough convictions, it would break the back of the United Mine Workers Union by portraying them as an anti-American socialist organization.

Renewed evictions began. Many miners attempted to conceal their UMW memberships, but bribes induced insider sources to produce UMW records. With lower demand for coal, the mines systematically terminated UMW miners from their payrolls. The coal mine operators' association heaped praise on Thomas Felts for his leadership against the UMW. As the tide of public opinion changed, Thomas Felts became emboldened.

Leland Atwood sensed his boss' change in attitude. The time was ripe to make the case for going after Burke and his troublesome wife. For Atwood, killing Burke rose to the level of personal obsession to exact revenge. For Thomas Felts, Keara Murphy was a public relations problem with her continued inflammatory articles that portray Baldwin-Felts as a sinister private force of hired thugs. Murphy even likened Baldwin-Felts to the Soviet Union's Cheka, the secret police inflicting a Bolshevik reign of terror during the Russian Civil War making newspaper headlines around the world.

The overthrow of centuries of rule by the Romanov dynasty in Russia gave rise to communist parties in many other countries. The international rhetoric of the Russian Bolsheviks produced a pervasive *Red Scare*. In the United States, labor strikes were on the rise across numerous industrial sectors. Terrorism from anarchist bombings also occurred around this time. The press sensationalized these acts as the work of immigrants. Organized labor movements suggested socialism and employed large numbers of immigrants. The merging of these factors provided a basis for fueling anti-unionism as leftist inspired with large numbers of immigrants among the working classes. Thomas Felts conservative nature made use of the national anxiety over the threat of communism making Keara Murphy's published attacks particularly galling.

Atwood resurrected his previous suggestion to go after Burke. After the failed assault on Murphy, he would propose something different. Atwood wanted Burke dead. Murphy was not his interest. However, he could use Burke's death in selling a new scenario to Felts for eliminating the irritation of the Keara Murphy.

Atwood said to Felts, "While the political environment is still heated and turmoil in West Virginia is still unsettled, we should take the opportunity to silence others that stand against us. I'm thinking of the writer Keara Murphy."

"Another try? Not sure we should go to all that trouble just to try to scare her off. Killing her may have unintended consequences. Killing a woman journalist could risky."

"Yes, Sir. I agree. What I'm suggesting is killing her husband, Marshal Burke. This might discourage her from continuing her crusade against the mine operators and Baldwin-Felts."

"Make his death part of an extension of the larger environment of violence while the situation remains unsettled. Specifically, we kill Burke laying the groundwork that it has nothing to do with Baldwin-Felts."

"And who would fall under suspicion for killing Burke?"

"Sheriff Don Chafin. A vendetta over Burke's going after his illicit liquor business. Chafin is a hot head with an outsized ego. Runs Logan County with absolute authority over everything. He hired great numbers of gunmen that he deputized to defend Logan from the marching miners on their way to Mingo. I can possibly convince Chafin to recommend several reliable men for the going after Burke. I hire them pretending to be connected to Chafin's bootlegging. Offer them an attractive fee to kill Burke."

"Killing a federal official might hold the same risk as killing a female journalist."

"Not if we leave no witnesses. I eliminate the assassins immediately following the incident when I link up to give them the remainder of their money. If any of them die in the process of assassinating Burke, their backgrounds connect them to Chafin. We will manufacture witnesses to testify this was about Burke going after bootlegging."

Felts pondered Atwood's proposal for several moments. This was no riskier than killing Sid Hatfield. "I would like to silence

Murphy. Who do you believe is helping her by taking all those damaging photographs that appear in her articles?"

"We suspect a Catholic priest in Williamson might be behind this. Father Patrick Geary. His parishioners are mostly miners. Geary's an outspoken critic of the mine operators in his sermons. The photographs come from various locations in Mingo County suggesting Geary used a network of people taking pictures. Burke has been observed visiting Geary on several occasions. The post office box Murphy uses in Charleston receives packages post marked from Williamson according to a postal clerk in our pay."

"Might be good if Father Geary suffer an *accident*."

"I'm sure we can arrange something. Mingo County is a dangerous place."

"Very well, Leland. Proceed against Burke. I will leave it in your hands. I don't want to know the details. Commit nothing to paper. Do not involve any Baldwin-Felts personnel. Keep it close and in the dark."

Felts knew Atwood held a personal animosity toward Burke as the cause of his disability in the incident at Mohawk. Felts suspected Atwood tried killing Burke at Mohawk and failed. Nonetheless, Felts understood Atwood's need for revenge. Should Atwood fail again, Felts needed plausible deniability. He would leave no paper trail nor confide in anyone about conspiring with Atwood to kill Burke. Should any question arise implicating Baldwin-Felts, enough information existed to portray this as a personal vendetta pursued by Atwood in a rogue operation. Incriminating evidence could always be created to support that allegation.

—

Atwood arrived by train in Logan City. His meeting prearranged, a deputy picked him up and brought him to Sheriff Don Chafin's office.

Chafin knew Atwood only by reputation as Thomas Felts right-hand man. A dangerous man and Felts' fixer. It was Baldwin-Felts gunmen that killed Sid Hatfield and Ed Chambers in

Welch. Undoubtedly that was Atwood's doing. A man to respect even though Chafin was surprised to see that Atwood had a disabled arm.

"What brings you to Logan, Mr. Atwood?" All Atwood said on the telephone was that he had something highly confidential but something that Chafin would find most interesting.

"I believe we have a common interest in eliminating Marshal Burke. My interests are more political, yours obviously are business related. With Prohibition a federal law, Marshal Burke has taken a particular interest in the illicit alcohol business in your county."

Chafin remained silent for a moment digesting what Atwood was suggesting. "By eliminating, what do'ya mean exactly?"

"Killing him."

Chafin was surprised with Atwood's frank pronouncement. "Why do you need my help? Baldwin-Felts has enough men good at killing."

"We can't even remotely risk becoming implicated given our business association with corporate coal mining interests."

"Neither can I. Killing a federal law enforcement officer carries serious repercussions."

"Neither of us will be involved. This needs to be about bootlegging. We're a detective agency, Sheriff. Regardless of your connections with Logan bootlegging, my information has it that your business interests in the liquor business are not directly linked to bootlegging operators. They don't work for you. It's from those ranks I want to find the men to do the killing. You will not have any direct involvement. All I need from you are some names of men that might be willing to make a fair amount of money by shooting Burke. I'll take it from there and do the recruiting personally. As long as you do not confide in anyone about this, there's no trail that can implicate you.

"I'll pose as a hit man hired by unnamed people in the liquor business from out of state to get rid of this marshal damaging the supply of liquor coming out of Logan County. Once they kill Burke, they become immediately expendable. I'll leave no witnesses. We float well-constructed rumors about this involving large scale illicit liquor interests wanting a free reign in Appalachia."

Chafin contemplated Atwood's scheme before replying. "That's one bold plan. This marshal is known as a tough lawman. How you goin' to do this?"

"Better that you don't know the details, Sheriff. All I need from you are a few names. Men involved in bootlegging. Men willing to shoot someone for serious money."

After a couple of moments, Chafin nodded in agreement. "How many you need?"

"Half a dozen should be enough from which to select those I need."

Atwood left Chafin's office an hour later to catch a train back to Bluefield. He was armed with six names and where to locate them. All had connections to Logan County bootlegging in addition to being temporary Logan County sheriff deputies during the recent crisis. Chafin provided enough about the character of these men and why they might be up to this work if paid enough money.

—

Chafin was cagy. The names he provided to Atwood all came from around Beckley in Raleigh County. While Chafin held a major stake in the bootlegging business operating there, he did so with another distilling operator in Raleigh County. Chafin and his partner jointly used Beckley for distribution to eastern markets. Should these assassins fail in killing Burke and either die or get arrested, it gave Chafin further plausible deniability of involvement. The fact they were temporarily deputized in Logan explained as a necessity given the emergency requirement to defend Logan. He considered the personal risk more than compensated by the opportunity of removing this aggressive federal lawman targeting him at a considerable loss of profits. According to Atwood, Burke sided with the miners and the United Mine Workers, therefore he was singling out Chafin for enforcement of the new laws targeting illicit alcohol.

Using Chafin's comments as a means of prioritizing which candidates to approach, Atwood selected four for the job. He approached each candidate separately making his pitch. "I've been hired by some people in the liquor business from out of state. Need a few men handy with a gun. Got wounded in my left arm in France in 1918. Hired out as a mercenary after the war. All I need is my good right hand for this sort of work. Killed my share of men for money. For this job I need more firepower. Each man gets $1,500. $500 up front, $1,000 when the job is complete."

Each man asked the same question. "Who's this fella we're to kill?" Atwood's reply, "Does that matter?"

Each agreed to do the job. This was serious money. Declining might also be dangerous if this guy feels that made them a risk. Atwood fortified that thought by adding, "Don't be stupid and shoot off your mouth. You don't want me coming after you."

To their question when and where, Atwood responded, "This will happen soon after I determine the best location for making the hit. Each morning you're to go to the closest telegraph office each of you gave me. I'll expect you at the location and time specified in my telegram. You'll have twenty-four hours. Take the train. Do not fail to show up or I'll assume you got cold feet and took the $500 calling off doing what I paid for. Don't even think about that. I know how to find you."

—

From local newspapers, Atwood learned that Burke and U.S. Attorney Northcott are to testify before a Senate subcommittee hearing investigating the recent violence in West Virginia. It gave a date of September 21. That could mean Burke might be going to Washington a few days before. Ever since the failed attack on Keara Murphy, Atwood maintained 24-hour surveillance on both Burke and Murphy. Killing Burke on the train to Washington offered a perfect opportunity. Burke will be in a fixed location. Seated. Easily approached by multiple assassins.

That it made it difficult for the assassins to get away became irrelevant. They were expendable. Soon to be eliminated by

Atwood's own people. If taken alive by law enforcement, they only knew that someone in the illicit liquor business was behind this.

He would wire each of the four assassins to be at the Charleston railway station every morning by no later than 8:00am starting the morning of the 18th. They are to look out for him at the station. He will be wearing a white Stetson hat. They are to come prepared with concealed revolvers ready to take the same train as the target. Atwood will have purchased round-trip tickets from Charleston to Washington each morning. That first morning, he will give them photographs to recognize Burke. Then he will explain how they are to approach and shoot Burke. When Burke shows up, the assassins will follow him onboard whichever train Burke takes. After that, they are on their own to make the hit on Burke.

Once the job is completed. They are to return to Charleston by train. He will be waiting at the Charleston train station to pay them the remainder of their fee. "It's a public place so have no concern about me double crossing you."

Atwood arrived in Charleston on the 17th. While at the train station he looked at the schedule of the route to Washington. The following morning all four gunmen appeared at the Charleston train station. Atwood took them outside to speak in private. He gave each a photograph of Burke.

Atwood said. "The plan is simple." Pointing to the man that most impressed him, "Polaski, you'll be responsible for locating this man. Once he boards the train, all of you board the last carriage. You and Esposito then walk forward through the carriages until you locate where Burke is sitting. You and Esposito continue walking to the next carriage forward of the target. Signal to Ziegler and Tucker behind you by removing your hat. They are to then turn around and board the carriage behind the target's carriage."

Polaski interrupted by asking, "Who's this we're to kill?"

"Name is Burke. He's a U.S. Marshal. The guy going after bootlegging. Any of you have a problem with that?"

The face of each man reflected the shock when learning the identity of the target. Seeing their reaction, Atwood said, "Does this trouble anyone of you?" After each man shook his head with a grim expression. Atwood added, "I see the concern on your faces. There's four of you. Burke will be seated. Just put enough bullets in him to make sure you kill him. I'll even sweeten your fee. You'll each receive an additional $500 when you complete the job."

Polaski said, "Once the train gets underway, how are we to do this?"

Atwood said, "You will be in charge of giving the signal then you and Esposito will make your move. You'll stand on the outside platform between the carriages, forward of the carriage where Burke is. Ziegler and Tucker, you will be on the rear platform on the other end of Burke's carriage. Keep a continual watch for Polaski's signal leaning outside the platform. All of you make entry into the carriage at the same time. To make the attack, Polaski and Esposito, enter the carriage and approach Burke from the front. Zeigler and Tucker, you'll enter from the rear of the carriage.

"Once close enough Polaski, you'll take the first shot. You and Esposito then fire as many rounds as it takes. Make sure you kill him. Ziegler and Tucker, you'll come in from the rear as backup to Polaski and Esposito should they fail. Remember that Burke will be armed. Don't fail. Act quickly. Give him no chance to pull his sidearm."

Polaski asked, "When do we make our move?"

"Any time after the train pulls out from the stop in Hinton, but before we reach Charlottesville. You've got three hours but don't wait until the last minute. After Charlottesville Burke must switch to a Pennsylvania Railroad train to take him into Washington. If that happens then you'll have to repeat the routine and start over while taking you further from getting back home."

"Once it's done, then what do we do?" Polaski asked.

"Get off the train. After the shooting the train should come to an emergency stop. Don't run and draw attention to yourselves. Just jump down and walk away from the train getting out of sight. Make your way back to the nearest train station walking back along the line to the nearest station. Take the next train back to Charleston. I'll meet you there at the train station the following morning and settle up with what I owe you. Then you disappear and keep your mouth shut."

—

On the morning of Monday September 19, 1921, Leland Atwood spotted Alan Burke walking into the Charleston train station. He recognized those accompanying Burke as Keara Murphy, U.S. Attorney Elliot Northcott, and Maude Burke.

Burke and Murphy appeared in good spirits. Both were anxious to deliver testimony at the Senate hearing. Murphy took charge of making notes for both their testimonies. They wanted to deliver persuasive presentations condemning the coal mining companies, Baldwin-Felts, and the pervasive local corruption endemic to the coalfield counties of southern West Virginia. This would become part of the congressional record. Excerpts likely quoted in the national press. The important forum would become another widely published article by Keara.

Beyond that, they were leaving this unsettled environment to resume life back in civilization. West Virginia would remain unchanged indefinitely until something extraordinary happened to cause fundamental changes to the backward socio-economic structure.

Burke understood how much Keara missed Brooklyn. As for him, they could begin a normal life. These factors overshadowed any uncertainty about his professional future. He would listen to what Attorney General Daugherty was offering by transferring to the Bureau of Investigations. Even that would be contingent upon a posting to New York City.

For Maude the trip was a celebration for the ending of the strife endured for so many years. With a mother's pride, she looked forward to watching her son appear before Congress. Then to enjoy the holiday season with Alan and Keara in Brooklyn. Noreen joining them for Christmas week would make a grand family affair.

CHAPTER 29

Bluefield, West Virginia | September 1921

Both Burke's and Atwood's groups stood on the station platform waiting for the eastbound train to arrive. Ever cautious, Burke looked around to maintain situational awareness. There were many other passengers waiting to board, but none appeared to indicate a potential threat. Atwood shielded himself from view. He dispersed his four assassins to avoid appearing together. They would proceed individually boarding after Burke stepped up into a carriage. Atwood would wait until the last moment before the train pulled out to board the last passenger carriage.

After those accompanying him boarded, Burke stepped up into a carriage situated midway on the train. Atwood watched as his four men boarded the train. Two in carriages forward of Burke and the other two behind. Since Burke knew his face, he wore a wide-brimmed felt hat pulled down to obscure his face as he crossed the platform to board the last carriage.

The carriage Burke chose was sparsely populated with just a half dozen other passengers. No one looked suspicious. While in a positive frame of mind with his new prospects, he remained vigilant. To Keara he said, "How about you sit next to my mother here in the last row. I'll sit with Northcott a couple of seats forward. Want to discuss our forthcoming testimonies with him.

Keara replied, "Sure." Before taking their seats, she touched Burke's face tenderly with her hand. "I'm glad we're doing this, Darling. I'm so looking forward to our new life together. In a more settled place." She then embraced him tightly and gave him a kiss.

Burke said still holding her, "You're armed?"

"Of course. You taught me well. Glad you are too. We're still in West Virginia. Enemy territory."

It was a glorious sunny day as the train pulled out of Charleston. The densely wooded hills of Appalachia carved by the many creeks feeding into larger tributaries that eventually dumped into major rivers made for a spectacular landscape. Within weeks the leaves would begin turning into autumn's brilliant display of reds and yellows. Burke smiled comforted by the thought that where he was going would also be spectacular this time of year. For all of them this was a joyous journey that held the promise of a happier future.

"So glad you are coming with us to Washington then to Brooklyn to spend the holidays," Keara said to Maude as she sat down next to her.

Maude smiled. "I am thrilled and thankful, Keara. Not to see New York but for what you mean to Alan. You seem so devoted to each other."

Keara touched the back of Maude's hand. "We are meant for each other. Alan loves me dearly. For a man that has seen so much violence, he is remarkably tender. And for a soldier, he is particularly well read. We engage intellectually as well as emotionally. We're a good match."

Maude placed her hand over Keara's, smiling knowingly. "You've truly become part of our family, Keara. Noreen thinks the world of you. Because of your example as a successful writer, you've given her the inspiration to try her hand at writing. Quite passionate about it. Gives her a life removed from the confines of our rural circumstances."

Keara replied, "Not necessarily removed from rural life, Noreen searches for deeper meaning that exists in every place. That's why she writes fiction. Characters moving through circumstances of any type using a storyline to portray how people interact. I'm more a reporter. Trying to explain actual events. Noreen uses her imagination to construct situations that she populates with characters. Good storytelling is creating an engaging plot populated with vivid interesting characters. I've read some of her drafts. There's real talent there, Maude."

Tears came to Maude's eyes. "She's never cared to show me any of her work. As you know, before I was injured, we had become distant. Things of course are much better now."

"Maude, ask Noreen to show you some of her work. Judge for yourself how talented she is."

Maude nodded, "Yes. I have been so foolish in so many ways since losing Joseph and Liam. Not much of a mother to Noreen or Alan."

"Forget the guilt and move forward with a new outlook, Maude. You and Noreen are reconnected. Make the most of that. You've both gone through a lot and changed by the experience. Alan is back in America for good. He and I are moving to New York away from this land of some much violence."

Maude said, "I know how that feels. Bluefield is a pleasant place. Not the overpowering feeling of living in Mingo County. Bluefield is anti-union in many respects. Can't say that I appreciate that perspective, but I've given up labor activism. Not as invested in organizing as much as Mother Jones. Found the subterfuge that Noreen and you concocted a more satisfying means of rebelling against injustice." Maude grinned at Keara.

—

As federal law enforcement officials working for the Department of Justice, Burke and Northcott shared similar views about the situation in West Virginia. Both were frustrated by the lack of federal authority under existing statutes to have an impact on remedying the most oppressive practices imposed on coal miners. Northcott had been at this far longer than Burke.

"This oppression has its roots in the merging of various factors," Northcott said, "But the foundation is a three-legged stool. The mine operators, the economic impact therefore leading to political influence of local and state officials, and Baldwin-Felts. These are the points we should emphasize in our congressional testimonies."

"Well, I can speak with specific examples from personal experiences," Burke said, "About Baldwin-Felts in particular. A violent bunch of thugs calling themselves detectives. Serving as quasi-law enforcement officers in some cases."

Northcott added, "Or the arrangement of mine operators funding local law enforcement giving legal cover to use deputized peace officers for private business interests."

"You mean Don Chafin and Logan County as a stark example?"

"Of course. You know you've made a powerful enemy of Chafin by going after his bootlegging interests."

"No doubt. Goes with the job. That is the one official duty I can perform that hurts one of the bad guys."

"I understand your wife is also going to testify. Didn't connect her professional name as Murphy. I read her magazine articles and her continuing column in the Sunday edition of the *New York Times*. She makes a very credible critic of mining corporations' oppressive working conditions. Her use of the term corporate feudalism as she explains that meaning is a powerful denunciation of unregulated capitalism. The photographs only add to the message. Where does she obtain such candid shots?"

Burke smiled, "Trade secret I'm afraid. Obviously, there's a network of people here in West Virginia that are looking to subvert the unhealthy rule of the mining interests."

Northcott added, "Your wife makes the strongest case for addressing all manner of constitutional rights violations for working class West Virginians. It will take federal legislation. to dismantle corporate feudalism. I look forward to her testimony.

"You know you will be the star witness when asked about those two violent gunbattles that made headlines. Not to mention those senators looking to heap praise on your military exploits and get themselves quoted in the press."

"That will be my last official act as U.S. marshal for the Southern District. I'm seriously thinking about resigning. Frustrated by the inability to make a difference as a federal law enforcement officer. I'm to meet with the attorney general. He's made overtures about me transferring to the Bureau of Investigations. Don't yet know enough about the BOI to determine if that holds any interest. Even then, I'm not interested unless I can be based in New York. That's where my wife is from. She wants to return there and so do I."

Northcott replied, "Hate to see you leave West Virginia but I can appreciate your reasons. Not been easy since you came here. Especially after serving all those years in war zones of foreign lands only to find West Virginia embroiled in similar circumstances. Based on your background, your military background and skills make you particularly suited for a position in security. You might want to consider the State Department's Bureau of Diplomatic Security. It's also a law enforcement service. Protecting foreign dignitaries but also going after fugitives that have left U.S. jurisdiction. I served in the State Department years ago. Still have friends there who told me about this new division that's only a few years old. Sounds right up your ally. If you're bent on leaving the marshal service, you might want to explore that opportunity while you're in Washington given your public recognition. Might be an option to the Bureau of Investigation."

"Thanks for the advice, Elliot. I just might look into that."

—

It was over two hours before the train made its brief stop in Hinton. Within an hour after departing Hinton the gunmen Polaski and Esposito left their seats in the carriage forward of Burke. Out on the adjoining platforms between the cars, Polaski said to Esposito, "Ready?"

Esposito nodded then pulled back his jacket extracting a colt peacemaker .45 from the back of his waist. Polaski did the same then leaned out to look back for the other two gunmen awaiting his signal. Ziegler was hanging out at the opposite end of the Burke's carriage. Polaski waved and turned back to Esposito. "Stay right behind me. Once I fire, reach around me and start shooting. Burke will be armed, and I hear he's good with a gun. We shoot him enough times to make sure he's dead. Then we back out of the carriage until the train begins slowing to a stop when we jump off the train. Don't forget to pull your mask up over your nose."

Polaski opened the carriage door and saw Burke in an aisle seat midway down the carriage. He began walking down the aisle while keeping his eyes fixed on Burke. As he got withing ten feet he slowed while fumbling to pull up a bandana from around his neck to cover his lower face with his left hand. His right hand held the butt of his revolver concealed behind his back.

From the moment Polaski entered the carriage, Burke noticed the man's eyes staring directly at him unwaveringly while approaching. One arm held behind his back triggered alarm in Burke. In a practiced move, Burke drew his Browning .45.

Polaski having pulled up the bandana over his nose now stared in terror at the .45 pointed at him. In the instant that it took him to bring his revolver around to shoot Burke, Burke shot him in the forehead.

As Polaski fell backwards, he collided against Esposito trying to get a clear shot at Burke. Burke fired twice in quick succession hitting Esposito in the face. Both Polaski and Esposito fell to the floor dead.

Ziegler advanced from behind Burke who was now standing looked down on the fallen assailants. Ziegler had advanced from the rear then stopped when Burke shot Polaski and Esposito. With Burke now standing and still facing forward, Ziegler extended his arm, and fired his .38 revolver twice. Both rounds struck Burke on the upper right side of his back. Burke fell forward trying to catch himself by grabbing the seat in front but collapsed to the floor onto one knee. Instinctively he kept hold of his Browning .45.

As all the shots unfolded in a span of only seconds, Maude Burke watched in horror as her son staggered forward falling to the floor. With Keara seated next to the window, Maude was seated next to her on the aisle. Ziegler was standing in the aisle only a couple of feet in front of her still holding his revolver after shooting Burke.

At the sound of the first gunshot, Maude reached inside her handbag and extracted a .45 M1909 revolver. The weapon was Alan's former service revolver from the Philippines given as a present to his father. The violence perpetrated by Baldwin-Felts long ago instilled in Maude the need to go about armed. Her husband insisted she carry it in her handbag. Even more prudent when she embarked on union organizing following his death.

Maude Burke extracted her gun from her handbag almost simultaneously as Ziegler shot her son. Without hesitation, she fired two rounds striking Ziegler in the back. At point blank range, the heavy caliber slugs dropped him to the floor immediately.

Maude immediately stepped over Ziegler to reach her son now in the aisle kneeling on one knee. Northcott was trying to give aide to Burke when a female passenger rushed from the front of the carriage. "I'm a surgical nurse. Let me help."

Burke was bleeding profusely however, the nurse said, "Get me something to compress the wound and stem the bleeding."

Keara pulled some handkerchiefs and undergarments from her overnight bag and gave them to Maude who was kneeing next to Alan and began helping the nurse by compressing the wound. "Hold on, Alan!"

The nurse said, "The bleeding looks bad, but the bullet appears not to have severed a major blood vessel. We need to get him to a hospital though quickly."

Northcott pulled the emergency cord. Moments later the train lurched as the wheels locked causing screeching with the wheels skidding on the rails rapidly slowing the train.

Maude and the nurse eventually slowed the bleeding by compressing the area of the wound while Keara knelt next to Alan taking over from Maude in assisting the nurse.

Northcott reached down to help a distraught Maude to her feet then took her to a seat in the back away from so many bodies causing growing pools of blood. "Let the nurse work on your son, Mrs. Burke."

The fourth gunman Tucker opened the rear door and peered inside the carriage. Seeing his associates down, he abruptly withdrew. Not about to make a try on his own after the other three failed, Tucker jumped off the slowing train then ducked into the cover of a wooded area.

After hearing the gunfire and the sudden stopping of the train, Leland Atwood made his way forward from the last carriage of the train. Outside the rear platform of Burke's carriage, Leland Atwood, opened the door to peer inside. Like the fourth gunman, he too saw bodies in the aisle. As to Burke, he could not determine if Burke was among the casualties. As he opened the carriage door, the conductor coming from the caboose burst onto the platform where Atwood was standing, "What the hell's goin' on! Who pulled the emergency cord?"

Atwood flashed his Baldwin-Felts badge, "I'm a private detective. I heard gunshots from this carriage. Took a look inside. There're bodies on the floor." Atwood opened the door. "See for yourself." The conductor took a couple of steps inside. Looking down at the gunmen in the aisle with blood pooling and two women ministering to what appeared a wounded man, he turned around to rejoin Atwood.

"There're bodies on the floor. Blood all over. At least another man wounded. Women crying. What happened?"

"I've no idea. I'm just a passenger. Seated in another carriage. Heard the gunshots and came to investigate."

The conductor said to Atwood, "I've got to report this. Get medial help. The nearest hospital is in Charlottesville. I'll tell the engineer to high ball the train. Be at least an hour though. Keep people out of that carriage."

Atwood nodded as the conductor jumped down to the ground and took off toward the locomotive on the run.

Atwood needed to determine if Burke was among the dead or wounded but couldn't risk getting a closer look. Elliot Northcott came out immediately after the conductor left. Seeing Atwood, he said, "Where's the conductor?"

"I told the conductor took one look inside Said there's men down, blood all over. Maybe wounded requiring medical attention?"

"That's right. Friend of mine is badly wounded."

"What happened?"

"Attempted assassination. Three gunmen. Looks like they're all dead or dying."

"How's your friend?"

"In a bad way. May not make it unless he gets medical attention."

"The conductor said he's ordering the engineer to get us headed to Charlottesville as fast as possible. That's the closest hospital."

"How long to Charlottesville?"

"Conductor said about an hour."

Atwood realized that again Burke may have escaped death. Three gunmen? What about the fourth? If three failed, the fourth hired gun no longer mattered. If Burke was to survive his wounds, then it fell to Atwood to personally kill him. Burke would be vulnerable as a patient in but likely protected by law enforcement. However, Atwood's obsession to exact revenge overshadowed concerns about personal risk.

The conductor stopped the train for a brief one-minute stop at the small town of Waynesboro. He handed the surprised station telegrapher a written message for law enforcement and medical personnel to meet the arriving train in Charlottesville.

As the train pulled into Charlotteville, a dozen police officers and emergency medical personnel were on hand as the conductor jumped from the train as it came to a stop gesturing toward the train carriage where the carnage took place.

Atwood discretely jumped off the opposite side of the train from the platform to avoid being seen. Coming around from the front of the locomotive, he took up a position to observe the medical personnel. Was Burke alive or did he die in route?

The answer came quickly, as medical orderlies wrestled a gurney off the carriage platform. It was Burke. Apparently still alive since his face was uncovered. At his side was Keara Murphy holding his hand and saying something to him with his mother on the opposite side. From the distance, Atwood could not make out if Burke was even conscious.

After loading Burke into the ambulance accompanied by Murphy, Atwood asked one of the medical attendants, "I'm a reporter, where are you taking the victim?"

"University Hospital."

"How bad is he?"

"Don't know. Gunshot wounds. Three other dead guys in there didn't fare as good."

—

Atwood found a taxi to take him to a hotel. He needed to regroup his thoughts. Construct a plan for how to kill Burke. It had been a long day. He needed food and some rest. Although Burke was now exceptionally vulnerable, the failed attack on the train complicated the circumstances. As a lone assassin, he stood a better chance than relying on others, but it would require a sharpened focus of all his faculties.

—

Burke's surgery lasted four hours with a team of surgeons. The wounds were serious. Even though the slugs were from a .38 rather than a .45, at a range of only a couple feet, there was extensive damage. Both rounds penetrated the upper area of the right lung but entered low enough to avoid severing major blood vessels. However, the loss of blood still proved extensive over the length of time it took before getting hospital medical attention.

One round was slowed by the scapula the other by a rib before entering the upper area of the right lung. The bones slowed the slugs enough to prevent an exit wound causing even greater soft tissue damage by extended cavitation of the wound track. Nonetheless, the surgeons gave him only even odds of survival as they began surgery. Their post-operative prognosis only marginally better.

Keara, Maude, and Northcott were sitting in the waiting room when the lead surgeon emerged. "I'm Dr. Hirsch. The surgery was successful to the extent that we stabilized Mr. Burke's condition. We removed two .38 caliber slugs from his right lung. Both were slowed by striking bones but did extensive damage to the lung and other soft tissue. Those repairs were the reason why the surgery took so long.

"Assisting me was Dr. Olsen. He served in the Army in France and therefore extensively experienced in treating gunshot wounds. Speaking of which, was Mr. Burke in the war? He has various scars from previous bullet wounds. There's particularly extensive surgical scarring on his upper torso both front and back near these recent wounds. Internally I encountered scar tissue in the right lung from that previous wound."

Keara replied, "He was in the U.S. Marines. Served in the Great War and other wars around the world. What is your prognosis, Doctor?"

"Guarded, Mrs. Burke. Your husband has sustained serious wounds. Infection is always the greatest concern. Then of course there is the question of recovering full use of his right lung considering the compounding effects of prior damage. Mr. Burke has led a violent life. However, his vital signs are relatively strong considering the degree of trauma. Right now, he is still under the effects of surgical anesthesia. That should wear off within the hour. When he regains consciousness, he will be in considerable pain therefore we are intravenously administering morphine."

"What are his chances, Doctor?" Keara asked.

"To be honest, Mrs. Burke, just fair. We'll be able to determine better in a couple of days."

Maude was exhausted and began crying quietly with tears running down her face.

Northcott interjected. "Mr. Burke is a United States Marshal. This was an assassination attempt on his life. He needs to be assigned to a private room. I intend to immediately request that local law enforcement provide around the clock armed security outside the room."

Dr. Hirsch replied, "I understand. Give me a moment. I'll see what I can arrange."

Hirsch walked down the hall to a nurse's station and made a call. Returning, he said, "I just spoke to the shift supervisor. She is making the necessary arrangements."

"When can we see him?" Keara asked.

"As soon as he regains consciousness, we will move him from post-op to a room. Probably in an hour or so."

Northcott said to Keara. "I will make arrangements for the local police to place a guard outside your husband's room around the clock. I'll join you when they move him into his recovery room."

Northcott found the office of the hospital director who was still in his office as evening approached. It had been a busy day. Northcott identified himself and both the director and another gentleman stood to shake hands. The gentleman was the county sheriff. Northcott described to the sheriff the attack that left three assailants dead and U.S. Marshal Burke in critical condition.

The sheriff listened to Northcott describe the broader violence plaguing West Virginia and possible enemies that might wish harm to the marshal. "Are you saying whoever tried to kill Marshal Burke might make another attempt?"

"That cannot be ruled out, Sheriff. As a U.S. attorney, I'm directing the opening of a federal investigation since this assault now becomes a federal crime. Can you provide an armed officer to secure the Marshal's room around-the-clock?"

"Certainly. I'll have a deputy situated there immediately."

"Thank you, Sheriff. Have you discovered anything about the identity of the three dead assailants?"

"No. Still working on it. I will let your office know once we learn anything. Any suspicion about who might be behind this?"

"Oh yes. However, I'd rather not speculate until we gather more evidence."

"Is Marshal Burke expected to survive?"

"That's not yet certain. The doctors are optimistic, but he was gravely wounded."

—

Leland Atwood checked into a hotel not far from University Hospital. Having not eaten all day, he felt better after a hearty meal at the hotel restaurant. Motioning to the waiter, he slid a twenty-dollar bill to the edge of his table. "Any chance you could find me some whiskey to top off dinner?"

The waiter smiled then nodded as he pocketed the twenty dollars. The whiskey settled his agitation over yet another frustrating encounter with Burke.

Calmed by the whiskey, Atwood walked to the hospital. Asking at the desk for a patient named Alan Burke, the receptionist replied, "Visitor hours are over. You'll have to return tomorrow."

"Very well. What is his room number."

The receptionist looked at the ledger. "Mr. Burke is in room 312. Says here he's not allowed to receive visitors. Are you a relative?"

"No. Just a friend. Heard about what happened. I'll check back tomorrow anyway. Thank you. Goodnight."

Back at the hotel, he procured another glass of whiskey to take to his room. Sitting by the open window he sipped the whiskey planning how he would kill Burke that very night. It did not matter that the murder could very well unleash a backlash that might compromise Baldwin-Felts. At this point it no longer mattered. Killing Burke transcended any concerns about personal repercussions.

Burke would be lying in bed. Unarmed. Perhaps not even conscious. Completely vulnerable. This remained Atwood's only opportunity to kill Burke. The failed attempt on the train would become headlines in the morning newspapers across the country. Burke was traveling to Washington to testify before a Senate subcommittee. Seated next to Burke on the train was U.S. Attorney Northcott. Narrowly escaping injury, Northcott's account of events would ensure Burke becoming famous. That also meant local law enforcement would likely place an armed guard outside Burke's hospital room.

Shooting his way into Burke's room might work but was suicidal. If not killed in the process, he would be recognized. Dying on the gallows was not to become his fate. Although willing to kill

Burke at great risk, Atwood nonetheless intended getting away, conceivably unidentified.

If there was only a single guard outside Burke's room, impersonating a doctor making rounds sometime after midnight offered a possibility to gain entry. All he had to do was get past the guard, shoot Burke, then shoot the guard to make his escape. Still wearing his white coat with a stethoscope hanging from his neck should give him a chance.

—

Leland Atwood slipped into University Hospital through a rear maintenance door. It was one o'clock in the morning. With minimal hospital night staffing he made his way through the first level undetected. To disguise his reason for walking about, he carried a small toolbox stolen from the hotel maintenance room and a shop coat with an embroidered name on the front. Sufficient to say he was maintenance staff if challenged. Eventually he found the doctors' locker room. No one present. Most lockers unlocked. After opening several he found a white coat with a stethoscope stuffed in the pocket. A nametag read Dr. James Richards.

Atwood shed his maintenance uniform jacket and placed the toolbox behind a trash receptacle. He had what he needed. Best to proceed without delay. Once on the third floor, he looked down the dimly lit hallway. The only person evident was a man seated in a chair leaning back against the wall smoking a cigarette. A police officer standing guard outside Burke's room. Without hesitation, Atwood walked up to the uniformed officer.

"Is this room 312?"

"Yes. And you are?"

"Dr. Richards. Supervising shift physician. I'm told that the patient is a VIP recovering from surgery just several hours ago. Need to check his vital signs."

"Go on in, Doc."

Atwood pushed the door open gently to avoid making any noise. The large room was even more dimly lit than the hallway. Most of the light came from a wall light fixture behind the patient's head. He could see Burke propped up with his eyes closed. An intravenous bottle hung from a pole next to the bed.

Atwood approached the bed slowly.

Suddenly from a darkened corner off to his left hidden from view as he opened the door came a female voice. "Who are you?"

Surprised, Atwood replied, "I'm Dr. Richards. Making my rounds. Checking on the patient's vital signs."

"Someone just did that twenty minutes ago. Turn around so I can see your face."

Atwood began turning slowly while reaching into his waistband and extracting a revolver. Thinking he concealed that he was armed in the dimmed lighting, when he turned toward the voice, he faced Keara Muphy' outstretched arm holding her .38 revolver pointed at him from only a few feet away.

In the fraction of a second it took to raise his weapon, Murphy fired, hitting Atwood first in the throat. As Alan had taught her, she followed immediately with a second shot striking his upper torso.

Atwood fell to his knees dropping his revolver to clutch his throat with his good right hand. Gasping for breath only brought forth spurts of blood.

Keara screamed, "Who are you!"

Unable to speak, Atwood could only look at her in disbelief with widening eyes before collapsing headfirst to the floor.

www.ingramcontent.com/pod-product-compliance
Lightning Source LLC
Chambersburg PA
CBHW030354030726
47497CB00002B/334